WYCKED RUMORS

Wycked Obsession – Book 2

Wynne Roman

WYCKED RUMORS
Wycked Obsession Series — Book 2
Copyright ©2018 by Wendy Ferguson
All Rights Reserved
Edited by Loredana Elsberry Schwartz
Proofreading by Kathy Hafer
Cover Design by Tatiana Vila, Vila Design

DEDICATION

For the Head Gypsy, JoAnne Mandel,
and the Worker Bee, Karen Henderson.

May we all do Grandma Grape proud.

TABLE OF CONTENTS

Prologue
Chapter 1
Chapter 2
Chapter 3
Chapter 4
Chapter 5
Chapter 6
Chapter 7
Chapter 8
Chapter 9
Chapter 10
Chapter 11
Chapter 12
Chapter 13
Chapter 14
Chapter 15
Chapter 16
Chapter 17
Chapter 18
Chapter 19
Chapter 20
Chapter 21
Chapter 22
Chapter 23
Chapter 24
Chapter 25
Chapter 26
Chapter 27
Chapter 28
Chapter 29
Epilogue

Playlist
Acknowledgements
About the Author
Books by Wynne Roman
Sneak Peaks

PROLOGUE

LONDON

THE RESTAURANT IS QUIET AND DIGNIFIED, everything I would expect from the finest French establishment in my namesake city. The table is covered with sparkling white linen and set with fine china, silver, and crystal. An elegant silver candlestick holds a flickering white taper, and the mood is perfect.

Colin has already ordered his choice of wine, it's poured and waiting, and so I take a sip. Anything to calm my nerves. They've put me on edge since he picked me up. Something in his voice, his demeanor, his choice of restaurant—everything—tells me he's up to something.

It must be something special, I think to myself. Colin Gilbert is somewhat stoic and unemotional—typically British, he always says—and romantic gestures aren't his style. Could tonight be the night he pops the question?

Do I even want him to? And if he does, how will I answer?

"Have you decided?"

I blink. I haven't looked at the menu.

"No." I shake my head as the waiter approaches. "You order for me. You know what I like."

Colin nods smoothly. He likes it when I defer to him, and in this case, I don't mind. I've been back in England for three days, and this is the first time we've seen each other. I'm hoping our latest separation might drag out of him whatever trace of romance he might have buried deep in his soul.

I can't help watching as he orders. He's slender, not soft but definitely not muscular. The perfect body for an English gentleman, he claims. I don't know if that's true, but I accept it if he's happy with himself. His hair is dark brown, curly on top and short on the sides, and his eyes are a shade lighter than his hair. He's maybe five inches taller than my 5'5", which seems comfortable enough, and dressed in a navy-blue-almost-black suit and coordinating tie.

We're a nice match, he says, although he does complain about my hair being too red. I laughed the first time he said it. Maybe I *do* have auburn highlights in my hair—they're natural— but it's just as much brown as it is red. My eyes are brown, too— hazel, they're probably called—but Colin says they're too gold. They make me stand out, and he'd rather I not draw too much attention.

He isn't the first one to wish that.

For myself, I'm through with that kind of thinking. I've lived most of my life under that pressure, and I'm done with it. Forever. I made myself a promise the day I turned eighteen. By the time I graduated from college, I'd no longer be the shy, innocent girl who faded into the background. I'd be strong and independent, a woman defined by nothing and no one except being my absolute and authentic self.

The time has come. I graduated with my degree in Communications a week ago.

Colin sends the waiter off and looks at me with a distant smile. Is it my imagination, or has he been preoccupied since he picked me up?

"Is everything all right?" I try to smile in an easy, understanding way.

"Yes. Why do you ask?"

"You seem...distracted." He's an attorney—a *solicitor,* I remind myself—and work frequently concerns him.

"No. Although I do want to have a word."

"All right." It's the British way of saying, *we need to talk.* Uneasiness snakes through me. That's not usually a sign of anything good, is it? On the other hand, maybe non-romantic Colin doesn't understand the usual clues. I learned long ago that he sees things much differently than I do.

"What is it?" I ask when he doesn't continue.

He shakes his head. "We'll save that for later. How was your trip?"

"Fine."

"Did you travel with your parents?"

"My mother. Dad...went ahead without us." I don't explain—again—that my father never goes out in public with us. Colin knows the situation. We've talked about the realities of my family dynamic more than once.

"Yes, of course. And your graduation?"

"Uneventful." I swallow the words that I really want to say, mostly because I've already said them and it was a waste of breath. I asked Colin to attend the ceremony, and he begged off. Too busy. Too far. Too expensive.

It's always too much *something.*

"And your plans now?"

I delay my answer while our waiter places an artfully-arranged vinaigrette salad before each of us. Colin begins eating immediately, while I wait.

"I've submitted a number of resumes, both here and in the States."

"The States?" He looks up. "Southern California?" He says it like he means the very pit of hell. The garbage dump of all humanity. I suppose, to Colin, that's the case.

"It's home," I remind him mildly. "Where I grew up."

"Yes, well..." His nose wrinkles up like he's just noticed a bad smell. It makes me want to push him a little.

"I've had some very promising interest from a record company in L.A. I interned there last summer."

"I thought you were staying in England permanently now."

"That depends."

"On what?"

I rest a flat gaze on his face. He ought to know; we've been seeing each other for months now. But I also recognize his unemotional reserve. Colin Gilbert never assumes *anything.*

"It depends on the job offers." I try to keep my tone patient. How difficult can it be to understand? "And how...fulfilling my life here can be. You know, because of *my father."*

"Right." He nods and returns his attention to his salad. "Have you thought about *not* working?"

"Not working?" I pick up my salad fork but then drop it back to the tabletop before I take a bite. "Why wouldn't I work? I worked hard for my degree! What would I do instead?"

He finishes his salad calmly and sits back in his chair. He looks at me after a moment, tilting his head as though he wants to see me from a different angle. "I'd like to set you up in a flat. Keep your time available for *me.*"

"I..." The words fall away. "Keep my time available for you?" I blink and pull my head back. "What the bloody hell does that mean?"

His expression tightens, and I know it's my language. Colin doesn't like ladies to curse. Right now, I really don't give a good goddamn.

"Exactly what it sounds like. I want to be your priority."

"My *priority?*" I have to repeat it, hear it again, to believe it. "My priority?" I say once more. "Do you mean *my priority,* or *my only concern?*"

He narrows his eyes. "London..."

Why doesn't he finish?

"What about me, Colin?" I ask stiffly. "Am I *your* priority?"

"London," he says again, and this time he shakes his head.

"What? We aren't engaged. Why should—"

"Engaged?" He frowns. "What do you mean?"

I blink and imitate his expression. "Engaged. As in we've made a commitment to each other. That we will have a future together. Why would I make you *the* priority in my life if I'm not one in yours?"

He stares at me long enough to make me uncomfortable, and then finally he sighs. "London, you must realize the impossibility of what you're suggesting."

"The impossibility of what? My being a priority in your life?"

"Of our becoming engaged."

An odd feeling races through me, like an electric shock sent straight through to my nervous system. I'm hot, then cold, then hot again. "What do you mean, Colin?"

He scowls and shakes his head. "Do I really have to say it?"

"Yes." I nod emphatically. "You do. Absolutely."

"It can't come as a surprise to you that a man in my position can't consider *marriage* to...Hugh Kennedy's illegitimate daughter."

"Hugh Kennedy's illegitimate daughter?" I repeat carefully, my throat suddenly dry. *"And a man in your position?"*

He tries to hold my gaze, but he can't do it. Brown eyes that suddenly appear weak and untrustworthy slide away.

"You know my goals," he finally says. "I have grander plans than to remain a simple solicitor for the rest of my life. With the right connections, the right wife, I can—"

"The right wife," I repeat. I don't give a damn if I interrupt him. "And that couldn't possibly be *Hugh Kennedy's illegitimate daughter.* So that must mean you're asking me to become—what? Your *mistress?"*

"London..."

I nod as though things suddenly make sense. And they do. They fucking do. "Your mistress," I say again. "You want to set me up in a flat where I can wait for you to have time to come round for a quick fuck."

He flinches but says nothing. I press on.

"This might come as something of a shock to you, Colin, but you overestimate the attraction of your cock, you asshole."

"London!"

His voice is strangled, his voice horrified, and I really don't give a damn. I rise from my chair with every bit of elegance my mother instilled in me, reach for my purse, and drop my napkin on top of my untouched salad. "I'll find my own way home, you wanker."

I don't turn back. Why would I? I may not have an undying love for this man, but my emotions *are* involved. I trusted him to believe that he at least cared enough to treat me *decently.* Hugh Kennedy's illegitimate daughter deserves *some* reasonable consideration. Some respect. Doesn't she?

Don't I?

It doesn't matter. I step out onto the street and look for a taxi. Quickly and oh-so-efficiently, Colin has destroyed whatever there might once have been between us. Shattered any hope that this time—this man—would be different.

I should have known better by now. Men want one thing, and women want another. Sex for security and commitment. Isn't that the exchange?

Maybe for others. Not for Hugh Kennedy's illegitimate daughter. Born on the wrong side of the sheets, as I've heard it whispered, means never aspiring to a *real* relationship apparently.

A man to love me for who I am, and no other reason.

Tears shock me when they begin to prickle behind my eyelids. I haven't cried in years, and I know instantly I'm not emotional over Colin fucking Gilbert. It's the reminder that the accident of my birth makes me...dirty. Not good enough. Someone to be hidden away or embarrassed over.

So maybe London Kennedy, embarrassment to her family and friends, ought to start thinking about herself, suggests a fierce voice from deep inside me.

I choke back a laugh, or is it more tears? Yeah, maybe I should. Instead of looking for trust, romance, or even respect, why not accept the obvious that life has laid out for me?

Work hard. Earn respect. Protect yourself, and forget about relationships. For that kind of thing, sex is the answer. Sex doesn't waste its time with love and happily ever after. Sex doesn't take your feelings and smash them into smithereens. Sex fills a physical need. The big O is the reward.

Isn't that how guys look at it? I know it is, so why waste my time expecting anything else? I ought to be *thanking* Colin! He did me a big bloody favor. Reordered my *priorities*.

Relationships? They aren't bloody worth it. I've seen what a mess they cause.

"Fuck love," I mutter as a cab pulls up to the curb. "Who needs it?"

Who, indeed? That's going to be my new motto, and if I do it right, it'll see me through anything.

CHAPTER 1

LONDON

THE PHOTOGRAPHER'S STUDIO BUZZES WITH ACTIVITY. I stop just inside the entrance, keeping well out of the way, and look for a familiar face. I recognize the guys from Wycked Obsession, of course; anybody in the music industry, or who hasn't been living under a rock for the last six months, would know them. They came out of nowhere, a sudden phenom from Austin, and now they're on tour with Edge of Return, the biggest band since Coldplay.

Not bad for a band with only two albums out.

I straighten my spine and resist the urge to adjust my hemline or tug at the fit of my shirt. I'll admit it: I dressed to impress. I'm wearing a white pencil skirt and a teal blue sleeveless blouse, with coordinating jewelry and three-inch blue heels. I don't expect Knox Gallagher, Wycked Obsession's lead guitarist and my contact within the band, to give a damn what I look like...or even notice anything about me. But Baz Calhoun, the band's manager, might, and I'm not taking any chances.

I want this job.

The photo shoot seems to be breaking up. I recognize every one of the band members: Ajia Stone, lead singer; Noah Dexter, drummer; Zayne Prescott, bassist; Rylan Myles, keyboardist...and Knox. I'd recognize him anywhere. He's one of the best guitarists playing right now, and, writing with Ajia, the creative geniuses of Wycked Obsession's biggest hits. He's also the best-looking guy in a band made up of some of the hottest men on the freaking planet.

The other band members disappear, while Knox continues to talk to the photographer. Baz explained that Knox acts as the band's unofficial leader, and I can see that must be true. From photo shoots to meeting with me about the band's marketing and PR needs, Knox exudes an element of *control.*

So, where's Baz?

I look around but don't see anyone who has that harried, I'm-so-busy-I'm-going-to-tear-my-hair-out look I've seen on other band managers. That leaves me to stare at Knox some more.

He's tall, maybe 6'2", and muscular. His arms and chest are tattooed, revealed because he's not wearing a shirt. The meaning and placement of his tattoos are of great interest to his female fans. I did a little on-line research before our meeting, and it left me both amused and alarmed at the information and speculation out there.

None of what I read about Knox seems to have done him justice. His hair is long, to his shoulders, and a deep sable color that looks so much richer in person. It's like strands of brown, black and ginger all tangled together, and some perfectly decadent part of me wants to discover for myself how soft it is. His lower face is covered with the scruff of a few days worth of whiskers, darker than his hair, and I have to admit it looks totally freaking *hot.*

His facial features are nicely proportioned. His nose is maybe a little wide, but his bottom lip is perfectly *bitable,* according to one online fan site. His eyes are lighter colored than I would have expected, sometimes gray and sometimes green, according to his fans. I can't tell the shade today, not from where I stand, and a part of me wants to move forward to see for myself. I almost take a step forward—and then I realize that he's staring back at me.

I can feel my reaction: my eyes widen and my cheeks flush. Damn. I've changed in so many ways from the shy, embarrassed girl I used to be, but I've never quite learned how to control that damned blush.

Knox grins, but it's more of an I-know-you-want-me smile than a friendly expression. Asshole. So he's like all rock stars. Sure of himself and his appeal, and not afraid to take advantage of it.

And why not? an impatient voice snaps inside of me. *He can get by with it. Every girl in America wants him—and if you had the chance, you wouldn't turn him down, either.*

Bloody hell.

I don't have time for this. More than that, I don't *want* to notice him as a man. That wanker, Colin, cured me of that kind of rubbish, and I'm *not* looking at Knox Gallagher any longer.

I pull my phone from my purse and glance at the time. I check emails and text messages. Nothing new. *Now, pay attention,* I tell myself. *You're here to meet with Knox and Baz as a* professional. *Not some daft cow looking for a quick dance in the sheets.*

Properly chastised, I look back only to discover Knox is gone. The photographer is bent over, messing with a camera case at her feet, and so I approach.

"Pardon me. Can you tell me where Knox Gallagher went?"

The photographer looks up at me through a tangle of long graying hair. "You supposed to be here?"

"I have a meeting with him. I'm from the label."

It's only partly true. Wycked Obsession's record label *was* interested in me for an in-house position, but they ended up hiring someone else. They think I'll be a better fit after some on-the-road experience, and so I'm here at their recommendation, hoping that Knox and Baz agree.

She nods her head toward the far corner of the room. "He's in the dressing room."

I turn. *Dressing room* is a generous term. The studio is one big loft, and there's an area partitioned off with a big screen that is, apparently, the dressing room. With Baz nowhere in sight, I head in that direction.

"Hello?" I step around the partition to find some odd pieces of furniture and a couple of rows of rectangular metal racks filled with men's clothes draped on hangers. "Pardon me?"

Clothing rustles, but I hear nothing else, so I try again. Politely. "Knox? Uh, Mr. Gallagher?"

My nerves ratchet up as I wait. I've met my share of famous people over the years, but this is different. Knox has the final say about whether I get this job—and the more arduous this whole process has become, the more I want it.

"Well, hell, honey. If you wanted to see my cock, all you had to do was ask."

He steps out from between two racks of clothes, stark fucking naked.

I try—bloody hell, do I try—to keep my gaze on his face. I fail. Dramatically. His chest is broad, tattooed with a Wycked Obsession logo over one pec, a colorful chest piece over the other—a dragon draped around a Celtic cross—and the words Wicked Is As Wycked Does angled over one hip.

That, of course, leads me lower. To his cock that—*oh, my God*—even in its only semi-hard state, is twice the size of Colin's in full erection.

What must it be like to ride him to orgasm? My panties become drenched and my nipples tighten at just the thought.

Jesus, luv, no more men! Remember?

I force my gaze back to his face and stiffen when I see his smirk. Bloody rock stars.

I swallow. A prissy part of me recognizes how completely unacceptable this is, but most of me knows I have to handle it just right. Rock stars—celebrities of any kind—live by their own rules. They pretty much get by with whatever strikes their fancy. If I want to play the game, I have to learn the system. After all, Baz made it clear that taking this job means working closely with Knox, and I can't do that if he's laughing behind my back at some prudish reaction on my part to a little nakedness.

"Well, hell, baby." I saunter close with an appreciative smile. "I didn't know you were offering such...personal service as part of the interview." I recognize a flicker of awareness in his almost-gray eyes, but that doesn't stop me. My research told me everything I need to know about the Wycked Obsession guys and their manwhore reputations.

I wrap my fingers around his shaft and stroke it up and down, just a couple of times. "I would have brought my camera if I'd known, and we could have posted a few pictures on Tumblr."

His gaze darkens to one of absolute awareness, like the two of us are suddenly and unquestioningly the only two beings on the planet. He closes his hand over mine and drags my palm up and down over his cock a few more times. His grin is a naughty smile that says, *What the hell do we have here?*

"Interview, huh? You must be…Kennedy?"

"London," I correct. "London Kennedy."

I pull my hand from his—and his now-hard cock. "I'd shake your hand," I say as casually as I can, "but I think we've already moved past that point."

His eyebrows rise. "We could try it again."

I can't help it. I laugh. "You'd like that, wouldn't you?"

He pretends to think about it, but then he laughs, too. "Hey, I'm a red-blooded American male. In my prime. What do you think?"

"I *know.*" I nod emphatically. "Now, if you want to put on some clothes, we can talk about this PR and marketing position you have available."

"What if I want to do it naked?"

I shrug. A very surprising—and mischievous—part of me wishes he would. "Your choice. You're the boss."

"And you?"

"Me?"

"Will you be naked, too?"

"Ah, no." I shake my head with as much emphasis as my earlier nod. "My girly bits aren't quite…agreeable to being naked for a first interview."

"Girly bits." He laughs and shakes his head. "Too bad. It might have been fun."

"I'm not sure your manager would agree."

Knox disappears between the rows of clothing racks. "About that," he calls, and I hear sounds that might indicate he's getting dressed. "Baz texted. He got held up at the label. It's just us."

"Oh." I swallow my disappointment, ninety percent sure it means I won't have an answer about the job today. "Are you all right with that?"

"Sure."

He walks back out, fastening a pair of skinny jeans over his remarkable hips. I got so caught up in the sight of his cock, I forgot about the rest of him. The man-scaping, the delicious V that starts above his hips and ends at his pelvis, the elaborate guitar tattooed on his thigh. I remember it all now, as clearly as if he hadn't covered it up at all.

I swallow. Part of me wishes I'd just said, *screw it, let's do this thing naked.* The rest of me fully appreciates the sight of Knox in those dark skinny jeans and vintage Jim Morrison T-shirt.

Hold on there, luv! I drag my thoughts to a halt. Or maybe it's my libido. Whatever, he's *dangerous.*

Knox Gallagher might be the hottest thing this side of the sun, but keep your mind on business!

"There's a Starbucks not too far from here." Thank God, he started to speak. "We can go there and talk."

"Out in public?"

"Why not?"

"Uh…" How exactly do I say it? "Fans? Interruptions?"

He shrugs. "It's Southern California. C-list celebrities are a dime a dozen here."

I smirk. "Not sure I'd classify you as 'C-list', but you're right about it being common to see celebrities here." I take a breath. "Okay, let's go."

"You got wheels?"

"Yeah." I send him a look. "You don't?"

"I got a tour bus." He waggles his eyebrows. "Otherwise, I hire a car."

"You trust my driving?"

He grins, and my heart stumbles. *Bollocks!* What is it about rock stars, and this one in particular, that makes me all hot and anxious and…*wet?*

And goddamn Colin for being such a douche as to drop the mistress bomb on me before we'd had sex in—what? Three months? Maybe if we *had,* I wouldn't be so…edgy.

"It's only a couple of blocks," Knox says easily. "If the label sent you, you must be safe to go at least *that far."*

I nod, wrestling my physical awareness of him to the back of my mind. I lead the way from the studio to my coppery-colored Audi R8 Spyder, parked just down the street.

He whistles. "Nice ride."

"A graduation present from my father."

"College?"

"High school."

He gives me a look I've seen before. It means anything from *you must be rich* to *who's your father?* I'm not about to explain anything about Hugh Kennedy and my cocked-up family life until I have to, so I just gesture toward the car as if to say, *get in.*

We do, and we're pulling into the Starbucks parking lot before I can think of anything else to say. Knox hasn't made any effort to speak, either, and I'm glad. It's hard to concentrate with the heat of his big, hard body so close to mine.

I order iced tea, Knox gets iced coffee, and we find a seat at a relatively private table. Well, private for Starbucks. He sits back in his seat and stares at me.

"Tell me about yourself."

I take a deep breath. *This is it.*

"I graduated from UCLA this spring. Communications. I interned with your label last summer. I know this isn't exactly a *publicist* position, that I'll be doing the actual marketing and PR." I pause long enough to organize my thoughts. "Heavy on computer work, which is fine. I'm well-versed with both Mac and PCs. I have experience in most software, and I'm familiar with all the social media sites online. I—"

"Baz can get all that shit from your resume. I want to know about *you.*"

"Me?" Why the hell does my voice squeak like Minnie Mouse? "What do you want to know about *me?*"

"We're on tour for a couple of months yet. You ready to live with the band twenty-four seven?"

"Yes. Of course."

"You ever been on the road living in a tour bus? It isn't easy."

"No." I shake my head slowly. "But I understand the celebrity lifestyle."

"The celebrity lifestyle?" He snorts. "What does that mean?"

Why does he have to sound so bloody *appealing,* even in his snark? I am *so* not noticing guys right now! And how many freaking times do I have to remind myself of it?

"Traveling a lot," I say quickly, talking fast so I can pretend that he doesn't make me nervous as hell. "Public exposure. Paparazzi. Fans. Screwing your way through—"

Oh, shit! Heat floods my face as the words die a sudden, humiliating death. *Jesus.* Was I really going to say *screwing your way through your fan base?*

"Screwing my way through...?" he repeats with a smirk. *Bloody hell.*

I fight the urge to close my eyes or hide behind my hands. They're shaking, and I don't want Knox to see it. *"Oh, my God! I am so sorry!* I didn't mean *you,* specifically, but that was completely uncalled for. I—*Jesus!* I don't know what I was thinking!"

He lifts one shoulder, along with one eyebrow. "Been known to happen."

If only I could smile, make light of it, but I know better. I fucked this up, and I have to own it. "I read some things on the Internet," I admit meekly, "but that doesn't excuse what I said. I'm terribly sorry."

He perks up. "Anything good?"

"What?"

"On the Internet. What'd you read? Anything good about us?"

Part of me wants to laugh. He's like a kid. The rest of me is busy fighting to keep a calm expression.

Don't blush. For God's sake, do not *blush!*

I take a breath. "About you? Just...you know. The tattoos and piercings."

"Which ones?" He flicks his earlobe, and for the first time, I notice he wears a diamond stud and a gold ring behind it.

"Not...there."

"Where, then?"

"Are you enjoying this?"

He shakes his head, his amazing sable-colored hair shifting to cover his earlobe, but I see the devil in his mostly gray eyes. "Nope. Just trying to find out what they're saying about me on the internet."

I settle back in my chair and cross my arms over my chest. *"You know what they're saying.* That your cock is tattooed. Or pierced. Or both."

He gives me a wicked smile that gives away just how much he *is* enjoying this. "Then you already know for yourself that it isn't either."

"That's true." I try to sound matter of fact, but my gaze drops like I'm looking past the solid wooden table and through thick fabric of his jeans. Picturing him naked again. And maybe I am—but he doesn't need to know that. I drag my eyes back upward.

"We don't need to confirm or deny those rumors on the Internet," I add desperately.

Knox takes a drink of his iced coffee and considers me with a look. "You say you know something about the *celebrity lifestyle?*" He uses my words again, sounding amused—or maybe irritated. I can't tell which. "Why?"

Here you go, luv. This is it.

I've known it was coming. I don't want to admit much about my past and my family; never have. Still, I thought I'd accepted that I'd have to do this. Faced with it, I'm not so sure.

Normal people with normal families don't run up against this kind of thing. I've whined about it most of my entire life. When your father is famous—*infamous*—it's a whole different ballgame. Full disclosure. In the long run, it's the right thing to do. The easiest.

And the hardest.

"My father is Hugh Kennedy. The movie—"

"Producer."

"Yes. You've heard of him."

"Everybody who's been to the movies in the last twenty years knows who Hugh Kennedy is. His string of hits is unprecedented."

I nod. "Twenty-two years."

Knox blinks. "That's a pretty specific number."

I shrug. "I'm twenty-two."

"Ahh…" He drags the word out. "You're his muse. His lucky charm."

"No." My laugh sounds more bitter than I mean it to. "My mother is."

He watches me for a heartbeat, and I see the instant he puts it all together. The stories and the gossip. Everything that's been said about my family—and me. True or not.

"London Kennedy." He says my name softly.

"That's right." I take a quick sip of my tea, mostly just to steal a few seconds to think. To breathe. "Illegitimate daughter of Hugh Kennedy." I say it like I'm reading a bullet list of facts from *USA Today.* "The result of his affair with actress Marisol Malone.

The relationship that has remained unacknowledged for twenty-two years. The mistress and daughter he only pretends to hide, while he remains married to Adele Southworth Kennedy, his beloved wife, and father to their three legitimate children."

I pause for a breath that takes too long and comes too ragged. *"That* London Kennedy."

CHAPTER 2

KNOX

FUCK MY LIFE. This girl is trouble…and, deep down, I know I'm going to hire her.

If she wants the job, it's hers.

Not because I want to fuck her—that much is absolutely true. I do. Not gonna waste my time pretending she doesn't make my cock hard as granite. Wanted her from the second I caught her staring at me from the other side of the photographer's studio. Fuck. I showed her my cock, just to see how far I could push her, and she stroked the fucker like a goddamn pro.

Jesus, it makes me even harder just thinking about it, but I can't go there right now. Not sitting in Starbucks in the middle of the day.

Besides, I can already tell this woman is brave, willing to take risks and no bullshit, and she deserves some respect for that.

Exactly the kind of publicist we need.

It isn't a true publicist's job. We're calling it that, but it's marketing and PR and publicity, all crammed together into a pile of shit and done from a seat on a tour bus. It's close, personal, and looking out for the band's interests instead of the label's. Somebody who, when they speak for us, says what *we* want to say and shows what we want to show.

Whatever the hell that means. Still figuring it all out. I'm shit at doing it. I like the control, but don't have the patience or finesse to say, "Go to hell," in a way that they won't figure out is an insult until it's too late.

I get the feeling that London Kennedy can manage that just fine.

She's been through some shit in her life. In some ways, maybe even uglier shit than we have, and for fucking longer. She knows how to keep a low profile. I know fuck all more about what her parents did than anything about London herself. She looks like any man's version of a wet dream, and I can't help running a slow gaze from her head to as far down as I can see.

She's got reddish-brown hair and oddly-colored golden-brown eyes. They see a lot, those eyes, and I want to know what that means. How does the world look to her? A lot of deep shit is going on in there.

A few freckles spread out over her nose and across her cheeks. Can't say I remember hooking up with a girl who had freckles, but on her, they're fucking hot. Her teeth are white and straight, like her old man paid for the best dentist in L.A., and her lips are full. Kissable.

Fuckable.

She blinks those strange golden eyes suddenly. "Is it too much?"

Looking at her without fucking her? Yeah, it's way too goddamn much.

"What?"

"My background. My...father." Her gaze slides away. "More than you want to take on?"

"No. Hell no. Why would you think that?"

She lifts one shoulder. "Not everybody feels that way."

"Fuck them."

She looks back at me. "You can afford to feel like that." She points in my direction. "You can get pretty much anything you want. Me? Not so much."

I sit back and look at her like I've been wanting to. Deep and hard and seeing every part of her body. A deliciously fine body it is, too. Full tits, tiny waist, hips and an ass that a man can really grab hold of when he fucks her, and legs that'd wrap around me perfectly.

But she's not a groupie, a one and done I'll forget as soon as I come. Or a fangirl who's heard I like things a little rough and wants to find out what that means. I've been known to hook up with a girl for more than a night...more than a few nights, even, but if she takes the job, she'll be around all of us *all the goddamn time*—and that means a little discretion.

My cock hates the restraint.

"What about your old man? He can't get you what you want?"

She pulls back like I slapped her. I get it. I hate that I understand, but I've got a fucking sperm donor who taught me everything I need to know about *fatherhood.*

"If I asked him, my father would give me whatever I want. It's easy to give...things. I've never asked him and never will, so if you're expecting some kind of special...favors from him—"

"Fuck no!" It's a harsh snap that suits my opinion of fathers just fine. "I don't take help from anybody. Not that kind."

She nods sharply, like we're in agreement, and I let it go. Don't want to talk about *fatherhood,* anyway. Just the idea ruins my fucking mood.

"Moving on," I mutter after a quick drink of my iced coffee. "Tell me what you know about Wycked Obsession."

"What?"

"You said you looked us up on the internet. What'd you find? And not the tattoos and piercing stuff."

She gives me a little smile. "Okay. Well, you're out of Austin, Texas, formed about five years ago. You and Ajia Stone were the founding members. You played the local circuit for a few years, put together an EP that went viral pretty quickly, and got yourself signed by a label. You went on tour after your first album, self-titled *Wycked Obsession.* You were on the road for a long time, almost six months, opening for anybody they paired you with."

I nod, and she keeps going.

"You took six months away from touring, except for local gigs and the occasional national appearance, and released *Wicked Is As Wycked Does* about a month ago. The first single is *Tonight,* hanging solidly in the top five on the charts. The video is concert and tour footage, but rumor has it that your next video will be a bigger production."

She pauses for a sip of iced tea, takes a breath, and then continues when I don't say anything. "You're on tour with Edge of Return, pretty damned impressive for a band less than two years out of Austin." She angles her head toward me like it's some sort of salute or something. "Your sister Bree is touring with you this summer, and your female fans are...not happy."

"What?" That part comes as a surprise. "Why do they care if Bree's with us?"

"You don't seem to be as..." She pauses as though searching for the right word. "Promiscuous with her around."

I laugh. I can't help it. *"Promiscuous?"* I shake my head. "Hell, English. They think we're not fucking enough 'cause my sister's along?"

"Apparently."

"Then they better be prepared to be disappointed for a while yet." My expression settles into something more serious. I never joke about what Bree means to me. "She's with us all summer, and my sister's way more important to me than some random fan's opinion."

"The two of you are close."

It's not a question, and I give a sharp nod. "Been there for each other through a lot."

"You could use that to...I don't know. Appeal to a different part of your audience." Her gaze slides away as she pauses. "Connect with the less horny ones?"

I give her a wicked smile that usually gets me my way. "Aren't many of those in our fan base, English. They're all hot for one of us."

"Lucky you."

"Jealous?"

"No." Her snort is damn cute, but then I feel myself tighten up. That's a description I usually reserve for my sister. "Just wondering how we can...upgrade that. Your sister—"

"Is off limits. Not using her for some media attention."

London angles her head, like she's seeing something new. Different. "All right."

I let it go. I'm a little touchy about Bree. She was just a kid when our sperm donor took off—eight and I was 12. Old enough to take up the slack, and I wanted her to stay a kid, fun loving and free of what the world is really like, for as long as possible. It worked for a while, but now she's complaining how she's grown up, and I'm too protective.

Bree might be almost 20, but...no. Screw that. Everything in me stiffens. I'm not ready for her to grow up. She pushed back against my *protective bullshit,* as she calls it, and I'm trying. Keeping my mouth shut as much as I can. It's easier when the other guys are there; we all keep an eye out for her and always have. I'm doing the best I can, but shit still gets out of hand.

Jesus! Our asshole stepfather, Gabe, is a prime example. He's been hitting on her for months now, for Christ's sake! Newly married to our mom, he thinks Bree ought to be some kind of sex toy for him.

Fuck, no. Fuck that—and him. He's the reason she's on tour with us, and I'm not letting anybody take advantage of his sick shit for some damn publicity!

"So what else do you have in mind for us?" It comes out as a snarky demand, but I don't care. This shit with Bree makes me crazy.

"What do you mean?"

"If you get the job." Deliberately, I make it sound less certain than it is in my mind. "What're your plans to get us out there?"

"Well..." She blinks, sips from her iced tea, and then relaxes against her seat to look at me. So, her ideas for publicity don't make her tense up. It says *confidence,* and I like that.

"I'd upgrade your website," she says finally. Slow and careful, like she's giving it serious thought before she speaks. "It needs a total redesign. Show off the album covers and your logo. I'd give you each a page, connect directly to merch sales and link to a YouTube channel for some video blogging. You've all got Facebook and Twitter accounts, but none of you use them effectively, so we'd change that. Post new content every day. Interact with some of your fan sites, maybe get the more serious ones to act like old-fashioned fan clubs used to. Start posting to Instagram, maybe some live feed, and—"

"Enough." I blow out a breath. "Jesus, I get it. Plaster us all over the internet."

"Pretty much."

"And where's this *content* coming from?"

She smiles. It's part daring and part naughty and hardens my dick again, just when it was starting to soften. *Jesus.* I want to know what the naughty part of her is thinking.

"Some from me. Some from you blokes. We'd set up a calendar—a system—and everybody participates. I'd organize and manage it, of course, and take up the slack on the days you don't post."

"Good luck getting the others to do anything. They don't listen to me."

She smirks. "They'll do it."

"You sound pretty sure of yourself."

"I'll...convince them."

What the hell does that mean? "Don't know how, but you're welcome to try."

Her smile widens. "Never dare a woman. Don't you know that?"

I drag a lazy, almost insolent gaze from her head as far down as I can see. She notices...and responds. I hear the sharp breath, cut off abruptly, and her nipples tighten beneath her bright blue top. Her smile fades.

"What else, honey?"

She swallows. "What?" Her voice is soft, ragged-sounding.

"What other dares you willing to take?"

Her eyes grow darker as she stares, narrow, and then her eyelids drift shut. Satisfaction mingles with an odd disappointment. I've seen women react that way a million times.

"Oh, you're good." Her eyes pop open, settling back to that unusual golden color, and she levels me with a harsh, serious gaze. "Bloody brilliant, actually. I don't know how you do it, exactly, but I see how you get your way."

"My way?"

She nods sharply, and a strand of reddish hair falls forward over her shoulder. "You give a girl *the look,* call her *honey,* and she falls in line with whatever you want. Clever wanker, aren't you?"

"Wanker?"

"Asshole." She lifts one shoulder in a casual shrug. "I've spent enough time in England to pick up some of their...idioms."

Idioms? She might use British expressions, but she doesn't have an accent. Sounds a little weird at times, but interesting, too. Can't help wondering what other contradictions London Kennedy hides deep inside her.

"You think that's what this is about?" I ask after a minute. "Some flirting so I can get in your pants?"

"Is it?"

"I don't fuck employees."

"I'm not your employee."

"You might be."

"And is this part of the interview? Deciding if you want to fuck me?"

Don't have to decide that. I wanted her from the second I saw her, and that hasn't changed. I *do* have something called self-control, however.

Why the hell don't people ever see beneath the manwhore reputation?

"Irrelevant," I snap in a cold voice, refusing to confirm or deny. I don't lie, but I don't give anybody any ammunition to use against me, either. "Who I fuck's my own business."

Uncertainty flickers in her eyes before she drops her lids to conceal it. I'm faster than that, smarter than that. Had to be, the way I grew up. Satisfaction that she got the message doesn't ease my irritation.

I'm a grown man, I haven't answered to anybody else since the sperm donor took off, and I don't have to tell her a goddamn thing about who I want to fuck.

Even if it's her?

"Anything else?" I demand.

"Pardon?" She pretends to look at me, but she doesn't really. Her voice is stiffly polite.

"Anything else you'd do?"

She swallows and takes a minute to answer. "Do you have a photographer touring with you?"

"No." I give my head a sharp shake. "Too intrusive."

She nods carefully, like she understands. "I'm not an expert, but I've taken some photography classes. I can manage internet-quality pictures and video. The label would hire a professional like today's photo shoot for the important things, anyway."

I stare at her like I'm expecting something more. And maybe I am. But I don't know what it is, unless it's for her to drop to her knees and tell me she wants to suck my cock—and that just pisses me off more.

"If we take you on," I snap, hearing the double entendre and glad it's only in my own freaking mind, "how soon can you be ready to start?"

"Immediately."

She does her best to hold my gaze but can't really do it. I know why. Been told often enough that my expressions intimidate the fuck out of people who don't know me well. I like it that way, have no interest in being subtle. What you see is what you get with me. I don't spill my guts of everything I know, but I don't pretend to be anything except exactly who I am.

God. I need to get out of here. I shouldn't be pissed off at her. None of this is her fault. She doesn't know I'm pushing her because of how bad I want to see her naked and spread wide open for me, her arms bound above her head while I eat her to more orgasms than she can count.

No, she's thinking any girl will do. And that's usually true. Something is seriously fucked up if I'm thinking I want *her,* specifically, over some random pussy.

My insides tighten, and I want to hit something. Kick it. Knock the ever-living shit out of it.

Forget all this ridiculous shit, I tell myself. *You played the relationship game once, and it was a goddamn disaster.*

Relationship? What the fuck? Just the thought pisses me off even more.

There was a girl. Once. After that blew all to shit, I decided never again. Even the girls I keep around for a month or two aren't real *relationships.* They're either convenient, or *that good.* They start expecting anything more than sex, and I'm outta there.

Every time.

Farren, the only girlfriend I ever had, taught me a lesson I've never, ever forgotten. No more girlfriends, no more relationships. Now I'm the kind of guy women want to fuck. To tell their friends they fucked a rock star with a big dick and a taste for rough, dirty sex. Permanent is never part of the game.

Romantic love doesn't exist. Pleasure—sex—makes a pretty good substitute, so I might as well get it wherever and however I can get it, and for as long as I want it. That means no emotions except knowing how good it feels to come. No need to explain shit. No reality except exactly the one I want.

Hey, all you motherfuckers. I'm Knox Gallagher. Songwriter, lead guitarist of Wycked Obsession...and manwhore.

CHAPTER 3

LONDON

I HAVE NO FREAKING CLUE HOW WELL THE INTERVIEW WENT. At first it seemed okay, despite the cock-grabbing incident. Then I pissed Knox off, and it went downhill from there. I'm not entirely sure how it all happened, but I know things didn't go quite like I hoped.

I've been trying to tell myself it's going to be *okay* for the last eighteen hours. I don't really believe it, not without some word from Knox or Baz. I know better than to expect to hear this soon, but I can't quite kill the hope that I might have somehow charmed my way into a job offer.

Don't be daft, I reprimanded myself with a snort of disgust. *You grabbed his bloody cock instead of shaking his hand! You gave him the impression he should use his sister as a media trick. You accused him of wanting to screw you as part of the interview. Great job, luv.*

God. When did I become such an idiot?

It's nine a.m., and I'm still in bed. I had a bloody hard time going to sleep last night, thinking about Wycked Obsession, the job—and Knox. About how he looked, both naked *and* in those damn tight jeans, and the tattoos that snaked over his body. I want to trace my fingers over them as he tells me what each one means, then drag my tongue along each image and taste him. Not only there, but I want to discover the wonders of his long, thick cock.

What is he? Nine, ten inches? And how big around? Could I even wrap my fingers all the way around him?

Jesus.

My lady parts clench, my pussy is unbelievably wet, and my nipples pop up like tight, aching buds. I shouldn't let myself think about Knox this way. It could jinx my chances—and if I *do* get the job, he'll be my boss...or the closest thing I'll have. Fantasizing about his dick isn't going to do either of us any favors.

But staying in bed, pretending that I'm not thinking about him, isn't helping, either.

Disgusted with myself, I scramble from the bed and start my day as usual. Coffee first thing, shower, and *then* find something to keep me occupied until I hear from Knox or Baz.

If *you hear from them today.* That damned snotty voice won't shut up.

Scowling, I hurry downstairs and wander into the huge chef's dream of a kitchen. My mom doesn't cook, doesn't have a full-time chef, but she *does* have a housekeeper who cooks and takes care of the ordinary household chores.

And me. Lucia takes care of me. She's more of a mom to me than my birth mother ever has been. It's mostly because of her that I still live in the house where I grew up. It's a mansion in the Hollywood Hills. I've lived here my whole life...and if I get the chance, I'll give it up for life on a rock band's tour bus.

In a bloody heartbeat.

"Good morning, sleepyhead."

"Morning, Luce."

She hands me a cup of coffee, with cream and sugar exactly the way I like it. I take a deep, long sip, and the sweet, smooth liquid warms my morning nerves.

God, that's good. Nobody makes coffee like Lucia.

"Your mama came home last night."

"She did?"

I plop down on one of the tall stools that fronts the counter where I've eaten most of my meals, done my homework, and listened to hours of Lucia's wise advice. Some of my favorite memories are of sitting here, across from her.

"*Sí.* Late."

Another sip of coffee, and then I say, "I thought she and my dad were spending the summer in England."

"Some meeting. Something business." Lucia shrugs. "Your papa follows her today. You know him."

Yeah, I do. Sort of. Enough that I can pretend to nod and drink more coffee without saying anything.

I can't say that I actually *know* Hugh Kennedy, the man. Or even Hugh Kennedy, the father. At least not the father that his other children see. His real, *legitimate* children. My half-sister and brothers, whom I've never met.

I know the often-absent papa who shows up *when he can,* he says. He smiles at me, gives me more money and presents than hugs, and talks to me sometimes. He doesn't listen when I talk back, though, and he *never* goes out in public with me.

Never, ever.

He doesn't actually go out with my mother, either. I don't know how they act with each other when they're alone; they don't show me that part of their lives. But while they might go out separately, they're very clearly *together.* They arrive individually, leave the same way, refuse to speak of their relationship in interviews, but everyone knows.

Even his wife in England. Or is it especially her?

When Hugh Kennedy is in L.A., he generally lives with Mom and me. They entertain here, he holds occasional business meetings here, and they spend many nights here alone. With me in my room most of the time. Or somewhere else—*anywhere else*—in the mansion. They like to be alone.

I'm their only child, but it's certainly a non-traditional upbringing. Hugh doesn't want me to mingle with other celebrities' kids, and so I don't. I mostly do what they ask of me, and live my life apart from their daily routine. It's been like this all my life, and I gave up wanting anything different years ago.

Then there's our English "life." My father lives on his grand estate with his wife, Adele, and their three children. That's a big chunk of the year, and so when I'm not in school, Mom and I holiday in England. We live in his manor house in London and see him whenever he can get away from his *family* obligations.

It isn't often, and it is clearly known that we are *not* his family.

I swallow a sigh and take a long drink of my now-cooled coffee. What the hell? Why am I thinking about this now? It is what it is, and I accepted the strangeness of it all long ago.

Maybe the *family* part of the interview with Knox put me on edge. Brought up realities I don't usually think about. How do you explain stuff like my life to somebody new?

Doesn't matter. It's too late now. Nobody else has to understand. I've been my father's dirty—and yet open—secret since the day I was born. Before that, really. From the minute that Marisol Malone got pregnant.

If anything still bothers me about it, it's that my father doesn't seem to feel bad—or guilty—about any of it. He has some odd, antiquated, and confusing sense of morality that only makes sense to him. The rest of us—legitimate and *illegitimate*—are some kind of collateral damage that have to live with the consequences.

And, yeah, it's a cocked-up way to grow up, but there it is. My life. My reality. I gave up trying to understand it by my sixth birthday.

"You want some breakfast, *chica? Huevos rancheros?*"

I'm glad for the interruption, because the direction of my thoughts is starting to piss me off. It's just a waste of bloody emotion and energy, and I gave it up a long time ago.

"Sí." I answer, finally. I don't want anything to eat, not really, but it's easier to let Lucia have her way. Besides, breakfast is *way better* than letting myself keep thinking about all that useless crap.

Lucia busies herself at the stove. "How was the job interview?"

"Okay. I think."

"You get the job?"

"I don't know yet. The band manager wasn't there. Maybe I'll hear today." *Or tomorrow.* The idea makes me frown.

"They would be *loco* not to hire you!"

I smile. I can always depend on Lucia's loyalty. "It's a rock band, Luce. I think they're supposed to be *loco.*"

She shakes her head and flips the tortilla she's frying on the griddle. Chorizo sizzles in a frying pan, while her special refried beans bubble in a saucepan at the back of the stove. They are smells of my childhood, as much as fish and chips in England, and In-N-Out Burgers in California.

I'm a real international girl, and I love all the differences.

At least that part of it came naturally from the way I was raised, and I'm glad for the experience. But now I have to find a place for London, the adult woman. A place where I fit in. Where I can be the person I am inside, depend on my own intelligence and actions, and not some false expectations that have nothing to do with me.

Not be included because of the people I know or who my parents are. Included, maybe, but never quite accepted. And if that means roaming the country with a rock band in their tour bus, bring it on! It might be better, actually. All the way around.

Maybe that's why my gut knows this is the perfect job for me. It's then, when my coffee is almost gone, that I realize I forgot my phone in my room. Damn.

"I'll be right back, Luce." I slip from the stool. "I need to get my phone."

"You and that phone." She shakes her head and cracks open the first of two eggs. "Go. Your eggs will be ready when you are back, *chica.*"

I race back to my room. I don't actually expect to hear from Knox, Baz, or even the record label this early in the day, but I'm a little superstitious. If my phone isn't nearby, I know the call will come and I'll miss it.

Maybe I should leave it upstairs, just to make sure it comes through.

I laugh to myself. I won't give in to *that* much superstition.

I grab my phone from its charger and glare at the screen. Nope. No missed calls and no texts waiting. But...what? A hell of a lot of notices about internet activity over Wycked Obsession. I okayed push notifications from some of the websites when I researched the band before my interview, and they're paying off big time right now.

I wander back to the kitchen as I pull up the first internet hit. *Wycked Obsession and Their Band Wife! Ménage a Cinq?*

What the bloody hell? I sink back onto my barstool.

Below the tawdry headline is a picture. Noah Dexter has his arms wrapped around the waist of a beautiful young woman who leans back against his chest. Rylan Myles and Ajia Stone stand on either side of them, and Zayne Prescott faces them with a huge, idiotic grin on his face.

I drop my gaze to the brief article printed beneath the picture. *Did Knox Gallagher give the guys in Wycked Obsession a major gift on this tour? Like...his sister? Our sources say,* yes. *Reports are that the band is involved in orgies and group sex with Breeanne Gallagher, Knox's younger sister, who's traveling with them on the summer's Edge of Return tour. The question is...is this simply a case of bandmates sharing the same woman, or are the rumors of incest true? Stay tuned!*

Bollocks and holy God!

I know two things almost immediately. The beautiful, dark-haired woman is Bree Gallagher, and Knox must be going out of his freaking mind. He made it very clear how he feels about his sister.

"The two of you are close."

"Been there for each other through a lot."

And then, later, when I started to suggest, *"Your sister—"*

"Is off limits. Not using her for some media attention."

There was affection, concern, even protectiveness in his expression and his voice. What I'd expect from a big brother. Nothing inappropriate or lustful.

Sure as hell nothing to hint at *incest.*

"Eat."

Lucia slides a plate in front of me. Two perfectly fried eggs decorate a tortilla heaped with refried beans and chorizo. *Pico de gallo,* sour cream and avocados top it all.

My favorite breakfast.

"Thank you."

I eat automatically, my thoughts racing to understand the paparazzi spin on the story about Bree Gallagher. More than that, guessing at the truth. I haven't a clue what started the whole thing, but somebody got the picture or spotted a story or...something. Whatever happened, it took off from there.

The good and the bad of the Internet all in one.

I'm not so mercenary to wonder what this might mean for me, but I do think about what I could do to help mitigate the damage. I probably won't get the chance, but it's exactly the kind of thing I should plan for.

Just in case.

♫

I'm just climbing out of the shower when my phone pings with a text. A couple of them, one right after the other. I wrap my hair in a towel and pad naked into the bedroom for my smartphone.

Knox: U been on the fucking internet today?

Knox: Seen the shitstorm?

I don't give myself time to think about my answer.

Me: Yeah. That sucks. Really sorry. Especially for your sister.

I dry myself as I wait for Knox's reply. It doesn't come, and so I dress in an ordinary bra and panties set. Okay, maybe not so ordinary, I think as I look at myself in the full-length mirror. They're white, but they're lacy and have some tiny pink bows. I bought them to cheer me up after Colin acted like such a douche. Even if nobody but me sees them, they make me feel good about myself.

Knox finally texts. *U free later?*

I frown at the phone.

Me: What do you have in mind?

Knox: Wycked Obsession party. Label's idea. Can U come?

Me: Uh...yeah. If you want me to.

Knox: Need 2 talk about this fucking PR shit. Can't have Bree's ass exposed like this.

Me: You hiring me?

Knox: Probably. Yeah.

I try to ignore a bubble of excitement in my chest.

Me: Terms?

Knox: Baz will text U with details. Email contract and NDA.

They want me to sign a non-disclosure agreement. I nod to myself. Not unexpected, and a good business decision.

Me: OK. Verbally agreeing.

Knox: Pack UR shit and bring it. UR with us now. 24/7.

I stare at the screen. With Wycked Obsession—and Knox—24/7 from here on out. It's what I wanted—isn't it?

I can't decide if I'm excited or scared to death.

Bloody hell.

Me: OK. See you at the party.

Knox doesn't reply, and part of me is glad. I hate the obligatory *ok* or *thumbs up* that people send when there's nothing left to be said. The rest of me wishes he'd send some little personal note. Like, *nice meeting you yesterday.*

Or a dick pic?

Don't be a wanker, I tell myself firmly. Not only do I not *need* a picture of Knox's cock—I remember what it looks like very well, thank you—but I don't *want* one. I don't give a damn if he's got a big dick, a hot body or is good looking as fuck.

You're off men—remember? I remind myself. At least for a while. The memory of Colin and his douchebaggery is enough to do that.

Besides, Knox is going to be my *boss.* If it's just sex I'm after, I can hook up with anybody on the tour except him.

As if there's any other guy on the tour who's worth considering.

And—what the hell? What the bloody fuck am I doing thinking about this now? *No men!* How many times do I have to remind myself?

I jerk my suitcase out of my closet and force myself to stare at my wardrobe. Dresses? Skirts? Is business casual too much? Ordinary casual too…casual?

I sort through my options, and then I remember. The one thing I'm not going to leave home without. Especially with Knox Gallagher around every damn day. Not considering my very traitorous thoughts.

I stalk back into my bedroom, open my nightstand drawer, and pack my one essential.

My rabbit vibrator.

CHAPTER 4

Knox

EVERYONE AGREES THIS PARTY IS SUPPOSED TO BE A GOOD IDEA. Baz; the label and their little mouthpiece, Marty; the band. Twenty-four hours ago, I thought so, too.

Now, it's all fucked up.

I stand near the bar, waiting for a Jack on the rocks, and look around the room. The label took over a restaurant for this thing, located on top of one of the fancy hotels in L.A., and the place looks like it's filled to capacity. The cynical part of me knows it's because of the free food and booze, more than because they give a shit about Wycked Obsession or our music.

I saw Baz earlier, but he's missing again. Probably taking care of a bunch of crap that I don't even know about. I grab the back of my neck and squeeze. It irks me a little, depending on Baz to do so much, but I can't do it all.

I can't control everything, as Bree likes to remind me.

I search the crowd until I find her, one arm linked through Ajia's as they drink champagne and listen to...who the hell knows? I haven't met the old geezer they're talking to, and I don't want to. Not interested in being bored to death like they must be. I can tell by the way my sister shifts her weight from side to side, and how Ajia keeps looking around the room, like he's desperate to get away.

Welcome to life as a rock star.

At least they look the part of the rich and famous. Bree's dressed in a black fuck-me dress with matching heels, and both piss me off. I can't bitch about it, though, because she didn't pick them out; Baz had some personal shopper send them to her room.

Besides, I promised to give her some space. I don't like it, but I get it. Kind of. She's almost 20 and says she's grown up. I just want to protect her, like our sperm donor didn't.

At least Ajia's dressed kind of conservatively. A lot like me, actually, in a suit and tie and his hair pulled back in a ponytail. I'm in gray, he's all in black, and I gotta admit they look fucking hot together. If I didn't know 'em, I'd think it was a great marketing campaign. Like they're each half of a pair. Seeing that pisses me off, too.

Is it a good idea for them to be together, hiding in plain sight, according to Rye? Bree's had a silly crush on Ajia for a long time. Putting them this close together...well, I don't like it. Especially because I have to give her some space right now. At least in public. Because of those goddamn rumors.

We had to do something, and I got outvoted on this one.

"Your drink, sir."

The bartender hands me a glass, and I kick up a corner of my mouth. Sir? They're way too freaking polite here.

"It's Knox," I say, and he nods with a smile.

I look around again. There was a time when we all dreamed about shit like this. A record label throwing parties for us. Crap like fancy tour buses, limos, and security. Videos, albums, traveling the country, playing sold-out shows, and having more pussy than we could ever fuck.

Well, we've got all that shit now. And the ever-loving gossip that goes with fame. Didn't plan on that.

Fucking paparazzi.

Who the hell would say shit like that about Bree? Sleeping with the band? Orgies and sharing her between them? And...*me?* Fucking my own sister?

Anybody saying shit like that makes me want to puke.

And Bree... She's innocent in all this. It's Gabe's fault, the motherfucker. If Mom's new husband knew how to keep his goddamn hands to himself, we wouldn't be in this position.

Only Baz and the band know about our stepfather wanting to fuck—hell, *rape*—my sister, and it's gonna stay that way. But, *Jesus!* Gossip and rumors about a band ménage and me fucking my own sister make it so much worse. It ramps up my temper to overload, but we're gonna deal with it.

Have to.

We're hiring London Kennedy. Today.

Knew I wanted to hire her from the get-go, but she pissed me off. Pushed me. Challenged me. Reminded me of shit I left behind me a long time ago. So I had a little tantrum and was almost ready to change my mind. Then this happened, and that made all the difference. *Nobody* is fucking with Bree.

I glance around the room again, just to look things over. Noah and Rye are making the rounds, chatting up execs and their women. Wives? Girlfriends? Doesn't matter. Those guys can charm little old ladies in wheelchairs. Even Zayne's doing his part, hanging with Marty and some other suits.

Weight shifts heavily on my shoulders as I watch Zayne. He's struggling. Drugs, alcohol, women. A fist forms in my gut. I don't know exactly what's going on with him; he won't say. Doesn't mean I can't guess. We agreed—no drugs. Ajia pushed us to agree to nothing more than weed, and nobody wanted to argue it with him. We understand his crap with it, and we respect it.

Now, we're a couple of weeks into the tour, and Zayne's using already. I'm sure of it—and it pisses me off for the band. Worse, it worries me for him.

Gotta figure this shit out.

I turn away, and it's then that I see her. London. Standing in the doorway, wearing her own version of a fuck-me dress. It's short and tight, hugging her tits and curvy hips in a very seductive way. Her dress is a dark-blue color with some lacy shit over the top, and her hair's all loose, falling just around her shoulders.

Jesus Christ. It's like my cock has eyeballs of its own and notices every fucking detail. I go hard in seconds.

She hasn't seen me yet, and I watch as she inspects the ridiculous posters plastered all over the room. *Fuck.* They're from yesterday's photo shoot. No idea how they got the prints made up so fast, but I guess the right amount of money can do anything.

I glance at the huge black-and-white posters. As a group, we look like we're ready to step onstage. I like the energy, the fire. The others—the stupid-ass individual shots—are different. I guess we're all supposed to look like we're ready to fuck the next girl we see—and we fucking do. I hate it.

I search until I find the one of me. Unshaven, hair back, the glint of my diamond earring caught by the camera. Worse, my pants are undone, pushed down over my hips just enough to leave you wondering if it's shadows or a tease of manscaping there. My thumbs are hooked over the waistband, fingers splayed wide over my hips. Looks like I'm ready to shove 'em off completely.

It could be worse, I suppose. I could have had to put my hand down my pants, like Ajia did.

And if it's all such a bad joke, why don't I laugh?

"Knox."

I blink and discover London standing in front of me.

"English. You made it."

She smiles faintly. "Yes, of course."

"Bring your shit?"

"I arranged everything with Baz. He had a car pick me up. I stopped by your hotel, checked in and left my luggage there."

"You didn't pack too much, did you?"

I'm being kind of a jackass, but I can't seem to stop myself. There's something about this woman that pushes at me, and I can't see how else to deal with it.

Her expression tightens, but she smooths it out so quickly, I almost miss it. Yep. I pissed her off.

"As I said, I arranged everything with Baz. He told me how much space I was allowed, and I packed accordingly."

I nod and let it go. It's the best thing all the way around, and for once, I try to follow some kind of good judgment. London Kennedy can help us, and I don't want to start out making things any more fucked up than they already are.

"Want a drink?" I gesture to the bartender.

"White wine, please."

I place the order and ask what I've been wanting to since I saw her. "You got any ideas how to handle this shitstorm?"

"I've made some notes and jotted down a few things. We can talk later, but for now—" she pauses when the bartender brings her wine "—making a public appearance like this is good."

"Group decision. Rye thought it would be good for her to be front and center with Ajia." I nod in their direction.

London glances across the room. They've escaped the boring old guy, and Bree's left Ajia, headed for...the bathroom? Looks like it.

"He's right." London turns back to me. "Hiding would indicate shame or guilt."

"I'm keeping my distance." Irks the shit out of me to say it.

"Also a good idea." She nods. "Like you trust her with Ajia and have no reason to...hover."

I snort. If she only knew the rest of it, what we left behind in Austin and how much I want to protect my baby sister. And, hell, that's the truth and nothing but the truth. It's my job to take care of everybody in the band. My responsibility.

"What about the rest of the guys?" London asks as her gaze slips through the crowd.

I lift my shoulder in a shrug "We all agreed Bree'd be best with Ajia and the rest of us would back off. No...group shit, you know?"

"Good idea. Looks like you've done a great job with your reactions so far."

"We all love Bree. Don't want anybody to fuck with her."

London rests a hand on my forearm, and my body goes into instant and total arousal. Like I wasn't already hard. Damn prick.

It makes me realize suddenly how much bigger I am than her. She's got a slender frame, looks almost too thin for her hourglass figure, and even though she's wearing heels high enough that her legs look so ridiculously long, she's still at least six inches shorter than me.

A sharp twist of protectiveness arcs through me, and I stiffen. All over. My cock likes the differences. And the idea of covering her. In every way.

What the fuck?

She's talking, but I can't make sense of the words. My brain is demanding an answer to that question. *What the fuck?*

I'm used to being bigger than the girls I fuck. I'm not a huge guy—not as big as Noah—but I'm a little over 6'2" and work out enough to have a body the right size for my height. Besides, chicks seem to like muscular guys.

Chicks? Like the one last night?

I don't remember a whole hell of a lot about that one. Not her name or her face. She was smaller than London in every way. Flat chest, no hips...and I picked her for exactly that reason. Didn't want to be thinking about London when I was fucking somebody else. But then, when that chick had her mouth around my dick, the sudden image of London's fingers wrapped around my cock grabbed me by the throat, and I exploded like a fucking roman candle. Came so hard the chick couldn't take it all.

Son of a bitch.

A sour fist knots in my stomach. Didn't want the girl anymore after that. Got her off with my fingers and a few slaps on the ass, and then sent her on her way. Didn't think of it again until now, when the memory carries a serious sense of revulsion.

What the fuck? The question comes again.

"Knox?"

"Yeah?"

"Did you hear me?"

"Uh...no." I toss back the rest of my drink and gesture toward the bartender for another. "Sorry. I was watching the crowd."

Her hand is gone from my arm, I realize, and I look down into her face. I wish she'd left it there. She smiles warily.

"I was saying that your instincts were good. Your group thinking is solid. There are other things we can do to protect your sister and turn attention away from this story. We'll make a plan."

"Like?"

"Like replace it with something else. A charitable act. Talk about the next single, the next video. Teasers about the photo shoot." She gestures toward the posters. "Lots of things. We can brainstorm later, and within a day or two, we can turn things in an entirely new direction. Your call which way they go."

I'm glad for something else to concentrate on. I hate this rumor shit about Bree, but I don't wanna go back to thinking about sex, either. Not when London's standing next to me. Can't really afford it now, and sure as hell can't afford it *here*.

I force myself to nod in agreement. "We'll have a band meeting tomorrow. Introduce you to everybody and figure this shit out."

"Okay." She pauses to sip her wine. "Good," she adds, like she isn't sure what else to say. I notice, but I'm also kind of distracted.

Where's Bree? I haven't seen her since she went in the direction of the restrooms, and now Ajia's missing, too. Did something happen? I snatch my fresh drink from the bar and start across the floor.

"Knox!"

It's London's voice, coming from behind me. I stop and turn back. "What?"

"Where are you going?"

"What?" I ask again.

"You have...a look on your face."

"What kind of look?"

She pulls in a breath deep enough that I can see the rise and fall of her breasts. And—goddammit! I shouldn't notice.

"Like you're ready to rip somebody a new asshole."

I blink. "Just looking for Bree. And Ajia. I don't see 'em."

"Relax." She comes closer, puts that same small hand over my forearm and squeezes. "They're all right. Just let the evening play out, and everything will be fine."

"But—"

"What do you think could have happened in a room full of people?"

"Somebody could have said something."

"Something worse than they've already said?"

She's got me there. "Probably not."

"Okay, then. You circulate, play the cocky rock god, and I'll find Baz. Let him know I'm here. Maybe he's seen Ajia and Bree."

I let out a breath. She's right. Okay. I can do this. I search my brain for a safe middle ground.

"You think I'm a cocky rock god?"

London looks at me until she gets this crooked little smile. "Bollocks." She snorts. "I should have known that's the part you'd listen to."

I'm surprised by an answering grin. What is it about London Kennedy?

"What can I say, English? We cocky rock gods have a reputation to keep up."

She shakes her head. "What the bloody hell have I gotten myself into?"

I give her a look, raised eyebrow and wide innocent eyes. She laughs.

"Keep trying, Rock God. Mingle." She waves her hand. "Give the people a thrill. I'll see you later."

She turns with a swing of her hips, working her way through the crowd with a smile and an occasional sip of her white wine. I watch, my eyes trained on her ass and wonder, not for the first time, what she'll look like, bent at the waist and waiting for my cock.

CHAPTER 5

LONDON

THE WYCKED OBSESSION PARTY IS A SUCCESS. At least, that's what Baz and Marty, the record company exec responsible for the band, tell me. I can easily believe it, if the energy in the room and excited expressions of the partygoers mean anything. Even so, a new buzz is humming through the crowd around me, and I'm not quite sure what it means. I can't pick up enough of any one conversation to understand what's behind it.

Mentally, I cross my fingers. *Please, God.* I send up a little prayer. *Let it be something simple like they ran out of champagne.*

I pass my empty wine glass to a passing waiter and decline a refill. Some odd nervousness scrapes through me, likely due to the band suddenly hiring me and the nasty rumors we're dealing with. More alcohol doesn't seem like a good idea at the moment.

I shoot an anxious gaze around the room but can't quite find anything that looks out of place. It's all ordinary enough, until I see Knox stalking out through the doorway.

Bollocks. He has a mean step in that stride. I don't know how I think I can tell the difference or what it means, but I'm not waiting to find out.

I rush across the room as fast as my heels will allow, whispering vague apologies as I work my way through the crowd. I catch up with him at the elevator.

"Knox? What's wrong?"

He punches the down button a few times.

"Knox?" I repeat.

"Motherfucker," he snaps without looking at me. "I'm going to kill that motherfucking asshole."

"Knox!"

Grabbing his arm, I squeeze. The hard-muscled strength beneath his suitcoat surprises me a little. I mean, I knew he was *built,* but I never really thought about it translating to such strength. Thank God, my touch gets his attention enough that he looks at me, and I can drop my hand.

"What?"

"What happened?" God, I need to sound anything besides *breathless.*

He smacks the heel of his hand against the elevator control buttons and mutters under his breath. I can't make it out, except to know it's more cursing. "What do you think?" he finally demands, glaring at me.

"I don't know." I say it softly. Calmly. Anything to take the edge off his temper. "I'm sorry."

"Ajia. Fucking. Stone."

"Ajia?" I blink. He's been nowhere on my radar, except as Bree's escort tonight. "What's he done? What happened?"

"That mother—"

The elevator dings, and he breaks off, waiting for the doors to open. I have no choice but to hop in with him. He jams a finger at the *Lobby* button, and eventually, finally, the doors close.

"Knox?" I say when he doesn't speak again.

"That motherfucker is dead fucking meat."

"You're pissed. I get that. I just don't know *why."*

"Why?" He stares at me like I've lost my mind. "You're asking me *why?"*

I glare back at him. "Well, bloody hell, Knox, this makes *no sense.* You've got to give me more than that. Ajia was Bree's date for tonight. He—"

"Don't fucking say that." His stare is lethal.

"Say what? You planned it! They were together tonight to keep—"

"Keep?" His voice is almost a roar. "Keep *her?* Keep her what? *Safe?* Motherfucker. He kept her for *himself."*

God. I swallow. I wish he'd stop saying motherfucker, because it just ramps him up, and I have no clue how to deal with

Knox Gallagher in a rage. All I've got is instinct and the very slight knowledge I have of dealing with him from the few moments since we first met.

"Something happened." I say it as a statement.

"No fucking shit. What was your first clue?"

"Don't be a jackass," I snap. This man might be my boss and the hottest thing this side of the planet, but his sarcasm pisses me off, and I don't give a damn right now.

"You're not taking your bad mood out on me," I add stiffly. "If you think that's part of my job description, then you can bloody well stuff it."

He doesn't respond, doesn't even look at me. He stares at the red blinking numbers until we reach the lobby and the elevator doors slide open. I expect him to stalk away to...wherever, but he surprises me when he waits after he steps out of the elevator.

A man in a non-descript suit stands a few feet away. The instant he spots Knox, he heads in our direction.

"The limo is waiting," he says simply. "It will return for the others."

Knox nods. "London, this is Kel." He waves a hand between us. "Kel, London. She's with us from now on."

Kel nods and takes my hand when I offer it. "Ma'am. I'm head of the band's security."

"Nice to meet you." Security? I didn't realize Wycked Obsession needed that kind of protection. "I'm PR. I...we should probably talk soon, so I don't make any security mistakes."

He nods seriously and gestures for us to proceed. "Just let me know."

Knox is right behind me. I can feel the heat of his body, and I catch a sudden whiff of something spicy and almost...chocolate. I noticed it yesterday, too, but I thought it was some delightful mix of a Starbucks' scent. Now I realize it's Knox, and I suddenly want to lean into him and breathe it in.

Don't be a daft cow! I give myself a mental jerk. *He was just acting like a cocked-up wanker, and now you want to* sniff *him?*

Yeah, so maybe Colin wasn't much good in the bedroom. That doesn't mean I'm not still pissed at him that he couldn't give me even one night of mediocre sex—one damn orgasm—to make up for three very dry months when it was just me and my little rabbit. If he had, maybe these first few meetings with Knox Gallagher wouldn't have me on such a sexual edge. I mean, once I get to know him better and get a regular dose of his horse's ass personality, my awareness of his hotness will fade.

Won't it?

God, I hope so. I don't want to spend the next couple of months on Wycked Obsession's tour bus, flipping between wanting to kill the guy and then screw him. But...oh, what a splendid screwing it would be! Everything in my woman's intuition tells me so.

Stop it! Just...stop!

We're going to be working closely; I know that much. I'm not sure about the rest of it. Baz said they have two buses and they're still working out my accommodations. *Please, God, let them put me on the crew bus and not the one for the band.*

That just might kill me. Horny after my dry spell and sleeping in the same space as five rock gods? No thank you!

The limo driver is waiting. He holds the door open, I climb inside, and Knox follows. I'm grateful for the diversion from my stupid, wandering thoughts and flop down on the long bench seat along the side. I catch an extra breath to soothe the rapid beat of my heart and steal a chance to settle myself.

It's when the limo pulls forward that Knox speaks. "Here." He shoves his smartphone at me.

I take the phone and automatically look at the screen. It's a picture, a couple dressed in black and standing close together in an elevator. I look closer. It's Bree Gallagher and Ajia Stone.

I touch the screen, and the video feed begins to cycle. They're still for a moment, and then Ajia turns to Bree. I don't get a chance to breathe before he's kissing the holy shit out of her. He drags her against him, her hands clutch his shoulders, and then he has her pressed against the wall. His head is bent, she's up on her tiptoes, and they're making out like they're on the Titanic as it's going down.

The video stops, loops to start over again, and I touch the screen to stop it. I stare at it a moment longer, but what can I do? Say? I hand the phone back.

"Where did you get that?" I ask softly.

"It's on the fucking Internet."

"The Internet?" I shouldn't sound as shocked as I do, but I know it's from tonight. They're wearing the same clothes as they were at the party. "What made you look?"

He shoves a hand into his hair, pulls some of it from his very civilized ponytail, and he looks suddenly wild. Entirely fuckable, that X-rated part of me notices, and pisses me off. Now is not the time, and, I do *not* want Knox Gallagher to be the man! Worse, my panties are damp, and I sense an odd new fluttering deep in my core.

Oh, no you don't! This is not acceptable! I shout the words inside my mind. Just because he's hot as hell and smells good enough to lick, I am *not* thinking about him that way!

"Some chicks were talking," he's saying, and I force myself to listen. "At the party."

That's it? "And...?"

He slants a fierce gaze in my direction. The evening shadows are growing, but it's still light enough that I can see his expression well enough. He's furious, but he's searching for some measure of control. Maybe the smooth limo ride, the forced time alone, or actually processing the events will help.

I want to reach for him, encourage him, but I know better. For both of us.

"I heard it third or fourth hand," he says irritably. "Fuckers. That Ajia said the shit on the Internet was bullshit, that he was keeping Bree all for himself."

I straighten in my seat. "Do you think he really said that?"

"Doesn't matter." One broad shoulder lifts. "Already learned how fast this shit can move. I pulled up the Internet, and there it was. Security feed from the hotel. That fucker kissing my sister."

I pull out my own smart phone, open the notes app, and start typing. *Who started the rumors at the party? Who from the hotel was working security? How would they get the elevator video and upload it so fast? Who leaked it to the internet?*

I slip my phone back in my clutch purse and allow myself a quick look at Knox. He's turned away from me, staring out the window, hands on his thighs, and one leg bounces up and down. Nervous tension, or feeling out of control?

"Knox?"

"What?" He doesn't look at me.

"How old is Bree?"

He swings his head around and scowls at me. The loose hair catches on his lips, and he pushes it away. "What?" he demands again.

"How old is Bree?"

"Nineteen. And I know what you're going to fucking say. Same shit she's been saying all summer."

I don't move. "She's old enough to kiss a guy."

"No—" He cuts the words off and closes his eyes. When he opens them again, he won't meet my gaze. "Maybe she is. But not fucking Ajia."

"Why not Ajia?"

"Why not?" His voice rises an octave, like he can't believe I asked the question. "You fucking researched us. You ought to know. He's twenty-four years old, and he's a manwhore."

"So are you." The words are out before I can stop them, so I add, quickly, "Not any worse than *any* of you."

"I know." He reaches up to squeeze the back of his neck. "I fucking *know*. I know exactly his type, because I'm the same fucker. I know how he treats chicks, because it's how *I* treat chicks. Hell, I've heard—seen—him fucking. He's seen me."

A bubble of emptiness keeps me from responding. Is it because of his level of personal truthfulness? Or is it the reminder of his manwhore reputation and this stupid feminine awareness I have for him?

"He's not the one for Bree," he says finally and allows me to catch his distant gaze.

"Don't you think that's her decision?"

"Her decision?" Knox sounds oddly tired, still angry, and yet tempered with a frustration that doesn't seem new. "What the fuck, English? How can she decide shit? She's nineteen years old. She doesn't...know."

"And you're twenty-three. *So much older.*" Sarcasm sharpens my voice.

He blinks. "You have no fucking idea."

"All right." I offer one hand, palm up, hoping to both learn something and prevent further argument. "Tell me."

"No. Fuck no. Not now. Not...tonight."

"Why?"

"I got other shit on my mind."

The limo slows, and I peer out to see that we're approaching the band's hotel. Damn. I'd hoped for a little more time. There's so much more to know, to understand. The rumors about Bree and the band suck, but the idea of her with Ajia doesn't seem so bad.

But...how can I know for sure? I haven't even met them yet. I'm assuming she's a normal 19-year-old, he's a normal 24-year-old, and they've connected after knowing each other for five years. It doesn't sound so strange or unacceptable, so what's Knox's problem?

I try again. "Knox?"

He's already opening the limo door, not waiting for even hotel security, and so I follow him awkwardly. I catch up with him at the bank of elevators, where he's already pushed the *up* button.

"Can we talk?" I try again.

"About what?"

"About...this." I wave my hand. "About your sister and—"

"No."

"But—"

"I'm talking to that fucker first. Ajia. After that—"

The arriving elevator cuts off whatever else he would have said. We're the only ones inside, and he punches the button for the same floor I'm going to.

"After that, what?" I ask.

He shrugs.

"What if they're together?" I ask the question as carefully as I can.

Tension radiates from him like a bomb just went off inside of him. "They probably are."

"What are you going to do?"

"My business."

"Knox..."

"My business," he repeats. His jaw is clenched so tightly I wonder that he doesn't break a tooth.

"If I can help—"

"Look, English." He shoots me a flat gaze. "We'll meet up tomorrow. Have that band meeting we talked about." He laughs harshly. "Ought to be real fucking interesting. I'll text you about it."

"Are you sure? How about if I go with you and—"

"No."

"Knox..."

"No."

I want to reach for him, but I know better. He's wound as tight as I've ever seen anybody, and I can't even guess what he'll do if I touch him.

"If you need anything—"

"I've got your number."

"Don't hesitate to—"

"I won't," he snaps just as the elevator dings our arrival. The doors swish open, and Knox is gone without another word.

CHAPTER 6

KNOX

I POUND ON AJIA'S DOOR BEFORE I STOP WALKING. "Goddammit, Ajia! Open this fucking door! Right this fucking minute!"

I wait, not long, I admit it, and pound again when nothing happens. I can only guess what's going on inside his room—and I don't want any of the details, thank you very much.

"Ajia, you fucker! Open the goddamn door!"

I wait seconds longer and am almost ready to break the fucking thing down when I hear the locks clicking. The door swings inward, and Ajia stands in front of me wearing a pair of jeans. Zipped but unbuttoned.

We're about the same height, the same build, but the similarities end there. Ajia is lighter, with blond hair and strangely colored brown eyes. He's got an easier personality, not boisterous like Noah but not as heavy as me. It's what makes us good songwriting partners.

That shit might just end. Tonight.

"Where is she?" I demand. I can't see shit around him, and the longer he stands in my way, the more pissed off I am.

Ajia stares at me, his gaze flat and almost...resigned. To what? He's the fucker who stepped over a line.

A big fucking line.

He steps back finally, spreading one arm wide. I shove my way inside and find Bree standing next to the unmade bed, her hair all tangled around her shoulders in that just-fucked look. She's wearing Ajia's favorite Led Zeppelin T-shirt—and nothing else, from what I can tell.

The details register in seconds. *"You motherfucker!"*

I spin on the ball of one foot, satisfaction zooming clear through me when my fist connects with his jaw. Ajia stumbles back against the wall.

"Knox!" Bree races across the room and shoves herself between me and him. "Stop it, right now! Goddammit!"

I pull my arm back, as pissed off as I've ever been, but I can't do anything more with my sister between me and that asshole. I'm hanging on to my temper by a thread, but it's strong enough to protect her. For now.

Something that fucker failed to do.

"Ajia, baby." She reaches for his face. "Are you okay?"

What the fuck?

He grabs her hand and lowers it between them, then links their fingers together. He's not looking at her, though; his gaze is focused totally on me.

"That's your free one, bro," Ajia says. "Maybe I even deserved it. But any more and I fight back."

Not wasting any time with this shit. "Get the fuck away from him, Bree."

"How did you find out?"

"That's your question? You got nothing else to say?"

"Knox—"

"No, A," Bree interrupts. "This is between my brother and me."

"Fuck if it is." That just pisses me off. "He's the one—"

"Forget it." She looks at me with a damn serious gaze. I don't want to believe my fucking eyes when she steps closer to him. "You have *no say* in this."

I shift forward and give her an ugly smile. "Oh, baby girl, I have a lot to fucking say about this. And you're going to listen to every fucking word."

Ajia pulls her close, like he's protecting her. *From me?* "Cool the fuck off, man," he says.

"Cool off?" I can't believe what I'm hearing, and my laugh sounds nasty. *"Cool off?* You have no fucking clue what's going on inside of me right now."

"Got a pretty good idea. I get it, man. Let's talk."

Then the asshole spoils it by touching her hair. "You okay, baby?" He says it so softly, I almost don't hear. "Why don't you go on back to your room, and—"

"Good idea," I snap. "You don't need—"

"Don't fucking tell me what I need to do! Either of you." Bree moves aside and frowns from him to me. "I'm a big girl now. *I* get to decide what I do—and that's *not* leaving the two of you alone to do whatever stupid shit you'd end up doing."

"Bree...c'mon." She's full of shit if she thinks I'll give up that easily. "You—this fucker—"

"What, Knox?" If I'm pissed, so is she. More than I can remember seeing her in a long fucking time. "What is it you think you have to say? Because I thought I put you on notice in Phoenix. Weren't you listening? My life, my body—*my decision!* You don't get to say one goddamn word about *anything.*"

Fuck! "You weren't talking that way when you wanted help to get away from Gabe." The words are out before I can think about what I'm saying.

"Son of a—"

Bree cuts off Ajia. "Knox, you goddamn *asshole!* That's not the fucking same thing, and you know it."

She's right; I *do* know it. I'm just so fucking pissed, it's all coming out wrong.

Pissed? A voice inside my head laughs at me. *You aren't mad. You're fucking scared. Like a little girl pissing in her pants. And maybe even jealous! You don't want to lose Bree, not to Ajia or anybody else. You want to be the one to keep her safe, like the sperm donor didn't.*

And that, I know, is complete and utter bullshit. The result of one too many Jack-on-the-rocks on top of all the other shit that's been going on. I'm not *scared* or *jealous.* Protective, yeah, I'll admit it. But this is Ajia fucking Stone, the face of Wycked Obsession and blue-ribbon manwhore.

Not the kind of guy I want my sister to date.

Date? Hell, it's past that. The kind of guy I want my sister to fuck.

I lose my train of thought when Bree stalks up to me and pokes my chest. "Listen to me, Knox," she says in a low voice that almost doesn't sound like her, "because this is the *last* time

I'm talking to you about any of it. That shit with Gabe wasn't about my choices, my life, and you damn well know it. It was about *our mother's husband* trying to force me into something sexual! *Something I didn't—and don't—want.* My relationship with Ajia is completely different."

I know the first part is true and open my mouth to agree, but the rest of it echoes in my mind. *My relationship with Ajia is completely different.*

"He's like your fucking brother!"

She laughs but doesn't exactly sound amused. "Do you *hear* yourself? I have *never* seen Ajia as my brother, and you damn well know it. Everybody in the fucking band knows it. Hell, probably half of Austin knows it! I thought I was so clever, keeping my little a secret, but y'all knew. Y'all must have thought it was so cute. Silly little Bree with her big crush on a *man* like Ajia Stone."

She shakes her head and sends a sharp look in my direction. "Well, the truth is, I've been in love with him since the first day we met. *Love,* Knox, not some stupid teenage crush. It's been five years—*five years*—and my feelings have only gotten stronger."

Five years? *Five fucking years?*

"So, all that shit you said in Phoenix?" The shit about *nothing happening?* "It was all fucking lies?"

"No." It's Ajia who answers as he steps close behind her. "It was all true. Every fucking word."

"So you didn't start fucking her until—"

"Knox, I swear to God I'm going to pound the fucking shit out of you!" Ajia's fury isn't anywhere close to what I'm feeling.

"Get over there, Knox!" Bree jabs her finger toward the table and chairs across the room.

"Fuck you! I'm—"

"Get your ass over there!" She goes up on her tiptoes to get in my face. "You two are *not* fighting over me!"

I don't want to move. It goes against everything I am. But Bree keeps glaring at me until I start across the room, to the table in the corner.

Does Ajia *have* to stroll over to the unmade bed and sprawl against the headboard?

Bree perches against the dresser opposite me. "Okay," she says. She sounds calm enough, but I know better. I know everything about my baby sister.

Or I thought I did.

"It's time for an actual discussion," she adds after a second. "An *adult* discussion. You're going to talk—and *listen."*

I'm too pissed off to do anything but stare daggers in response.

"You never answered me. How did you find out?"

I open my mouth, want to ask the same question as earlier. That's *your question? You got nothing else to say?* Jesus Christ, how did this all get so fucked up?

"Answers, Knox," Bree insists before I can say a goddamn word. *"Adult conversation."*

I shake my head. "How do you think? The fucking Internet."

"Again?" snaps Ajia.

My look should incinerate them both. "What the fuck did you expect? You tell some chicks at the party that you're keeping Bree all to yourself, and you think that isn't going to run the room in, like, five seconds? Then the photographer—the legit one—got all kinds of shots of the two of you together."

"It's what Marty wanted," says Ajia stiffly.

"Yeah? Including one of you *kissing* when you got on the elevator together?"

"That doesn't sound so bad," Bree says, her voice softer than it was earlier. Good. Maybe she's finally getting what a shit storm she's gotten herself into.

"Then maybe it was the video of the two of you making out in the fucking elevator."

"What the fuck?" Ajia straightens on the bed.

Bree stares. "What video?"

"Security footage."

She turns her look to Ajia, who shrugs. "Never thought about security cameras in the elevator."

"How'd anybody get that?"

My sister sounds kind of lost, and so I shrug. "How do the tabloids get any of that shit? Somebody knows somebody who…fill in the blank. I guess somebody had an in with security at the hotel."

She nods, and I can see she's trying to process all this shit. Welcome to the world of stardom. I don't say it. I know it'll come out shitty, because that's the way I feel.

"So," I say instead. "You gonna answer my questions now?"

"As long as they're reasonable. What do you want to know?"

I shoot Ajia a look that should kill him right there. "How long?"

"Recently," Bree says carefully. "A couple of days, actually."

"C'mon, baby." Ajia leans forward with a soft smile meant totally for my sister. "You know things have been different since we left Austin."

"Austin!" It explodes from me. "Jesus, Bree! You saw some chick sucking him off there! He's a goddamn manwhore and you—"

"Who was there to comfort me when I had that nightmare, Knox?" she snaps back. "It was Ajia, because you were too busy fucking your one-and-done for the night. And last night? *Last night* I came to Ajia's room, because I was sick of listening to you and your fuck of the night. 'Spank my ass, Knox, and make me come on your cock!' Or maybe it was when you said, 'Take my cock down your throat!'"

Jesus Christ! That chick I fucked so I wouldn't think too much about London. I was drunk, pissed off, and—fuck! Bree *heard* that?

"You're such a goddamn hypocrite, Knox," she says before I can process it. "You're fucking anything with two legs and a pussy. No different from what you say Ajia was doing. Yeah, I get it. But if he and I want to see what we've got between us—you don't get a say!"

"See what you've got?" I don't know if I'm more pissed off at the idea of her trying for something with Ajia, or if it's a delayed reaction from the idea that my baby sister heard me fucking some one-night stand. *Jesus!*

"There are no guarantees, bro. I know that. But we'll never know unless we give it a shot. And we're only a couple of days into *that."*

"Bree..." Her name comes out soft. "You're different from most girls. Different from most chicks we see on tours. You—" I shake my head. "He's no good for you, baby girl."

"He's right about that, kitten," Ajia agrees. "We all know damn well that you're too fucking good for me."

"That is such bullshit, and you both know it!" She pierces me with narrowed eyes and points. "You two wouldn't be such good friends, and Ajia and I wouldn't have this *connection,* if it were. So don't try to pull any of that crap on me."

Something changes, some softness in her or something, and she says quietly, "Knox, sweetie...here's the deal. I'm twenty in a couple of weeks. Not a teenager any longer! Most girls lose their virginity in high school, the back seat of a car or some party or— who the hell knows? They're with a boy who hasn't a clue what he's doing, they're lucky if he has a condom, and the only thing a girl gets out of it is the fact that she isn't a virgin anymore. I—"

"Uh...Bree," Ajia interrupts. "Kitten?"

Bree keeps talking. "I was actually lucky. That wasn't the case for me. I—"

Tension shoves its way through me, and I straighten, stiff enough that every one of my muscles *hurts.* "You telling me he busted your cherry?"

"Son of a bitch," Ajia sighs.

I see the instant she realizes what she admitted. True to everything I know about my sister, she pushes forward.

"That is *not* what I'm trying to tell you," she says primly, "and it's a disgusting way to think of it, but, yes, Ajia was my first. That's because I *wanted* him to be. I...waited. I had other chances, there were other boys. I didn't take them."

"Because of *this motherfucker?"* I don't plan to say the words, but there they are.

"Because I wanted to be with Ajia, yes. And you're just gonna have to get used to it. Accept it. He's your friend, part of the band. Those things aren't going to change simply because I slept with him."

Jesus, I want to move. Hit something. It takes every ounce of self-control I have to hold myself steady and not destroy everything in this goddamn room. Including—or especially—Ajia Stone.

"There's shit you don't know, Bree." My voice is low and rough. Doesn't sound anything like me. Doesn't matter. There's shit that she has to know, shit she clearly doesn't or she wouldn't have let him *touch her.*

Jesus.

"He's not the guy you think he is."

"Knox, let me do it."

Ajia's voice sounds weird, and even I can see the pain in his eyes. Too damn bad. This is about *my sister.*

"Ajia?" She looks at him.

"I'll tell you everything, baby. I was going to tonight, anyway."

I snort. He's had days, weeks—*years*—to tell her the shit the band and I know, and he hasn't done it. Won't do it now, if he can run away from it. Asshole.

"I know everything I need to. He's not some stranger I just happened to run across, you know," Bree insists, but is that a trace of uncertainty I hear in her voice?

I speak to Bree, even though I aim my pissed-off glare at Ajia. "He's got secrets, baby girl. Shit you don't know. Shit that—"

"Well, fuck me, Knox." Bree scowls. "We've all got shit, and you know that as well as anybody. Ajia's can't be any worse—"

"Don't kid yourself, Bree. If you knew the truth about this fucker, you wouldn't say that."

"Don't start with your drama queen shit, Knox. Now isn't the time."

"You gonna tell her?" I snap.

Ajia's sitting straight and stiff on the bed. "Yeah," he says. "I said I would."

"What?" Bree look between him and me. "What are you two talking about?"

"Your *boyfriend* here." God, I hate that word.

"Knox…"

"Let me get the conversation started." Something inside me feels like it's going to explode, and I know I've got to say it and then get the hell out of here. Everything inside of me wants to either fight or fuck—and I have just enough self-control to know I can't do either.

"About what?" Bree asks carefully.

"The girl."

"What girl?"
"The one he killed."

CHAPTER 7

LONDON

MY HAIR IS PULLED BACK IN A LOOSE PONYTAIL, my teeth are brushed, and I slip on an oversized tank top and sleep shorts. My phone pings as I pull the shirt over my head. It's a text message from Knox.

Knox: What's UR room

Me: 715

I stare at my phone, but he doesn't text back. Strange, maybe, but not all that surprising, either. Knox likes to know what's going on, but he doesn't waste time with chitchat.

Heading back into the bathroom to remove my makeup, there's a knock at the door. It doesn't take a genius to figure out it's probably Knox, and so I open the door without thinking.

His eyes flare, but then he just stares. "Let me in?"

I blink. I'm dressed. I mean, everything's covered, but the neckline of my top is a little low, the underarms are cut a little deep, and the shorts are a little...well, short. Still, we're both adults, and it's not completely inappropriate. He can see way more on any beach in the country.

Besides, I *have* seen his cock.

"Sure."

I step back, and he brushes past me. Automatically, I lock the door. It's something I always do in a hotel. When I turn, Knox is standing just behind me.

"Knox?" I say, but there's no time for other words when his mouth crashes down onto mine.

Surprise lasts only a second before absolute sensation takes over—and why not? I've been lusting for Knox since I first saw him. His mouth is hot, his lips are demanding, and his tongue plunges forward to steal past my gasp. He's deep in my mouth, licking his way all around, and I can't help myself. I suck on his tongue, and it earns me a growl deep from his throat.

He bites my bottom lip, sucks it into his mouth, and then soothes it with his tongue. I moan as sensation races through me, tightening my nipples, and sending a sharp surge of pure lightning deep to my core. I'm wet, completely so.

How can he do that with no more than a *kiss?*

He shoves his hands into my hair and pushes me back against the door. He holds me still, his eyes flashing a stormy gray, and I can't look away. I can only stare and try, with the ragged bits of mind available to me, to decipher whatever is going on behind that dangerous, passionate face.

I reach for him, to do...what? Something. I don't know; I can't think straight. I'm only sure that I need to touch him. The chance never comes, because he grabs my hands and jerks them up over my head. He clenches both wrists in one fist, while his other hand splays wide over the plane of the door, next to my head.

"You touch me, and I'm gonna fuck you." The words are like a harsh bite through the air, and he doesn't blink as he says them.

I swallow, barely able to breathe. "I thought you didn't fuck employees."

His eyes darken. "I'll make an exception."

This is it. A moment of truth. *The* moment of truth? I don't know how far-reaching this truth goes, but I'm *sure* I have a choice to make.

How can I be sure which is the right one? And do I really give a damn if one of them means that Knox will do exactly what I pray he will?

My mouth is suddenly dry, and I run my tongue over my lips. Knox's eyes flare and he lets out a soft grunt. "What if I want to touch you?" I whisper and lean my head forward. It's the only part I can move easily, and I stroke my tongue over his bottom lip. "What if I want you to fuck me?"

His hips slam against me at the same moment his open mouth smashes over mine. His kisses overpower me almost immediately, deep and wet like he's going to eat me whole. I don't care. I want that—and more. Sweet baby Jesus, so much more. Especially when I feel the ridge of his very large, very hard cock press firmly against me.

He licks his way from my mouth to my jaw, my throat, my collar bone. I gasp and squirm in his hold, but he doesn't release my hands. Instead, he leans down to take one breast in his mouth, tank top and all. He sucks me deep, brings my nipple to almost painful hardness from the mixed abrasion of his tongue and the interfering cotton fabric, while his free hand shoves its way beneath the waistband of my sleep shorts.

I don't have the attention span to be embarrassed because he'll find me wet and aching. I can't hold back the gasp of pleasure as his callused fingers slide through the slickness, stroking over my lower lips, and avoiding my clit with a teasing game of hide and seek. I don't mean to push my pussy against his hand, but I do all the same. Again and again. He lets out a satisfied chuckle and then bites the crest of my breast as he does it again.

"Knox," I groan. Asking...begging, encouraging? I can't be sure, and what does it matter? They're all the same, because I can only be sure that I need his touch like the air that I breathe.

Like nothing else I've ever wanted in my whole damn life.

He bites my other breast while he slips one finger deep within me. A guttural sound comes from deep in my throat—I have no knowledge of it before it echoes between us—and I shove myself against him again. He pulls back just enough to drag the pads of his fingers over me and then shove two inside. That same needy sound escapes my throat, and then he moves them in and out in a slow, steady rhythm.

I flex with his shifting hand, unable to stop myself. It's been so long since a man touched me with any sort of attraction. Lust. Physical need. Whatever. Colin was too tidy, too reserved, to show that much emotion, even when he was in the throes of passion. He never really went after what he wanted, and any orgasm I had was purely accidental on his part.

This...Jesus, this is different. Knox is focused totally on me. I can feel it in the way he licks and bites my tits, not caring if the fabric of my tank top is in the way. The way he teases his way around my clit. The way he pumps his fingers in and out of my pussy, as though he can think of nothing else.

I find myself up on my tiptoes as he fucks me with his hand, and I lose my breath. "Knox." I try to say his name, but I don't think he can hear me. Or maybe he can, because he brings his mouth back to mine and slips his tongue deep as I pant. I want to bring my tongue to life, stroke his, caress the ridges of his teeth, but all I can do is suck him deep and groan again.

Knox growls deep and then his thumb strokes boldly over my clit. Again. His fingers move faster, go deeper, and his other hand tightens around my wrists. My hips flex against him, and I'm vaguely aware that I'm trying to find that place of release. Orgasm. What a thin, non-descriptive word for what I want. So much more than that waits beyond the lure of Knox's touch, his kiss.

He drags his fingers from me, stroking hard over my clit, and I jerk. For a moment, his hand is gone, and then I feel the loss of my sleep shorts as he pushes them down over my hips. I wiggle enough to get them to my ankles, where I can get at least one leg free. A metallic sound comes from far away. It should mean something, I suppose, but how can I concentrate when Knox's mouth, tongue and lips seduce me, devour me, drag me deeper under his spell? A very distant part of me knows I've lost complete control of myself, but I really don't give a bloody goddamn.

This man is doing things to me and my body that I've only ever fantasized about!

Knox shifts against me, and then his hand is back at my hip, my thigh. He brings my leg up, curls it around his waist—his very naked waist—and I follow with the other leg. My shoulders and back press against the solid wood of the door, while the rest of me wraps around him. I know damn well my pussy is exposed to his cock.

He releases my mouth just long enough to move, and then I feel the head of his dick press against my soaking entrance. He pushes in just a enough to remind me just how big he really is, and then he shoves all the way in until his pelvis rests solidly between my legs.

I groan, or would if I had any breath left. All I'm really sure of is that Knox is inside me, stretching me, and the friction as he pulls out drives me insane. He snaps his hip forward, he's deep inside me again, and I feel myself tighten around him.

"Knox."

His mouth is on mine again, his tongue plunging deep, just like his cock, and I'm so bloody full of him, I can't tell where I stop and he starts. I bite his tongue, hoping he'll understand what I can't say.

Harder. Deeper. Faster.

He does, if the powerful thrust of his hips is any indication. I feel him drive against my cervix, a mix of pleasure and pain I've never experienced before. Never had a man built like him before. A man who knows how to strum my body like he owns it.

Jesus.

It's like I'm outside of myself, unable to control my actions, reactions or emotions. I'm only distantly aware of anything so rational. One second I'm caught in a building maelstrom of something I've never experienced before, and the next I'm soaring, screaming Knox's name, my arms and legs trembling, and yet completely unable to move. My head and shoulders grind back against the door, and my hips are thrust forward to seal my crotch against his. It goes on and on, white lights flashing behind my eyelids, and tremors tighten the walls of my pussy around his cock.

"Oh, fuck, English," he grunts against my mouth and keeps moving.

I try to catch my breath, but the orgasm doesn't stop. It goes on and on and then builds again.

"Knox," I breathe when he finally releases my mouth. "Oh, Jesus, it won't stop! You're gonna make me come again!"

"That's it, baby." He dips his head to bite my neck. "Give it to me. Come all over my cock."

I don't know if it's his words or the hard flex of his hips. His dick shoves up against my cervix again, and the sharp pain of it sends me back over the edge of sensation that never really stopped. I'm lost and can only cling to Knox with my legs around his waist.

He strokes again, that same frantic rhythm, and I hear a hitch in his breathing. Satisfaction sharpens my physical reactions to the point that I'm all nerve endings. He's on the verge of orgasm. With me.

For me.

"C'mon, baby," I mutter, my lips against his hair. His teeth close over the place where my neck meets my shoulder, and I feel the sharp sting of the bite as he suckles on my flesh. "You're close," I pant and tighten my pussy around his cock. "I can feel it." I do it again. "You wanna come, baby? Do it."

He growls against my shoulder.

"Do it!" I urge again, and then he slams into me with enough force to rattle the door.

"Oh, Jesus Christ, English!" He keeps moving like he can't stop, and I feel the surge of his cock inside of me. Pulsing. Releasing.

Giving me exactly what I asked for.

I'm vaguely aware of moving—being carried—and then I'm laid out on the bed. Knox follows me down, but only after pulling my tank top over my head.

"Jesus, English, you have gorgeous tits!"

"What?"

I can't really think beyond the vague question. I shift against him, seeking his physical warmth. Or some kind of connection. Instead, I find the barrier of fabric.

He's still dressed.

I blink and try to sharpen my gaze on him. He lost his suitcoat somewhere, and his tie is loosened but still in place. Beneath that, his gray shirt is still buttoned which, under the circumstances, looks far too orderly.

A short breath of disbelief shoots from my lungs. "Oh, no. No way."

"What?" It's his turn to ask.

I moisten my lips and shake my head. "You just fucked me to within an inch of my life, and you're still *dressed?*"

His eyes flare, darkening to more gray than green. "You gonna do something about it, English?"

"Oh, yeah."

One of my arms is pinned beneath him, but I can maneuver the other one just fine. I unfasten the top button with an ease that surprises me, and then I move down to the next. The next. And again, until my fingers become clumsy from working one-handed. Or maybe the buttons just get harder to manage as they get closer to his waist. I can't tell for sure—and Knox doesn't do a damn thing.

"You *could* help, you know." I peek up at him through lowered lashes as I concentrate. "This would go a lot faster."

He moves then, so fast I don't realize his intent until he's on his knees. He tears open the rest of the shirt front, and buttons fly across the room. I can't help smiling as he jerks the thing off and throws it across the room. His tie still drapes loosely around his neck.

"That better, English?"

I push up to a half-sitting position and rest one hand over the Celtic cross tattoo on his pec. I want to trace it with my fingers and tongue, ask him about it, take in all the detail, understand this small part of him...but not now! My core tightens, my breasts feel heavy, my nipples ache, and I can only think about the splendor of his broad, muscled chest and those amazing six-pack abs that guard his happy trail.

"Almost," I mutter breathlessly as my hand falls to the waistband of his dress pants. Odd how I continue to find myself moving without thinking about what I'm doing, but right now, I can't bring myself to care all that much about it, either.

Seconds later a piece of reality strikes me. I catch his eyes and just stare. "You didn't even take your bloody pants off?"

One corner of his mouth quirks. "You didn't notice until now?"

I close one eye, tilt my head down, and take a breath. "Touché."

I drop my gaze and find the button undone, zipper down, and his dick proudly exposed. Not completely hard now, but at least semi-erect again. Or still? I'm not sure, and then it moves with my continued stare.

"Bollocks," I whisper to myself. "No wonder you poked against my cervix."

"What?" It seems an off-hand question, maybe even automatic, as he wriggles to shift around and shove his trousers farther toward his ankles. A moment later he kicks the whole mess from his feet, including his shoes and socks.

Holy Christ, he looks even bigger without the backdrop of his pants to conceal anything.

I swallow. "When you went deep…" I have to pause, suddenly a little embarrassed to find myself saying the words. I've never once in my life had a particularly frank discussion with a lover. Certainly not with Colin.

"What?" He leans forward, his attention fully on me again, and brushes his thumb over my bottom lip. "What happens when I go deep, baby?"

"You…go all the way…to my…cervix."

Please, don't blush! Please, God, not now.

Knox's expression reveals nothing other than a flicker in his eyes that conceals more than it reveals. He drops his hand to splay over my tummy. "Did it hurt?"

I nod once. "Kind of."

"Kind of?"

I'm a little amazed as I watch my hand reach out to push a strand of dark hair back from his eyes. It's mostly to delay having to say anything, but I'm a little surprised by the bravery of making such a seemingly tender gesture. Maybe I *was* joking when I called Knox a cocky rock god, but it's true—and he's *so far* out of my league. He's an amazing man, an amazing talent, and he's so bloody hot.

So how in the hell could he have wanted to fuck me so bad that he took me against the freaking door without taking his pants off? And now that he has—*we have*—why can't I be more sophisticated about it? I'm almost 23 bloody years old and shouldn't be so awkward when talking about this stuff. Just because nothing was open for discussion in my so-called family—ever—doesn't mean I have to carry that fucked up habit into my adulthood.

"English?" he prompts me.

"Uh...well, yeah, there was a sharp pain. At first. But then—" I grin in spite of myself "—once I came, it was like my orgasm just kept going. Every time you smacked up against my cervix, things...intensified."

I blink and give him a look that feels kind of shy, and I suppose it is. This kind of raw honesty is new territory for me. "I'm not sure if I came three times," I add softly, amazed by the memory, "or if it was one long orgasm that just kept starting over."

"That never happened to you before?" He looks kind of smug.

"Uh, *no.*" I shake my head sharply. "Don't think it happens to most women. But then...I've never been with a guy who's built like you."

He glances down at his chest. "Built like me?"

I laugh. "Wanker. You know what I mean." I point. "Your cock is...impressive."

"Thank you."

"You're laughing at me."

"No, baby. Not at all." He leans forward to drop a quick kiss on my lips. He licks his way over my jaw, my throat, between my breasts, past my belly button to stop just above my pussy. I've trimmed it to a small, tidy V that he gives a quick kiss. "I know my dick is bigger than a lot of guys," he adds with another kiss and peers up at me through lashes that are unfairly long. "I use it to my advantage."

"I'll bet you do," I gasp as his tongue traces the perimeter of my V.

Knox chuckles and darts his tongue lower, coming closer and closer to my clit, until finally he swipes a line over my seam upward and then back down again. "You taste good, baby," he mutters as he does it again.

"That's us," I murmur, because I can't really speak—or think for that matter. "You and me."

"What?" He pulls back suddenly and pushes up on his forearms. "What did you say?"

I stare at him, at the hair that's mostly come loose from his ponytail and hangs down around his face. It keeps me from getting a clear view of his face. "That's us," I repeat slowly, the relaxed satisfaction that's kept me in a sensual web beginning to dissipate. I swallow. "Why?"

"Motherfucker!"

Knox is up and standing next to the bed before I realize he's moving. He shoves his hair away from his face and grips the back of his neck with one hand. His chest heaves as he breathes.

"Knox?" It's barely more than a whisper. "What's wrong?"

"Wrong?" He closes his eyes and then drops a fierce glare on me. "Wrong?" he repeats. "What the fuck could be *wrong?* We just fucked without protection! I forgot to use a goddamn condom!"

CHAPTER 8

KNOX

FUCK.

I stare at the gorgeous woman sprawled out before me. My chest heaves as I look at her. Her body is amazing: full tits, tapered waist, and generous hips. Exactly the kind of figure that makes me hard and hot, and she responded to me perfectly. Maybe the most amazing goddamn orgasm of my life.

Without using a condom.

I squeeze the back of my neck. *Fuck, fuck, fuck.*

"Whoa." She swallows and pushes herself up to a sitting position.

"Yeah." An understatement if I ever heard one, but I swallow the snarky comment. It isn't London's fault. It's mine. All mine. I'm the one who stormed into her room, pinned her to the goddamn door, and fucked her without one damn thought about *anything* except getting inside her.

"Hey." She crawls to her knees and curls an unsteady hand over my arm. "It's okay. It's…it'll be okay."

"Okay?" I snap. "What's okay about it?"

Fuck. Nothing has been okay in my life since our stepfather went after Bree. I was glad to get her out of Austin and away from him, but that somehow shoved her into Ajia's bed. Now she's sleeping with him, and who knows where that will lead? Worse, those rumors about Bree, the band…and me are making me seriously crazy.

I told myself I was holding it together, but that was just another lie. I can't think straight about anything, have no control over the shit going on around me, and now I just made it so much worse by fucking the band's new publicist.

Without protection!

London offers me a careful half-smile. "Does it help if I tell you I'm on birth control?" she asks softly.

The pounding in my heart changes. "What?" I force the question out.

"The shot. I get a shot every three months."

I blow out a long, ragged breath that makes me feel only a little better. Her strange golden gaze lingers on mine. "Thank God for that."

Her lips shift to a slightly more genuine smile, and she lifts one shoulder. "I'm clean, too. I get tested when I get the shot, and I haven't—well..." She drops her gaze and pulls her hand away. "I haven't been with anybody in a while."

A girl who looks like her? Hard to believe.

"How long?" I ask before I can stop myself.

"Months. Since last time I got the shot."

My heart's starting to settle down, and I can breathe more normally again. "You don't know the right kind of men, baby."

She snaps off a harsh laugh. "That's the bloody truth."

"What?"

She shakes her head. "Never mind. What about you?"

"What about me?"

"Are you clean?"

"Yeah. I get tested every six months, and I *always* wear a condom." Every. Single. Fucking. Time.

"Except tonight."

I snort, a rough sound that doesn't come close to describing the shit churning through my gut. I shove my hair back from my face and nod. "Yeah. Except tonight."

"Hey, Knox."

London holds out her hand, steady this time, and waits for me to move. She doesn't flinch, doesn't get impatient, doesn't lose her cool, and so finally I twine my fingers around hers. She pulls me toward her.

"It's okay." She scoots back to the middle of the bed, and I follow until we're both crouched on the mattress. "Things got a little...hot." I slant her a look. "Okay, bloody, amazingly hot," she adds with a soft smile. "It got away from us, but that doesn't have to mean anything."

"Doesn't have to mean anything?" Why should that piss me off?

"The sex was fantastic." She smiles almost uneasily. "As for the rest of it, we can both get tested again if you want."

"Tested again."

Her eyes narrow. "Why do you keep repeating everything I say?"

I shake my head, feeling somehow like I've been caught up in some vague line of circular thinking that makes absolutely no freaking sense. "Sorry." I know I don't sound it, so I add, "I'm just...a little fucked up, I guess."

She drags her gaze slowly from my face and down over my body. I feel it like a hot, electric touch, and my dick twitches awake.

"C'mere." She pushes me onto my back. "Let's release some of that...tension."

"Tension?" I repeat. Her tits sway with her movements, and I can't look away. Who would want to? They're gorgeous tits! And then, fuck me if I don't feel my muscles loosen, my shoulders and legs begin to relax.

"Tension," she agrees, and then she's straddling my hips, leaning forward until her mouth almost rests against mine. "Let me take care of you, luv."

Her tongue traces the outline of my lips, pretending to be a seductive tease right up to the moment she turns aggressive. She seals our lips together and slips her tongue into my mouth. I welcome her with a sweep of my tongue and then swallow a low groan as she follows with a thorough discovery of the depths of my mouth.

Who knew a kiss could be so fucking sexy?

We trade control, back and forth in my mouth and then hers, until, finally, we're both panting. She pulls back with a naughty smile and breathy gasp for air, and then scoots down to drop kisses at my throat, my shoulders, my chest.

"Someday," she says, licking her way around the Celtic cross tat I have on my left pec, "you're going to tell me all about your tattoos. Why you got them and what they mean to you."

"You think so?" Is it the temptation of her tongue or my ever-hardening cock that makes my voice sound so winded?

"Yep." She takes a soft bite of my chest, then soothes with her tongue. "But not now."

"No?"

"Nope." She drags her open mouth down, over my chest and abs to my belly button. My cock, hard as a rock, waits there anxiously. "I have something else in mind now."

She kisses the tip of my dick, swipes her tongue over it, and licks up the drops of pre-cum that gather there. Her soft noise, maybe one of satisfaction, echoes through the room, and then she takes just the head into her mouth and sucks. Hard.

"Jesus!" My hips flex upward, but she moves with the movement and holds me off until, finally, she swirls her tongue all around me.

I shove my hands into her hair, ripping it from the tidy ponytail, and holding her close. She laughs and pulls back enough to start at the tip again, this time licking her way up and down the shaft until she's bathed every fucking inch. My balls are next, and she gets to know them very up close and personal. She sucks them into her mouth, licks them all over, and at the same time strokes a firm, steady hand up and down my cock from tip to base.

"Goddamn, English." My hips shift again, and I guess she approves, because she sucks and strokes harder.

I lose a soft groan, and she changes her tactics. She licks up to the head, and in one deliberate movement, swallows my dick as far as she can. Never had a woman who can take me all the way, but London goes farther than most. I press against the back of her throat, and after a moment, she relaxes to let me go a little farther. Once there, she holds me with a little bob of her head until she gags.

She does it again. Again. And again, until finally she pulls back to haul in a long, panting breath. Saliva collects at the corners of her mouth, stray tears dot her cheeks, and she sniffs like her nose wants to run.

I wipe her tears with my thumbs. "You okay, baby?"

She smiles and swirls her tongue around the head of my dick again. "Oh, I'm good. Real good, luv." She does that thing with her tongue again. "You're just…well, I told you. Never had a man built like you."

I can't help grinning. "You saying I have a big dick?"

"The biggest." She sucks me deep again, and then sighs when she comes up for air. "It's perfect."

She does it again, swallowing a little more each time, until I have to move.

"Hold still, baby." I hold her face between my hands and give a twist of my hips to bring them up from the bed. "I'm gonna fuck your mouth."

She groans deep in her throat, and I start to thrust. I have to. The soft, wet heat of her mouth makes it impossible for me to do anything else. I'm not gonna let myself come, but, holy hell, I just have to feel her *surround me.*

She gags from time to time, and I feel her try to relax her throat more and more. I try to pull back, but she's having none of it. If I don't fuck her mouth, her mouth is fucking my dick.

"Stop, baby, before I blow your fucking head off."

I force her up and catch her mouth with mine. Our kiss is as deep and hot as those from earlier, thinning my control over my prick even further.

"Knox," she whispers, her lips against mine. "I need you inside me. Bad."

She slips away, and then she lowers herself over my cock. I've hardly touched her this time, except for kissing, and she's soaked. Ready for me. *Needs me,* she said.

"Holy fuck, you're tight, baby."

I wrap my hands around her waist and try to thrust up, but she's in control of the action. She doesn't go all the way down, and some vague, ragged voice reminds me of her admission. *You go all the way to my cervix.* And, later, *I've never been with a guy who's built like you.*

"You doin' okay, baby?" It takes everything I have to hold still as I ask.

"Yeah. But…Jesus, Knox. You're so goddamn big!"

"Too much?" I hate asking. How many times have I had to hold myself back from chicks who can't deal with ten inches?

"No! God, no! *Never!*"

She throws her head back, and her hair flies all around her face. Her breasts thrust forward, and I reach up, palm her, then twist my fingers until I can take her nipple between them. I roll it, alternating soft and then harder, and she groans. That's all I need to hear, and I pinch it tight.

London gasps, and the next thing I know she's dropped herself all the way down. I feel a little resistance at the tip—her cervix?—but then she's moving again, and this time I have to move with her. She groans deep in her throat.

"Yeah." She makes a strange mewling sound. "Please. Jesus, Knox. Fuck me! Please. Just…fuck me."

I thrust up. "Like this?"

"Yeah. God. Just…like…that."

Yeah. Just like that.

I have a better idea. I twist up and off the bed, and then London is beneath me. I haul her legs up over my shoulders. I all but impale her on my cock, and I don't stop. I can't.

"I'll fuck you, baby. I'll fuck you till you can't walk tomorrow."

Until my dick falls off and *I* can't walk. I have no other choice. I have to.

I cup her ass in my hands, raise her up and shove myself in and out. She makes a ragged, keening cry and grips my shoulder with one hand, the other grabbing for my ass. She squeezes in rhythm with our other movements. My lungs heave in response.

I have to move. *Jesus.* Even if I wanted to stop, I couldn't. Sensation charges through me, my balls tighten, and I know I'm not going to last long.

I free one hand and slip it between us, amazing myself at how easily I find her clit. It's a hard little nub, and my thumb settles there firmly. She shrieks, arches toward me, and I trap her mouth with mine.

"You gonna come for me, baby?" It's a demand I make against her lips.

"I…" She breathes more than says anything else.

"C'mon, English," I mutter hoarsely as I pound into her. My thumb works its magic. "You know you want it."

And if she doesn't, I do.

"Knox."

Never heard my name in quite that grunt, groan, and moan combination, but it affects me like no other sound. My cock tightens, maybe even expands, if I can guess by the way the walls of her pussy tighten around me.

"That's it, baby. Come for me." I keep up the pace, rubbing her clit and plunging in and out of her.

"I…" She pants and surges against me. "Knox! Yeah. C'mon, baby. Fuck me!"

I slam into her once more, and then she's screaming and her cunt pulses around me. I'm only good for one, maybe two more strokes, and then I bury myself in her, cum filling her like a goddamn fire hose.

"What the fuck do you do to me?" I ask as I collapse over her.

"What do *you* do to *me?*"

I can't answer as reality fades.

CHAPTER 9

Lᴏɴᴅᴏɴ

A KNOCK ON THE DOOR WAKES ME.

"Housekeeping."

I'm naked, in bed, and under the covers. I stretch out one arm to grope around me, but the other side of the mattress is empty and cold.

Knox is gone, and has been for some time, apparently.

"Uh...I just woke up," I call warily. "Can you give me about an hour?"

"Yes, ma'am."

There are no other words, no sounds, and eventually I relax under the covers. Housekeeping must have moved on...and so did Knox.

Bollocks. *What did you expect?* I lay there berating myself in typical British fashion. *What were you thinking to let Knox in, to fuck him, like some kind of slutty tramp? You've* never *let your hormones do the thinking for you.*

Except last night. Last night, I allowed—no, encouraged—my pussy to take control and welcome Knox with open arms. So to speak.

And, good Lord above, was it ever good!

My body responds to the memories with tight nipples and a new dampness between my legs. I squirm a little. It was good? That doesn't even come close! It was bloody amazing, and I know damn well that there is no other guy in God's creation who can do that to my body.

Despite what I see on Tumblr, how many ten-inch cocks am I ever really going to meet personally? And, narrowing it down even farther, how many men will I ever get close to who know how to *use* their ten-inch cocks?

And who has everything else that Knox has going for him? Who looks like him? Who sends my pulse soaring with no more than a naughty smile. And who's so protective of his baby sister that he gets all cockeyed when things go wrong.

Men in my experience just don't give a shit anymore. Colin didn't. My father hasn't in my entire life. Other men—boys—I've dated over the years have always looked out for themselves. Men take care of themselves first and pretty much ignore anything and anyone else. Knox Gallagher is a whole different species, and I want to know him better.

Oh, don't worry. You will. That sometimes annoying voice of reason won't let me alone. *He's your boss...remember? You'll see him every damn day for the next two months. You'll practically be living in each other's pockets. Touring the West Coast on a damn bus!*

I throw back the covers and climb from the bed. I can't lay there and think about this stuff anymore; it screws with my equilibrium.

I glance at the clock. Almost 9:30. Past time I get up, anyway.

I wander into the bathroom, take care of the most urgent need, and then glance in the mirror as I shove my hair back from my face. The dreamy eyes, the messy tangle of hair...and the hickey where my neck curves into my shoulder give me a well-fucked look.

Hickey?

"Bollocks."

I lean forward to look closer, fingering the little bruise. Yep. A hickey. Knox is a biter.

A choppy sigh fogs the mirror. Do I laugh or get pissed? I haven't had a hickey since Darren Andrews tried to get all hot-and-heavy with me in tenth grade. I kneed him in the balls, but not before he left a mark...that was nowhere near as large and noticeable as the one Knox gave me.

I shake my head and give into the laughter, but the sound quickly dies. What's so bloody funny? If anything, this could present some serious difficulties for me. It's not like I think Knox has some sudden, undying love for me, and we're a couple now. We aren't, and I know it damn well—but I just fucked my boss…and he marked me!

I close my eyes and take a couple of deep breaths. Okay, first things first. A shower, makeup, and get dressed. Maybe something will occur to me by then.

The shower is hot and renews me, so I don't hurry. We'll be at the hotel at least another week, according to the schedule Baz gave me, and so I unpack and arrange things for my convenience. Next is makeup, and I spend a little extra effort to cover Knox's hickey as best I can. It doesn't cover as well as I hoped it would, and I glare at the offending spot.

He's too good at that shit. I can still see it.

"Wanker," I mutter but don't waste any more time with it. What's the point?

I dress in summer-weight white slacks and a blousy lavender shirt with tiny cap sleeves. It's not overly professional, but not as casual as jeans and T-shirts, either. I leave my hair to fall around my shoulders and keep the jewelry to a minimum, silver earrings and a silver cross necklace. It's a decent compromise until I have a better idea of where I fit in within the workings of the Wycked Obsession world.

Now what? I don't really want to wait in the room, like I'm hiding out. Besides, sitting here, staring around the room, all I can think about is Knox and how expertly he fucked me. Against the door. In bed. How many times he made me come, and the breathless growling sound he made when he came. It makes my core tighten all over again.

What did he think when he woke up? I don't want to wonder, but I do. Did he watch me sleep? Want to stay? Or was he anxious to get away? Like I was one of his one-night-stand, groupie girls.

An anxious hole opens up in my stomach, robbing me of breath. Knox doesn't have staying power. Longest I've heard of him being with a woman is a month or two. He's a manwhore, and I knew that before I ever applied for this job. He's been with hundreds of girls, and there is *nothing* about me that makes me stand out from most of them. His emotions were stirred up last night; the stuff with Bree made him crazy. I was convenient…end of story.

Besides, who said I want anything more? So why do I still taste him? Remember his hands and mouth on me? Feel him inside of me?

And how the bloody hell am I going to face him again?

Bollocks. I can't stay here!

I grab my phone, my laptop, and my purse, and stalk from the room. I know the band and other assorted personnel such as Baz and myself are all on this floor, but I don't know their room numbers yet. I haven't even met anybody except Knox and Baz. I look up and down the hall like a fish out of water, and hate knowing how familiar that feeling is.

God, I hate never fitting in!

I storm down the hall to the elevators and punch the down button with emphasis. I wait, counting as I tap my toes. It keeps me from thinking about the shambles my life seems to have become.

How did that happen? First Colin, and then losing out on the record company job. I almost thought I'd resurrected things with this job. Wycked Obsession is flirting with huge success, and it's a tremendous opportunity for somebody like me. Fresh out of college, traveling the country, and experiencing things from a front-row seat. I'd hoped to find my place, my future in the music industry.

Then I went and fucked my boss, arguably the hottest guy in the band.

The elevator arrives before I can process that any further, and I all but rush inside the cab. I watch the descending numbers ferociously rather than let my mind return to thoughts of Knox. In the lobby, I find a trendy little bistro in one corner where they serve breakfast all day.

The hostess seats me and takes my drink order, while I force myself to look at the menu. I don't give a damn, but I know I could use a little protein. When the waitress arrives with my skinny vanilla latte, I order an egg white omelet with fruit and then pull my phone out.

Bollocks! The push notifications have gone crazy again, all with updates about Wycked Obsession. Reactions to Ajia and Bree making out in the elevator, rampant speculation about him stealing her from the rest of the band, Knox's supposed reaction, and reports that Ajia and Bree were seen at LAX, running away together.

I massage my brow as I shake my head. *Motherfucker,* to quote Knox. What now? What's our next step? How will the band want to handle this? What will they want me to do?

I worry the questions but eventually put the phone away. There have been no texts, not from Knox or Baz, and I don't even want to think about that right now. We're going to have to do something...but what? And when?

I'm glad when my omelet arrives and I can distract myself with food, but it ends up not working all that well. I can't stop thinking, waiting, checking my phone for a text. I tell myself I'm expecting to hear from Baz, but in my heart, I know it isn't true. I want to hear from Knox. Anything. Just...contact.

I pull my napkin from my lap, drop it on my plate, and sit back, suddenly feeling like I'm going to throw up. *What?* What the hell is wrong with me? Waiting to hear from a man after what's most likely a one-time thing? Like I spent my whole life waiting for some attention from my father? Like I spent my time waiting for Colin to romance me?

No. *No way.*

London Kennedy isn't playing that game anymore. Knox and Baz *should* have contacted me first thing about today's latest round of gossip. It's now my job to handle this shit. They didn't. So if they're not going to come to me, then I'm taking charge, and *they* can play catch up for a change.

I call a band meeting for one o'clock. I leave it up to Baz to gather the band, including Bree, in a small meeting room I convinced the hotel to let us use. They're all there when I arrive, lounging in chairs all around the table. All except Ajia, who's nowhere to be seen.

Knox sits at the far end, arms crossed over his chest and a look on his face that says, *don't fuck with me.* I don't let myself look any further than that. Bree, on the other hand, looks a little...fragile.

A sympathetic ache settles in my chest. Being the target of tabloid gossip sucks, however you look at it, and nothing that's ever been said about me or my family is as bad as what Bree's been going through now. Still, I know exactly how it feels to be somebody who's forced into some kind of celebrity by association.

Not that telling her any of that's going to help. Not now, anyway, and so I look at the others around the table. I'm sitting opposite of Knox, with Zayne and Rye on my right, looking stiff and vaguely pissed off. Is it because of the meeting, or something else? Noah and Bree are on my left, and he looks like he's keeping a very close eye on her.

Interesting dynamic, these friends seem to have.

"Where's Ajia?" I ask in my most businesslike tone.

The room is silent until Noah says, "Gone." It's just the one word, flat, followed by a fierce glare shot in Knox's direction.

I blink. "Gone where?"

The silence returns, and I find myself automatically looking at Bree. She and Ajia are...together. Something. Whatever. She's looking down at her hands.

It's Rye who answers. "Texas."

"Texas?" I look around the room. Professional or not, I make no effort to regulate my tone or words. "What the bloody fucking hell?"

One corner of Zayne's mouth twitches. "Exactly."

No one says anything else, but the other four are staring at Knox like he's the second coming of Satan. He stares back without blinking, like a stone statue.

"What happened?" I scramble for composure, but the words come out sharp and bitten off.

"Knox," says Noah, his voice carrying its own bite, "and his usual charming asshole personality."

"You don't know a fucking thing, Noah," snaps Knox.

"Fuck you! I know enough. We all do. *Motherfucker.*"

God, that word again. Don't these guys know anything else? I know I caught them at a bad time, but...*Jesus.* We're gonna have to work on their communication style.

"You. Weren't. There," Knox says, his teeth gritted, and I search the sound of his voice for any nuance of what he *isn't* saying. I struggle to concentrate as other words crowd into my brain. Words *I* was there to hear.

I'll fuck you, baby. I'll fuck you till you can't walk tomorrow. You gonna come for me, baby?

God, please! Not now!

"I was."

It's Bree who speaks, and it's like all the air in the room has been sucked away. I don't know why, but there's some special connection she has with these guys. I feel it, know it instinctively—and know absolutely it isn't about sex. It's love, yeah…like a family.

It's dangerous territory for me. I have no experience to fall back on.

"I was there, Knox," Bree says softly, "and Noah's right. You're my brother and I love you, but I don't think I've *ever* seen you act like such an asshole."

"Big statement there, baby girl." This from Rye, across the table.

She nods. "I know."

"Enough!" I hold up my hand. A glance in Knox's direction tells me nothing. His hair falls around his face, almost like he'd like to hide behind it, but I know better. He doesn't retreat.

Besides, why hide? His expression shows nothing. His body, on the other hand, is stiff and stoic, like a soldier facing a firing squad.

Uncertainty tightens my nerves. Maybe even a sense of unfairness. Part of me wants to demand why they're all ganging up on him like this. The rest of me is divided, remembering my own interactions with Knox. He *can* be an ass, but he also wrung a passion from me that I didn't know existed.

"Do you want to tell me what happened?" I lay a heavy gaze on each of them, and they all stare back in undisguised defiance.

It's Bree who finally sighs. "You'll have to get the details from Ajia. It's his story to tell, and I won't break his trust." She glares past me at Knox, as if to say *he* did just that.

"I *can* say that my brother pushed in ways he shouldn't have," she adds a moment later. "He made everything sound worse than it had to be, and he did it deliberately."

"Bree—"

"No." She holds up a hand. "No explanations. Nothing from you until you apologize to Ajia. Until you get your shit together and accept that my life isn't yours to control. You are not my *father.*"

Something changes in Knox's demeanor. I don't know exactly what it is; I don't know him well enough and shouldn't be able to tell anything at all, but sleeping with a guy gives a girl some insight. Or did for me. It's withdrawal, a…shutting down. Not anger. Not disappointment.

No…something far worse than that.

"Okay." It's a throw-away word that I toss out there just to fill the silence. Something to draw attention away from Knox and give me a second to gather my composure.

I look at the others. "Can we assume Ajia will be back?"

"Tomorrow," says Noah, his eyes on Bree. "In time for the concert, according to Baz."

"Do we need to make any kind of a statement?" I glance in Knox's direction, but he's looking past me, like the door has some fascinating design other than its natural wood grain.

"What's your recommendation?" Rye asks.

I take a breath. "I say no. Not yet. Not about this. We proceed as though you don't have time to pay attention to…silly rumors. You started off on the right foot last night, so if we make any statement, it's about that. I'll check with Baz to see what plans the label might have for a follow-up, if any. Something about the party and *nothing else.*" I make a note in my tablet.

"They had a photographer there," says Knox stiffly.

"Great." I nod and add the information to my list.

When I look up, I spread my gaze among them. "Tonight you'll attend the Edge of Return party as planned. It would have been best if Ajia and Bree could go as…partners—" I can't find a better word at the moment, but it probably only matters to Knox "—but that won't be possible now."

I glance across the table at Rye. "Bree should stick with you, Rye. You have the least…notorious reputation."

He stares at me, his eyes dark and knowing. There's a fathomlessness there, a depth that intrigues me…and tells me nothing that he doesn't want me to see. Then his lips twist in a parody of a smile, and he says, "Anything for Bree."

There it is again. That sense of family. It warms me and freezes me at the same damn time. What must it feel like to be cared for with such love?

"You don't have to stay long—" I force myself back to the issue at hand "—but an appearance tonight is mandatory. Once Ajia is back tomorrow…we can bloody well plan what we want to say then."

"Are we gonna address the elephant in the room?" asks Noah.

"The elephant in the room?"

"The other rumors," says Bree softly. "About orgies and…stuff."

"No." I don't hesitate. "Absolutely not. That's all bullshit. The paparazzi would love to get a reaction from you, and then they'll twist it into whatever they want it to be. No, we concentrate on showing a different side of the band and respond only if we have to."

"What *different side?*" Zayne asks.

"I'm not sure yet," I admit. "I'll introduce myself on your social media sites, give your fans a name and someone to talk to. I'll distract them with some trivia, vague teasers about what's coming, ignore anything we don't want to answer. Make it strictly *our* agenda."

The others are nodding, all except Knox, who's back to being a statue, and so I continue. "I ought to be able to waste a day or two that way. I can always pretend I'm such a newbie that I don't know what I'm doing. By the time that excuse is played out, Ajia will be back and we'll have made our plan."

Rye gives me that same little smile of approval, while Zayne and Noah are still nodding.

"Anything else?" I ask.

"You going tonight?" asks Knox suddenly.

"Yes." I nod. "Just to keep things headed in the right direction. This is Edge of Return's party, which means it could go either way. The press might ignore you for the most part, or the gloves might come off where Wycked Obsession is concerned." I don't say it, but I expect it to be the latter.

"You meant they aren't already?" Bree sounds a little breathless.

"Don't worry." I give her a smile that better be damn well full of encouragement. "This'll all be over soon."

The words seem to signal the end of the meeting. Or maybe the others are just ready to be done. Whatever explains it, they all stand except Knox.

"C'mon, baby girl," says Noah as he slings an arm around Bree's shoulders. "Let's go spend an hour by the pool and let the sun bake us to crispy critters."

She smiles and looks over her shoulder at Rye and Zayne. "Y'all coming?"

They both nod. "We go where you go, baby girl," says Rye, and Zayne nods again.

"That's a lousy fucking idea," calls Knox as they leave. Noah flips him the bird, and they keep walking.

He slides a look in my direction. "Somebody could see 'em."

"Maybe," I agree. "But the hotel's fairly secure. Kel can watch over them. And you can't really expect them not to live their lives, Knox."

He looks at me, the first time we've really made eye contact since sometime last night, and though he doesn't say a thing, I see a riot of emotion coursing through him. I can't identify any of it, but the shit boiling under the surface is tearing him apart.

As much as I want to ask him about last night, about the *us* that isn't really an us at all, I know better. Now isn't the time— but will it ever be?

CHAPTER 10

KNOX

THE LIGHTS GO DARK AS SCREAMING AND APPLAUSE CROWD OVER US LIKE LIGHTNING AND THUNDER. Satisfaction soothes my itchy nerves. The show went great, much better than I expected. Ajia didn't fucking show up until less than thirty minutes before we went on, and nobody else in the band is talking to me.

But once we got on stage together, all that shit fell away.

I hand my guitar to Bobby, the only guy I trust with it besides myself. He takes care of all my shit.

"Great job." He smacks me on the back.

"Thanks, man."

I head off stage, glancing to where Bree usually sits. She was there tonight with London, but they're gone now. Probably waiting in the green room, where it's safe. Well, *safer*. Backstage is chaos, just like it always is. We're coming off, Edge of Reason is going on, roadies and equipment people are racing around, and fans who got passes are everywhere.

It's always the same, and I usually play the game. Sometimes I even like it, but not tonight.

Everything's just too screwed up right now.

I don't need to go over it, like some stupid to-do list. All I need are names. Bree. Gabe. Ajia. Zayne. Well, the whole fucking band.

And London.

Jesus. I've been thinking about her for two days. Wanted to see if a second time could be as good as the first, but shit's been going down and I've been busy. Now I'm harder and hornier than

I've been in a long time. The memory of being with her makes me want to come again.

Hell, I had to stroke one off in the shower just thinking about her. She let me fuck her against the door, she went down on me better than any blow job I ever had, and I came so hard I thought my head would explode.

All without even *thinking* of a condom.

What the fuck?

That part still screws with my head. Yeah, we're both clean, and she's on birth control, but it was still goddamn reckless. I might be a lot of things—bossy, demanding...asshole—but I'm not irresponsible. I take shit like fatherhood and family seriously.

Good and bad.

So, yeah, it's reassuring that we're safe, but it doesn't let me off the hook for not making *sure*.

"Knox!"

Some chick screams my name, and other screams follow. I sigh to myself and step out from the shadows. Zayne and Rye are surrounded by a group of fans, and a couple of girls peel themselves away to race for me.

"Knox! God, I love you!" They grab for my arms and pull.

"Hey, ladies, watch the merchandise!" I pretend to laugh and raise my hands in surrender. Before we were famous, this shit sounded so cool. And at first, it gave me a real surge of sexual energy. Hot chicks eager to bang us. Blow jobs a dime a dozen. I've shared girls and watched every one of my bandmates while they're fucking. They've seen me.

Now, it's all intrusive and irritating. I like to *invite* women into my personal space, not be mauled by them.

The thought sends me back to memories of London, about how I practically *mauled* her...and she welcomed me. She gave me what I needed, and then she seduced me with her mouth, her hands, her pussy. She was everything I needed, and I can't stop thinking about fucking her again.

The girls around me laugh and settle down, but they still want to be close. Touch. I force myself to tolerate it with a smile, because I know it's expected of me. Especially with Noah and Ajia nowhere to be seen. That fucker Ajia is probably already in the green room with *my sister*.

I start walking in that direction, and my little minions are right there with me. The others follow with Zayne and Rye, and then we're in the green room with everybody else. The door closes behind me as I hear the first notes of Edge of Reason's set. It reminds me where we are, *who* we are, and a new burst of energy races through me.

Knox Gallagher, lead guitarist of Wycked Obsession. *Cocky rock god,* London teased me. I got this shit.

The crowd moves around us like a living organism, and I'm not sure if it psyches me up or pisses me off. It's too early in the tour to be pissed, so I try to let it all flow around me and search the room while pretending that these fangirls matter somehow. And they do, in the overall scheme of things. They're fans, and I love that about them. But they don't own me—and I don't want to fuck them.

I give them my music, everything I have when I'm on stage. The rest of it...well, it's only been a couple of years of relative success, but I'm already jaded. Maybe it's my need for things to go my way, and this part of fame makes me feel real *out of control.*

Or maybe it's the rest of it. The thing with Gabe pissed me off, but the rumors about Bree and the band really pushed me over the edge. Plus, being with London totally screwed with my head. It was better than a year's worth of sex with a different groupie every night.

Blinking, I look again and find her standing with Ajia and Bree across the room. They're huddled in a corner behind the crafts table, looking like they're in serious conversation. Hope she's chewing Ajia's ass out for taking off like he did, leaving us all wondering what the hell was going on.

Fuck you, asshole. The voice that never lets me lie to myself speaks up with its typically confrontational attitude. It's the one way I know I can hold myself accountable. *You know what's* going on, *and don't act like you had nothing to do with it.*

It's true. I maybe don't know *exactly* what happened to Ajia years ago or how it all went down. I only know that he had to come clean with my sister. Bree deserves better than him keeping secrets from her, and so I pushed him to do *something.* Maybe the way I handled forcing him to tell Bree shit wasn't nice or fair. I don't give a shit! I'm not abandoning my sister to some lying player like Ajia Stone.

As much as I hate the idea, if she's going to make the choice to be with him, then it better be after she knows *everything*.

So why the hell does he have his arms around her *now?*

"You're so hot, Knox!" One of the fangirls squirms a little closer and leans in to whisper, "You make me...wet."

Why the fuck can't they ever tell me they like the way I play the guitar? They never do. It's always about me and my dick.

And why not? asks that pissy voice inside me. *Isn't that the way you've always treated them? Ever since you got fucked over by Farren, you've made it your mission to return the favor to every girl you meet. What did you expect?*

And why didn't I ever think about any of this shit until the rumors about Bree?

"Thanks a lot, honey." I don't know how else to respond to the chick.

"You got any plans for later?"

Fuck. I know where this is going. A few days ago, I might have been all over it. Her. Now...not.

"Hadn't really thought about it yet."

"I'm free." She slides one hand up my chest to my shoulder. "We could find a quiet place and—"

"I hate to interrupt your little...rendezvous, but you're wanted elsewhere, Romeo."

London's voice comes from behind the crowd around me, thick with irritation. Does that mean she's been thinking about fucking me again, too?

"English." I give her a lazy smile. "What's up, baby?"

The chick pressing herself against me shoves her hip against mine and tries to get closer. It isn't possible. "Who the fuck is this?" she demands.

I don't answer, and London all but ignores the fan, too. "Band meeting," she says shortly. "Mandatory. Ajia's room. He and Bree are going on ahead. Get the others."

She spins around and stalks away. Pissed. No doubt about it.

Interesting. I swallow a grin, the first real smile that's even tempted me in a while.

"Sorry, honey." I extricate myself from the clingy chick. "Gotta go. Duty calls and all that shit."

"But...I thought..." She sounds kind of screechy.

I shrug. "Thanks for coming out, honey. Enjoy Edge of Reason's show." And then I walk away without a backward glance.

♬

The limo ride to the hotel is silent. Nobody says a word. London sits across from me, her arms crossed over her chest like some disapproving mother with a carful of brats. She's dressed in a ruffly black skirt and white lacy tank top with thin little straps, and somehow looks both hot and conservative. It's all I can do to keep myself from shoving my hands up her legs to her pussy so I can find out if she's wet under that skirt.

Another time, another woman, I'd have done it. It wouldn't make a bit of difference if the rest of the band was here or not.

It's all different now.

The ride to our hotel is relatively short. We ignore the shouts, the cameras, and the crowd itself as hotel security escorts us straight to the elevator. Still, nobody says a word until I pound on Ajia's door.

"Open up!"

Ajia lets us in. I step back for London to go first but follow right on her heels. Noah's just behind me.

Bree's propped up on the bed. "You doing okay, baby girl?" Noah asks as he walks over.

"Of course." She smiles, the first I've seen from her in a couple of days. "I didn't get to tell y'all at the venue. It was a great show!"

Noah climbs onto the bed and pulls her next to him, one arm around her shoulders. I recognize the way he smirks at Ajia. Noah likes to stir up shit, and he wants to get a response out of our singer. He's shit out of luck. Ajia just skirts to the other side of the bed and scoots up next to Bree on the opposite side.

The rest of us shift around the room. Rye takes the soft chair, Zayne stretches out on the floor, and London sits at the desk. I perch on the top. Nobody says anything until Noah laughs.

"Well, look at this. We got ourselves a Bree sandwich."

"Different for you, huh?" She laughs back.

"What do you mean?"

"You're usually with two girls. I guess that makes you the meat in *that* sandwich."

Bree's face goes bright red, and there's a moment of weird silence. Everybody is trying not to laugh, and it pisses me off. Royally. Being on the road with us, she's learning too much sexy shit.

"Shut up, you fuckers," she laughs, and the rest of them join in. Even London.

Traitors.

I let my irritation settle over my expression and spread a fierce look around the room. "Okay, Pipes." I glance at Ajia. "You wanted a fucking band meeting. We're here."

"*I* called the meeting," says London, sounding all prickly. She doesn't look at me. "This kind of thing is *my* responsibility, and we need to talk about what's going on and plan some strategies."

I tighten my mouth, but it's Rye who asks, "Strategies about what?"

"Well, we have a couple of things to explain." She touches the screen on her tablet. "First, we need to talk about Ajia's unexpected trip to Austin."

"It was personal," says Bree.

Ajia kisses her head with a smile. "No, it's not a secret. Not anymore."

He waits a minute before he continues. "I was in a car accident as a kid. Fifteen, back when I was invincible." He lets out kind of a choked-sounding laugh that bugs me. Don't tell me *he's* after sympathy here. I don't have time to think about it, because he's talking again.

"It was bad. The friends with me...two were hurt, and one died." He shrugs. "I've never really gotten over it and carried a shitload of guilt over it. I had to...clean that up."

Clean it up? I snort. How do you clean up *killing* someone?

London only nods. "Any reason you had to go *now,* mid-tour?"

Ajia grabs my sister's hand suddenly. "Bree and I are together. It's not a one-night stand, and we're not fucking around." He glares at me. "Our relationship isn't open for discussion."

There isn't a thing I can say about it—now—and that asshole knows it. So, *what?* Am I just supposed to accept the fact that my sister's *with* this guy?

"About fucking time," says Noah, and I know I'm in the minority here.

"What?" Zayne pops up from the floor and looks around like he just joined the human race. "You two are fucking?" My jaw clenches as he points at Ajia and Bree.

"Among other things," says Ajia.

"Huh." He shakes his head. "So she's your…girlfriend?"

"Fuck," says Rye. "You killed too many brain cells, Zayne. Ajia said they're *together."*

"Right." Zayne nods. "Together—as in girlfriend."

"Right," agrees Ajia.

I watch the others, and we all exchange a stiff, what-the-fuck look. It's got nothing to do with Ajia and Bree, and maybe the only thing we can all agree on right now. It's Zayne. He's still messed up. Whatever's going on with him, it's not getting better. I glance at London.

We'll talk about this later.

She nods as though she understands.

"The truth is half-assed out there," says Ajia, letting Zayne off the hook for the moment. "At least the questions are. We haven't confirmed or denied. Correct?" He looks at London.

"Correct. Although you gave a pretty good indication of how things are in the green room tonight."

"What happened?"

"Fuck, Knox, you were there." It's Bree who snaps at me. "Too interested in your groupies to notice anything else? Ajia kissed me."

"Is that all?" I don't like it, but it could be a hell of a lot worse.

"You should have been paying attention," London says calmly. "In this case, it's enough."

"I was there."

London shakes her head stiffly. "Maybe physically. But your bloody attention wasn't. A few too many groupies for you to concentrate?"

What the fuck? I remember then when she came up to me in the green room.

I hate to interrupt your little rendezvous, but you're wanted elsewhere, Romeo.

She sounded pissed. Don't tell me she's…jealous.

No way.

Ajia's saying something that I miss, but I tune in to London's answer.

"Being a typical Texas man, you couldn't wait. For anything. You had to go to Austin *immediately,* come back just in time for the concert, and then make out with Bree like you hadn't seen her in a damn year."

"Well, yeah." Gotta admire Ajia for the way he ignores London's sarcasm, even though his attitude pisses me off. "Bree helped me see it's time for me to find a way to put the accident shit behind me, so I took the first step."

"All right." London takes a quick breath. "Anything else I need to know?"

"Besides the fact that Knox is pissed Ajia and I are together?" Bree asks.

"Is that true?" London looks at me, but she already knows the answer.

My sister won't let it go. "You tell me. He told me things about Ajia—about the accident—in the worst possible way, hoping it would end things. It didn't, and he's been pouting ever since."

"I'm not pouting." My look ought to incinerate anybody in a fifty foot radius.

"Oh, you're pouting, man," laughs Noah, but his expression is hard. "It was a dick fucking move to say that shit to Bree, and now you're twice as pissed. One cause they're together at all—" he points at her and Ajia "—and two because you couldn't break 'em up."

"Well, we aren't going to share any of that," London says quickly, before I can tell him what a dumbass he is. He doesn't know shit, and—

"And in public," she adds, cutting off my thoughts, "you're going to act like it's the best thing that's happened all tour."

"Fuck me," I snap coldly. "Bree is *my* sister, and—"

"And she's an adult," London interrupts with a frown. "Unless you want fans to be worried about problems within the band, you're going to act happy as fuck that your sister and your best friend are a couple. Got it?"

The room falls silent we stare at each other. I can damn near see the tension crackle between us, and at that moment, the only thing I want more than to walk out of the room is to fuck her.

I take a breath and nod. "Understood."

"Good." She glances around. "Anything else?"

Nobody else answers, and so I push off the desk. "Mom's divorcing Gabe." I don't look at anyone when I say it.

"When did she tell you that?" Bree's pressed against Ajia's chest, her eyes suddenly watery.

"This morning."

"And you didn't tell me until now?"

"You knew it was coming." I'm not accusing her or anything, but it's true. "You had to expect it, after you fucking told her about him."

Ajia and Bree whisper to each other, while London glares at me.

"Details, please." She doesn't sound like she's in an encouraging mood, all of a sudden.

I don't say a word, and it's Rye who finally answers. "Bree's stepdad was hitting on her."

"Okay." She nods briskly. "More personal stuff. Not going there, either." She stands, like we're all a bunch of kids, and she's dismissing us. "Let me do a little work. I'll see what I can put together for strategies, and let's meet again in the morning. We'll start our own campaign and direct attention to where *we* want it."

"Thanks, London." Bree smiles

She smiles back. "Hey, you're stuck with me now. I'll do whatever I can for you."

"Great!" crows Noah as he climbs to his feet. "Welcome to the family! Looks like you got yourself a sister in crime, baby girl."

"It's about time." She laughs.

"And it's about time for the rest of you fuckers to get out of here. I wanna be alone with my girl."

The others laugh as we crowd toward the door. I don't see anything funny about it at all, but Rye shoves me out the door all the same.

"Night, kiddies. Sleep tight." Noah laughs and heads down the hall like the shit-stirrer he is.

CHAPTER 11

LONDON

MY ROOM IS ABOUT HALFWAY DOWN THE HALL FROM AJIA'S. I'm almost there when I hear my name. Well, my apparent nickname.

"English! Wait up."

I stop just outside my door, waiting as Knox strides up behind me. He hasn't changed since being onstage, wearing leather pants and a vintage Nirvana T-shirt. They fit him like a bloody glove, he still has guyliner outlining his eyes, he hasn't shaved in a couple of days, earrings glint from his left ear, and the whole package just pisses me off.

No man should look as good as Knox Gallagher does, be so goddamn entitled to the title Cocky Rock God, and fuck like he invented it.

"What is it?"

He blinks. My tone is cold, and I mean it to be.

"Let's talk."

"Talk."

I stare at him. The eyeliner makes his expression more intense. His gray-green eyes flicker with...something, but I can't tell what. Then again, I'm not trying that hard to figure it out; I'm thinking about the last time a man told me he wanted to talk. Colin said he wanted to *have a word,* but the result was the same. The disrespect, and the end of our relationship.

"About what?" I ask stiffly.

"Couple of things. Let's go inside." He nods toward my door. "I don't want to do this in the hall."

Do what? But I don't ask. I unlock the door and step inside. Is he going to fire me? Tell me it was a mistake to sleep together? Or just grace me with his presence and pretend like nothing happened?

I stalk across the room to stand between the dresser and end of the bed. Like my little fortress, I guess. The image that pops into my mind should make me smile, but it doesn't.

"What is it?" I ask again. "What do you want to talk about?"

He locks the door behind him and steps to the middle of the room. "You're damn prickly tonight, baby. What's wrong?"

Wrong? And why the hell is he calling me *baby?*

I blink and huff out a sharp breath. Mostly I'm trying to buy time, a few seconds, at least. Tonight was the first time I'd seen Wycked Obsession perform live. Watching Knox and his Les Paul left me amazed, breathless...so bloody turned on, my body wants to take control from my mind.

I shouldn't be alone with him in my room.

"It's late." It's a bullshit answer, and I know it, even if he doesn't. "What did you want to talk about?" I ask the question again, because I can't think of anything else to say.

"Okay..." He lets the word fade away like he's trying to figure me out, and then finally he adds, "Let's start with taking control of some of these rumors."

"All right." It takes everything I have to keep the words coolly professional. "Which ones, specifically?"

Knox narrows his gaze like he's tightening his focus. On me? Probably. He's into that kind of control.

"Like Ajia's trip to Texas." He says it deliberately. "You gonna say something?"

"I can. How do you want me to handle it?"

He keeps looking at me with those deep gray-green eyes that see too much. "Isn't that your job? To tell us what we should say?"

I shrug, like his words don't strike a tender part of me. They do, maybe even should, but I'm not admitting to a bloody thing.

"All right. We *should* release a statement that says Ajia made a brief trip to Austin for personal reasons, and that he and his family appreciate his fans respecting their privacy."

"Why bring up his family?"

"To hint that it has nothing to do with the band. Or Bree."

"Yeah. Okay." He nods slowly. "Makes sense. I like it."

"I'm glad to hear it." I can tell Knox is smart enough to hear the sarcasm in my voice, but I don't wait long enough for him to comment. "What else?"

"What do you mean?"

I glare at him. So he's playing the bullshit game, too. I can read his expression well enough to know the question means nothing. He's buying time, but why?

"What else do you want me to do?" I ask deliberately.

"Well…" He looks me up and down as though he's measuring me. Weighing something. Sorting through the details for…what?

"Let's talk about Bree."

I try to treat him to the same careful observation he gave me, but I'm nowhere as good as him. "My first choice would be to arrange for an interview with her, but—" I hold up one hand when Knox opens his mouth "—she doesn't have the experience or public persona for that. *Somebody* has to go on record, though, and it can't be you. Your bloody temper will ruin it. I'm suggesting Ajia."

"Why him?" His gaze darkens, but it makes his direct attention on me less intense.

"He's the face of the band. The frontman. He jacked up the rumors with that stunt at the Wycked Obsession party. He can take the heat."

Knox lifts a shoulder as he shakes his head, and so I add, "I'll work with you *all* tomorrow about the message we want to get across."

"And Bree won't be a part of it?"

"No." I say it flatly. "Now, what else?"

He takes a step toward me. "What the hell's wrong with you?"

"What do you mean?"

"You're all stiff." He slants me a look. "Cold."

I give my head a quick jerk. "Just following your lead."

"My lead? What are you talking about?"

I shrug. "I guess maybe I don't know the proper etiquette of being your one-night stand. You avoid me and don't speak, so I'm trying to *follow your lead."* I want it to sound pithy and emotionless, but the words come out sharp and almost bitter.

"One-night stand? Avoiding you?" He sounds as confused as he looks. "What the hell, English? I'm not avoiding you."

"You've hardly said a word to me in two days."

"Well…fuck me. I've been busy." He flings one hand aside. "You know, my sister telling my mom that her scumbag husband's been hitting on her, and Mom filing for divorce. The lead singer of my band going AWOL. My baby sister being crucified on the internet. Finding out we've got an unscheduled video shoot coming up. Shit like that—or am I not supposed to have feelings about anything except when my dick gets hard?"

I stare at him. I probably shouldn't—it isn't exactly safe for me—but I can't help it. He has a point, and I need to be sure I understand it correctly. Everything *has* been in an uproar since he hired me. Actually, it's one of the reasons he hired me when he did.

So…is that it? He was just…busy?

"Uh…you're sure? You haven't been—"

"I don't lie." His voice sounds as cold as mine was earlier, and his gaze is frosty. "Never needed to."

"Uhm…okay. I…uh, I'm sorry?"

The words sound more tentative than I want, but Knox has me completely off-center here. I believe him. I really *can* see the truth in his expression, and everything I know about him, from my internet searches to the few days I've known him, tells me he's sincere. He *doesn't* lie. He is, in fact, brutally honest at times.

But that's not the worst of it. I'm a hypocrite, and a selfish one at that. I told myself I was going for sex with no emotional ties or obligations. Colin's asshole stunt gave me the chance to make a choice, and I took it.

So what the bloody hell do I think I'm doing acting like some woman scorned?

You can't have it both ways, luv. You're either going for sex and a good time or you're looking for a relationship. Which is it?

A relationship with Knox Gallagher. Yeah—right. I could almost laugh. Not gonna happen in this lifetime.

"I...uh..." I shake my head and force myself to look at him. He looks pissed, and he deserves to be mad. "Bollocks! This is awkward! I am *so* not used to this."

"Not used to what?" His voice is sharp, and he takes a step toward me.

"You." I lift my shoulder. "I mean, I get it. You fuck women and move on. You don't have to see them again. But...here I am. I should have thought about that before I gave it up."

"Didn't give you much choice, English." His bearing changes, eases, and he gives me a half-smile as he moves closer.

My smile isn't as confident as I'd like, but I make do. I owe him. My earlier apology sucked. "Maybe not," I agree. "You *were*...irresistible."

He grins then, surprising after the last couple of days and our salty exchange. "It's a curse."

I blink. "You are also incorrigible."

He takes another step, and then he's right next to me. Close enough that the scent of spicy chocolate and Knox himself hits me like a ton of bricks. Close enough that he can reach out and trace the backs of his fingers down my cheek. It's a surprisingly tender gesture, and I'm not quite sure what to make of it.

"Who said I wanted to move on?"

I wet my lips and swallow. "Don't you always? Fuck a girl and then on to the next one. The gossip sites say so. Like you did tonight." I don't have to close my eyes to see the groupies crowded around him, grabbing him like they own him.

He frowns. "I didn't fuck anybody tonight. I—" he shakes his head "—haven't fucked anybody since you."

"Wow!" I widen my eyes and try to smile, but it feels fake. It *is* fake. "Two days and a night. You sure you can go that long?"

His frown gets fierce again. "So we're back to that? Manwhore with no self-control."

"I didn't say that."

"You're thinking it."

Am I? I think about it. Is my attitude about me and my insecurities, or my disapproval of Knox's lifestyle?

A lifestyle you said you wanted for yourself, a voice of honesty snaps. *You said no more boyfriends. Sex for the sake of the physical release. The big O, remember?*

So why am I being so bitchy about this? He didn't do anything wrong.

And neither did I.

"Sorry." I let out a low breath. "You didn't do anything, Knox. It's me. I told you—" I try to smile, but it's a complete failure "—I'm out of my comfort zone here. It's my problem, my mess. I'm making things harder than they have to be."

"Well, hell, baby. If you need it hard—" he grabs his crotch through his leather pants "—I can make that happen."

I don't mean to laugh. I don't want to laugh. But I do.

How the bloody hell does he do it? Pissed off, arrogant control freak one minute, and then flirty rock god the next?

He steps close, pins my hips against the dresser and completely fills my little pseudo-fortress. The strength of his abs, his pelvis, his thighs hold me in place while he leans close enough that I can feel a soft puff of breath over my skin. "Does that mean you forgive me for what I didn't do wrong?"

I open my mouth to answer, but it's too late. His lips are on mine, his tongue slips inside, and I have zero willpower to do anything but kiss him back. I bite his bottom lip when he acts like he's going to pull away and then suck his tongue deep in my mouth.

Who the hell taught him how to kiss? Are cocky rock gods born knowing this shit?

He shifts against me, and the hard ridge of his cock presses against my stomach. I want to reach for him—it—but he has my arms pinned to my sides, and then somehow I can't think straight anymore because my tongue is in his mouth. He circles it with his, bites down lightly, and then strokes it again and again.

"Jesus, Knox." I pant more than speak. "What is it about you? You're like a freaking drug in my system."

He drops his forehead against mine, his breathing as heavy as mine, and we stand there panting. He drops a quick, light kiss on my lips and then steps back. He grabs the back of his neck and drops down onto the end of the bed behind him. "Fuck."

"What?" I swallow, try to regroup. "What's wrong? Did I do something?"

He shakes his head, then shoves his hands in his hair to push it back, away from his face. "Much as that was damn fine...there's something else."

"What?"

I circle around the bed and sit a little farther toward the head. I'm at a disadvantage around Knox, and if I don't want to immediately jump his bones, I need a little space. Clearly, he has something to say.

"Zayne."

"Zayne?" I repeat. Why the hell are we talking about him now? Mid-kiss?

"I think he's using again."

"Drugs." It makes sense then. Awful and clear. Zayne's odd behavior; other, less prominent rumors; and why Knox stopped kissing me.

You're like a freaking drug in my system, I told him.

"Tell me about it," I say softly as I try to resettle myself. I want to reach for him, encourage him, but I don't. I'm afraid the next thing I know, I'll find my hand on his cock, and I can't do that to him. He needs—*we need*—to have this conversation.

It's important to Knox, to the band.

"We did shit on the first tour." He slants a knowing gaze in my direction. "Lots of it. Sex, drugs, rock'n'roll, you know?"

I nod.

"We got back to Austin pretty fucked up. Straightened ourselves out, but once we were clean, Ajia took the drug use pretty hard. He's got a friend fucked up on prescription pain killers. It led to other shit, and the guy's a mess. Ajia made us promise to give up that shit. Alcohol, a little pot, nothing stronger."

"And Zayne didn't keep his promise."

"Thought he did. Now I'm not so sure. Definitely not since the tour. We've been there. We know what it looks like."

I don't have to guess; I know he's right. I haven't had all that much to do with drugs personally; I don't have that many friends, people who would introduce me to it, and it wasn't something I sought out on my own. But I'm no dummy, and in the short time I've known him, I recognize Zayne's impairment for what it is.

"What are you going to do?"

"No choice. Confront him."

"Can I help?"

He shakes his head, but says, "Yeah. Keep it out of the gossip sites."

I nod. "Consider it done."

And I will. After everything else, the last thing Wycked Obsession needs is rumors of drug use.

Knox turns on the bed, surprising me when he tugs me close and gives me an oddly serious look. "I don't talk about my shit," he admits slowly. "I just take care of it. So why did I tell you anything? And why do I feel better now?"

"I...don't know." What else can I say? I *don't* know. In fact, I don't know shit right now.

"Maybe because it's my job to help keep you guys out of trouble," I suggest softly.

"And why do I want to kiss you so bad it fucking hurts?"

I lose my breath and can only shake my head. "Knox..."

His lips descend over mine, and he takes my mouth in a purely sexual kiss. It's everything we have, tongues and teeth and lips, and I can't get enough of it. I want to push myself against him, feel his hardness press back—*all of it*—but before I can appreciate any of it, he jerks me close. He's all sharp angles to my soft curves, and we fit together in a way that reminds me men and women were always supposed to be so.

He sucks my tongue deep into his mouth, and my nipples go all hard and demanding. My core tightens, and my pussy wakes up with its own sudden demand. God, what this man can do with his mouth, his hands, his cock. The other night was the best sex ever, in the entire world, for anybody who ever lived. Another night in bed with Knox would make up for a lot of the frustration I felt over the last two days.

The frustration I felt over the last two days?

The words splash over me and dampen the sharp physical reactions of my body. I don't mean to, but I find myself pulling back, struggling for a long, labored breath, searching for enough concentration to put my brain back in working order.

Bollocks!

"Knox." I pant his name.

"What is it, baby?" He shoves a hand in my hair and tries to pull me closer.

"No. I...I'm not sure we should do this."

He blinks. "Do what?"

"Kiss. And...stuff."

"Stuff." He shoots me a seductive grin. "It's called fucking, baby, and you liked it the other night. A lot, I think. I know I did."

I close my eyes. "Yeah. I, uh, did." I have to look at him, see the seductive fullness of his face, and remind myself what a bloody fool I can be. "But I'm not sure I can do it again."

Hearing those words—*I'm not sure I can do it again*—tells me that my subconscious has some things figured out. I couldn't see it before, but suddenly I understand my hypocrisy all the way to my soul. It isn't so much about the one-night stand; it's about seeing him again so soon afterward, and knowing he has been, or is going, to other women.

No matter what I thought I wanted, it just makes me feels...used.

"I see that brain working, English." He wraps one hand around the back of my neck and holds me in place. "Tell me."

I swallow. "Well, it's the...the whole one-night stand aspect of it, I suppose. It would be one thing if we went our separate ways, but I don't think I'm cut out to fuck you randomly when I know we're going to see each other again the next day. And it might be when you're going off to fuck another girl."

"Who said I want random? Or a one-night stand?"

"But...isn't that how you usually operate. The gossip sites say—""

"I don't give a damn what they say. Yeah, I've done that. Maybe even a lot. It's kind of the nature of the game when you're on the road. But I'm not a one-trick pony. I've stuck with girls for longer."

"How long?"

He hesitates. "I don't know. A month or two."

"And..." I don't know how to ask it. It sounds so...*needy.* "How long do you think you can...*stick* with me?"

"You looking for rules, English?"

Rules? How do I answer, when I don't know myself?

"Maybe."

"Stand up."

His voice is an unexpected and sharp demand. I don't argue, confused about where the tone came from or what it means.

"Knox?"

"Stand up," he repeats, sounding even shorter and harsher.

I do it, but only because I don't know what else to do. That doesn't explain why my nipples get even harder, and are my panties seriously damp?

"Take off your blouse."

"What?"

He frowns. "Don't make me repeat myself again, English. You won't like the consequences."

It hits me then, like a bolt of lightning. He's a Dom. Or at least he likes to be dominant. Everything about him screams it, and has since I met him. How could I have missed it? And, now that I see it, how far will he take it?

I'm not normally submissive, never fantasized about being with a guy who took control that seriously, but I can't deny that something about his tone, the demanding look on his face, sends my sex drive into high gear.

I've never had a man like Knox Gallagher fuck me before, and I'm not giving him up until I have to.

I peel my lacy camisole-type top over my head and toss it to the dresser. It just so happens I'm wearing my white bra and panties set with the tiny pink ribbons, and I realize suddenly that I feel sexy and desirable.

"Now the skirt."

I don't hesitate. I unzip the black pleated skirt and shimmy out of it, tossing it to land with my top. I'm still wearing my bra and panties, and my strappy black sandals, but I don't take anything else off. I don't think I'm supposed to.

"Come here."

I step closer, enough that he grabs my arm and tugs me to stand almost between his knees. He slips two fingers between my legs, stroking over my slit through the layer of cotton.

"You're wet, baby."

"I...yes." I swallow.

"But you want rules."

Do I? I don't know. I don't know what the hell is going on. But maybe rules would be good.

"I...yes," I say again and nod. "I think so."

"Okay, English." He strokes over me a little harder, but still on the outside of my panties. "I'll give you some rules."

He slips his other hand inside the cup of my bra and teases my nipple until it aches. Still, he doesn't say anything, just keeps rubbing his fingers over me until I think I'll scream in frustration.

"Rule number one," he says finally, slowly. "We both get tested, just like you wanted. No fucking until that's done."

My mouth is dry, my breathing ragged, and so I can only nod.

"Rule number two. We go exclusive, until the end of the tour. No groupies for me, no roadies for you."

I lose a ragged breath. *"Exclusive?"*

"It's what you wanted, isn't it? You don't like the one-night shit?"

"Yes, but...I didn't expect you to—agree."

"I don't give a shit what the gossip sites say. I don't fuck just anything with two legs and a pussy. I don't find women like you very often, and I want you. So I'll make a concession."

A concession. I'd laugh if I could, but he looks perfectly serious.

"What happens at the end of the tour?"

He shrugs and pinches my nipple. "What normally happens. We'll still work together, but you'll be in LA or wherever you live, and I'll be in Austin. We'll go back to our separate lives, and everything will be normal again."

Normal. Do I even know what that is anymore?

"Okay," I agree softly. What else can I say?

He nods. "Rule number three, no condoms. You're on birth control, and when we're sure we're clean, no reason for it. I had you bareback the other night, baby, and I fucking *liked it.*"

I never knew what it meant when books described someone as looking wolfish. Now I do. "All right."

"And rule number four." He pauses.

"Yes?"

"The most important one of all. The others hinge on this one."

"Yes?"

"Tomorrow." He pulls his hands from my body, and I want to cry out at the loss of his touch. "Wear a dress. No bra, no panties, just you under that dress. You find me sometime when I'm not alone and show me just how good you are at following the rules."

CHAPTER 12

KNOX

THE CONFERENCE ROOM IS FULL, and I have no freaking clue why half these jokers are here. Somebody from the label called the meeting, and so here we are. Even London came—to get a feel for shit, Baz said. He wants her to see how it all works, to know what to look for when the band differs from what the label wants to put out.

I'm all for having her with us, and I smirk in her direction. She sees me; I know she does. She's sitting across from me, pretending to look at her phone, but I see the half-smile she tries to hide. She's been fighting it since we met up in the hotel lobby for the thirty-minute limo ride to the label's offices.

She's wearing a white dress decorated with smeary-looking flowers. It's short and tight, some kind of wrap-around thing that crosses over her tits and fastens at the left side of her waist. The straps are thin enough, and the V neckline shows enough of her cleavage that I'm damn sure she's not wearing a bra.

But panties? Haven't figured that out yet. The wrap-around style means the front hem rises up in a V that stops only a couple of inches south of her pussy. She hasn't shown me shit yet, and I get hard just thinking about it.

Down boy, I remind myself with an inner groan. *No fucking till you get tested.*

Why the hell did I say that? Dammit! I swallow a growl as another inner voice pipes up.

You could always use a condom. It'd be worth it.

Fuck, yeah, it would be. And I'm used to condoms. I use them 100% of the time—except with London, apparently, and that still shocks the shit out of me. Was it *her,* or was I just too worked up over Bree, Ajia, and all the rumors? I can't decide and want to believe it doesn't matter. It isn't true, but I don't have the fucking answer.

It isn't easy to accept, and now I told her no sex until we got tested. *Fuck.* But I gotta stick with it. It's important that she understands I stick to my word.

It's my brand of control.

Voices are arguing around me, but I haven't been listening. They don't know what the hell they're talking about, anyway. Marty got us all together in this large, tight ass-looking conference room that sucks the life out of the creative process. I don't care about any of this shit, except why these fuckers think they get a say in our next video.

"Stop!" I make the demand in a voice as loud as I need to in order to get them to shut up. I'm a little surprised when the room goes silent in an instant.

I look at Marty. "This is fucking ridiculous," I snap. "I mean, thanks for being so gung-ho about our music, but how closely have you listened to the song? Have any of you ever thought to ask me or Ajia about *our* vision for *Lost?* Or don't you give a shit what the songwriters meant?"

I can feel their stares, but I'm busy looking at the guys in the band, one by one. They look back without flinching.

"Knox—" Marty begins, but I cut him off.

"Play it."

"What?" He frowns.

"Play the song."

"Knox…"

"Play it."

Marty looks around the room like he's lost. So do the other label suits. It's London, finally, who pulls out her phone and finds the song.

Lost. One of the best songs Ajia and I have ever written. The label wants to release it next, and we all like the idea. It sneaks up on you, this song, but it rocks. We screwed with the arrangement for days, starting out soft. Just Ajia's voice sounding all ragged and Rye understated on the piano. The rest of us hold off, patient, and just before the bridge, Noah and Zayne kick in with a heavy drum and bass line. I follow with a short guitar solo, and then we're all together again.

That's when the thing fucking takes off into the stratosphere.

It could be a blockbuster. It's why we wanted to release it while we're on tour. None of these assholes had a thing to do with it.

I almost smile as the song starts with Rye's piano opening. Then Ajia.

Turn my back,
Walk away.
That's what I want to do.
The past is pain.
Future looks empty.
The world is only cruel.
I'm lost.
She's gone.
Where do I go from here?
Alone, afraid,
All by myself.
I pray the end is near.

We worked our asses off, and *Lost* sounds just like we wanted it to. I fucking love it that the room stays silent as the last note fades away. I recognize the pride on my bandmates' faces, because I feel the same. Marty has it, too. Even the label's suits look pleased, like they finally recognize the possibilities of the song.

The stunned look on London's face makes my dick hard. Some deep, purely masculine satisfaction surges through me. Maybe she isn't my girlfriend, but some part of me likes knowing how well she responded to our music.

"I'm gobsmacked," she whispers and shakes her head.

"What the fuck is that?" Noah asks.

She blushes just a little, and it's fucking adorable. "Overwhelmed," she admits in kind of a breathy voice. "Blown away. That's, like…the most amazing song I ever heard."

I nod toward Ajia. I'm still pissed at him, but I can't deny the truth of his lyrical genius. "He wrote the words."

He stares at me for a few seconds and then blinks. "Wouldn't mean shit without the music."

We haven't resolved shit—he's still fucking my sister—but we can at least recognize each other's contribution.

"What's it about?" London asks, sounding kind of awestruck. I frown, not quite sure how that makes me feel.

Ajia shakes his head. "Not my place to say. Somebody else's story. It...inspired me." He's been saying that same damn thing since he first showed me the lyrics, and I still wonder if it's true.

"I know how we do it."

I stare across the table at Rye. He rarely says anything in these meetings. He only watches and listens, so when he does speak up, I listen.

"You got a concept?"

He shakes his head. "No. I got *the* concept."

"Go ahead, man," says Ajia quickly, almost anxious, and it makes me wonder.

I look between them. Does Rye know who or what inspired the lyrics? Could it even be him? He's had his share of shit in his life, just like the rest of us, but he keeps his stuff secret. At least from me.

"Black and white," says Rye. "A couple in love. They're so fucking happy." He blinks. "Then switch to a cemetery. She's dead, and he's wrecked."

"Dude..." Words fail me. It sounds heavy, dramatic...and maybe fucking inspired.

Nobody else says a word as the idea sinks in. Images flash through my mind. A couple at the beach. Having a romantic dinner. Snuggled in bed together. Then a headstone. Surrounded by other headstones.

"It's brilliant," whispers London, like she's reading my mind.

"Yeah," say Noah and Zayne at the same time.

I pull myself from the movie going on in my head and look around the table. Marty has this weird look of satisfaction on his face, and the guy who's supposed to be the director—can't remember his name—is all zoned out. He's scribbling notes on a pad of paper, nodding and muttering to himself.

"Do we get actors or use the band?" asks Marty, glaring at me. I can read his look: *keep your mouth shut!*

"The band. Definitely," says the director. "Ajia's the guy," he points, "with the band playing in the background. Especially in the cemetery. Just need the girl."

"We'll do some screen tests," suggests another guy. No clue who he is. "Find the right look, the right chemistry with Ajia."

"Bree," says London suddenly.

We all stare at her. "What?"

I add a couple more words. "The. Fuck?"

She looks only at me. "The actress doesn't need to be anything but happy." She angles her head toward Ajia. "In love. She and Ajia won't actually have to *act*. They'll just do stuff a normal couple in love would do."

"Who's Bree?" asks the director.

"My sister," I snap.

"What's she look like?"

I hold up my palm toward the director but shoot a fierce glare at London. "Give us a minute."

I shove back from the table and stalk over to the far corner of the room. The one that puts the most distance between me and the table. I turn in time to see her stroll in my direction like a queen on a red carpet. Maybe mixing shit up there, but the idea is the same. She's calm, composed, and so goddamn fuckable I think I'll lose my mind.

"Yes?" she says, even sounding like a damn queen.

"English," I snap and pull her around until she's in the corner and I'm looming over her. My back is to the rest of the room, and I lean down to bite off the rest of my words. "What the fuck are you thinking?"

"Knox." She reaches out, places her palm on my chest, and if wasn't for the AC/DC T-shirt I'm wearing, she'd be touching me skin to skin. I can almost feel the soft heat of her hand, anyway.

"Don't you see?" she asks, dragging my attention back to the conversation. "It's the perfect answer."

"Perfect for who?"

"Everybody!" She smiles, but there's something almost naughty mixed in with her certainty. "This stuff with Bree's all over the internet. And, yeah, Ajia's going to make a statement later today. We'll keep it as innocent as possible. Something like

Bree's been a part of the Wycked Obsession family from the beginning, and you're all...close."

"Like that's gonna satisfy anybody."

"It won't." She nods. "So we put her in the video and give her some legitimacy with the band. And if fans want to take it to mean that Bree and Ajia are together...well, they are."

"But—"

"Knox." She licks her lips—those goddamn lips!—and gives me a little smile. "Best we can do at this point is keep the attention on them together. The ugly stuff will get buried under the speculation about them as an actual couple, and we won't comment on that after Ajia's statement."

"I don't know..." I blow out a harsh breath. "I still don't like it."

"How about this, then?" She leans back just an inch or so and grabs my hand like she needs it for balance.

"English?"

"Remember the rules, Knox? You listed them out for me. Are you wondering if I followed them?" she whispers.

"Shit, baby."

I can barely keep my voice down as she drags my hand to the hem of her dress, that curvy upside down V that's been taunting me all fucking day. The tips of my fingers barely touch the skin of her thigh, softness smooth against years of guitar-string calluses. She takes a half-step forward, tugs on my hand at the same time, and then I'm there. Her tight, wet pussy at my fingertips.

"So you're a good girl," I approve as I stroke over her and almost slip one finger inside.

"Your good girl." She corrects me with a sigh, and this time I do push in. She's as tight as I remember, and wetter by the second.

How far do I want to push it with the crowd behind me? The band? It wouldn't stop me. Marty, the video director, the others? Wouldn't give a shit about them, either, except I want the label's support for this video and our third album.

Finger fucking our publicist in the middle of a concept meeting probably won't do that.

"You got an appointment yet?" I demand.

She shakes her head. "I'll make it when we're done here." The muscles of her pussy tighten around my finger. "I'm almost due for my shot, anyway, so I'll do it all at once."

I nod and move my finger just enough to earn a gasp. I grin.

"Asked Baz to find me a doctor in L.A. He said he'd make the appointment."

Her eyes darken, losing some of that glittering gold and becoming heavy. Needy. I can use that to my advantage, so I slowly pull my finger from her tight channel and stick it in my mouth. I swirl my tongue around it, showing how much I savor the sweet taste of her, and watching her gaze grow wild and heavy.

"Knox..." She swallows.

"Mr. Gallagher."

The voice comes out of nowhere, from behind us, and I jerk around like somebody pulled me on a rope. I step back toward London, giving her a few seconds of extra privacy, praying nobody notices my woody, and stare around the room. A girl, maybe 20, stands just inside the doorway.

"Yeah?"

"Mr. Gallagher," she says again but keeps her eyes down, like she's afraid to make eye contact.

"What is it, honey?" I try for an easy voice.

"You...uh, you have a phone call."

"A phone call?" I blink and look from Marty to all the members of the band. They shake their heads in confusion. "Who the fuck knows I'm here?"

"Bree," says Ajia, and we both whip out our phones. Nothing. If it's my sister, why wouldn't she call me on my cell?

"I don't know, sir." The nervous chick answers, and her voice wavers. "It came in through the...uh, switchboard and got forwarded up here."

"Where can I take it?"

"Over there." It's Marty who points to a phone sitting on a long, low table against one wall. I stalk over, see a blinking light and connect the call.

"Hello?"

"Well, if it isn't the son who I never thought would amount to shit."

My breath all but dies, and my heart starts pounding like a fucking jackhammer. "Who is this?"

"Who do you think, jerkoff?"

I don't answer. I can't, because it can't be *him.*

"What do you want—" my voice isn't as hard as I want it to be, but it'll have to do "—and how did you get this number?"

His laugh is ugly. "I'm not the dumb fuck you must think I am. You and your sister are hot gossip."

"What the fuck do you want?" I demand again.

"Guess."

"I haven't a clue. I haven't thought about you in years." So maybe that's a stretch. I *do* think about the sperm donor from time to time, but only to thank God that he disappeared from our lives.

"Well, start thinking, dickwad. You got money, and I'm thinking you could share some with your old man."

"You're crazy." I don't have to think about it. "I got nothing I'm giving you."

He laughs, that same goddamn ugly sound. A memory, thin and vague, sneaks over me. I remember hearing the same thing as a kid, when he'd talk shit to my mom.

"You might want to think again, *boy."*

"And why the fuck would I do that?"

"'Cause I could go to the press and tell them all kinds of shit."

"Like what?" I scoff.

"Like how you're all rich and famous now and let your old man live like a fucking bum."

"Hey, you live like a bum, you deserve it, asshole."

"Then how about you started sneaking into your little sister's room as a kid, and I caught you messing with her."

My heart is pounding so hard, I think it's gonna beat right out of my chest. I'm shaking with rage, and I wish to holy hell he was here, right in front of me. I'd smash in his ugly face and rip off his nuts.

"That. Is. A. Fucking. Lie."

There it is, that same hideous fucking laugh. "Who the fuck cares? It'll be too fucking late by the time anybody figures it out."

"I'm not giving you shit."

"Figured you'd say that. You always were a hothead. So I'm gonna give you a chance to think it over."

"I don't need to think about shit."

"Take the time, anyway, sonny boy. I'll be in touch."

"When?"

"When I'm good and goddamn ready." He laughs, and the line goes dead.

I pull the receiver from my ear and stare at it. Count to three. Five. Ten. Then I slam it back in its cradle with a shout.

"Motherfucker!"

CHAPTER 13

LONDON

KNOX DOESN'T SAY A WORD ON THE RIDE BACK TO THE HOTEL. He's stoic, arms crossed over his chest, and staring straight ahead. I want to say something silly to lighten the mood, like comment on his vintage AC/DC T-shirt or ask who his favorite guitar player is, but everything about him warns me off.

Whatever happened in there, he does *not* want to talk about it. Or anything else.

It was Ajia who put an end to the meeting and got us out of there. I can't even remember what he said. Knox just stalked out of the room, Ajia made some kind of excuse, and we all got the hell out of there. Now we simply remain quiet in deference to Knox's attitude.

What the bloody hell went down during that phone call? I don't know Knox or the band well enough to even guess. Even my online research doesn't give me a clue, and asking him seems like a terrible idea. Just his gaze freezes me, and the tension radiating from him tells me not to take the risk.

At least not now, not in front of the whole band.

We ride for almost thirty minutes like that before we reach our hotel. The instant we pull to a stop, Knox exits the limo without a word. It worries me as much as relief soothes over me. The awkwardness is gone, but uncertainty ramps itself up. I exchange a variety of looks with the other guys, mostly *what the hell?* Or, in the vernacular of the band…*what the fuck?*

Rye helps me from the car and escorts me into the lobby. These Texas boys. I smile gently to myself. They're very polite, more so than most guys I've known *without* long hair and tattoos.

It gives me a surprising amount of pride to walk into the hotel surrounded by this group of tall, well-built, and handsome dark-haired men, any one of whom could top any Sexiest Men Alive list.

Noah points to a corner seating area that looks relatively private. "Let's talk."

I assume he means just the band until Rye places a light hand at the small of my back and encourages me forward. "Are you sure you want to include me?"

Ajia nods. "You as much as the rest of us."

"But…" I slip into a comfy chair and look among the others. "You don't really know me. I'd understand if you—"

"You pretty much know all our secrets." Noah sits across from me, and Zayne laughs.

"Maybe not all of 'em," he says with a smirk. "But it's just a matter of time."

Ajia leans forward from his own seat and looks at me seriously. "We've been doing this for a little while. Did stupid shit and put up with the fallout, but this crap with Bree and the orgy rumors…" His voice dies and he shakes his head. He's the only blond in the group, and he stands out. Or is it the emotion I hear in his voice when he mentions Knox's sister? "We're still learning, and this shit came fast and hard."

I nod. "A bloody shitstorm."

Ajia smiles, and I see firsthand why female fans love him so much. His smile is like a little bit of magic. It hits me then: he's the light to Knox's darkness. But does it have to be that way? Can't Knox find his own lightness?

"Now we know we have to be ready for anything," he continues. "That means you have to know what to watch for. So, you just earned an open-ended pass to pretty much everything in our lives."

I try to smile, but I don't think it's very good. I swallow and take a breath. *Bollocks!* That's a bloody huge lot of responsibility.

"I hope you know I'll do my best for you, but…well, you haven't known me for long. Are you sure you trust me?"

"Knox does." Rye's voice is emphatic, and he pins me with his dark gaze.

"Do you think so?" There's a thin anxiousness to the question that I hate.

"He hired you," says Ajia flatly. "He pulled you into this stuff with Bree. He wouldn't hire you if he didn't trust you."

There might be more to it than that, like the sex that nobody knows about, but I sure as hell am not about to say anything more!

"Okay." Truthfully, I'm not quite sure *what* to say. "Uh…thanks." I take a breath so I can be sure my smile is genuine this time. "And just so you know, you guys have all been great."

Noah smiles and wiggles his eyebrows, but it's Zayne who asks, "So, anybody got any idea what that was about?"

There's a general consensus of shaking heads.

"No clue," admits Ajia.

"He didn't like it, that's for sure," says Noah.

"And he didn't expect it," Ajia adds as he lifts a questioning shoulder. "Whoever it was didn't have his number. They called the *label.*"

"He doesn't like surprises," says Rye, and it sounds almost like a warning. I'll remember that.

"You don't have any idea who it might have been?" Instinct tells me it's important to know.

Rye shakes his head, but then Noah scowls. "Fuck."

"What?"

"I hope to God it wasn't *Farren.*"

The men share almost comical looks of horror and disgust. They look like little boys being asked to eat broccoli or liver or something, and that puts me immediately on edge. "Who's Farren?"

They hesitate. Every bloody one of them. Like they're keeping a State secret or something.

"Hey, I get it if you don't want to gossip." I'm not exactly sure that's true, at least about this, but I'll give them the benefit of the doubt. "But this is just us. And if it's something I need to be prepared for, like you said, it'll be easier if I have the facts."

Ajia sighs heavily. *"Damn.* Well, Farren's his old girlfriend. From high school. They were still together when we first put Wycked Obsession together."

His old girlfriend.

Why did the idea of an *old girlfriend* never occur to me? Of course he must have loved someone in his life. Someone other than his sister and, presumably, his mother. It explains why he doesn't stick with a girl longer than a couple of nights—or even a couple of months, like his proposal to me. An old girlfriend whose phone call would upset him.

That means something bad happened between them.

My breathing is a little erratic and there's a surprisingly empty place in my stomach, but I push through it.

"How did it end?" I ask carefully.

"How do you think?" asks Noah without hesitating. "Shitty. Ugly as you can get. He caught her fucking some other dude and cut her off. She tried to get him back a couple of times, begged and cried, even claimed she was pregnant with his kid, but he never caved."

"Holy Christ," I mutter, imagining a variety of scenes and instinctively knowing how Knox would have hated them all.

"Yeah," agrees Rye. "She finally got so pissed off, she blew it and admitted she was lying. Said a bunch of nasty shit, and that was pretty much the end of things. He was done the instant he saw some other dude's dick in her pussy, but it took a while for her to get the message."

"How long ago was that?" I don't want to ask, but I have to know.

Ajia shakes his head. "Uh...maybe a couple of years? Definitely before things started to hit for us."

"So you think maybe she's interested again, now that you blokes are famous?"

"Sounds just like her," snaps Noah. He's pissed; everything about his tone and his expression says so. I blink, realizing I've never seen him quite like that. Even when he was mad at Knox.

This is deeper. Angrier. So maybe these guys have a soft spot for Knox after all.

"So what do we do now?" I ask softly. Instinct tells me to go to him, to comfort him, get him out of his head and—

"Leave him alone." Rye's tone is emphatic.

I blink. "Are you sure? I mean, maybe we could...I don't know. Help him. Take his mind off things. Give him an outlet for..."

My voice fades away as I notice four pairs of eyes staring at me with equally amused expressions.

"Hey, go for it, honey." Noah grins.

"Go for what?" They don't know anything. *Do they?*

"You and Knox. Bet you can get to him like none of us can."

I swallow and shake my head, but the sound of my words comes back to haunt me. *Maybe we could help him. Take his mind off things. Give him an outlet.*

Did I give something away? The words don't seem like it, but maybe my tone was too anxious or needy. I know these guys and how they think. Like maybe I'm offering to fuck him into forgetfulness?

Am I?

"Guys, I..." What can I say?

"Hey, don't worry about us." Noah stands, towering over me, and smiles a naughty grin. "You know what they say about Knox. If you're into it, he is, too. He could use a distraction."

Rye's smile is crooked. "Hey, maybe it's a fix none of us have figured out before."

"Like any one of us is gonna fuck him," snorts Ajia.

Zayne laughs as he stands. "Like anybody can ever figure Knox out."

Ajia and Rye rise with matching smiles, and the four of them start to walk away. They're a few feet behind me when Rye turns and calls back in a soft, sing-song kind of voice. "Give him an hour or so. Then go *take his mind off things.*"

Go take his mind off things.

Is that what I really want to do? Why I'm standing outside his room, wearing the same dress as earlier, still sans underwear, and trying to decide whether I should knock?

It's been more than an hour, more like two, and my stomach is crawling with nerves. Is it because I'm not sure which Knox will answer the door? The cocky rock god, the pissed-off alpha male who doesn't give a shit what anybody else thinks...or the man who got a phone call from hell, from the sound of it?

Which one do I want it to be?

Pull yourself together, luv, reminds that practical voice that I've come to depend on. *You know bloody well you don't want to face him feeling this indecisive!*

Can't *face him feeling this indecisive!*

My smarter self is right. If I'm going to do this—whatever *this* ends up being—then I need to do it from strength. Knox deserves the very best I can give him...and so do I.

If he needs my help, I'll be there for him. I remember what he said...was it just last night? *I don't talk about my shit. I just take care of it. So why did I tell you anything? And why do I feel better now?*

I knock on the door before I can back out.

I hear movement, but it takes a minute before Knox opens the door and stands before me. He looks...blank. Like nothing at all. Like a mask has come down over his face, a suit of armor all around him. He stares at me and doesn't say a word.

"Can I come in?" I sound more tentative than I want, and so I clear my throat. "Seems like you might need a friend right now."

"A friend?"

I angle my head in his direction. "All right. Maybe more."

"What about the rules?"

"Who said this breaks them? I'm just here to..." I pause. I can't say *comfort him.* He'll bloody hate that. I finally settle on a different choice. "Support you."

He doesn't say anything. He doesn't even stare anymore. He just steps back, and I follow him into the room. It looks a lot like mine, both of them with king-sized-beds and typical hotel décor.

"Do you want to tell me what happened?" I know I shouldn't ask, but it comes out, anyway.

"No."

"Do you want to talk at all?"

"No."

He's standing behind me at the end of the little hallway leading from the door and past the bathroom. His hair is mussed, like he's been shoving his fingers through it, and his eyes are almost a dark gray. I smell that vague scent of spicy chocolate and something entirely Knox, and my body responds with what's become a predictable awareness of everything about him. It ramps up a degree when I realize that, despite wearing the same jeans and T-shirt, he's barefoot. Something about it turns me on, even though he looks cold and distant.

And terribly vulnerable.

Jesus, I never expected Knox to appear so...exposed.

"Uh...how about...I'll give you a massage!" It comes out too high-pitched and chirpy. It was the excuse I'd come up with before I ever came to his room, but it sounded a lot more innocent in the silence of my own head.

"A massage?" His eyes narrow, his gaze sharpens. I don't need to hear his thoughts to guess what's going through his head.

"Sure." I nod with a confidence I don't feel. In for a penny, in for a pound now. "I can see the tension in you from across the room. I can help with that."

"You can help me with my...tension."

I reach for a wicked smile that might be a little bit of bravado—okay, a lot of bravado—but I rely on some old advice from my mother, of all people. *Fake it till you make it.*

"Get your mind out of the gutter. I..." Realizing that anything I say is going to come out as a double entendre, I try to give my smile a little boost. "I'm just going to rub your back and your shoulders."

Somehow, the mood seems to lighten maybe a fraction, and I almost believe Knox's half-smile. "All right, English. You're in charge." He throws his arms wide.

"Do you have any lotion?"

"Lotion?" His expression looks like I might have asked if he wears women's underwear on stage.

"Never mind." I can't help but grin. "I'll look in the bathroom. The hotel put some in mine."

I have to brush past Knox to get to the bathroom. He doesn't say a word, just smirks a knowing grin as I grab a couple of towels and the tiny travel-size bottle of lotion I expected to find.

"Here." I stride casually over to the bed like I've done this a thousand times and spread a bath towel over the comforter. "Take off your shirt and lie down on your stomach." I straighten and look at him. Is that a dare I feel flaring at the corners of my smile?

He's still silent, just staring and hiding a world of emotion behind his distant gaze. He blinks, his eyebrows raise, and then he reaches behind him to pull his T-shirt over his head. He tosses it aside without looking and stalks across the room to stand next to me.

"You sure you want to do this, English?"

"What?" I struggle to sound innocent. "It's just a massage."

"Right."

He crawls onto the bed and stretches out on his stomach, legs slightly spread and his arms on either side of him. Like he's been in this position before.

Don't be daft! Of course he's been in this position before! He's probably been in every bloody position in and out of the Kama Sutra.

I hear the naughty laughter inside my head. *I thought this was supposed to be* just a massage.

It is! It is, but...*fuck!* I don't use the word very often, but nothing else will do. He looks so goddamn hot! His shoulders are broad, his arms well-muscled. His waist is tapered, and his ass is round, perfectly shaped.

And he has a huge tattoo that covers his upper back.

I'm drawn forward despite knowing better and drop light fingertips over one shoulder blade. "You have a tattoo," I murmur dumbly.

He doesn't raise his head, but he turns to look in my direction. His hair shifts and falls on each side of his neck. He has a small tattoo there, too, the shape of Texas in red, white, and blue, with a star in the middle of the blue part.

"Couple of 'em."

"This big one...it's amazing!"

He lets out a long breath. "Archangel Michael. You know, the kick-ass one."

"I know."

Wings spread from shoulder blade to shoulder blade, with a muscled, broad-shouldered, and long-haired angel positioned over the middle of his back. Michael the Archangel wields a sword pointed downward, to where a snake curls dead at his feet. The only color is Michael's armor, which is blue, and the tip of his sword dripping red blood.

I trace the fine detail of angel's wings on the shoulder closest to me. It looks so realistic, a part of me almost sees it as a photo. "I..." I take a breath and rethink my words. "I guess I never pictured you as an angel kind of guy."

He lifts a shoulder, and the wing shifts with him. "Ajia got the first one. St. Cecelia, the patron saint of musicians or some shit. I liked it."

"So you got Michael the Protector."

A second too late, I wish I hadn't phrased it that way. I press my lips together in a tight frown, like that will make a difference. Bollocks! I mean, it makes total sense; how else would a control freak of Knox Gallagher's caliber see himself? But that doesn't mean he's not sensitive about hearing it.

"I told you," he says mildly, and I let out a soft sigh of relief. "He's kick ass."

"And that's a guy's main requirement? Kick ass?"

Knox lifts his head just a fraction. "Don't know about that. I just liked it."

I nod and find myself staring at him, at the sideways glance he spreads in my direction and the way his lips are parted slightly.

"So you giving me this massage or you just trying to get me on the bed for...whatever?" He smirks.

"Uh...right. Sorry." I shake my head and pray I'm not blushing, figuring all the while I'm a lost cause. The heat warms my cheeks, and I hate it.

I crawl onto the bed next to him, moving so slowly and carefully, you'd think the bed was made of the finest crystal shot through with fiery nails. I'm aware of it, but I'm also smart enough to know I can't do anything about it. I'm in so far over my head with a man like Knox Gallagher, I'll rely on every little caution I can force myself to take.

Finally, I'm close enough to sit back on my heels for balance and squeeze a blob of lotion in my hands. I rub my palms together to warm the lotion, then lean forward to brush them over Knox's shoulder and shoulder blades.

His skin is warm—Christ, it's *hot*—and his muscles are tense and hard. Not the kind of hard that speaks of double entendres and cute, blushing giggles. Hard like he's holding in all the stress and anger and frustration and every other emotion from the last few days, and it's settled throughout his body.

I straighten a bit and lean forward, rubbing my hands over the delicious warmth of his skin and leaning in to put a little more pressure where he needs it.

"How's that?"

"Okay." He doesn't move or say anything more.

"Just okay?" I keep rubbing.

He nods once. "You need to do it harder."

"Harder."

"Yeah. If this is supposed to...what did you say? Release my *tension?*"

"Uh, okay. Yeah. Sure."

I try to balance myself well enough to put my weight and strength into what I'm doing, but I'm in an awkward position. Off-center and really only reaching one side of him.

Well, shit.

You know what you have to do. You're *the one who offered the massage.*

I do. And I was.

I swallow. "Uh...I'm just going to reposition myself. Get a better reach."

"Okay."

I pull in a deep breath and climb over Knox's hips. I settle myself at the small of his back, my knees automatically tightening against his sides, and I start to lean forward.

"English?"

I settle back, straddling him anxiously. "Yes?"

"Tell me, baby." His voice sounds unnaturally raw. "After the meeting today. Did you go back to your room and put panties on?"

CHAPTER 14

KNOX

FUCK!
   Goddammit to hell.
   You lucky son of a bitch.
   It all shouts in my mind at the same time.
   London doesn't need to answer the question. Fuck no. I can feel her pussy, all soft and wet and teasing, perched against my back.
   Fucking hell.
   The silence between us is charged until finally she answers.
   "Uh...no."
   "Why not?"
   She waits long enough I'm almost sure she's not going to answer. "I didn't have permission."
   Fuck my life. My cock's been hard from the second she said the word *massage*. Now I could pound nails with it.
   Rule number one. We both get tested, just like you wanted. No fucking until that's done.
   Why the hell had I said that? Made it a *rule*? Backing down from that shit...I don't do it. But she's sitting on my back, pantyless and braless under that too tight dress, and I want her like no woman I've ever been with.
   No one...ever.
   She moves a little, and I feel every minor twitch.
   "You didn't have permission?"
   Not sure how I'm able to ask the question. My voice is all hoarse and softer than it should be, but...goddamn. Yeah, I've

developed a reputation for some kinky shit, but it's not really true. Not entirely. Oh, I'll spank a chick if that's what she needs, and I might use some restraint from time to time, but I'm not a true Dom looking for a sub to hook up with. I'm just...*dominant.* I like to be in control, and it turns me the fuck on when a chick follows my instructions.

"You said it was important." Her voice sounds all wavery. "Everything else depended on this. So..." Her voice dies away, and then I feel a soft fluttering of her lips against the back of my neck. "I followed the rules."

My dick grabs every bit of the blood flow in my body, and I'm fucking glad. For once in my life, I only want to *feel.*

I don't hesitate. Not sure how I do it, but suddenly London is on her back, and I'm straddling her thighs. Those expressive golden eyes are wide, dilated, and her breath is caught in her throat. She doesn't move, only stares at me.

"You were a good girl?"

"Your good girl."

She said that before. *My* good girl. Like being even a little submissive isn't something she usually does.

My dick gets harder.

"You want more rules, baby?"

Her eyes darken, and a little breath sneaks out. "Yes."

I climb off the bed and stand next to her. "Get up.

She does, and I'm struck again how small she is next to me. Her shoes are off, like mine, and the top of her head only reaches my shoulder. The difference explodes something in me. I want to protect her—and dominate her.

"Undo my jeans."

Her chest heaves, but she takes a breath and licks her lips as she reaches for my waistband. I want to catch her mouth with mine, seal our lips, and suck her tongue deep into my mouth, but I want to watch the magic of her fingers more. Her fingers tremble as she struggles with the metal fastening, but then she gets it open and releases the zipper. My cock surges forward.

"You're not wearing underwear, either." Her eyes raise to mine.

My grin is wicked. "It's only fair."

"Sweet baby Jesus." It's no more than a whisper, and then she reaches for me, stroking her fingers lightly from the tip to as far as she can reach. "Ten inches, Knox." She swallows. "What the fuck do I do with that?"

My hips flex. "You handled it pretty fucking good the other night."

"I think I was in shock."

"And now?"

Her hands rest on my hips like she wants to push my jeans down, but she doesn't. Those incredible eyes seem trapped by mine.

"Now I want you in my mouth."

Precum dots the tip of my cock, and my hips flex on their own. Jesus, I'd give up everything to be in her mouth right now.

"Take off your dress."

I miss her touch the instant she drops her hands. She fumbles with some kind of fastening at her side, and part of her dress flops open. There must be another button or something, because she reaches inside, and then the whole thing falls to her sides.

Jesus. Those full, gorgeous tits. Amazingly small waist. Hips that beg for my hands. I curl my fingers into my palms.

"All the way off, beautiful."

Her movements are slow. Does she know how fucking hot that is? She shrugs her shoulders until the skinny little straps fall down her arms, and then the dress is gone. It falls to the floor in a puddle, and she stands before me like I've been dying to see her.

"You?" Her voice is hoarse.

"You want these gone?" I point to my jeans.

"Yeah. Uh...yes, sir?"

I grin. I can't help it. "You been reading some sexy shit, English? Or watching porn?"

Her cheeks flush, but she doesn't answer.

"I don't need that *sir* shit. My kink doesn't go there." I open my arms wide. "But if you want me naked, you're gonna have to take care of it yourself."

She doesn't wait. Her small palms are on my hips, and she pushes, sinking to her knees as she drags my jeans down with her. I lift one foot and then the other, and she shoves the pants away before I can.

She drags her hands up my thighs, and then she's there, cupping my balls. She massages gently with one hand, while the other goes to my cock and strokes lightly. Fucking tease.

My groan seems to please her. She leans forward with a smile, peeks up at me, and slides her tongue out to lick just below the head. God*damn,* but she knows *the spot.*

My cock twitches, and she smiles. She licks up and down the shaft, all around it, like it's some kind of ice cream treat. I don't even try to pretend that I don't love it, but I want more.

"Suck it, baby. Deep."

She licks up to the tip, swirls her tongue around, and then does it. She takes me in slow and steady, and I feel myself at the back of her throat. She holds me there for a few seconds until I feel her muscles relax enough that she can take me even deeper.

She stops, one hand still cupping my balls and the other tight around my shaft, until her gag reflex takes over and she pulls back. Her head bobs up and down, her hand stroking in rhythm, and she takes me deep every few beats.

I hold myself steady as long as I can, but it's a losing battle and I fucking know it. I shove my hands through her hair, hold her face between my palms, and mutter, "Jesus, baby. Let me do it."

Her movements stop, and her eyes lift to mine. Even as fucking turned on as I am, I can see desire and something more, something deeper—Christ, is it trust?—in the flickering gold. I can't begin to stop moving, and I'm thrusting like I've wanted to since the first touch of her tongue.

Her hands go to my thighs, clench at my muscles to hold her steady. Tears leak from her eyes as I go deep and she gags more often than not, but she does nothing to stop me. I feel like a dick, know I shouldn't push it when I'm losing control, but it's all getting away from me. I've usually got wicked stamina, but not this time.

"Goddamn, baby, I'm gonna come."

The voice doesn't sound like me, and that breaks my trance a little. I need to find my control again, try to pull back, but London tightens her grip on my thighs.

I massage my fingers over her scalp. "Running out of time here, baby," I grunt. "Pull back unless you want me to come down your throat."

She sucks harder, pushes against my thrusting, and in seconds it's too late. I shoot a load of cum down her throat and roar her name.

"English! Goddammit, baby!"

My heart's pounding, chest heaving, and it's all I can do to stay on my feet. She holds me in her mouth, her palms against my ass cheeks, and gradually I begin to soften. My hands flex against her head, fingers tangled in her hair, and a low groan comes all on its own.

Hell. Things were *not* supposed to go that way.

I pull away, scoop her up in my arms, and follow her down onto the bed. I catch her mouth with mine, push my tongue into her mouth, and kiss her like a man starving. Or who just had the best blowjob of his life.

I taste myself on her tongue, and my hips press her to the bed. I drag her arms up over her head as I kiss her again. "Time to return the favor, baby."

She kisses me back but starts squirming when I drag my mouth over her jaw, her throat.

"No! Uh, Knox." She wiggles her hips. "No. Please."

I pull back with a frown. "What is it, English? What's wrong?"

She smiles almost shyly, touching her tongue to her top lip. "No on returning the favor. That was all for you."

"And it was amazing." I offer her a satisfied grin. "But I want to do this. I barely got a taste of your pussy the other night."

I force myself to smile through the memory of my little freak out that first night. Yeah, it worked out okay in that case, but what about the rest of it? Is that what my life has come to with this fame shit? Everything out of control from day to fucking day?

Nothing has been *in* my control for months now.

London smiles back, happier, more relaxed, and I feel myself respond.

"You'll get your chance, luv. Plenty of 'em over the next couple of months, I think. But this..." She shakes her head and spares me an oddly deliberate look. "This was for you. All you. You know. Friend to friend."

"Friend?" I send one eyebrow high.

This time she grins. *"You know."*

She takes advantage of my distraction and wriggles from my grip. Pushes me back on the bed. Settles in next to me, her softness pressed against my side.

"Still didn't expect it, English."

"No?" She turns her head to smile up at me. "What did you expect?"

I drag an idle finger up and down her arm. "Expect?" I shake my head. "Don't think I expect much of anything anymore."

Her eyes narrow, and she shakes her head. "No. That isn't true."

I stare at her, at the certainty in those whiskey-gold eyes that are warmed by encouragement and not a bit of judgment. This girl...

I lift a shoulder. "Yeah, I suppose you're right. My expectation is to expect the unexpected."

She watches me, her gaze flickering over me like a damn microscope. "Is that bullshit?"

"No." I shake my head. "This tour was supposed to be easy. We'd been through it, knew the ropes, made a plan. Had some extra time built in for shit like this when we're in L.A. A lot of pride in the new album, and we were hot to get the songs before a live audience. We weren't even out of Austin before it all started to go to shit."

The same list of names cycles through my brain. Gabe. Bree. Ajia. Zayne. London herself.

And now, the sperm donor.

Fuck.

London reaches for me, pushes hair back from my forehead, and smiles sadly. "You don't have to go through it all alone, you know, luv. You can share the burdens with others."

I shake my head. Not these burdens. The only people I have to share them with are the people I have to protect. Nothing'll change that.

"Nobody to tell." I settle on that.

"What about me?"

"What about you?"

"Is there anything you can tell me? Share with me?" She shrugs. "You might not be able to tell, but I've got some pretty broad shoulders."

I smile a little, push hair back from her face. "I'm sure you do, baby. You're probably even really scary when you wanna be. But..."

"But what? Nobody can do it all alone forever, luv."

Do it all alone forever? Maybe not, but I've been doing *it* alone for a long goddamn time. Don't think I know how to share this shit anymore. Never had anybody even offer before.

She smiles sadly when I don't say anything, just tucks herself closer to my side and kisses my chest. "It's okay. Just know that I'm here for you."

We lay that way for a while. A few minutes, half an hour? I have no clue. She seems contented enough, kissing my chest from time to time, and wrapping her arm securely around my waist. I haven't felt this close to a woman—to anyone—in a long time.

It feels good, and I know I shouldn't let it.

"It was the old man."

"What?" She looks up at me.

"On the phone. The sperm donor."

She doesn't blink, but her expression turns to an odd combination of both relief and horror. "Sperm donor. I take it you and your father aren't close."

My laugh is disgusted, even ugly, but I do nothing to stop it. "Nope. Haven't seen or talked to him in about...oh, eleven or twelve years." I swallow. "Until today."

London doesn't say anything until, finally, "What happened?"

I shrug. "He disappeared. Went to El Paso and never came back. Never heard from him again."

"How old were you?"

"Twelve. Bree was eight."

She flinches, almost like she can feel what it was like. The fear. The not knowing. The pain on our mom's face. And maybe she can. She has a fucked-up family life, too.

"What did he want?" London asks quietly.

"Money." I cup her head for a second, hold her against my chest, and then stroke my hand down her arm and back up. Rather do that than remember the ugly words from the sperm donor.

"Money." Her nose wrinkles as she repeats the word. It's kind of cute, but I don't have time to appreciate it when she tilts back her head. "Are you going to give it to him?"

My head snaps back like it's on a spring. "No! Fuck no!"

She nods, like she expected me to say that. "Will he accept that?"

I've been keeping my hand moving up and down her arm, but I can't do it anymore. Anxiousness scraps over my nerves, something in me wants to smash shit.

"No. I...no." Tension seeps back into my muscles, my very bones. "Said he'd tell everybody that he caught me messing with Bree as a kid."

"Knox!" London pops up onto her knees in an instant, her hands on my face, and a look of horror darkening her eyes. "What kind of father would do such a thing?"

I shake my head. "Not a father, remember? *Sperm donor.*"

She sits back on her heels, giving me a great view of her tits, her waist, her lush hips. I want to grab her, pin her beneath me, but I know her well enough already to guess she probably won't let this go that easily.

"What are you going to do?" she asks with a frown, proving my instincts.

"Not give him any freaking money, that's for sure."

"Good." She smiles with something that looks almost like pride, but it's followed by a little sigh.

"What?"

She shakes her head. "I thought my family was fucked up. My father has his issues, but he would never try to extort money from his *children.*"

"Welcome to life in the Gallagher family." I don't even try to smile. "A stepfather who hits on his stepdaughter, and a sperm donor who's only after the money. Who the fuck knows what I'll turn out to be like?"

"Knox..."

I shake my head. "I've done everything I can to protect Bree and keep her from knowing the shit that's gone on. This gossip about a band orgy…" My jaw clenches, despite trying to remain calm. "It shook me."

"Of course it would." Amazingly, London leans forward and drops a quick kiss on my mouth. "But I'm here now, luv. I know you like to take care of stuff yourself—" she shakes her head when I open my mouth to say something "—but it's *my job* to help you. So let me!"

I let myself relax against the headboard. This woman. She's nothing like anybody I've ever known. Pisses me off one second, soothes me the next.

"Don't know what you can do, English. You said it yourself, speaking out is what the paparazzi wants us to do."

She nods. "Yeah, well, I've been thinking about that. Knowing this—" she waves her hand "—about the…*sperm donor,* I think we should take charge."

"Doing what?"

"I want to take your biographies, the ones you blokes gave to the label, and expand them a little. Put them on your website. Make them more personal. Maybe add a couple of pictures from when you were kids."

"What's that supposed to do?"

"We take the first step. Strike before anybody else can. We'll start with you, open up about growing up with a single mom who worked *hard* after your dad disappeared one day."

I'm shaking my head before she finishes. "You know how I feel about that shit, English. I don't wanna use my family for—"

"I know," she interrupts, her expression and her voice so sincere, I have to listen. "And we don't have to go into much detail. But we can still show a father who leaves his family—who *disappears!*—isn't a good guy."

The subject fucking exhausts me. "You really think that'll help?"

"I don't know. But he doesn't get to make all the rules."

"Rules." The word shoots a different energy through me, my dick perks up, and slow smile comes eases across my face.

"Rules," I say again. "Goddamn rules."

She nods like she's encouraging me.

"Okay, English. Don't mean to change the subject here, but you know what we talked about? *The rules?"*

"Yes?"

"Well, dammit, English, I really wanna fuck you!"

CHAPTER 15

LONDON

THE DOCTOR'S OFFICE IS CROWDED, which doesn't really surprise me. Dr. Jackson is working me in as a favor to my father—not that I asked for any special treatment. I never do, but the doctor's office must have a note on my account. Something like: *Hugh Kennedy's daughter! Handle with care!* I hate that, but Dr. Jackson is my mother's gynecologist, too, so I guess I shouldn't be surprised.

It took me four days to get this pseudo-appointment. Four days since Knox and I have slept together. After his somewhat aborted massage and the sex that followed, he refused to do it again.

Him and his bloody rules.

I can't help smiling as I think back to the things he did to my body after he said what he did. *Dammit, English, I really wanna fuck you!* How do you say no to a plea like that?

I didn't. Couldn't. *And thank God for that,* I think now. The man's got a strength of will that's hard to believe, and he was a little bitter that I *made him* break his own rules. His words, not mine, and my smile grows.

Like anybody can make Knox Gallagher do anything he doesn't want to do, or convince him *not* to do what he wants to.

But good Lord, the things he *can* do. With his mouth, his tongue...his cock. My nipples tighten and I feel a familiar twinge in my core. Dammit, but he's going to bloody well pay for making me wait like this!

And how the hell does he manage to always get the upper hand?

"Ms. Kennedy?"

The nurse calls my name, and I take a breath. It's just as well. I need to stop thinking about that cocky rock god before my blood pressure goes through the roof.

I follow Gloria, Dr. Jackson's nurse, into the back. We go through the usual pre-exam stuff: weight, blood pressure, questions about my last period, and my reasons for the visit. I'm soon alone in the exam room again, waiting for the doctor, and glad a pelvic isn't scheduled this time.

I hate those things.

I'm flipping through a year-old *People* magazine when Dr. Jackson arrives. She's a tiny woman with one of those faces where you can't tell if she's 50 or 70 years old. Her graying hair is pulled back in an old-fashioned French roll, and her jewelry—costume necklaces and bracelets—must weigh as much as she does.

"London." She smiles in her typical no-nonsense way and flips open my chart. A paper chart, not an electronic device like the nurse used. It doesn't surprise me that Dr. Jackson is fighting the transition to digital records. She's unique, headstrong, and unconventional.

I'd have her as my doctor even if my mom didn't. Maybe even especially then.

"Hello, Dr. Jackson."

"I wondered when I'd see you again."

"You'll never get rid of me." I smile, thinking about the truth behind that statement.

"I meant because you're late."

"Excuse me?" I blink uncertainly. "I'm about a week early for my quarterly appointment, I think, but I'm leaving tomorrow for the rest of the summer."

She takes a seat and glares at me. I'm used to her fierce expressions; she's that way about most things in life, I think. This time, I'm sitting on the exam table, she's in a chair that puts her at least a foot shorter than me, and I'm intimidated as hell.

"Dr. Jackson?"

"If you're talking about your birth control shot, my girl, you're *late.*"

"I'm sorry?" My brows draw down, and my eyes have narrowed. I know it, feel it, but my thoughts are stuck on the last thing she said.

If you're talking about your birth control shot, my girl, you're late.

"I'm late?"

"Almost five weeks," she says with a firm nod and glances back at my chart. "Yes." She nods. "You were due here almost five weeks ago for your shot."

"Five weeks!"

She nods again, more decisively this time, and gives me a look that is equal parts chastising and irritated. "This is only your third shot, London. If you want this to be an effective method of birth control, you have to get your shots *regularly.* We talked about this! You can't be five weeks late like this and expect it to be one-hundred-percent effective."

"But...I can't be five weeks late." My voice too soft, but I can't manage anything more.

How the bloody hell could I be so wrong on the date?

"London?" Dr. Jackson snaps. "What's wrong with you?"

"I...I'm trying to understand. I got my last shot a couple of weeks after I got back from spring break, when I went to England. That should put me right on time."

She frowns and glances at my file again. "According to your chart, you were leaving in a few days. I made detailed notes of our discussion, because it was only your second shot." She jabs a finger at the paper and reads, "'Patient reports no problems with first shot. Requests second dose early, because she leaves for spring break in ten days.' Does that sound right?"

I stare at her in horror and try to ignore the sudden heavy pounding of my heart. "I got it early?" The words sound ragged. "But...no. I'm sure I came in when I got home."

Dr. Jackson doesn't exactly look impatient, but she doesn't look happy, either. She taps her finger on the file. "Not according to my records."

"Five weeks."

I can't stop saying it. I know what it means. I read the literature. In the first year, the shot can lose its effectiveness quickly if you don't stick with the schedule. I'm responsible. Dependable. Trustworthy. Staying on a simple routine of doctor's appointments was going to be so easy.

So why wasn't it?

How did I get it confused?

And why am I so freaked out? But I know.

It'll be okay, I told Knox that first night. And then I asked, *Does it help if I tell you I'm on birth control?*

A voice of reason speaks up to calm my racing nerves. *Don't get carried away. Even if you're late getting the shot, it doesn't mean you're automatically pregnant. I mean, it was only a couple of times.*

Oh, no? demands a hysterical reply. *What are the chances that my girls would tell Knox's swimmers* no?

"I see you requested a full range of STD testing." Dr. Jackson interrupts my rollercoastering thoughts, and I reach for composure with a couple of slow, deep breaths. "Can I take that to mean you've had unprotected sex?"

"Uhm...yes."

"Recently?"

"Yes."

"How long ago?"

"The first time? Uhm..." I count back, but it's all a blur. "Eight or nine days ago."

"Eight or nine days." She nods, staring, and finally takes a deep breath before she stands. "All right. Well, we might get something. We'll do a blood test, and, since you're leaving tomorrow, I'll call in some favors to get the response immediately. We'll do the same with your STD results."

"The same? You mean...there's something more?" I know the answer, but I'm determined to pretend it isn't possible.

"A *pregnancy* test."

It'll be okay. Does it help if I tell you I'm on birth control?

I reassured him. Knox trusted me, and I made him feel better about skipping the condom. Me, too. At the time. But now I'm sitting here with Dr. Jackson's words rattling through my head.

You can't be five weeks late like this and expect it to be one-hundred-percent effective.

I know, I know, I know. I did my research. Paid attention. Made an informed decision. And now…

Holy fucking Christ!

"I'll call the lab," Dr. Jackson says as she walks to the door. "I'll have Gloria escort you."

"When will I have the results?"

"A couple of hours."

"That soon?"

She turns back to me, and for the first time, I see a flicker of sympathy in her expression. "I told you. I'll call in a few favors." She almost smiles. "Good thing we're in L.A. and I have connections, because they're big favors." She angles her head in my direction. "I think you need them."

I sit in the waiting room of Dr. Jackson's office, anxious and totally unable to calm my racing thoughts. It's been—I look at my phone—over two hours since I returned from the lab, and I've been lingering here in a constant state of anxiety. Dr. Jackson recommended I go do something—shopping, she suggested, or maybe get something to drink—but I can't leave.

Not before I know the truth.

I've never been this close to a pregnancy scare before. I'm always meticulous about these things, just like Knox claims he is. Something about the two of us together sent us off on totally uncharted territory. Neither of us could think about anything but the other, apparently, and now I can't think at all. I can't function, can only pretend to look at my phone and scroll through the pages, switch apps, and pretty much stare blankly at the changing screen.

What if I'm pregnant?

I can't be pregnant!

It was only a couple of times.

Five weeks late.

You can't be...late...and expect it to be one hundred percent effective.

And then, when those thoughts lose steam, there are others eager to take their place. Ones that make me feel even worse.

The band, talking about Knox's old girlfriend. *Claimed she was pregnant with his kid,* they said, *but he never caved.* And how did it resolve? *Admitted she was lying. Said a bunch of nasty shit.*

Yeah, that ought to make him trust me. Give him an interest in the possibility of fatherhood.

And what was it that he said? *Welcome to life in the Gallagher family. A stepfather who hits on his stepdaughter, and a sperm donor who's only after the money. Who the fuck knows what I'll turn out to be like?*

I know damn well he doesn't plan to find out. At least not now, and not with me.

My stomach clenches and my breathing stumbles. I try to talk myself calm again.

Just stop! You don't even know if you're pregnant. The possibilities have *to be slim, right? It was only a couple of times. And what are the chances you were ovulating when you slept with him?*

Yes, ovulating. The internet is a wealth of information. Some good and some bad, as I've learned very well. It's the one thing I could concentrate on while I've been sitting here, and I did a little digging. I now know that, even this early, a Quantitative hCG blood test can tell if I'm pregnant. Some hormone will tell the tale right away.

Thank, God, because *I need to know!*

Dear God, how did things come to this? And what a stupid question, because I was right there for all of it! Things didn't happen *to me;* I was a willing participant in every bit of it!

I take another deep breath and shift in my seat as I look around the room. It's remained pretty full as other patients have come and gone. No one pays any attention to me, which means I must be handling my shit pretty well. Right?

At least on the outside.

Good thing they can't see the hurricane going on inside of me. Withstanding it is taking everything I have—and I can't get away from it.

What is wrong with me?

The questions start a new rotation, but I shut them down as much as I can. I open up the app I use for my notes. It isn't the first time I've done it this afternoon, but this time I try to concentrate with a new resolve and review all we've accomplished in the last few days. Ajia made his statement to the press, and while it didn't really answer any questions, the media is now focused on trying to figure out exactly what he was and wasn't saying. I've rewritten the band members' bios, and they're reviewing them now. I've put together their individual pages for the website, and we'll go live as soon as the new bios are ready. Next will be to freshen their Facebook pages, give them each some individual personality, and create Instagram accounts for Zayne and Rye.

There will be other things, other sites and new content, but I started where I thought the guys could do the most good. Become more personal. Make changes that would be quick and obvious. Start to interact with their fans in a way that seems almost intimate and doesn't involve any face-to-face contact.

Or fucking.

I frown.

Fucking. I close my eyes and swallow a ragged sigh. Fucking leads to pregnancy. Pregnancy leads to babies and…

Oh, God, I can't be pregnant!

I don't know how much more time has passed since the last time I checked out the waiting room's clock, and I refuse to look now. Maybe or twenty or thirty minutes. An hour? It doesn't matter. I'm *dying* for the results…and just as contented, anxious even, to sit here and wait. Numb in my uncertainty.

Just a little longer…

"Ms. Kennedy?"

Gloria calls my name, and I stand. My hands are shaking, alarmingly so, and for a minute I think I'm going to pass out.

Don't be so dramatic! I tell myself. *You don't know anything yet.*

I follow her back into a different exam room. Her face is…well, blank. Not happy, unhappy, encouraging, or horrified. Just purely professional, an expression I'm used to seeing from her.

It shouldn't piss me off now, but it does.

"Have a seat." She gestures toward the patient table. "Dr. Jackson will be right with you."

I nod and climb up, reminding myself to never play bloody goddamn poker with Gloria.

I wait another ten minutes or so, and then Dr. Jackson finally walks in. She can't play in my poker tournament, either, I decide almost immediately, and with supreme annoyance, because her expression is that same serious and yet ferocious look she always wears.

"Well?" I can't help myself.

She pulls a piece of paper out of my file and hands it over. "Clean. No STDs."

I clutch the single page, wrinkling it, but I don't care. I was certain before I ever stepped foot inside the waiting room this morning that I'd be clean. I knew it about myself; I hadn't slept with anyone except that wanker Colin in *months*. More than that, I'd never doubted Knox's claim that he was clean, too. He is a man too much in control for it to be otherwise.

His test results, received back yesterday, had proved it.

But we're just circling the thousand-pound elephant squatting in the middle of the room. We both know it, and I stare at the paper file in Dr. Jackson's hands. Neither of us move.

"And the rest of it?"

She doesn't open the manilla folder. She simply waits until I drag my gaze up to meet hers.

"Pregnant."

CHAPTER 16

KNOX

WE'RE BACK ON THE BUS, and I'm glad. Real glad. Not that I didn't like the privacy of the hotel, because I did. If we hadn't been there, I might not have had the space to get with London. But we were in L.A. for almost two weeks. Too damn long. Too many parties, meetings, and photo shoots.

Business shit. Label shit. Shit that was never on our radar when we were rock'n'roll wannabes.

Now I'm ready to get back to the reason we're on this tour to begin with. Playing in front of a live audience. We only played a few shows in the L.A. area while we did all that other crap, and it's time to hit it again.

Besides, I need to do something other than think about all the other shit that's going on right now. It's like hell opened its gates and threw a few nasty surprises my way just to say *fuck you.*

It better be done.

"Who's got the bedroom?" I ask as I step into the bus, my backpack slung over my shoulder. I'll do whatever it takes to get hold of it so London and I can spend the next few nights together. I don't give a shit if the others know we're fucking; never spent much time trying to keep secrets about my sex life. Not sure I like the idea of my baby sister knowing the details, but I lost control of that shit the second she got on the tour bus.

Fuck. Inside I'm frowning, but I keep it to myself. *Forget about it,* I tell myself. *About Bree and Ajia. Think about London.*

I want her like I haven't wanted another woman in a long, long time.

If ever.

We haven't fucked in four...make that five days. The waiting sucked, but I had to hold firm. She wanted rules, I gave them to her, and then she seduced me away from them. I couldn't let it happen again.

Rule number one. We both get tested, just like you wanted. No fucking until that's done.

It was a dumbass rule to make, but I still couldn't break it. Again.

Give yourself a break, says a sturdy voice of encouragement. *You were shook up. The sperm donor threw you off. Everything's good now. You got this shit. Again.*

I do, but it's still a good damn thing that her doctor's appointment was yesterday. I've had enough waiting.

Maybe she got the test results expedited like I did.

"It's Bree's turn in the bedroom." Noah smirks at me, finally answering my question. He's been staring at me, and I've been staring back.

Well...fuck. No way is my sister giving up her turn. She and Ajia'll hole up in there, fuck every chance they get. I know it, I hate it, and there's not a goddamn thing I can do about it.

Okay, no way I'm gonna get the kind of privacy I want for English and me. At least not right now. Hell, I'm not even sure I could get it if it was one of the others who had their turn. Nobody in the band is all that happy with me these days, and I don't figure that's gonna change anytime soon. Bree wants me to apologize to Ajia, but no way am I doing that. I'm not sorry for looking out for my sister's safety first.

Even if she doesn't see it the same way.

I grunt and head for my bunk, throw my backpack onto the mattress to unpack later. We don't have all that far to go on this first leg, only as far as Sacramento, but we're there only one night there and sleeping on the bus. Then on to the Bay Area and...shit. I can't remember the rest of our schedule. Haven't looked at it since we hit L.A., and right now, I don't really give a damn, anyway.

I can't get rid of all the shit on my mind—and not just about my cock, either.

The rumors about Bree and the band have scraped my nerves raw since the day they started. They're not completely over, but the worst gossip seems to have died down. They're too busy trying to figure out what Ajia's doublespeak statement meant. I twist my lips in a half-smile. They're also pouring over the new bios London wrote for us. Digging up old pictures from high school year books and senior prom dates.

What a bunch of shit, but…okay. Fine. If that changes the attention for a while, I'm glad for it. It gives me the space to concentrate on other things, like making sure Mom stays strong through filing for divorce from that prick Gabe.

And the sperm donor. Can't forget about that asshole.

He'll be back and demanding money. I have no freaking doubt. He's a piece of shit who never deserved the family he had—*could have had*—but always wanted something more. Something different.

Something he didn't deserve.

Like money he didn't earn. *My* money. The band's money.

Wycked Obsession's success didn't come from some magic bean or wishing on a fucking star. We worked our asses off for it, and the asshole isn't getting a goddamn dime.

I don't have a plan yet, like what I'll fucking do if he does the shit he says he will. Claiming that something *inappropriate* happened between Bree and me? Just thinking it makes me fucking sick. The only thing I *ever* wanted for my baby sister was to keep her safe.

Even, or especially, if that means from the sperm donor. And that means keeping this latest bullshit a secret. I don't want her to know that all we are to him is a chance for a paycheck.

My temper rises to a sharp edge, and my fingers curl up toward my palms. Part of me wishes the asshole were here, right in front of me, so I could beat the fuck out of him. The rest of me wishes he'd disappear back under the disgusting rock he crawled out from, never to be heard from again.

"London!"

Noah's welcoming shout interrupts my thoughts. She steps up into the bus. Her eyes are dark, the color of whiskey, her expression wary.

"Baz told me to report here."

Noah smirks at me. "That so?"

I shrug and offer a simple, "Yeah," and don't explain further. The others can think what they want. Truth is, I told Baz that London was with the band.

With me.

"Whatever." He smiles in London's direction. "Welcome aboard."

She smiles back, but it's a little uneasy. Like she isn't really sure of herself. It's cute and makes me want to smile myself, but I don't. If she thinks she has an idea of what it's like to tour with a rock band so far, she's in for a shock. A couple of days on the bus with us, and she'll be a pro.

Maybe disgusted, but still a pro.

"Where should I put this?" She nods toward her a small suitcase on rollers.

"C'mon, English." I hold out one hand. "I'll show you."

Her eyes widen, but she moves toward me. I wasn't bullshitting myself earlier; I got nothing to hide where she's concerned. We agreed. We're fucking through the rest of the tour, and I'm not pretending otherwise.

"My bunk's here." I point when she gets close enough to take my hand. "You can take this one." I gesture toward the one below mine.

"You're sure?" Her eyes dart around the bus. "I don't want to be an...inconvenience."

"Take it, honey." Noah waves a careless hand before I can answer. "Nobody was using it before, and if Knox wants you close..." He grins and lets the words fade as he throws himself on the sofa. He picks up one of the video game controllers and ignores us.

I shrug. Typical bus behavior.

"You can unpack if you want," I suggest. "Storage under the bunk." I lift mine to show her. "Bathroom's there—" I point behind her "—and there's a bedroom. We each get a turn. Guess you'll go at the end of the line. Bree's got it this week," I admit grudgingly.

London nods as she follows my gestures, but she still seems...remote. Distant. Not quite there.

What the hell?

I narrow my eyes and look at her. She's beautiful, her reddish-brown hair falling all around her shoulders. Her jeans are tight in all the right places, and she's got a sexy-looking white tank top under a loose gray-and-white plaid shirt. Makes me want to slip my hands under that shirt, that tank, feel her skin hot against my hands and…

Well, shit. My dick notices my thoughts, but now isn't the time. Maybe I *do* want to do a lot with that body, but she's not in the moment with me right now. Looks almost like she's gone inward. Away from here, the bus…me.

A lot like she acted last night, and I thought *that* was strange.

I figured it was because of the no sex rule. I got it and didn't push. Knew better. It's hell when a woman like London Kennedy wants to fuck you, and you gotta wait.

"You okay, baby?" I lean close and whisper in her ear.

She looks at me with a ragged smile. "Uh…yeah. Sure. Just…" She waves a hand around us. "Nervous, I guess."

I catch her earlobe between my teeth and bite. Not hard enough to hurt but definitely sharp enough to get her attention. "It'll be okay. You know these guys. It's just a little bit…closer quarters on the bus."

She nods and shoots me a look that's oddly relieved and distracted at the same time. Makes me wonder…

"You get your test results back yet, baby?"

She blinks. "Yes." Nods. Pulls up her phone. "I'll email them to you."

I shrug. "Whatever. All I need is your word."

She takes a deep breath. "I'm clean. I knew I would be."

"Me, too." I lift a shoulder. "But I've learned to be careful."

"Careful…" She repeats the word in a whisper, letting it echo between us. "Yes. Of course. Careful."

"What's wrong, baby?" I slide my hand into her hair, cup the back of her head. "You seem tense."

She swallows and glances up at me, but then her gaze drops away. "No. I'm—fine." Her smile is weak. "Just…adjusting to this." She flips her hand through the air around her.

"This?"

"Life on a tour bus." Finally, a crooked grin. "Part of Wycked Obsession's entourage."

"Entourage?" I shout a quick laugh. "Oh, baby, that doesn't even come close to describing what you are."

Really? And what am I?

I can see the question in her eyes, but I step back and look away. Not answering that right now. Not for her, and not for me.

♪

We settle in pretty easily after that. Bree cooks one of our favorites, chicken spaghetti, and London helps with the clean-up. Tomorrow night is the show in Sacramento, but the next free night on the bus, Ajia and I are tagged for clean-up duty. Bree insists, and I'm not arguing over it.

It's cute to see London and my sister ganging up on us, and so it's easy to let it go.

We're gonna start out for Sacramento during the night. Less traffic then. I don't care one way or the other. Baz has the whole thing so damn well organized, I don't need to keep up with anything. Not sure how that makes me feel. Normally it'd irritate the crap out of me, but right now, I've got too much other shit going on, I guess.

I'm learning to trust Baz, and that's a goddamn miracle.

Noah and Zayne settle in for an intense game of *Resident Evil*. Rye hunches over a notebook, scribbling something. Bree and Ajia disappear into the bedroom, leaving me with London. We're just...waiting.

For what?

"Going to bed."

I grab her hand and pull her toward the back of the bus. The others mumble behind us, but I don't look back. Got nothing to hide, and I give no fucks about what they think.

"Knox!"

I grin. "Aw, c'mon, baby. None of their business, what's going on between us. They'll figure it out quick enough, anyway."

"But—"

I tumble her onto her bunk, and she squeals my name. I crawl in behind her and pull the curtains closed with a grin. "Knox!" she squeals, but I just grin as I snap on the small bulkhead lamp.

"Knox," she says again, softer this time, one hand reaching up to push my hair back from my face.

"What?"

"They'll…"

"They'll what, baby? Know we're fucking?" I drop a quick, hard kiss on her open mouth. "They're gonna know, anyway."

"You…don't mind?"

Her eyes are wide and shimmery. Something's there, something deep, but she shifts against me, and my cock doesn't give a shit about anything except getting closer to her.

"You think I was gonna keep you a secret?"

Her eyelids drop. "I…didn't know."

I tip her head back with one finger under her chin. I don't say a damn word until her whiskey eyes meet mine. "I might not be the guy you want to bring home to daddy, but you'll *never* be my dirty little secret. We're exclusive, however long it lasts, and I don't give a fuck if everybody knows. In fact, I hope they do."

"Knox…"

The same inexplicable look tears at me.

"You don't believe me?" She just stares back.

I lean to one side, sticking my head out through the drawn curtains. "Hey," I shout. "London and I are together through the rest of the tour! We're fucking, and it might get loud, so if you don't wanna hear it…earphones."

A small moment of silence echoes back, and then Noah shouts, "You think we didn't figure that out already? Losing your touch, fucker!"

I pull my head back inside and give my girl a quick grin. "See?"

"Jesus, Knox." She tucks her head against my chest. "I can't believe you just did that!"

"Why not? I stroke a hand over her hair. It's more of a comforting gesture than I usually make, but something about London makes me want to give it to her.

And more.

She stepped up for me, for Bree, for the band. I owe her, and not just a good time in bed.

"C'mon, baby."

I wait until she looks at me, and then I dip down for a kiss that goes far deeper and far longer than I meant. My dick isn't just awake, it's harder than it's been in days, and it wants inside my English.

Bareback. Just like we've been so far. And why not? She gets the shot, we're both clean, and I want to feel her tight, pulsing walls around me. Again. And we're not stopping until she screams my name at the top of her lungs.

CHAPTER 17

LONDON

AN ODD, MUSICAL TONE WAKES ME. It takes a few seconds, maybe half a minute, to figure out where I am and what the sound might be.

Reality sinks in slowly. I'm on the tour bus. Knox is sprawled over me, one leg slung across mine and an arm curled around my waist. His skin is hot against mine, the hair on his legs rough. We spent the night together, we're in my bunk and…the noise…

My phone. My cell phone is ringing. It's the opening of Wycked Obsession's *Tonight,* a ringtone Rye sent me.

I fumble around, searching for my phone, and wake Knox in the process.

"Wha…" he grumbles.

"My phone," I breathe, still searching.

"Who the fuck is calling *now?"*

I shake my head. "We don't even know what time it is."

"I don't give a damn. It's still too early to *talk."*

He pushes up, flicks on the little light, and we both squint as he searches the space. His cheeks are rough with a couple of days' beard, and his eyes are an interesting dark green. I haven't seen that look before. Is it normal for the morning? Because of the shadows? The remnants of the best sex *ever* last night?

"Here." Knox reaches above my head into a little cubbyhole storage. I remember leaving it there now, but wish to bloody hell I'd lost it for good.

He hands me the phone, and I check the screen. Baz. I hand it back to him.

"It's Baz. He's probably looking for you more than me."

Knox shrugs and connects the call. "What?"

Most of me zones out then, because…well, Knox. We're naked. Pressed together in the most delightfully intimate way. His chest smashes my boobs, while his dick is glorious with its morning wood presses against my mound. It brings back memories of the things he did to me last night—his mouth, his hands, his cock—and I want them again. Now. For as long and as loud as we were last night.

I smooth one hand over his ass, squeeze, and his hips flex against mine. Automatically? I glance up and see, no…his eyes are fixed on me with a promise of what's to come. Is he even listening to Baz?

"Repeat that."

No. He's concentrating on *me*.

Oh, God.

The rest of my reality crashes back with all the finesse of a bomb. *What am I going to do?*

How do I tell him I'm pregnant? *Pregnant?* I can't tell him until I have some semblance of control, or even acceptance, over the knowledge. I have none of that. The least provocation, and my thoughts, my emotions, surge through me in chaos, like that tiny metal ball in the old-fashioned pinball machine my father has in the game room. Bouncing everywhere, landing nowhere.

The questions swing back and forth. *How can I tell him? How can I not tell him?* Honesty is important to Knox, and keeping this kind of secret from him…how long can I do it?

I can't! I don't *want* to keep this secret. But how do I tell him? He trusted me, and it was all a lie!

And then, last night? *You think I was gonna keep you a secret?* he asked. Like my father does, even as an open secret, but I doubt Knox thought about it that way. He merely proved his intentions, revealing our relationship. Plainly.

And, yeah, maybe it *is* temporary. But he didn't hide it.

How can I do anything less?

But how can I tell him?

"Motherfucker!"

Knox's outburst puts a quick halt to my rambling thoughts. I gaze up at him, at his dark, stormy eyes, narrow and fierce. His forehead is wrinkled.

"Knox." I whisper his name, but he doesn't respond.

"Send me everything. Send it to London, too."

He ends the call, tosses my phone back into the cubbyhole, and his chest heaves as he breathes long and heavy. *"Motherfucker,"* he mutters again, under his breath this time.

"Knox?" I try again.

He blinks without answering, crawls over me, and out of the bunk. He's standing in the passageway naked, but he doesn't seem to care. He stands there for a minute, two, his dick reduced to a more normal size right before my face. He fumbles in the bunk above mine, and then he pulls on a pair of ragged sweatpants.

"Noah?" he shouts and stalks away, toward the front of the bus. "Front and center!"

Okay, it's something bad. Maybe not about Bree or their father, but it's something serious. Whatever it is, I'm not letting Knox face it on his own.

I dig around in the covers until I find a shirt. Knox's. I don't care, pull it over my head. A little more searching and I come up with yesterday's panties. They'll work for the moment, and I tug them on, too. I'm out of the bunk at the same time the others come straggling out of theirs. Ajia and Bree, he in boxers and she looking much like me, are the last to join us.

"Knox."

He's pacing around the front of the bus, and I slip up next to him. We're stopped and parked in a venue parking lot. We must be in Sacramento, but I only notice with half my attention. The rest is strictly on Knox.

"What's wrong, luv?" I whisper and try to soothe him with my hand on his back. His chest heaves, but he doesn't pull away.

"What the fuck, Gallagher?" demands Noah from behind us.

I look at the others. The guys are all in all boxers like Ajia, with the exception of Knox, and they were clearly asleep. Bree and Ajia have that just-fucked look about them, and I wonder suddenly if that's how Knox and I look. I let the thought go as quickly as I can, because the tension radiating from Knox is enough to knock any one of us over.

"We didn't have enough shit to deal with? Now you have to do *this?*"

"What are you talking about?"

Knox may be too pissed to see Noah's confusion, but I read it clearly. He's a big guy, all muscular and tattooed and long-haired, but he's a good-natured pussycat, too. He loves Bree, the band, and his mates, not necessarily in that order, and he's not screwing around.

"What's going on, Knox?" I ask softly. "What did Baz say?"

"Baz?" repeats Noah with a frown.

Knox drops to the nearby sofa and grabs the back of his neck, squeezing until his knuckles are white. "Some chick," he grunts and falls against the back of the couch. "She's accusing you of giving her crabs."

"What the fuck?" Noah's shout rivals Knox at his best.

I sink down next to Knox. "Crabs?"

He shakes his head and looks at Noah. "Some STD. I don't know. Baz is sending us the shit. She went to some gossip rag, and it's all over TV and the internet. She fucked Noah Dexter with some other chick, and they both came away with some nasty disease."

Noah hasn't moved. He looks like he's made of stone, in fact, with no expression at all. Not even when Bree scoots up next to him, wraps an arm around his waist, and lays her head on his chest.

"Noah, sweetie," she whispers and reaches to tug his head around until their eyes meet. "What can we do?"

An odd, ragged sound rumbles from his chest, and then Noah's arms are around Bree. Ajia steps up next to them, trapping Bree between the two men, and laying a strong hand of support on Noah's shoulder.

They stand there for a long time. Silent time. It stretches out long enough that both Rye and Zayne squeeze past with a shoulder bump for Noah. Guy encouragement. I recognize it, appreciate it, might even congratulate it if I wasn't so gobsmacked.

This is a family in every way, and some deep, lonely part of me longs to be included in it.

We all sit and wait. For what? Instinct tells me that Noah needs time. The chance to process this information. To…feel.

Maybe we all do.

I understand how it feels, struggle with my own version of needing to think—but I'm not going there now. I can't.

This is about a band crisis. Not a surprise pregnancy that *I could have prevented!*

A couple of minutes, maybe even five, and Noah finally pulls away from Bree and Ajia. He takes a step forward, just one, and then shakes his head.

"I didn't give anybody *shit*. I don't have an STD. Never have. I wear a condom. Every. Fucking. Time. Always have."

"Okay," I agree. Instinct, women's intuition, whatever it is, tells me to take the lead in this. I'm not as emotionally attached as the rest of the band, and—Jesus! I need something else to focus on at the moment.

"We'll find a doctor in Sacramento and get you tested." I start planning. "We'll get it done ASAP, the test results expedited. We'll release the results to the media immediately."

"And in the meantime?" Knox demands.

"We issue a denial. A *strong* denial. I'll put something on social media and arrange for Noah to give a statement, like Ajia did. Better, *this* is something we can follow up on, and quickly. No wanker hiding away to leave us boxing at shadows. *This* gives us a target. Some groupie who came forward for a quick buck or notoriety or whatever. Doesn't matter." I shoot a hard glance at the others. "We strike back. And hard."

"What do you mean *hard?*" asks Noah.

I shake my head. "I have to talk to Baz first. And maybe the label. But if they agree, we threaten to sue for defamation of character."

It's Zayne who laughs. His eyes look clearer than in L.A., and I hope that's good news. Permanent news.

"Fuck, you think that'll get anywhere?" he demands. "We're all known as fucking manwhores. Who's gonna give a shit if some chick says she fucked Noah and got crabs?"

I toss off a half-serious, half amused expression. "Sleeping with you guys is one thing, irresponsible as it might be. But doing it without condoms and a disease…that's a whole different level of carelessness. If Noah's as careful as he says, we might have a case. But…" I hesitate. "That doesn't necessarily mean anything. The lawyers might shy away, Baz and the label might say no. They might think that a clean health report is vindication enough. We'll just have to see."

I stand and go to Noah. "I'll do everything I can to get control of this today."

He flicks me a surprisingly weary gaze. I don't know exactly what's behind it, but I figured out pretty quickly that there's more to every one of these guys than meets the eye.

"Thanks, London." He wraps me in a quick but genuine hug that surprises me. He turns to stare at the line of bunks, one hand on his head, and he seems to drift a million miles away.

"Noah?" Bree slips up next to him, wraps him in a hug of her own, and smiles up at him. "How about some breakfast?"

He takes a breath, his massive chest moving with the effort. "Let me shower first, baby girl?"

"Sure." She turns back to the rest of us. "Requests?"

We all shake our heads. It's Ajia who says, "Noah?"

He blinks, seeming to come back to the moment. "Pancakes?"

"And bacon?" Bree asks in a teasing voice.

"Crispy," Noah agrees.

It's not over, things aren't better. But Wycked Obsession is pulling together, and I'll do everything I can to walk this new minefield of celebrity life with them.

I take my turn in the shower and dress far more casually than when we were in L.A. Jeans and a fitted T-shirt, plain cream colored and not the retro band T-shirts the guys mostly wear. Unless I'm called on to meet with someone outside of the band, I'll fit in better if I look like everyone else.

Part of the team.

The smell of bacon greets me when I step out of the bathroom. I don't appreciate it as much as I normally would, which makes me think. Because of the baby? I'm not that far along; it must be the size of...well, nothing. Yet. That can't explain it.

But what about nutrition? Is bacon okay to eat? Drinking coffee? I know there are dietary restrictions, but what are they? Dr. Jackson gave me some prenatal vitamins that I've been taking and literature that I haven't read yet. Guess it's time to get serious about this stuff. I need to figure it out.

Am I keeping this baby? Not?

I have no bloody clue, can't believe I'm asking the question. I'll never make that kind of decision without Knox. It's his baby, too, and he has every right to be a part of whatever happens. But...God.

Knox.

Jesus, I've got to tell him. But I can't do it now. Not today. Not with this new crisis looming.

Wycked Obsession is *his* baby. He's had plenty to worry about with it, and this new strike against them is bound to wear on him further. We've got to get this sorted and a retraction of the accusation, at the very least. Then I can tell him.

It's better that way.

A day. Maybe two. Right? And I can use the time to get my own thoughts together about it.

But...bollocks! I *hate* keeping this secret. On the other hand, I can't bring myself to add to his burden.

I tip back against the wall next to the bathroom door as the word echoes in my head. Burden.

His burden? Is that what I'll be? What my—*our*—baby will be?

I have no bloody clue. We don't know each other well enough for me to be able to answer that. So what the bloody fucking hell am I doing pregnant with this man's baby?

Too late to ask that question, luv, my better sense reminds me. *You should have thought about details like that when you were playing free and easy with your schedule. You should have known* for sure *when you were due for your shot.*

Maybe so. I take a deep breath. I can't deny the very irresponsible truth to the fact that I wasn't. But it wasn't deliberate. I thought I knew!

And how many accidental pregnancies are the result of that kind of thinking?

I bang my head back against the wall and close my eyes. What the hell am I going to do? *When* am I going to do it? And how?

"Hey, English." Knox is next to me suddenly, his arm around my waist, and he drops his head for a quick kiss. "What's wrong?"

I straighten and look at him. He's showered and dressed, too, in a pair of tight, hip-hugging jeans and a well-washed Metallica T-shirt. It cradles his chest, his biceps, and I just want to fall into him. Take comfort from his body and pour out the whole sorry tale.

"Nothing." I force a smile and shake my head, but I do sneak a quick hug against him, my head on his chest. "Just thinking of how best to make this rubbish go away for Noah."

Knox drops a surprisingly tender kiss on the top of my head. Surprising, because he was so angry before. Not at me, no, but he's a man of strong emotion. I didn't expect softness from him so soon.

"Talk to Baz. He's a miracle worker. If anybody can get control of this shit, it's the two of you."

I smile up at him. Gratified surprise warms me. "You think so?"

"I know so." He doesn't smile, which would probably be too much under the circumstances, but his expression seems lighter somehow. "We're lucky to have you."

Lucky to have you.

He says that now. But will he feel the same way when I tell him I'm carrying his baby?

CHAPTER 18

KNOX

THE SHOW IN SACRAMENTO GOES BETTER THAN EXPECTED. Yeah, paparazzi line the path between the venue and the bus, but Kel and the rest of our security team keep them under control. They shout their questions.

Ajia, did you steal Bree from the rest of the band?

Knox, how do you feel about your sister and Ajia hooking up?

Noah, some girl says you gave her a disease. That true?

We ignore them. Already agreed we're not answering any more questions about Ajia's and Bree's relationship, and that pretty much takes care of orgy questions, too. No. Fucking. Comment.

The shit about Noah giving some chick an STD? London worked her ass off getting ahead of that. She and Baz got Noah in for testing, with the results promised in twenty-four hours. It cost a few extra bucks, but it's worth it. She posted a carefully-worded denial with the promise that Noah would issue a statement with his test results. She put it everywhere online, and she and Baz made some deal with the label to get better coverage with Noah's statement.

Video, we decide, and not a press conference. Don't want to make any more of it than it needs to be. Less chance of him being blindsided by some jerk out for blood. We're using the excuse that we're too busy with the tour.

Next up are a few dates in the Bay Area. Won't be there as long as we were in L.A., about a week. Thank freaking God! Plus, there won't be any label bullshit to deal with. Just this goddamn gossip, like somebody put a damn target on our backs.

Is this what fame is like?

Can't believe I'm thinking this, but why can't we just write and perform our music? Didn't think I'd get so jaded so fast—but didn't think I'd have to deal with all this gossip shit, either.

Baz gets us back in a hotel after only a couple of nights on the bus. I was glad to get back on the road, but not crazy about Bree and Ajia sharing the bedroom. The least noise, and my gut clenches. Jesus, I know what they're doing...and it's none of my business!

Bree says so.

And even though they're sharing a room at the hotel, there's at least some real estate between us. I'm glad and not pretending. Which is why London and I share a room, too.

She seems happy about it...but somehow nervous as hell, too.

"What's wrong, English?" I asked her when we first checked in. "Something bothering you?"

She gave me a surprisingly weak smile. "No. It's...nothing. Just...we're so new, and there's all this other stuff going on. It's like we're, I don't know, getting to know each other in front of an audience."

I pulled her close then and dropped a quick, hard kiss on her mouth. Maybe a little too sweet and caring for Knox Gallagher, manwhore, but I like London. She doesn't pull her punches, and she looks out for all of us. Especially Bree. That means something to me, so I gave her words, too.

"You know how it is with celebrity, baby. Even B- and C-list rockers. Put us on tour together, and you can't find much privacy."

"I know." She smiled then, seemed more at ease, and she's worked like a pro ever since.

Now we're setting up for sound check at the venue in San Jose, and London is drifting through the backstage area, talking to everybody there. Roadies, managers, merch people. What the hell?

What's she up to now? Just getting to know everyone?

"Knox!"

I have to let it go when Rye calls my name. Just as well, and I lose track of time while we go through the actual sound check and get set for the night's concert. I actually *like* the process, making sure everything is set up right.

My *control-freak tendencies,* Bree would say.

I almost smile. She's right. I do like things a certain way—*my* way, I suppose—and feel easier when I'm in charge. If that makes me a control freak, I wear the title proudly.

After sound check is over, I head from the stage to the green room. Accommodations have been decent all over California, but it's still backstage. Still Grand Fucking Central most of the time.

London's alone there, hovering over her tablet.

"Hey, baby."

She looks up, shooting a glance behind me. The rest of the band drags in, Bree tucked close against Ajia's side. I hold my frown and stare at London. Still not used to the sight of them together, but at least I don't want to punch my fist in Ajia's too-pretty face anymore.

I'd rather look at London, but the heavy, whiskey-gold light in her eyes makes me curious. They're deep, uneasy, and my gut tells me something's wrong.

"What?" I say in a low voice.

She stands with so much grace, my breath catches. What the fuck? Jesus, am I going all poetic or something now? I grab the back of my neck and shoot out a short breath.

No, nothing like that, but what the hell is she doing with a long-haired, tattooed rocker like me? She's beautiful, intelligent, naughty at all the right times, and in all the right ways. Too good for an asshole like me.

She slips close enough that I can smell the faintly exotic fragrance that I associate with her. No damn clue what it is, just all London.

"Can we go somewhere?" she whispers. "Private? We need to talk."

"Okay?" It's more of a question than agreement. What the hell?

"We'll be in the bus," I announce to no one, and Zayne laughs.

"A little afternoon delight, kids?"

London blushes adorably, and I toss off a quick grin. Maybe—who knows? She has something on her mind, I know that much, and we have to get through that first. I can wait. I hold the winning card.

No matter what happens on the bus—or doesn't—I get her to myself in the hotel room tonight.

We head for the bus, the metal barricades already in place. A few hardcore fans lounge in the parking lot, and security is stationed at both the venue and bus doors.

We brought the bus for privacy. Relaxation. A place to rest or get away from the crazy atmosphere backstage. I'm glad now, because something's eating at London. In fact, she's been acting weird for a couple of days.

Is she finally gonna tell me why?

"Knox!"

Some super fan notices us and starts racing toward the metal barricade. Security nods toward the bus, encouraging us inside, and then ambles over to intercept the screeching girl. I don't hesitate and urge London up the steps into the bus.

She shakes her head. "I'm gonna have to get used to that."

I grin but don't really feel it. "Good luck. I'm not used to it." Not sure I ever will be. I mean, who really *likes* women—people—coming out of the woodwork, screaming their name, grabbing at them, their clothes, their hair? Who doesn't want a say in who touches you, where, and how?

I drop onto the sofa, grab London's hand, and pull her down with me. She's still a little off-center, so I start out easy.

"Saw you ghosting around backstage."

Her smile is easier than any other I've seen today. "Yes. I thought I'd do a little…snooping. We still don't know who leaked that original picture of Bree with the band."

"Any luck?"

She shrugs. "Not yet. I've only talked to about half the crew, yours and Edge of Return's. If it was a jealous fan, we might never find out anything. But maybe somebody from the crew saw something. Heard something. It's worth following up."

I want to smile back. My girl is going all the way for my sister. That means a lot to me. A hell of a lot. But I stay serious.

"Thanks, English. It means…a lot." Can't think of any other words.

She twines her fingers with mine. "I'd say it's my job. And it is! But there's more to it than that. I *hate* that sneaky, behind the veil kind of stuff."

We sit for a minute. I tell myself I don't like the feel of her hand, so small and soft in mine, but it's a lie.

I love it.

"Knox?" She says it softly. Carefully. "There's something else."

"Figured." I nod once. "What is it?"

"I…" She drops her gaze and sighs. "This."

She shoves her tablet into my hands, and I glance down. It's Wycked Obsession's Facebook page. I see London's original response to the accusations against Noah. Heartfelt but professional. Perfect under the circumstances. I look farther down and see the little private message window.

Fuking digenrates. Group sex w/ my dau w/ dirty dicks? Im coming for my $$ an want 50 grand. Tell Knox the ole man always git his way.

I stare at the words, misspellings, the stupid shorthand. My gut fists, ending up at the same time empty and too full. My heart thuds an extra beat, and I try to swallow.

"That motherfucker."

The words come out soft but hard. Granite. I can't find the pissed-off shout I'd normally give. Don't have the breath for it.

This isn't normal for me. Or acceptable, considering the churning emotions inside me. It's totally, completely wrong, and on so many levels.

Fucked up in every way.

I want to be pissed. To let my rage erupt. To punch something, someone. Destroy shit. But it's not there. Right now, I'm just fucking tired. Tired of fighting. Tired of the sperm donor and his bullshit. Tired of these assholes coming at us from all angles.

The fury will come. I know it, and I can't wait for it. It'll help me. Motivate me to do what I have to. I need it.

All I ever wanted was to keep my family safe, write some music, and play my fucking guitar. What's so wrong about that?

"Knox?"

I blink. London's expression is intense. Concerned. Afraid?

"He's not gonna give up," I say finally. Tiredly.

"I…" She shakes her head. "No, I don't think so."

I stare at her, at the genuine emotion in her eyes, the way her hair curls around her shoulders in auburn-colored waves, the tight-fitting tank top with old-fashioned looking flowers that suit her so well. She's so hot, beautiful with a smokin' body, but she's so much more.

She's strong and committed to her beliefs. She's smart. She's kind and caring. She's genuine and giving, and she's helping me take care of my Wycked Obsession family.

I let out a sharp breath. "He screwed with us our whole lives. When we were little, he'd fight with Mom and then disappear for a few days, weeks. Whatever. Then one time he didn't come back. Ever. He left us with questions and bills, and Mom working her ass off to pay 'em because she had two kids to support."

"She sounds like a remarkable woman."

"She is." I nod. "Bree's a lot like her, but she was so scared at first. Hurt. Couldn't understand why he 'didn't want us anymore.' She was eight years old, and that's how she said it. *Didn't want us anymore."*

I hate those fucking memories. Of the nights when Bree would cry herself to sleep, and I'd sneak into her room to calm her down. Didn't want Mom to hear. She was upset enough. So I'd crawl into Bree's bed, wrap my arms around her in the awkward way only a twelve-year-old boy can do, and lay there until my sister fell asleep. Then I'd go back to my room and curse the asshole who made my mom and my sister cry.

The sperm donor.

I swallow, and finally find some rage in the tone of my voice. "I'm not giving him a goddamn dime."

"I know. But…do Bree and your mom deserve to know about this?"

"No!" I stiffen and pull away. "Absolutely not. You didn't see them, English. Don't know what they went through when he abandoned us. No." I shake my head sharply, and my hair whips across my eyes. I shove it back. "Not after all these years. He doesn't want to see them. Didn't ask about that, did he? No!" I answer my own question. "He's only after *money."*

"Right." She agrees softly. "Okay. I understand. But…maybe we should bring Baz in on this."

"Baz?" But I'm still shaking my head.

"Knox." She reaches for me, scoots closer. For some reason, that makes me feel better.

"I know you want to handle this yourself," she admits. "Like you do with everything. I get it. But this has the potential to spin so bloody far out of control. I'm not sure if I have the knowledge or know-how to contain it. Baz has other contacts, more experience. Between the three of us…"

Her words die away, and I know it's because she doesn't quite know what to say. Who would? It's a screwed-up situation, no winners, and she's caught right in the middle of it.

Just like me. Along with all the other bullshit going on in my life.

I nod. "Yeah, okay. Baz. We'll talk to him tomorrow."

I know how to get my head back in the game, channel my adrenalin, and by the time we leave the green room for the show, I'm Knox Gallagher, guitarist and co-founder of Wycked Obsession.

Cocky rock god.

A corner of my mouth twists up in a half-grin, and it let it. London's voice fills my head, and I glance over my shoulder to where she and Bree perch on a couple of chairs to watch. She's been with us for a couple of shows now, but I'm suddenly aware of her watching me perform.

Not as a band employee or a new acquaintance. As English. My lover. The woman who can touch me and make me go off like a damn Roman candle. Who knows more about me than just about anybody.

The show goes well. From our standard opening of *Run* to the last song, our most recent hit, *Tonight.* Soon as we get the details for shooting the video of *Lost,* we'll switch up the playlist and end with that.

But now, tonight, I have something—someone—that matters more. I grab London's hand as I stalk off stage. "C'mon."

She hurries to keep up. She's wearing a cute skirt that's maybe a little tight—for my benefit?—so I slow down a little. "Where are we going?"

"Away from here." I stop long enough to press a long, deep kiss against her mouth. Just enough of a taste to hold me until we get back to the hotel.

Or maybe just the bus.

I wrap an arm around her, because I know what's waiting. The groupies crowding forward, screaming and grabbing. I can already hear them up ahead.

"Noah!"

"Ajia, wait! Are you really with *her?*"

"Zayne!"

"Rye!"

And my name, when we get up around the corner. I'm already tense, and the whole circus pisses me off.

Why? I used to play the game, liked it even. Then everything got all screwed up with the first rumors about Bree, and it all started to change for me.

I love Wycked Obsession. The band. I love making music, performing. I'm grateful for the fans, and the groupie chicks have been good for business. Good for me. But...fuck.

Not now. Not tonight. Not anymore.

Too much other shit on my mind, and I've got a woman next to me who has my back. Who knows how to make it all go away.

At least for a little while.

"Knox!"

The inevitable happens, and the crowd descends on us. I keep London tight against me, her arm around my waist. She's smart enough to hook her thumb through a belt loop on my leather pants, and I smile down at her. She smiles back, but I can see the uneasiness in the depths of her eyes.

Who wouldn't freak out a little with a hoard of women all pushing close, grabbing, shouting?

"Sorry, ladies," I call with what I hope sounds like real sorrow and give them my I-wish-I-could-fuck-you-all grin. It usually works.

"Got other plans tonight," I add and tighten my grip around London's shoulder. "Thanks for coming out. You're the reason we do this."

It's bullshit. We do it for ourselves. *I* do it to calm the noise in my soul. But they want to be a part of it all? What's the harm?

A chorus of groans follows us. Literally. They're right behind us, on into the green room where the rest of the band and the hangers-on are milling around. Ajia's got Bree on the couch, protected by his arm around her, and Noah's just coming out of the bathroom. Zayne and Rye hold court on opposite sides of the room, ever-present red Solo cups in their hands and one-and-done chicks jockeying for position.

I've seen it a thousand times, but something about it scrapes over my nerves tonight. Maybe it's the rumors. Bree and Ajia and Noah. Or Mom's divorce. She has to handle that shit on her own while we're on tour. Or the next video, the one the label is putting money and talent behind, and that we're going to have to fly back to L.A. to film.

Or the sperm donor. No matter what else is going on, I know that jerk and his bullshit have pushed me over the edge.

Irritation and anger rise in me, probably worse because of the adrenalin that started before the show and is still there. Always is after a performance. And maybe a dose of testosterone, tuned up by the need to smash my fist into the old man's face. Stirred by the groupies who act so desperate just to be around us. Refined by the woman standing so close next to me.

"Let's get out of here." I look down at her, and I can tell by how her eyes widen that my expression carries the ferocity I feel inside.

"Go where?"

"Back to the room. I...need you."

I fucking hate admitting it, but I don't have it in me to say anything else tonight. I just need to get that sexy, flirty skirt and white, short-sleeved top off her. I need to get her under me, ready and waiting for my cock. My hands. My mouth.

I need *something* in my control, and English is the only one who can give it to me.

CHAPTER 19

LONDON

I WAIT NEXT TO KNOX AS HE SLIPS THE CARD KEY IN THE SLOT ON THE HOTEL ROOM DOOR. I fight to keep my breathing easy, regular.

I need you, he said. It seems significant, because he doesn't admit to needing anyone or anything. At least not often. I've learned that much about him already. Oh, he might say it in bed, when the sex is good enough to push him over the edge, but otherwise, he's a very self-contained man.

And he *needs me.*

I didn't know how much I ached to hear the words until he said them. Not because I take them as any great undying declaration of love. I wouldn't believe him if he said those three little words. *I love you.* But this pregnancy has me so off-center, I need...something. Some sign of...I don't know, affection maybe? A hint that we're going to get through this.

Whatever that means.

You have to tell him, my conscience reminds me, and I agree.

I know, and I groan a little inside. *But how can I do it* now?

We haven't resolved the rumors about Noah. The test results came back, negative, as he promised, and we've worked on the script for his video, but there hasn't been time to film it yet. Now Knox's father has made another appearance.

I just can't add to his burden. And news that I'm going to have a baby—*his baby*—will be like a missile soaring straight through him to destroy parts of his life I can't even imagine.

He's been through it before. I remember the story Noah told me about Farren.

He caught her fucking some other dude and cut her off. She tried to get him back a couple of times, begged and cried, even claimed she was pregnant with his kid, but he never caved.

So his old girlfriend lied—and I'm telling the truth. Will that make a difference? Will memories of her betrayal make believing me, *trusting* me, more difficult? How could they not?

I can't do that to him. Not now.

Besides, I justify to myself. I'm barely pregnant. Most people wouldn't even know yet. I got myself into some strange *Twilight Zone* set of circumstances that put me in the right place at the right time to find out I was pregnant practically *immediately.* I'm just a couple of weeks along, my only symptoms are a slight soreness in my breasts and a sudden sleepiness, so I can afford to wait a little while.

Can't I?

Knox's hand on mine brings me out of the dangerous territory in my head. I'm grateful for the reprieve. I want what he wants: to lose ourselves in each other for a few hours and leave the bloody outside world behind us.

Far, far behind. For now.

I enter ahead of him and scoot across the room to turn on the bedside lamp. The instant the softer glow of the lamp fills the space, the bright entry light goes off. I turn to look at him. He's still by the door.

"Knox?"

"Take it off."

His voice is low, rough, and it produces an instant physical reaction in my body. My nipples tighten, and my core twinges with awareness. I'm damp between my legs.

What the bloody hell? I'm not a submissive woman, but damn if I don't respond to his dominant voice. This isn't the first time, and I find it as damn sexy as I did before.

"What?"

He nods toward me, his expression almost harsh. "Off. Take it off."

"My clothes?"

Why am I questioning him? I wonder when his mouth hardens.

"Everything."

Swallowing, I don't say a word, but I know almost immediately how I'm going to do it. I'll follow his commands, *ache* to do it…but I'm going to make him as crazy as he has me.

I slip off my woven canvas wedges and place them precisely next to the dresser. I reach behind me slowly, find the zipper of my tapestry-type embroidered skirt, and tug it down one tooth at a time. It slips a bit, and so I push the fabric down over my hips. I shift my weight from one leg to the other as I step out of the circle, bend down, and then carefully fold the skirt before I place it on the dresser.

I keep my eyes trained downward, not so much because I'm being submissive to Knox, but because I need to concentrate. I can't do that if he catches me in the heat of his gaze.

I cross my arms in front of me, each hand grabbing hold of the hem of my peasant-style blouse, and then, oh-so-slowly, I pull it over my head. I take my time, folding the white cotton with the same attention I paid to my skirt.

Only then do I bring my gaze up to met Knox's. His eyes are narrow with a raging fire burning deep within. His mouth is heavy, lips parted, and his chest moves with the weight of his breath. I smile.

"All of it."

His voice is ragged, and he twirls a finger in a circle, apparently indicating my very sexy lace bra-and-panty set. It's a blue so pale it looks almost white, and I wore it on purpose. I admit it. Not just for him, but for me. Because I knew it would make me feel feminine and sexy and deserving of a man like Knox Gallagher.

It seems he approves.

What to remove first? He can't seem to take his eyes from my breasts, so I make him wait. I slip my fingers under each side of my thong and push it slowly down over my hips. It falls to my ankles, and I extend the teasing by leaning down flat-footed to step out and fold it with the same care.

I train my eyes on his as I reach behind me for the fastening of my bra. The hooks give way easily, the lacy fabric falls forward, and I slip my arms free. It's my last line of defense, if I'd needed it, and I take my time folding the lingerie and then placing it on top of the other things.

I turn to face Knox, finally naked. I raise my head, push back my shoulders, and give myself permission to present myself with the proud bearing of a woman who is desired. There may be nothing else between us, but he wants me.

He *needs me.*

"Jesus, English." He swallows. "You're so fucking gorgeous."

I smile, but it's heavy with my arousal. I know it, can feel it. How could it *not* be?

He stares at me, just stares and doesn't move. I look back, search his expression for...*something.* Why doesn't he say or do something?

His eyes are dark. I see desire. Need. Something I don't understand, but I don't need to, I decide abruptly. I only need to be here for him.

I hold out my hand with a soft smile, wait patiently, and after a minute, he walks toward me. He reaches behind his neck to pull his T-shirt over his head as he moves.

His chest is everything I've learned it could be. Hard and muscled, broad and tattooed, and I plant my palms on his pecs. His gaze sharpens, and I slide them up to his shoulders, his neck, cupping his face in my hands.

"Let me take care of you, luv." I lean forward to plant an open-mouthed kiss on his chest.

"I...that's not—"

"Not your brand of control, I know." I give him a wicked grin tinged with understanding. We touched on this before, when I gave him the massage. But this time...

"I'm giving you *full* control, luv. You don't have to do anything. Just let me...pleasure you."

He grunts, like the idea turns him on. I kiss his chest again, licking him this time, and continue.

"You like what I do? I'll do more of it. You don't, I'll do something else. It's all about you, baby. Let me do this for you."

Something wild flares in his eyes, something I haven't seen before. It's deep and visceral and primal. Everything that makes Knox the man he is. I know in that instant that, as much as he's struggling for the control that's so important to him, I have an answer he hasn't considered before. Even better, he *likes* it.

Especially with all the things in his life that have become frantically unpredictable.

But *I* can soothe him. Calm him. Reassure him.

Give him an unexpected measure of control.

Give him that release.

I sink to my knees in front of him. I unfasten his leather pants and struggle to release him. He's enormous the way it is, and a hard-on inside the tight leather isn't easy to manage, but finally I work him free.

I push his pants down over his hips, his thighs, his calves, only then remembering his boots. I tug them from his feet, and then finally drag him free of the constricting leather.

God, he's naked, and he's magnificent.

I tilt my head back to peer up at him. The fire is there, the desire hot enough to burn me where I kneel. I wish I could smile, but the moment is too deep for that. I can only drop my gaze as I reach for him.

His dick is hot and hard, and I spot a tiny drop of precum at his tip. I lick him clean and then lean forward to take him between my lips, resting my hands on his thighs. He sucks in a sharp, harsh breath that both satisfies and excites me. I circle the full, round head with my tongue, stroking that special place at the front, where nerves and sensation draw a groan from him. His hips flex a little, and my own arousal spikes.

It makes me feel strong and powerful and desirable that I can do that to him.

I take another swipe around the blunt tip, and then I bob my head forward, taking him as deep as I can. Deeper than I have before, and I gag. My eyes tear, but I don't stop. I pull back, go deep, pull back again, and then Knox's hips are moving in rhythm with my mouth.

"Goddamn, English," he mutters and cups my head.

I grip his thighs and keep my pace steady, with the occasional deeper push that makes me gag every time he reaches the back of my throat. My jaws ache with the need to keep them open wide enough to accommodate his size, but I don't care. I never wanted to take a guy's cock in my throat the way I want to take Knox as deep and as far as I can.

"Oh, Jesus. *Like that.* Suck it deep, baby." He groans. "All the way."

He adjusts his hands, shoves them into my hair, holding my head steady as he moves. He fucks my mouth. Again. Again. Farther than he's ever gone. Tears run down my cheeks, but I open my mouth wide and relax my throat as much as I can. Knox groans, gives a good, hard thrust, and then pulls out completely.

"Knox?" I gasp. "Luv?"

He shakes his head. "No more," he grunts. "You'll make me come, and I'm not ready for that."

I sink back on my heels, stare at his long, hard cock, covered with my saliva. It looks as wet as my pussy feels.

"No." I lean forward, swipe my tongue around his balls, one and then the other. "I told you." I peer up at him. *"I'm* taking care of you. You liked it well enough to come?" I lick him again. "Well, guess what, luv? You don't get to be a cunt tease."

I straighten and take his dick back in my mouth, my throat. Massage his balls with one hand, stroke him with the other. He picks up my rhythm almost immediately.

"Jesus Christ, English." He thrusts, and I suck. We do it again, and I close my eyes at the deep emotion that bursts through me. My pussy is wet, my nipples are hard, and I want nothing more than for this man to come down my throat.

Incredibly, he goes harder in my mouth, I feel a twitch, and so I work harder for him. I want him to have this release.

I *need* him to have this release.

And then it comes. Thick and salty and so much of Knox, I swallow greedily. His fingers grip my hair, and he moans a low, guttural sound that is both surrender and satisfaction.

I hold him in my mouth until he begins to soften, and I settle back on my heels with a lingering swipe of my tongue. I peer up at him and smile.

He runs a hand over my hair. "Christ, English. You know how to wreck a man."

I go to stand and he helps me up, his hands on my arms. Even with us both barefooted, the top of my head still reaches just to his shoulder, and I rest my head there. He wraps his arms around me.

"You needed the…release," I whisper.

"Is that what you're calling the best fucking blowjob of my life?"

I tilt my head back to look up at him and wink. "Among other things."

He drops his mouth to mine, captures it in a kiss that blisters my soul, all tongue and lips and his hands squeezing my ass. I lose the certainty of where I end and he begins.

"I want you." He bites my bottom lip. "On the bed."

I leave him with a quick kiss and crawl onto the bed.

"On your knees."

I respond immediately, and why wouldn't I? Knox has never put me in a position where I couldn't trust him, and I have the same confidence in him now. If he wants me from behind, I'm his. No matter what that means...even if it's any of those things I've heard he likes.

I'm his.

The mattress dips, and I feel the heat of Knox's body behind me. His hands wrap around my waist, and he tugs at me until my butt is resting on his thighs, my back against his chest. He's kneeling, sitting on his heels, and I'm sprawled over him.

What...?

"You surprise the shit out of me, English." He nuzzles the side of my neck, and my nipples tighten hard enough to cut glass.

"Why?" It's more breath than question.

"I came up here expecting one thing. Not even sure what it was, but you totally turned the tables on me...and I fucking loved it."

I turn my head enough to peer up at him. I give him a smile that I hope is both wicked and satisfied. "You were *supposed* to love it."

His response isn't what I expect when his dark gaze drills into mine. "I have a reputation. I like...kink. I tie girls up. Blindfold 'em. Spank 'em. Do shit that not everybody does."

I bring one hand up to tangle in his hair, heavy on his shoulder. "Well, you've swatted my ass a few times."

His smile is brief.

"Do you want to do more? Bind me? Blindfold me?"

He blinks. "Maybe. Yeah. I like the feeling of..."

He hesitates, and I finish for him. "Control."

"Yeah."

The ideas he's putting in my head scare me a little but not as much as they excite me. They excite him, too. I know, because I feel him begin to harden again against my back.

"I trust you, baby." I stroke my fingers along his hairline, behind his ear, fondle his earrings. I reach the other hand around to grab his ass and squeeze. "I'll try anything you want."

He brings his hands around to cup my breasts, forced forward by the arch of my back. "That fucking guts me, baby."

I blink. "What? Why?"

He blows out a harsh breath and drags his thumbs over my nipples. I swallow a groan of arousal.

"I'm a manwhore, English. More chicks than you can count."

I swallow, fighting the hollow that forms in my chest. My heart trips, and my nerves feel a little achy. I hate thinking about those other women. What he shared with them.

And I have no right to feel that way. Pregnant or not, this thing between Knox and me was always meant to be temporary. Lots of people have children and no real relationship other than being co-parents.

So why do I feel like all that's changed for me?

Hormones, I tell myself. Maybe pregnancy hormones start right away.

Rather than follow that train of thought, I force myself to speak. "I know," I admit softly. "I've...always known." *And hated it,* but I swallow that much.

"Jesus, I'm such a piece of shit. I don't remember any of them."

Hearing that doesn't necessarily make me feel better. In fact, it bothers me that Knox sounds so disgusted with himself.

I can't quite reach his cheek, but I can turn my head far enough to kiss his jaw. "Hey, that's the life of a rock star. Isn't it?"

He doesn't respond to my lighter tone. "That shit I did to them. Tying them up. Spanking their ass. I never gave a shit if they trusted me. If they wanted it. It was what *I* wanted, they never said no because they wanted to fuck a rock star, and so I did it."

"Knox...baby..." I'm not sure what to say, and then I can't think all that well when his arms wrap around my waist and he nuzzles my ear, my neck, my shoulder. The tenderness in the gesture twists my heart, and tears prickle behind my eyelids. I blink them away.

"It's different with you, English."

I swallow. "What do you mean?"

"I want to do those things with you. To play. Indulge that stuff a little. But...it's not *the thing*. I want something different with you." He pauses, and I almost don't hear the last word. "More."

More.

He's killing me. He wants more, too? What does that mean? What *can* it mean? He doesn't understand what he's saying, or how I'm hearing it. Not until he knows the truth. Everything.

I have to tell him about the baby.

But right now...tonight? I need something else. We both do.

"Knox?" I whisper softly, and wrap my arms over top of his.

"Yeah?"

"Make love to me."

CHAPTER 20

KNOX

THE SEATTLE CONCERT GOES WELL. It's a special show, Bree's birthday. Ajia planned something different, making their relationship public and official, and that irritates the hell out of me. Can't fight it now, though, with everything out in the open.

Not like there'd ever been a snowball's chance in hell of changing anything, anyway.

I play along with him for Bree's sake. We all do, and my baby sister is happy. No mistaking it. I suppose that made everything worth it. The show of band solidarity. The secrets I'm keeping.

And especially keeping the sperm donor's threats from her.

He's been in touch twice more since the first message. Through Facebook again and once through our website. The second Facebook message said only, *Get ready, asshole,* while the website email was more rambling. *Aint heard no more rumors. Got ur dicks clean? Time runnin out. Get the 50 grand ready cos I'm comin 4 it. Just waitin 4 u to get closer.*

London saw the messages first, and we've kept them between just us. The asshole must live somewhere near one of our tour stops, but that could be anywhere. I don't give a shit, as long as he doesn't get to Bree. Doesn't matter when, where, or how he comes at me, it means nothing. Less than nothing. He's not getting any fucking money. More than that, Bree and Mom will never know anything about it.

I tighten my mouth, satisfied. It's dark in the hotel room, and I'm in bed with London. She's been there for me, always, and somehow that lets me worry less about having control. I don't get it; it's weird. She doesn't really have to *do* anything, just be there if I need her. She's been with us a month now, and I don't question that she has my back. Has from the very beginning.

Something's up with her, though. She gets kind of quiet sometimes, and I don't know what she's thinking. A darkness fills her eyes, and her smile disappears. I've asked a couple of times, and I almost think she's been ready to tell me. Then we get interrupted or something else comes up, and it gets forgotten until the next time I notice her pull back.

Is it that fucked-up family of hers? The tour? The groupies? The band?

Me?

I turn on my side and pull her closer. She pushes against me with a soft sigh, and snuggles the delicious curve of her butt against my groin. Son of a bitch, that feels good!

We're still in Seattle. We have another show here, a schedule delay while we fly back to L.A. to shoot the video for *Lost,* and then we head out for Spokane. Except for Seattle and L.A., I don't remember all the details of whether we're in hotels or on the bus, and I don't really care right now. Last week was my turn in the bedroom, and this is London's week.

I fucked her every night.

We haven't tried any of the things I'm supposed to be known for: light bondage, blindfolds, spanking. We've been too busy fucking in every position designed by man. It's like something in me needs to get its fill of her before we start messing with other shit.

Never felt that way before, but I guess there's a first time for everything. As long as the sex is *hot,* I don't give a shit.

I palm her hip and anchor her tight against my hard-on. Don't know what time it is, don't really care. No early appointments, so my morning wood gets top priority.

I slide my hand around to her find she's wet for me—and then like the devil is playing another of his fucking tricks on me, my phone chirps.

"Goddammit," I mutter. Part of me wants to ignore it, let it go to voice mail, but when I'm still in bed, it's usually Baz and something important.

I twist around to reach the nightstand behind me. I don't even look before I connect the call. "Yeah?"

"It's Zayne." Noah's voice is sharp.

Fuck. I don't need to hear more. I've been dreading this goddamn call for weeks. I shoot up straight in bed, my dick forgotten while everything else in me goes hard.

"What the fuck?" It's more of an automatic reaction than a real question, but I need a minute. "OD?" I demand.

"Yeah. No." He blows out a harsh breath. "Could have been. Got here in time."

I squeeze the back of my neck. Hard. "Who found him?"

"Me and Rye."

"Where?"

"In his room. We're with him now."

"On my way."

I disconnect the call, look at the blank screen for a second, and then throw the fucking thing across the room. It smashes against the wall. I don't give a shit.

"Motherfucker!"

"Baby?" London's hand caresses my side. "What happened?"

"Fuck." I push off the bed and stalk over to my suitcase, digging for a pair of sweatpants. "Zayne."

She's up almost before I get his name out, reaching into her own suitcase.

"Don't know the details," I add, talking but not really thinking about what I'm saying. "Noah and Rye found him. OD or—fuck, I don't know."

By the time I pull a T-shirt over my head, London's got a pair of shorts and tank top on. We're both commando, barefoot, unshowered with bedhead hair, and I don't give a shit. Pretty sure she doesn't either.

"You wanna stay here?" I ask. "I can go find out what hap—"

"I'm coming."

"We can probably keep this quiet, so you—"

"I'm coming."

"English—"

"Goddammit, Knox, I'm coming! I might be new around here, but Zayne is my friend, too!"

I stop and shove my hand through my hair, pushing it away from my face. "Shit." I grab her and pull her close. "Sorry, baby. I didn't mean anything by it. I just—"

She snuggles against me and kisses my neck. "You're being protective, I know. But you aren't doing this alone. *None of you are.*"

She follows me from the room, down the hall to Zayne's room. The door's propped open by the locking bar, and everyone is there, all dressed pretty much like London and me. Zayne sits on the side of the bed, naked, but nobody seems to give a shit. He's leaning forward, his head low, and his hair covering his face.

My sister is kneeling in front of him. It'd piss me off to think of her that close to Zayne's naked dick, but that means nothing right now. Besides, Ajia's right there, and Zayne's not in any condition to even know he's naked, let alone do anything about it.

"Zayne? Sweetie?" Bree takes his hand between hers. "Talk to me. Come on."

He raises his head just enough to peer at her. His hair hides most of his expression. "Thaa you...baby girl?" He sounds more out of it than aware.

"Yeah. It's me." She smooths a hand over his cheek, pushes his hair back, and moves a little closer. "What happened, sweetie?"

"Whaa...yaa...mean?"

I shoot a look around the room. Ajia stares back and then takes a seat next to Zayne on the bed.

"What'd you take, bro?" he asks carefully.

Zayne turns his head just enough to shoot a knowing look in Ajia's direction. "Y'know...dude. Juss a li'l...smack." His smile looks oddly euphoric. "Juss...a...li'l."

"Okay, man. No problem."

I nod. Ajia could have hassled him about the no-drugs rule— he feels that strong about it—but he didn't. I pretty much plan to beat the shit out of Zayne over it myself, but now's not the time.

"Listen, sweetie," Bree's saying. "We're going to get you some help." She rubs his hand with hers.

He shakes his head. At least it gets the hair out of his eyes. "Doan...need...no help."

"Yeah, I know," Ajia says like he agrees. "We just wanna be sure."

"Sure?" Zayne asks, looking from Bree to Ajia and back. "Sure...boouu...whaa?"

"Noah's on the phone with Baz now," my sister says softly. To Zayne? Or to all of us?

I glance over to Noah, who's intent on his phone conversation. Rye's nearby and nods in my direction.

"Not...goin...to no...hospital."

I hear Zayne's slurred speech again. Well, shit. Been worried about Zayne from almost the beginning of the tour. Never thought it would get this far, and now we gotta think about the rest of it.

Hospital. Rehab. More shitty press.

But...*fuck!* This is Zayne. My friend. We can't just let it *go,* no matter what that means.

Thoughts fade, and the inner wrestling match disappears when I catch sight of London heading for the group around the bed. "Zayne?" she says and kneels next to my sister. I'm no more worried about her seeing his naked cock than my sister. Zayne's *that* fucked up

He raises his head a little more. "Hey...there...Lon...don...Kennedy."

She smiles. "Listen, sweetie." She borrows Bree's endearment, and the women share a clearly understanding smile. "We need to be sure you're okay."

"I'm...fine."

She nods. "I know you think you are. But how about you let us at least get a doctor to come by? It'll make *us* feel better. Just to make sure."

He tilts his head back far enough that I can see his eyes, his pupils so tiny I can barely find them. "Make sure...o' what?"

"That you're okay."

"I'm...good."

Ajia throws an arm around him. "I know it feels like it, dude. But you need to let us help. We need to be sure. Dope can be tricky."

Zayne shakes his head. "Nah. That ain...right, Aj. H's...my frien'."

Bree surges up suddenly to sit on Ajia's lap, pulling Zayne against her so she can wrap her arms around him. *"We're* your friends, sweetie. Noah and Rye and Knox and London and Ajia and me." She strokes a trembling hand over his hair. "All of us. We're here for you, and we're gonna take care of you."

He nuzzles his head against her. "Course...you are. You're...the wife."

Jesus, not that again! But Bree just laughs softly and keeps stroking his head. "That's right. I'm the wife."

"Heeeey...whaaa 'bou...London?" He twists around to look at her. "Sorry...baby. We...doan...wanna...leave her...out." He frowns.

English looks at me, confused, but then she shrugs. "No, I'm here, Zayne. It's okay."

"But...whaaa are...you?"

What is she? I look at her, at Bree, at Ajia. *What is she?* What the hell is he talking about?

Bree's eyes widen. "You want another wife, sweetie?" She shrugs. "A different wife?"

"Nooo." Zayne cuddles back against her, and he tilts his head back to look at her. Sort of. "Yer...the wife. Only one." He looks at London again, squinting. "Buu...who's she?"

She takes his hand. "Oh. The...uh—the mistress. I'm Knox's mistress. He can't really have Bree as his wife since she's his sister."

"Oh..." He nods almost seriously, like that makes sense to him. "Buuu...jusss...Knox's? Or all o' ours?"

She laughs, but it sounds forced. "You're not in any bloody condition to worry about mistresses, Zayne Prescott."

He fumbles for his dick but gives up pretty quick. "Maybe...yer riiii."

"Baz is on his way," Noah says under his breath, coming up beside me. "He's looking for a doctor."

"Right." I nod in Zayne's direction. "So all we've gotta do is keep him awake and talking till then."

Noah nods, and we get to work.

We leave Baz in charge when he shows up with the doctor. The rest of us go to Rye's room next door.

"Gonna have to do something," Ajia says the minute the door's closed.

"What?" Bree's scared. I can hear it in her voice, see it in the way she tucks herself against Ajia's side like she won't let go. "What can we do?"

"Rehab." Rye's voice is flat.

"Now?" I ask, knowing as I say it how much I sound like an asshole. Like the tour is more important than Zayne. It's not, but we gotta think about this shit.

Noah looks at me, pissed off, but London holds up a hand. "Let's think," she says, her tone calm.

"About what?" Ajia asks.

"Let's not rush into anything. Let's hear what the doctor says. Talk to Baz. And Zayne. He gets a say in this, too."

"Fuck," says Noah. "You know what he'll say."

"Maybe." She nods. "That doesn't mean he gets the last word. Just that he gets to be a part of the discussion."

We go quiet, not normal for any of us, but none of us ever got this close to the edge before.

"What about tonight?" Rye finally asks.

I blink. "The show."

"Think he'll be able to go on?"

I shrug. "Who knows?"

What are we going to do? I play with the bass a little, but I'm not good enough to switch, even for one night. Besides, who'd play guitar? Ajia can play, but not enough to take on the complicated shit I've written into our songs. Not with a day's notice. Same with Rye, who toys with the guitar, and, far as I know, Noah only plays drums.

"Our shit's arranged for all of us," Ajia admits. "Can't pull anybody out on a day's notice."

"Bollocks."

London's curse makes me want to smile, but I don't. Love that she takes our problems on as hers.

The room goes quiet again, until she asks, "Can we get somebody to fill in? Like...Ayden. He's the bass player for Edge of Return, right?"

I look at the others. A fill-in?

"Never occurred to me," I mutter. Never had anybody fill in. Never needed it. Never even thought about it. We might get messed up from time to time, but we can always play.

"Learn our shit in a day?" asks Noah.

I shrug, wondering. "Ayden's good. He and Zayne have talked music shit. Like some fucking mutual admiration society or something."

"What do we say?" Noah demands. "Zayne almost OD'd and can't go on? Who wants an opening act with that kind of shit going on?"

"Uh...food poisoning?" suggests Bree after a few silent seconds.

"Brilliant!" London nods enthusiastically. "That's enough to knock anybody out for a day or two. It's the first time it's happened, so I bet nobody would even question it."

I'm not crazy about the excuse, but I don't have anything better to suggest. "Okay. Let's talk to Baz."

Ajia shakes his head. "Never thought we'd be here, like this."

Bree whispers to him, something I can't hear, and he kisses her.

Fuck it. I look away, grab for London's hand and pull her close. She's there for us. Again. Feels a little weird to have a woman to trust.

So why do I like it so much?

CHAPTER 21

LONDON

I'M ON EDGE FOR THE REST OF THE DAY, just like everybody else. Relief took over when Baz arrived with the doctor, but the whole shitstorm isn't over. We all know it.

That's what Knox called it. *A shitstorm.* And he's right. Not much we can do about it today, though, so we spend the rest of the day at the venue. We're all here, except for Bree, who's staying at the hotel with Zayne. Even Ajia couldn't get her to leave.

The food poisoning excuse worked, and Ayden agreed to fill in tonight. He and Zayne have been playing each other's stuff for weeks, but they still have a lot of rehearsing to do.

At least we have some peace of mind. The doctor did his thing, checked Zayne out, and gave him an injection of something to help him recover. I don't know all the details, and as long as I don't have to write a press release, I don't need them. Even then, the less I know, the better, it seems sometimes.

No, Knox and Baz need to know what's going on, but the rest of us only care about Zayne. About making sure he recovers enough to get some sort of control over his addiction. Whatever that takes.

Everybody's suspected that Zayne's been using for a while. Even me, joining the group so late, but I suppose that's because of the way I came into things. The middle of another shitstorm created by Zayne being high.

I swallow, watch the guys shift around on stage as they get ready to rehearse another song, and shake my head. Staying true to the Knox I'm coming to know, he's taking it personally. Pissed at himself for missing or ignoring the signs. Pretending it wasn't serious.

Ajia's taking it just as hard. He's the driving force behind the no-drugs rule and thinks he should have seen something. Tried harder. Done something more.

That isn't true. I don't have a lot of personal experience with addiction, but I grew up in Hollywood, for God's sake. I saw friends and friends of friends get bloody messed up. I saw what happened, and if I know one thing, it's that this is totally on Zayne.

If I do anything, it'll be to make sure these blokes know it, too. No one else is responsible, and Zayne has to be the one to pull himself together.

I hear Noah count off the beat and the band kicks into *Tonight,* a kind of heavy, melancholy song that's been on heavy rotation for over a month now. *Lost,* the next release, is just starting to get some airplay, and the band and Bree fly out to L.A. to record the video in a couple of days. Will Zayne be up for it?

I hope so, because I know how this will go. Knox will assume responsibility himself, just like he does with everything else. Not only take responsibility, but take over. Take charge.

Take control.

This time it isn't going to happen that way. Not while I'm around. I'll do my best to make sure every one of us, Zayne included, does our part.

Knox doesn't get to isolate himself over this.

I rest one hand over my abdomen. It's a symbolic gesture more than anything, but I can't resist. The life growing there is so tiny, I probably wouldn't even know about it yet under normal circumstances.

But...nothing about my circumstances with Wycked Obsession has been *normal,* and it just bloody got *ab*normal to the extreme. I've now got one more reason to keep my mouth shut about the baby.

For the time being, anyway.

Bollocks! Bloody fucking hell! Dirty, rotten arsehole.

I swallow a litany of curses. I don't care how early in the pregnancy it is; it's killing me to keep it from Knox. But...how else can I handle it? He's got so bloody much else on his mind.

The last thing I want is for the peanut and me to become an added burden.

Stop it! Stop thinking that way! There's nothing you can do right now. Just wait a few more days...after the video is done. That will be a perfect *time to tell him! He'll be all high, satisfied and feeling in control, after that. It'll still be early, just about the right time to tell him!*

I listen to the advice from my hopefully wiser self and nod. It makes sense. It'll be the best way to handle things, for Knox and for me and the peanut. The band has three or four shows in quick succession after the L.A. trip, then about three days off. I'll tell him then.

I look around resolutely, searching for something—anything—to take my mind off my thoughts. A couple of Edge of Return merch guys are joking around, standing next to a pile of boxes, and I smile. I haven't talked to either of them about the orgy rumors.

It isn't a wasted effort, but neither of the guys give me anything to go on. They both seem to genuinely like Bree and the guys in Wycked Obsession, and promise to warn me about any other gossip.

Just like everyone else I've talked to.

I find a couple other guys, drivers for Edge of Return, but their stories are the same. Nobody knows anything.

"Hey, Steve!" I spot a familiar face.

He's a roadie for Edge, young, fresh out of high school, I'd guess. He's nice enough, I suppose, but shy, with lank, unwashed hair and a face scarred by acne.

"Hi." He doesn't meet my gaze, but I'm not surprised. He keeps to himself and doesn't say much.

"You bring stools for Bree and me to sit on, don't you? When we watch the shows."

He colors and nods.

"Well, thanks. I know we usually say that, but I want you to know how much we appreciate it. Bree said she used to have to stand before you gave her something to sit on."

"Yeah. She…" He lifts a shoulder. "She's nice."

"She is." I smile softly, thinking of Bree back at the hotel, caring for Zayne. *Nice* doesn't begin to cover it.

Still, something about Steve's tone bothers me. A slight harshness, almost an underscored bitterness when he says *nice.*

"It's too bad she's had that trouble lately."

He steps back and swallows. "Trouble?"

"Yes. Somebody started some rumors about her. Pretty bad ones about her and the band."

"That's…too bad." He looks anywhere but at me.

"It is. They were some pretty nasty rumors, especially considering they're all *just friends.*"

Steve shifts from one leg to the other. "Rumors."

He doesn't sound as surprised as some of the others. Most don't have the time or interest in following paparazzi reports and Internet gossip about the people they see every day. But Steve is different, and I swear his voice cracks on a squeak.

My shoulders stiffen, and I look closer. It's clear he's painfully shy, awkward and skittish at his best. He's not the only one around here with a personality quirk; maybe all musicians, roadies, and their road crew are a little weird. But Steve's the *only* one who's acted this uncomfortable when I asked my questions.

Every single one of them said they like Bree and hate the gossip about her.

"Steve?" He won't look at me and keeps sort of sliding backward. "Do you know anything about it?"

"A-about…what?"

"About the rumors."

"I-I don't know what you mean."

"Are you sure?" I work hard to keep the accusation from my voice. "Somebody took a picture of her with the guys in Wycked Obsession. They sent it to the tabloids and made up some pretty awful stuff about her."

He shakes his head and takes a real step back. "That's—" he pauses, swallows "—bad."

I move forward. "It really hurt her feelings. The story was a lie. Those guys are like brothers to her."

"Not Ajia," he snaps, the first real emotion I've seen from him.

"No," I agree carefully. "Not Ajia. She loves him. She has for years. Long before this tour."

"He..." Steve pauses, and his gaze shoots past my shoulder. "He's not good enough for her. No way. He fu—sleeps around. With all the chicks."

I nod with either agreement or understanding. He can choose whatever makes him comfortable enough to keep talking.

"He'd agree with you that he's not good enough for her," I add. "But he doesn't sleep around anymore. He's with her now. He loves her."

"Does he?" Some emotion I can't quite place flares in his eyes. "Then why does he let them call her their *wife?*"

"It's a joke," I say gently. I never suspected Steve until we started this conversation, but now I *know*. Faced with direct questions, he isn't shrewd enough to lie.

"Some joke."

"She takes care of them," I remind him. "Like a sister. Because she loves them."

He frowns but doesn't say anything.

"Bree's really nice. Isn't she?"

"Yeah." It's a grudging admission as he keeps looking anywhere but at me.

"She made you cookies the other day, didn't she?"

He nods slowly. "Peanut butter."

"Your favorite." It isn't a question. Bree told me. She wanted them to be a thank you because he always found her a seat.

"But you weren't so nice in return, were you?" I step closer, and now he looks at me. "You took that picture and started the rumors. Didn't you?"

He swallows and his face screws up for a minute. Then his thin shoulders drop. "She...hurt my feelings. She didn't even see me when he was around. It was only *him.*"

I slip up next to him and put an arm around his shoulders. He's barely taller than I am. "You know we have to tell the others."

"Who?" He looks at me, panicked. "I-I'll get fired!"

"Well..." He's right. He probably will. No famous rock band is going to want a snitch around them. If he gets pissed off at somebody else, what other gossip could he start?

"That's true," I finally admit. "You *could* get fired. But we don't know anything yet."

As long as I keep him away from Knox and Ajia. I sure as hell don't want to bring *them* into this. Either of them would probably want to beat Steve into a bloody pulp, and that's the last thing we need right now.

"Come on." I sigh and spot Maddox Spencer, Edge of Return's version of a cocky rock god, disappear into their dressing room. "Let's go talk to Mad. He'll..." I pause. I don't know what the hell he'll do, but I pretend, anyway.

"He'll help us."

The show goes better than expected. Ayden picked up what he needed to know quick, and the friendly rivalry between Zayne and him helped a lot, according to Ayden. They'd played each other's stuff, talked about developing bass lines, and whatever else musicians shared.

It doesn't matter now. Ayden pulled it off, and the band's regained a bit of euphoria.

Maybe everything *will* be all right.

None of us hangs around backstage after the show. We head straight back to the hotel and congregate in Zayne's room.

He's in bed, pale and bare-chested, tattoos on display. He's got the same Wycked Obsession logo tatted on his right pec, but I don't have time to look at any of the others.

Bree sits on the mattress next to him, cross-legged. She smiles with clear relief when we come in, and then scoots from the bed to throw herself into Ajia's arms.

"Uh...how you feeling, man?" Noah is the first to speak, though the words are slow and careful, like he isn't quite sure how to act.

"I'm...good." Zayne's gaze flickers around the room, darting near all of us but not really stopping anywhere. Definitely not making eye contact. "Better."

Ajia has his arm around Bree, and she's tucked close against his side. "You know we gotta talk about this shit."

"Ajia—" she starts, but Zayne cuts her off with a wave of his hand. Sighs.

"I know. But can we do it...later? Tomorrow? I'm not still fucked up, but..." He pauses, shrugs. "I need a day."

"You taking this shit serious?" asks Knox from behind me. I turn and realize I've never seen him more determined.

This thing with Zayne hit him harder than almost anything else.

"Yeah," Zayne says softly. "I'm taking it serious. Just...give me tonight."

The rest of the band and Bree share looks of uncertainty. I can almost read the exchange.

Is that the best thing for him?

For us?

Is he just avoiding talking about it?

Can we trust him?

I don't have the answers, but a look at Zayne's weary and almost fearful face, and I decide to give him the benefit of the doubt.

"I have something to tell you."

Knox steps closer, tilts his head, his dark eyes searching mine. "About?"

"I found out who did it."

"What?" asks Noah, but Bree gasps at the same time.

"The rumors?" she breathes, her eyes wide.

"The picture?" demands Ajia, his oddly golden eyes dark with sudden fury.

Knox grabs my hand, his fingers tight, and he pulls me around to face him. "Who?" he growls.

"A roadie for Edge. His name's Steve."

"Steve!" Bree's eyes pop wide, and she sags against Ajia. "Steve?" she repeats. "I...I made him cookies. I thought he liked me!"

"Steve?" Ajia says the name carefully, like he's trying to place it. Or maybe commit it to permanent memory, because his voice is like granite.

"The guy who brings me a stool so I can sit when you're on stage."

"Steve." I've never seen Ajia's expression so fierce.

"That motherfucker," snarls Knox, his fingers squeezing mine even tighter. I don't have to look at his face to know how perfectly his expression matches Ajia's.

"What the hell?" demands Noah with a frown, and though Rye doesn't actually speak, he looks as angry as the others.

"He has a crush on Bree," I try to explain. "He's…well, he's young and shy and has acne, and he doesn't know how to talk to girls. He was jealous when she and Ajia got together, and when he heard Zayne joking about her being the band *wife,* he…overreacted and did something stupid."

"Stupid?" Knox bites off. "This is way past fucking *stupid.* "

"I know." I sigh. I pull my hand from his and cup one hand over his cheek. As comfort? To calm him? I can't say for sure, so I add, "I took him to Mad. Left them to work it out."

"Work it out?" Knox and Ajia demand at the same time, sounding equally pissed.

I nod and pull my hand free. "But don't worry. Mad took me aside later and said they let him go. Steve understands that the NDA he signed including everything and every*one* on the tour, and lies are never acceptable."

"Mad said all that?" Knox's gaze flickers between rage and a certain dark humor.

"Well, not in those words, no." I give him a crooked smile. He was a little more…colorful in his explanation, but that's the gist of it."

"I'm sorry," Bree says suddenly, and we all turn like in unison to look at her in surprise.

"Kitten, you don't have anything to be sorry about," says Ajia, kissing the top of her head.

"I feel like it's my fault. I tried to be nice to him, but…he got the wrong idea, I guess. I didn't know he had feelings for me. I—"

"If it's anybody's fault, it's mine." Zayne's still stretched out on the bed, eyes closed, and he doesn't move, but he's still the one who spoke.

"Zayne—"

"You know it's true, baby girl." He cuts Bree off.

"Look, let's not do this." I work hard for a firm but understanding tone. "Nobody knew that Steve was going to react like that. Nobody did anything malicious—except Steve himself. It's his own fault he turned into a bloody wanker, so let's just let it go at that."

"Bloody wanker," shouts Noah with a laugh, and the rest join in.

No one notices when Knox comes up behind me and plants a lingering kiss just where my neck curves into my shoulder. "Thanks, English," he whispers in my ear, his teeth strong over my earlobe before he swirls his tongue in apology. "I needed this today."

CHAPTER 22

KNOX

BOISE. Fucking. Idaho.

We got here overnight and are parked behind the venue. Seems like a cool enough place, even if the schedule here is a pain in the ass.

It's not Boise's fault. The tour brought us here after two shows in Spokane. Just one night, according to the original schedule, but a second show got added somewhere along the line. Baz says the venue schedule got screwed up in the middle of it all, and so we've got a show, a couple of days off, and then another show.

Either somebody called in a favor from the label, like they did in El Paso, or they're just really into Wycked Obsession and Edge of Reason in Boise.

Who knows? More than that, who cares? A couple of days off right now isn't such bad duty, no matter how or where it happens.

We head inside about mid-morning to set up for tonight's show. It's chaos—the usual pre-show controlled chaos—and it kind of soothes me after a week in L.A. This is familiar; the gig in L.A. was our first big-production video, exciting and dull and repetitive in turns and yet all at once. At least that's how it felt to me.

Maybe I was just anxious because London stayed behind with Baz and the rest of the tour. Or maybe the dull, repetitive parts gave me way too much time to think about all the shit going on around us.

None of it will give me any peace. It's all been haunting me since Austin, one thing on top of another on top of another. Solving one, like Mom deciding to divorce that scum Gabe, or London finding the asshole who lied about Bree, only seems to open us up to other shit.

The sperm donor won't give it up.

Zayne getting himself strung out on heroin.

What happened to the rock star dream?

I glance over to the band. Ajia's laughing at Noah, who's trying to do some fancy twirling shit with his drumsticks. Rye's running the scales on his keyboard, and Zayne's tuning his bass. I watch him longest. He looks okay, clear-eyed and alert, even if he's a little jumpier than usual. Far as I can tell, he's held it together since the OD in Seattle, but he's edgy. Brittle. Not himself.

Withdrawals?

Shit. I blow out a breath. Can't put off talking to him any longer. It's the one thing Ajia and I agree on. After tonight, we've got two days to pin Zayne to the wall. He holds it together through the rest of the tour, or he's going into rehab.

No negotiating.

I grab the back of my neck. What else? Gotta call Mom, make sure she's doing okay with the divorce shit. Haven't had a chance yet, but I should sit down with London and Baz to figure out the other stuff. Everything dead and buried with the rumors about Noah and STDs? That asshole Steve really fired? Any retraction or press release we can put to help?

And the sperm donor. He was quiet while we were in L.A., but I don't trust that asshole. He's gonna make a move, crawl out from under whatever rock he's been hiding, and it won't be pretty. He doesn't operate that way.

Hit and run, that's him. Pissing me off, like he's done all my life, and now I think he's wearing on English, too. She's been feeling kind of crappy for a couple of days, probably due to his shit.

I just want that jerk gone so we can find a new normal.

"I'm gonna check on London," I call out to nobody in particular.

Bree waves from where she stands next to Ajia. "Do you think she's all right?"

I shrug. "Dunno. Probably. Said she's been feeling a little shitty. Maybe the flu or something?"

My sister nods. "Let me know if you need anything."

I almost smile to myself as I head for the back door. My two girls get along. First time I've had a woman I'm fucking who didn't act all jealous of Bree. Never made any sense to me, but I never spent much time worrying it. Fuck buddies were temporary; my sister's in my life forever.

And London? I can't answer that right now except I'm glad she and Bree are friends.

Weather's decent in Boise, sunny and warm. Not like Austin in late July—thank God! I can almost enjoy walking to the bus. The metal barricades aren't up yet, and security's working inside this early in the day. The routine of knowing Kel will have his team set everything up in a couple of hours satisfies me.

I'm a couple of steps away from the building when a scratchy voice scrapes through me. "So there's the cocky little shit who claims to be my son."

I spin on my heel before I think about moving, and I'm staring at the face of a man I haven't seen in almost a dozen years.

The sperm donor.

I narrow my eyes, look him up and down. He's old, used up, and beat down. Everything about him shouts it, and it clings to him like a stink. Head shaved, eyes sunk in, skin wrinkled and weathered. Jeans are ragged, shirt stained, wearing some cheap brand of tennis shoes that've seen better days.

Too bad, motherfucker.

I don't give a shit what his life's like now. If that's his truth, it's what he deserved. What he asked for.

What he earned.

"You got it wrong, old man. You're disowned. You don't have a son, and I don't have a father."

I like the sound of the words. No emotion, and yet more honest than anything I've ever said in my life.

"Your cute little baby sister agree with that? Or your mom?"

"Shut up," I snap in spite of myself. He can say anything about me, but Bree and Mom are *off fucking limits.*

"You don't get to know anything about them," I add. "You're not allowed to mention them. Even think about them."

"Still a pissy little mama's boy?" He smirks.

"You're a motherfucker, you know that? Now, what do you want?"

"You know what I want."

I laugh, loud and disgusted and probably the ugliest sound I've ever made. Shaking my head, I take a step toward him. "Too bad. I'm not giving you a dime."

"Then you know what that means." His tone, his dark eyes, are cocky enough to tell me he thinks he still has the upper hand. Guess he doesn't follow social media close enough to know that the orgy rumors are pretty much old news.

Or else the sperm donor just doesn't care. He'll just bring it all up again.

"You really want to do that to your own kids? Your own daughter?" It's less a question than it should be, because the man doesn't have a conscience.

I'm right. His eyes narrow, and something ugly snakes down my spine. Everything shitty I've ever thought about him seems like nothing in comparison to the nasty look on his face.

"You got a lot of room to talk, dickwad. You're fucking her—"

My hand is around his throat before I actually have the thought to move. "Shut the fuck up, old man."

His arms shoot up under mine, and he flexes out to break my hold. An unholy glee dances in his eyes, and he laughs.

"Hit a nerve, did I, dumbass? You don't want to share?"

"SHUT. THE. FUCK. UP."

My voice is a roar, and every bit of fury and hatred I've ever felt for this man over the last dozen years snarls out in the sound. He abandoned us, left Mom as a single mom paying off *his* bills, and he broke Bree's heart. He is *not* going to come along now, years later, to trash talk any of us.

His expression doesn't change. He found my kryptonite, and he knows it.

I don't give a fuck.

I grab him by the shirt collar and jerk him to within a couple of inches. *"Shut. The. Fuck. Up,"* I repeat. "You're a piece of shit who isn't fit to think about them. They don't belong to you. *You. Are. NOTHING."*

My voice grows, becoming a shout again by the end, and I don't give a damn if this shitty excuse of a man knows what matters to me. He's not getting close to Bree, to Mom, and he's not getting any goddamn money. Anybody he tries to talk to is going to see him for the greedy, scum-sucking loser he is.

Somebody needs to take a stand against him, and I'm just the man to do it.

"That what you think, Knoxie-boy?" He laughs in my face.

"Knox!"

London races up from behind him, and I blink. Shit. She must have heard me shouting. I give no fucks if she knows he's here—she already knows everything—except I want to protect her from being contaminated by his disgusting presence.

"Go back to the bus, baby." I don't look at her again. "We're finished here."

The sperm donor slides an ugly gaze in London's direction. "Baby? You got a girl you're fucking besides your sister? How's *that* go over? You got a threesome going with both of 'em?"

My body keeps moving without any conscious effort on my part. One second I'm standing there, worrying about English, and the next my fist connects with the old man's nose. A satisfying *crunch* makes my skin crawl, and then blood gushes over his face, my hand.

"Son of a bitch!" he shouts, and it's like a wild man is suddenly released in him. He head butts me, his forehead banging against my chin before I can jerk my head back. I try to twist away, but he's stronger than I expected, wiry, and almost my height.

We grapple, and I'm not really sure whose fist pummels who. I think I'm getting the better of him; I've got maybe an inch or two and probably forty pounds on him. The more we struggle, the more my aggression comes out. But he's not giving up—and neither am I.

"Knox!" I hear London's shout, but I can't focus on anything besides the sperm donor and his totally unwelcome presence here. He's here, contaminating her, Bree...all of us.

He has to go!

"Please, Knox, stop!"

But we don't. Instead, the old man goes down, and I follow him. We roll across the ground, him pulling my hair and me going for his eyes. Anything to end this farce, to get rid of him, to keep the women in my life safe.

To get rid of this man *forever.*

Other noises join the sounds of our grunts and London's shouts. Some part of my brain notices them, but most of me only cares about punching the ever-living shit out of this man. I connect with his jaw, his gut, and take out on him every bit of rage that I've stored up for the last twelve fucking years.

"You're an asshole," I pant. "You left...a wife and kids...who loved you...for some fucking reason. You want money...? Too fucking bad.... Too late for anything...except this!"

I feel a little ragged, but I have a pretty good right hook left in me. It works, stuns him for a second, and then somebody is pulling me back. Away.

Kel. He's got a fierce look on his face, and he glares in the direction of my old man.

Off balance, I plop down on my ass, breathing hard, and London drops to her knees, throws herself against my chest. "Are you okay, baby?"

I nod but don't answer.

"Is this...him?" she asks, smoothing a soft hand over my cheek. It hurts, but I wouldn't stop her for anything.

I nod again.

"Kel?" She turns to look at our security chief. "Call the police and then get Baz." Her voice hardens. "This man should be arrested. Extortion and assault."

She starts to rise, pushing herself between the sperm donor and me. If I felt better, I'd smile. It's like she thinks she's protecting me from him

Nobody's ever done that for me before.

I open my mouth to tell her...what? Not quite sure, and before I can decide, a growl that doesn't come from me tears through the air.

"You bitch!"

The old man surges to his feet quicker than I thought he could, and he swings wildly. His fist catches London on the jaw, and she stumbles. Before I can do a thing—one fucking thing—he kicks out and catches her square in the stomach. She screams, grabs her belly, and goes down like a lead fucking balloon. I hear the crack of her head against the pavement an instant before I understand what's happening.

She doesn't move again.

♫

Shit's happening all around me, but I barely notice. I can only hold London in my arms and whisper her name.

"London. English, c'mon. Wake up, baby."

She still doesn't move.

My knuckles are raw and bleeding, and some of the sperm donor's blood splashed over the backs of my hands. At least I think it's his, 'cause broken noses can bleed like water in a river. But the blood that really scares me covers my palm.

It's from the back of London's head.

Her reddish-brown hair is draped over my arm, matted at the back of her head where I hold her steady. "Baby, c'mon," I whisper, but...nothing.

A shout draws my attention, and I jerk my head back, looking for the threat. Two of the security guards have the old man restrained while he screams and twists in their grip, and Kel shoves his phone in his pocket.

"Police and ambulance on the way," he calls to me, then turns to intercept Bree and the rest of the band as they come racing from inside the venue. My sister drops to her knees next to me.

"Knox!" she cries. "What happened?"

I glare at the sperm donor. *"He* happened! *That* motherfucker happened."

She follows my look, then glances back at me. "Who is it?"

"Don't recognize me, girlie?" The old man's laugh sounds like a maniac, but he doesn't have the chance to say more when the security guys jerk him back and drag him farther away.

"Knox?" Bree frowns. I can read her confusion so well.

Fuck.

I drop a quick kiss on London's forehead and cradle her close. To show I care? Hoping to wake her up? Or maybe for strength.

"The old man," I finally admit.

"Who?"

I scowl. "Sperm donor. You know, the asshole who ran out on us."

"Our...*father?"*

She sits back on her heels and looks around like she isn't quite sure where she is. I know the fucking feeling.

"Shh, baby."

Ajia puts his arms around Bree, comforts her. Jesus, I didn't even know he was around. For the first time I'm glad he's there for my sister. I gather London closer in my arms. He can see after her, 'cause I gotta take care of English.

Sirens scream in the distance, and my relief grows with the sound. Thank fucking God! I smooth a hand over London's hair.

"Help's on the way, baby. Hang on."

"Knox." Bree's voice, her hand on my arm. She squeezes. "I know you're upset. Worried. We all are. But..." She pauses. Swallows. "What the hell's *he* doing here?"

I want to shout that *he*—the goddamn waste of human flesh sperm donor—is the last of my worries right now. It's true, and I even open my mouth to say the words. But then it's like my English is whispering in my ear.

It's not Bree's fault, luv. She's scared and confused. Help her.

I tilt my head toward the rest of the band, mostly bunched up around Baz and Kel. "Talk to Baz. He'll tell you everything. And I...I'll talk to you later."

She blinks, stares into my face, nods and finally goes to stand. I grab her hand, ignoring the blood staining mine. "I promise. Okay?"

My sister gives me a sad, crooked smile. She leans forward, kisses my forehead. "Okay."

Ajia helps her to her feet, she takes a step and then turns back. "Knox?"

I look up. "Yeah?"

"I love you."

"I love you, too, baby girl."

It's about the last peaceful minute I have for a while. Is it chaos around me after the police arrive, or is it just scrambled inside my head? I'm pissed, no doubt about that, and it's worse when the cops take me aside while the EMTs look after London.

"Goddammit!" I shout, staring in her direction. "Let me go! I have to take care of my girlfriend!"

"Calm down, Mr. Gallagher," says the officer next to me. "Let the professionals do their job, and you help us by telling us what happened."

I tell them everything I know. More than once. I can't take my eyes off my girl as they lift her onto a stretcher. Agitation urges me to punch somebody else, to shove the cop away and rush to London's side. Can't say where I get the control to stop myself.

Don't do anything to put London in any more danger, I remind myself. And so I answer all the questions in as much detail as I can. I suck it up and try to follow the rules until they start loading her into the ambulance.

"Hey, man." I step back. "I gotta go." I gesture behind me.

"We're not done here, Mr. Gallagher."

"But they're...*fuck!*" I shout, sudden panic threatening to choke me as they start to close the ambulance doors. "I don't know what the fuck they're doing. Where they're tak—"

"Knox?"

Bree's beside me again, looking from London to me to the cop. He nods.

"Listen, sweetie." She puts her hand on my arm again in that same comforting way. "You stay here and answer all the questions. Do whatever you need to do. I'll go with London. I won't leave her. I promise."

"But, I..."

She squeezes. "Take care of this part. It's the best thing you can do for her right now."

I swallow. "You...sure?"

"I'm sure."

Don't think I've ever seen such a look of confidence on my baby sister's face. It releases something in me. I trust her like few others, and I know she'll look after London until I can get there. She'll do what I couldn't.

She'll keep my girl safe for me.

CHAPTER 23

LONDON

ALL AROUND ME IT'S DARK AND QUIET. I like it, I think, but…something about it feels wrong, too.

What?

I think, wrinkle my brow, and then I know. Yes! It's a bloody damned headache that's pulsing through me. I take a breath, praying for it to go away, but that's all I can do. Anything else seems beyond me.

Nothing changes.

I stay quiet for a moment, eventually deciding that I must be lying down. That's probably good, under the circumstances. I notice the bed isn't moving, so I guess I'm not on the tour bus. I shift a little, to the left and then to the right. Knox isn't next to me, and a thread of panic bubbles up in me.

Am I in a hotel? If I am, where's he? He's back from L.A. I'm sure of that.

My thoughts race, stumbling through the questions and making my head hurt worse. I know better, try to calm my breathing, but my mind doesn't cooperate so easily. It wants answers.

What do I know for sure?

I'm touring with Wycked Obsession. Doing PR. Knox and I are…something to each other. We have to talk about that. We're in…Spokane—no, Boise! And…what?

There's nothing more.

I pull in a long breath. My chest, my stomach hurt, but the pain is dulled, like it's old or medicated. I breathe again, same result, and so I force my eyes open a bit to look around.

Yes, I was right. I'm in a bed. But…it has rails on it. I'm covered by a thin sheet and blanket, my hands resting at my sides. A needle—an IV?—sticks in the back of one hand with tubing taped down at my wrist. I follow the tube with my eyes, tracking to where it leads to a bag hanging on a tall, metallic stand.

Hospital. I know in a moment that's where I am but…what the bloody hell?

I swallow and look around with a little more interest, and that's when I see him. Knox is slumped in a chair in the corner of the room, eyes closed. Asleep.

"Knox?" My voice is rusty-sounding and hoarse, so I try again. "Knox?"

His eyes pop open and he stumbles to his feet. "English!"

He blinks and stares at me. He looks…bad. Worn. He's got a black eye, his lip is cut and swollen, and his cheek and chin are bruised. His T-shirt is stained with…is that *blood?*

What the hell?

"Jesus, luv," I gasp, reaching my free hand toward him and ignoring the renewed throbbing in my head. "What happened to you?"

"I…" He takes a step toward the door and shakes his head. "Gotta get the doctor."

I drop my hand as he strides from the room like a man on a mission. I suppose he is. That's how he always is when he wants to get things done.

When he returns, he's accompanied by a man in a white coat.

"Ms. Kennedy." The man smiles. "I'm Doctor Brown."

I don't smile back. "What happened?" I ask instead.

The doctor glances toward Knox, who shakes his head slightly.

"What?" I ask.

"You don't remember?" asks the doctor.

I shake my head.

"You were involved in an…altercation." He angles his head sharply in Knox's direction, as though giving him a direct order. "Your boyfriend can explain that part of things in a minute. I'm here to tell you that you've had a fairly serious concussion. You'll be fine if you take it easy for a few days. You may have headaches for a while, but I'll give you something for that."

Boyfriend. My mind snags on the word. We haven't used that term—or anything—to describe what we are to each other. Should I correct the doctor? I don't want to embarrass any of us. Will he make Knox leave and if he thinks we aren't seriously...together?

"All right." I keep it simple. Isn't it important to pay more attention to the doctor and his words than look at Knox's somehow odd and awful expression?

"You have a couple of bruised ribs, but there's not much we can do about that. Again, pain meds will help, manage your breathing, and ice the area to help with pain and swelling. If you take it easy for a few days, you'll feel much better."

"Okay," I agree when Dr. Brown seems to expect some response from me.

"Lastly, I'm afraid that the blow to your midsection was severe enough to terminate your pregnancy. I'm sorry."

Terminate your pregnancy.

If I had any color in my face before the words, I know it's gone now. My mouth hangs slack and my gaze pins itself to Knox's face. He stares back with absolutely no expression at all. It tears at my soul badly enough that I have to look away, and I glance back toward the doctor.

Seconds later my own emotion hits me.

The blow to your midsection was severe enough to terminate your pregnancy.

Terminate your pregnancy.

No more peanut to grow into a healthy baby boy or girl? Knox's baby.

Our baby.

"I..." My voice dies, broken, a cross between a struggle for breath and a sob. "I lost the baby?" It's only a whisper.

"I'm afraid so." The doctor glances between us, pats my hand, and smiles in what I suppose is meant to be an encouraging way. "But there's no permanent damage. You and your boyfriend can try again. Just give your body a few months to recover from all this. Check with your regular gynecologist. I'm sure things will be fine."

I swallow. Emotion radiates from Knox, but I can't look at him again right now. Worse, I can't think of anything to say. Nothing. Tears collect under my eyelids and I blink them away. They keep coming.

"All right," Dr. Brown says briskly as though trying to end the moment. He pats me on the shoulder. "We're going to keep you another night or two for observation. We don't take that concussion lightly. I'll be back to check on you later."

The room is unnaturally quiet after the doctor leaves, and yet it's filled to bursting with Knox's presence. He's always a force to be reckoned with, but now it's somehow *more*. So much more. I stare at my hands, the IV, the thin tan blanket covering me. Anywhere to keep me from looking at *him*.

"You were six or seven weeks along," he says finally. "Did you know?"

I don't have a choice. I have to look at him.

"Yes."

"When?" He sounds a little hoarse, and he won't meet my eyes.

"From almost the beginning," I admit softly. I kept the truth from him; I can't lie *now*.

His gaze slams into mine, his eyes stormy and gray without a hint of green. "How?" he demands.

I take a breath, as deep as I can manage, and close my eyes. To soothe my headache? Maybe, but mostly to block the sight of the growing pain and disbelief in Knox's expression.

"When I got tested. I was late—for the shot, I mean. I got my dates mixed up somehow, and Dr. Jackson wouldn't give me the shot without a pregnancy test. It came back...positive."

His eyes narrow as I explain, and he shakes his head with the words. His stubble has grown to almost a beard, but he still looks almost gaunt. His dark hair shifts over his shoulders with his movement, and I want badly to hold him, to push his hair back from his face, to soothe him into a softer expression, and kiss his pain away.

"Fuck," he mutters. Then louder. *"Fuck!"* He pins me with a dark, fiery gaze. "Goddamn it, London."

My name sounds so foreign on his lips. He calls me *English* and *baby*. I know then that *they* wouldn't have kept that kind of secret from him. London...*she* must be the one who can't be trusted.

"I'm sorry." I have nothing else.

"That was like a week after we fucked the first time."

I nod. "Eight days. There's a special blood test they can do that early."

"Eight days." He blinks. "Eight. Fucking. Days. Were you even gonna tell me?"

He sounds so hard. So cold. I understand, but my stomach plummets all the same. If I know anything about Knox, it's that he doesn't trust easily...and he forgives even less.

"Yes." My voice is thick with tears. "I was. I promise. I wanted to, so many times, but..."

The words die away when he holds up his hand. "No more." He's looking anywhere but at me again. "Not now. I can't do this right now."

"But, Knox, I want to tell you. Everything. I *need* to tell you everything."

"Maybe you should have thought about that before."

"I *did* think about it. I just..." How can I explain that I was trying to protect him, that I was afraid and confused and—

"Then you should have thought about it a little harder. Maybe if you'd told me, I could have protected you from shit like what happened today. Maybe if you'd told me, our baby would still be alive inside you."

I jerk back, the pounding in my head renewed suddenly, and the sharp sound of all my breath leaving my body fills the air.

Maybe if you'd told me, our baby would still be alive inside you.

God, does he mean that? And does it matter? Probably not, because it's true.

I nap throughout most of the day, except when the nurses wake me up every couple of hours. They take my temp, my blood pressure, check the bandage on the back of my head. I try to contain the hope, but it's no use. It comes over me before I even open my eyes…and discover I'm always alone.

Knox isn't here. Is he coming back? Or did I ruin everything with my lie?

You didn't lie. I try to defend myself. *You just didn't* tell *him everything you should have.*

But that's not the truth, and I can't pretend. Maybe I didn't lie to his face, but it was still a lie. A lie of omission, maybe, but it still makes me as guilty as if I'd actually done the deed.

Maybe if you'd told me, I could have protected you from shit like what happened today. Maybe if you'd told me, our baby would still be alive inside you.

Knox's words stay with me, pound through me, steal my breath, bring tears to my eyes, and destroy me with their point-blank accuracy. I have no good argument against them, and I can't blame him for feeling that way. There's more than a good chance that things would have turned out differently—so very differently—if I'd been honest with him. The way it is now…

Well, the way it is, the only thing I'm sure of at this moment is that I'm in love with Knox Gallagher, and I just lost his baby.

I'm in love with Knox.

I lost his baby.

Which tears at me the most? The knowledge that my selfishness destroyed the innocent life that Knox and I created in our white-hot heat? Or that there's no way Knox will want my love after this, and I've just destroyed any chance at true happiness I ever had?

I swallow a sob and blink away the tears that just won't cooperate. I can't seem to do anything else. Just sit here and…grieve.

Will I ever get the chance to tell Knox all the things I want to say? Not that I love him—I can't burden him with that—but explain why I didn't tell him about the baby? My reasons may look shitty now, when it's too late, but can I make him see that I didn't do it to hurt him?

I only wanted to protect him.

The night passes in much the same way, with a constant disruption by the nurses. The only good thing about this concussion is that it makes me groggy enough to fall back asleep after each time I'm awoken. I *like* the escape of sleep, I realize around the middle of the night. It frees me from reality, and that's pretty bloody welcome right now.

In fact, it strikes me after the second or third time, I'll even put up with the odd, disjointed dreams that I can't quite remember. They make some kind of terrible sense in my dream world, but they drift away when I wake up, leaving me only confused and somehow at odds with everything around me. It's like reading a road sign through the dense British fog.

I probably don't deserve the easiness of either, but I'm grateful for it, all the same.

By late morning, I've been awake for a couple of hours, and the grogginess seems to have disappeared for the most part. I keep hoping that Dr. Brown will come in to release me, but I haven't seen him since last night.

Are you sure you want to be released? I can't help but ask myself the question. Where will I go? Am I still a part of the band's entourage? And where's my phone? Without it, I can't call Knox or Baz or anyone else.

Who am I kidding? I don't have the courage to call Knox, anyway.

Do I?

I close my eyes and rest my head against the pillow. How could I *ever* have let things get so bloody out of control? For the first time in...maybe ever, I'm starting to feel like I was part of a family. The Wycked Obsession family. They accept me, I contribute to the well-being of the whole, and I have a sexy, complicated man who makes me feel special and desired.

Had, I remind myself, even as I accept the truth. All of it.

Knox is the man I love, more than anyone else ever. Colin's like a cardboard stick figure in comparison.

And what did I do?

I acted like a goddamn coward and fucked it up. Royally. As bad as anyone ever fucked up any relationship—or wanna-be relationship—in the history of relationships.

"Hey, London."

The voice interrupts my maudlin thoughts—thank God—and I discover Rye coming into the room.

"Rye," I breathe with more relief than I can disguise. "Hi."

His smile is crooked and sad at the same time. "How're you feeling?"

I take a breath and close my eyes in a slow blink. *I will not cry!*

I lift one shoulder. "I've been better."

He nods as he approaches the bed, takes my hand in his, and he squeezes. "I'm sorry about the baby."

My eyes pop wide. "You...know?"

"We all know."

I close my eyes for real this time. "You must all hate me."

He squeezes my hand again before he lets go and drags a chair next to the bed. "No, sweet thing. Nobody hates you."

I open my eyes. Rye, another rock god, looks at me with kind, caring eyes. They're dark, like his hair, and he's big and muscular like Knox. He doesn't affect me in the same way, but something about him makes me feel...cared for.

"Knox does," I finally say sadly. "Knox hates me."

Rye shakes his head, his hair shifting over his shoulders like Knox's does, and a wave of longing pours through me. God, what's happening to me? My feelings are so confused right now! Even more than before.

"He might be kinda upset," Rye admits, "but he doesn't hate you."

"Are you sure about that?" My voice cracks on the question, and I need a minute before I can continue. "He hasn't been back to see me since I first woke up."

Rye nods, but his voice is careful. "Yeah, well...that's not entirely Knox's fault."

"What do you mean?" I'm almost disinterested in the answer.

"Shit's been happening."

"What kind of shit?"

Rye leans back in the plastic chair, crosses one ankle over the opposite knee, and slants me a serious gaze. "I dunno, honey. Not sure you're up to hearing about it."

I half-snort/half-laugh, neither all that convincing. "What are you talking about? I've been stuck in this bed for close to twenty-four hours now. Slept most of that time. I'd say I'm pretty rested."

"What about emotionally?"

I shake my head. "I'm fucked," I admit in the band's vernacular. "But that isn't going to change any time soon. What's going on?"

"You name it. Knox and Baz have their hands full."

"And not with me, you mean?"

"You remember what happened? How you ended up here?"

I blink and think for a second, and then shake my head. "Uh...well...no. Not really. I haven't even thought about it at all until you mentioned it."

It's true, and how screwed up is that? I just accepted where I was, never wondering *why*. It was enough knowing I miscarried. Admitting how much I love Knox. What else could matter?

Maybe if you'd told me, I could have protected you from shit like what happened today. Maybe if you'd told me, our baby would fucking still be alive inside you.

"The concussion—" nods Rye, as though it makes sense, and I'm glad he can't hear my thoughts "—screws up your memory. Your thinking."

"Okay, so what happened?" Suddenly it matters. "How'd I end up here?"

"You got in the middle of a fight between Knox and his old man."

"The sperm donor?" Knox's description of his father is out before I can think about it.

Rye's lips twist, like he might have smiled, but he remains serious. "Yeah. You were trying to play peacemaker, and the old man took it out on you. Knox didn't have a chance to stop it, and when Mr. Gallagher kicked you..."

"I lost the baby."

Rye nods. "I'm sorry," he says, not for the first time. "You went down, hit your head on the ground, and, well, shit snowballed from there."

I don't realize my hands are fists until my knuckles start to ache. I release them, flex my fingers, and try to remember the details of what happened. *The sperm donor. A fight. Being hit. Falling...*

There's nothing. I remember Knox showering that morning, going into the Boise venue while I spent a little more time in bed. I didn't know if it was morning sickness or what, but I was feeling kind of lousy for a few days. If I stayed in bed till late morning, I'd be okay.

Had it worked yesterday? I didn't know.

Then there's…no more until I woke up here.

"The cops arrested Mr. Gallagher," Rye adds after a minute. "The EMTs brought you here, and Knox wouldn't leave your side until you woke up."

I don't remember any of that. "I haven't seen him since then."

Rye leans forward. "He isn't just ignoring you, sweet thing. He was stuck at the police station. Filed charges. Bunch of label and attorney shit to go along with it. And then—"

The words end abruptly, and Rye's expression hardens with an underlying sadness that doesn't fit at all.

"What?" I demand.

He doesn't answer.

"What happened, Rye?"

"Uhm…shit. It's Zayne."

I shoot straight up in bed, sending a new throbbing through my head. I don't give a damn. *Zayne?*

"What? Wait! What happened to Zayne?"

Rye's gaze tracks the perimeter of the room, like he can't look at me. Finally, though, he doesn't have a choice.

"We cancelled our part of the show last night. No choice," he adds when I open my mouth to protest. "Too much shit going on. It worked okay. Edge extended their set, and everybody was real supportive. But…"

"What?" My heart's pounding, my voice hoarse and afraid. Zayne's a nice guy, but shit gets to him. It makes him vulnerable, and he doesn't handle it well. We all know it. "But what?"

"He took everything…pretty bad. He…shit, he got himself some dope, London. Bad shit, or else he just didn't fucking know when to stop."

"Oh, God." I can't find any other words.

"He did it again. OD'd. Noah got to him, had to call the ambulance this time. He's gonna survive, but we can't let him finish the tour like this. Label's having a shit fit, so Baz and Knox are doing damage control."

"Zayne." My heart aches for him. We aren't close, but he's always been sweet to me. I've seen him with Bree, and I see how deeply he feels for those he loves. Even Knox.

"Rye?" I swallow but force myself to say the words that want to choke me. "This is my fault, isn't it? I know Zayne takes things really personally, and knowing what I did to Knox—"

"No!" Rye's out of his chair and next to the bed faster than I can blink. He grabs my hand with his. "Stop it, sweet thing. This ain't your fault. It's Zayne's. His way of…coping when things go to shit. It's just a goddamned excuse."

I blink away the tears stinging behind my eyelids. God, every one of these guys—and Bree—are becoming like the family I never had. And family lets you off the hook when you don't deserve it.

I breathe, but not too deeply. Bruised ribs teach you quick just how far to go.

"Thing went to shit pretty good because of me."

"Nope." Rye shake his head, squeezes my hand, pulls free. "Lots of other blame to go around. Mostly Zayne's."

He's got a stubborn look that I haven't seen often, but I give into it all the same. I just don't have the strength to fight one more stubborn man.

"What happens now?" I ask finally.

"He's going into rehab. Knox found him a place in Austin. Noah's taking him."

Bollocks. This is serious!

"And the band?"

Rye smiles, but there's a forced cheerfulness about it. "We're skipping the Boise shows, going on to Salt Lake as soon as we get shit wrapped up here and you get sprung from this joint." He waves his hand toward the door.

"You want me to go with you?"

The question is out before I realize how pitiful it sounds. There are so many other things I want to ask, like who's going to play the bass with Zayne in rehab, and is there a chance that Mr. Gallagher can get out of jail on bond? But the one I asked—*You want me to go with you?*—is the only one that matters right now.

"Shit, sweet thing! Course we do! You're part of the group now."

I can't help myself. "You think Knox feels that way, too?"

Rye smiles. A real one this time. "I know so, honey. Just give him some time. He'll come around."

CHAPTER 24

KNOX

THE BOTTLE OF JACK SHIMMERS IN THE BRIGHT SUMMER SUN. I'm camped out in the tour bus, empty glass and half-empty bottle of whiskey on the table in front of me. The Jack started out full this morning, and now, at—I claw for my phone to check the time— 2:17 p.m., it's half gone.

I frown. Shit! Been like three hours since I started drinking. I ought to have more of a buzz than this!

I pour myself another drink and pound it back. It don't burn anymore, my gut don't churn, my head don't swim. I don't get the feeling of satisfaction I'm looking for, either.

I don't feel a fucking thing.

I drag my eyes around the empty bus. No wonder! It's no fun to drink alone!

"Fuckin' shit," I mutter to no one and about nothing in particular.

Or maybe it's everything.

I'm tired. I admit it. Exhausted. Sick and tired of all the shit that's destroying everything I love.

I flop back against the seat and grab the back of my neck. How did it all end up like this? I'm an ordinary guy with some kind of talent for playing the guitar. I write songs with my best friend—jury's still out on how I feel about Pipes right now—and I work my ass off to make us and Wycked Obsession a success.

So how the fuck did all this bad shit happen?

And there's a shit ton of it.

I stare at the bottle of Jack Daniels like the answers are there. They aren't.

Big surprise.

It makes me think of our first tour. It was hard. We had no fuckin' clue what it would be like. But when we got home to Austin, we got our shit together. We thought. This tour was supposed to be fun. *Different.*

Different? A different town every night. Different crowd. Different girl. Every thirteen-year-old boy wannabe rock star's dream.

What a buncha shit! Instead, it's all fucked up. The shit with Gabe. Ajia and Bree hooking up. Those fuckin' orgy rumors. Noah and the STDs. Zayne ODing.

What else could have gone wrong?

I laugh, a fucked-up sound, and pour myself another drink.

"The sperm donor." Can't forget about him.

I toss back the shot and try to force his ugly face from my memory. It doesn't work, and that just pisses me off. Why couldn't he just stay a faceless jerk that I practically forgot?

No, he had to come back, looking better and worse than I expected. Better in that he's just a disgusting excuse of a man, not the larger-than-life asshole he grew to be in my head. Worse in that he *is* just that disgusting excuse of a man.

And, like always, he fucked up everything.

Bree knows about him now. Saw him. And Mom knows, at least some of it. Then there's London…

Fuck.

"Fuck, fuck, fuck."

"That good, huh?"

Ajia steps up into the bus, and a second later he helps Bree inside. I shoot 'em both a sour look and pour another shot.

"Knox?" My sister frowns, heads straight for me, scoots into the booth across from me. Ajia slides in next to her.

"What?" I swallow the whiskey.

"Did you…" She slants a gaze at Ajia. "Have you been drinking all day?"

I laugh. "Nope. Only a cuppla hours."

Her eyes pop. "More than half a bottle of Jack in a *couple of hours?*"

"Hell." I grin, but it feels all fucked up. Don't let that stop me. "Last tour, any one of us coulda pounded the whole bottle back in less time than that."

Ajia gives her a nod that looks all too sheepish for me. "What? You got no balls, Pipes, now you're with my sister?"

"Knox." Bree's voice is a little sharp. "Don't...you know, be that way. Everything's going to be okay. You know that, right?"

"Ya think?"

"I know." She nods. *"He*—Dad—won't be getting out of jail anytime soon. The D.A. told Baz they're looking at more charges. And he's got warrants."

"He can't afford a lawyer," Ajia adds. I almost wanna laugh, 'cause he sounds so satisfied the old man ain't doing so well, but then he continues. "He's got a public defender. The D.A. figures he'll go for a plea, so you won't have to come back to testify in a trial."

Too bad. Love to come back here and pin his ass to the fuckin' wall.

"You see him?" I shoot a gaze at Bree.

"No." It's flat. Emotionless. Different from how she used to sound about him. Kinda makes me sad. Not for him. Never him. But her. She really *has* lost her innocence this tour.

Ajia slips an arm around her, hugs her tight. Kisses her head. I'm glad.

What the fuck?

I blink and narrow my eyes. Either I'm getting used to them as a couple, or I'm totally shitfaced. Could be either.

"I thought about it," my sister admits after a minute, "but for what? He didn't want to have anything to do with us. He just wanted...money." Her eyes look damp, but the tears never fall. "I get it. Better than before. He doesn't want us? Well, fuck him. We don't need him."

She snuggles against Ajia's side, adding, "We've got each other."

She looks from him to me, smiling, and even in my half-drunk state, I don't miss the love in her expression. Not just for him, but for me, too.

It soothes a small, ragged place in my heart. Maybe I couldn't protect her like I wanted to, but she's...okay. And Mom might've had to hear about it, but she didn't have to see it.

See him.

Asshole.

I frown and pour another shot. It don't make me feel as good as I wish it would.

Bree lays a hand on mine. "Don't you think you've had enough?"

I stare at her tiny hand covering mine. No matter what I did or didn't do—anything I've ever done—she's there for me. Always has been. Loves me. And I love her. But...that ain't enough right now.

It just ain't enough.

I pull my hand free and throw back the shot. "Not even fuckin' close."

Nobody says anything for a minute. What's there to say? If she don't get it, Ajia will.

Till the whiskey's gone, I'm incoherent, or I pass out, ain't had enough.

"Noah's taking Zayne to Austin tonight," Ajia says finally. "Label ponied up for a charter. He'll stay a couple of days to get it all settled, then meet us in Salt Lake."

"We leave soon. Early evening. Edge'll do their last show here and then—"

"No business." I interrupt Bree.

"What?"

"Tomorrow. Don't wanna hear it now."

She stares at me, eyes narrowed and probing. Frustrated.

Doesn't she get it? I just can't do it now.

"London's being released today. Baz is taking care of the arrangements."

I stare back at her, giving her...nothing. It's all there, in my head, my heart, and that's where it's going to stay. Don't understand it, and so not ready to bring it out into the open.

"You haven't mentioned her name. Once."

I lift a shoulder. "Nothin' to say."

"You wouldn't leave her side until she woke up. Since then…" Bree lets the words die away but pierces me with a look. "You haven't gone to see her again."

I shrug again.

"Rye saw her yesterday. We thought she might be released, but they kept her another day. Ajia and I went this morning."

I stare from my sister to Ajia, and then out the window.

It's quiet. I don't move. They don't, either. Not until Bree suddenly smacks her palm on the table. "Goddamn it, Knox! What the fuck is going on?"

"Baby," Ajia soothes, but she hardly seems to notice.

"You two are close," she adds, but I cut her off.

"Were."

"No. *Are.*" She plants her palms on the table and leans toward me. "You didn't see the look on her face when it was us this morning and not you. So what the hell happened?"

I skip the shot glass and pour Jack straight down my throat. It burns this time—I cough—and bang the bottle back to the table. I glare in a way I know is pissed off, and I don't give a shit. In fact, I hope to hell it is.

I know my sister, and she don't give up when she wants something. Her thing with Ajia is a prime example. So why fight it?

"She lied to me."

"About what?"

I shoot the room an *are-you-fucking-kidding-me* look. "What do you think?"

"The baby? But it was so early. She—"

"Knew. She knew. And she didn't tell me."

"How long?" my sister demands in a frosty voice. For me or for English?

I shrug, but Bree repeats, "How long did she know?"

"Long enough."

Ajia snorts. "Well, fuck. Do you blame her?"

"What?" I snap.

"Jesus Christ, dude, think about it for a second. Lot of shit been going on since you met her. Fuck, it's *why* you met her. The orgy rumors started it all. Then there was your old man, which you fucking kept from *everybody else,* and Zayne's shit. When, exactly, d'you think she'd of had a chance?"

"She had plentya chances."

"C'mon, Knox, put yourself in her shoes." Bree's irritated. "You two haven't been together that long. It must have been a hell of a shock. She probably needed some time to figure it out for herself."

I pour myself another shot and swallow it before I answer. "She had time." I'm not telling 'em anything more.

"She was probably scared." Ajia looks serious. "You're kind of..." He pauses.

"Intense," Bree supplies. "We're used to your shit, but somebody who isn't...well, it can't be easy."

"Plus, after the shit with Farren—"

"What the ever-lovin' fuck does *that* have to do with anything?" I snap, glaring at the others in a way that should fry them.

"She knew."

"What?" I stiffen up straight, and my pissed-off stare transfers straight to Ajia. "Whaddya mean, *she knew?* She knew *what?"*

"That Farren faked a pregnancy to try to get you back."

I flop back against the seat. "And how would she know *that?"*

"We told her."

"We told her? Who is *we?"*

"Knox..." I hear the soothing tone in my sister's voice, but something—rage, fear...uncertainty?—races through my blood. I can't do a damn thing but stare.

She knew Farren faked a pregnancy.

"Pipes?"

He lifts a shoulder, like it's no big deal.

No big deal? It's a *huge* fucking deal!

"It was after that phone call when we were at the label," he finally says. "We didn't know who called. Never in a million years would have guessed your old man."

He shoots a tender gaze in Bree's direction, like he's sorry for mentioning the sperm donor or some shit. She gives him a soft smile, all romantic and loving, and it just irritates the hell out of me.

"And?" I prompt impatiently.

"And London was worried about you. She wanted to do something. Help. You were so pissed off, and she...well, fuck, man, she was upset. Confused. Worried. I don't know."

He shakes his head. "Anyway, we—the band—ended up telling her the shit we thought it might be, and somehow Farren came up. So we told her what happened."

"Well, shit." My sister glares at me. "No wonder she didn't tell you right away. Jesus, Knox."

"What?" I glare back.

"C'mon. Think about it!"

"What?" It's almost a shout this time.

"She knows you. We all fucking *know you,* Knox." Is that a growl from Bree? "You're pissed off half the time, intimidating as fuck, and you hold grudges. So, yeah, I get it if London needed a little time to come to terms with that kind of a surprise."

I grab the bottle of Jack. "Fuck. You." I shoot another death-ray gaze at my sister and her boyfriend. *"Fuck. You."*

I chug every bit of the whiskey left in the bottle, stand, and ignore the way the room sways around me.

"Fuck you," I say again, balancing myself with one hand on the table. "You wanna take London's side? Go ahead."

"Knox!" Bree's tone should probably tell me something, but I can't make it out. "That is *not* what we're doing!"

"Sure looks like it ta me."

The words—Bree's and mine—sound kinda funny, like they're coming from far away. Shake my head, proud of the way I can hold my booze, so that can't be it.

"Knoooooox."

Sounds kinda long and drawn out. I blink, see Ajia moving, Bree right behind him, even feel my ass plop down on the floor. Then...nothing.

CHAPTER 25

LONDON

THE TOUR BUS LOOKS JUST THE SAME. As much as I hate seeing it, I like it, too. Yeah, everything's different, like a big, bloody explosion blew up everything around me, but a sense of peace soothes me from knowing some simple things in life haven't changed.

"London?"

Rye comes up behind me, smiling softly.

"Rye! Hi."

"How are you?"

I try to smile, but it feels too weak. I'm grateful when Rye doesn't mention it.

"I'm…okay. Baz just dropped me off."

"You ready to go inside?"

"Uh…yeah. I guess so."

He smiles again and takes my arm, helps me inside like I'm elderly, or maybe broken. I do feel a little bit fractured in places, fearful and sad and guilty, and yet trying somehow to stay strong.

How am I ever going to do that?

Reaching the top step, I discover Ajia and Bree are snuggled on the couch, watching a movie. It's…*This is Spinal Tap.* I surprise myself with a smile.

Rye laughs. "How many times have you seen that, man?"

Ajia grins. "A few."

"Hundred," adds Bree.

"Hey, it's a classic!" Ajia defends their choice.

"Well…yeah." Rye shakes his head, still smiling. "Yeah, okay. You got me there, bro."

"London, sit down!"

Bree pulls herself from Ajia's arms and rushes over to give me a hug. She takes me by the shoulders and seats me on the couch opposite from where Ajia sits. She takes my hand in hers and squeezes.

"How are you?" Her sparkling green gaze carries all the intensity of her brother's. Her look is caring.

"I'm okay."

"You're sure?" The guys are silent, letting Bree take the lead.

"Positive." I nod.

"And aftercare?"

"Baby," calls Ajia, and she slants her eyes in his direction. "Give the woman some privacy."

I smile, maybe a little crooked, but I can't help it. It feels good to have these people care about me. It's bloody soothing after Knox—

Nope, not going there right now. Only when I'm alone.

"I just want to help her," says Bree primly, and my smile straightens.

"It's okay. Thanks. Really. Physically I'm good. I'm free to follow my normal routine. The doctor gave me some pain meds for headaches if I get them, and I have to be careful of the ribs for a while. Ice if they hurt, no carrying things…you know." I don't mention the huge bruise just below my ribcage.

Bree hugs me carefully. "You let us help you, okay? We're here for you. However you need."

"Okay…"

The word sounds a lot more tentative than I mean it to, but…how can they be so nice when Knox was so angry? Aren't they upset with me, too? They have every right to be.

As if sensing my dilemma, Rye plops down on the other side of me. He lays a light hand on my knee and repeats Bree's words. "We're *here for you,* sweet thing." "Whatever happened between you and Knox stays between you two, unless you want it different. But you're our friend, too. We ain't gonna abandon you."

Tears prickle behind my eyelids. They all know enough about what happened; I can tell by the tender look on Ajia's face, the way Rye squeezes my leg and lets go, the way Bree hugs me again.

"Where is…everybody?" I ask to ease the mood.

"Noah's in Austin with Zayne." Ajia seems to take up the role of leader when Knox isn't around. "He'll meet up with us in Salt Lake tomorrow. Knox is—"

"Passed out in the bedroom," inserts Bree, disgusted. No doubt about it.

"Passed out?" I repeat. "As in…drunk?"

"As a skunk," says Ajia.

"But…" Knox drinks. I've seen him drink a fair amount and still keep himself under control. But for him to get drunk enough to pass out?

Shit.

"Knox doesn't get drunk." The words are unnecessary, but they come out on their own.

"Not often," Ajia agrees, "but when he does, it can be epic."

Epic. Is he that bad off this time?

"I…" I look among the others. "Should I go to him?"

Don't be an idiot! A voice of self-preservation shouts in the back of my mind. *He turned his back on you when you needed him. Why should you go to him now?*

But another part of me knows that the things eating at Knox are my fault. They eat at me, too, and I understand how they can seem bad enough to drink enough to pass out.

"What do you want to do?" asks Bree.

I don't answer for a minute, and Rye offers, "You can hang out here with us if you want to. Or just rest in your bunk. Whatever you want."

"You can let Knox come to you," suggests Ajia. "He owes you that."

I consider the words. *Let Knox come to you. He owes you that.*

Let Knox come to you.

God, how I'd love that to happen! For Knox to make the gesture to talk to me. Give me the chance to tell him everything I couldn't say when I should have, and that he wouldn't listen to the other day. But I know better than to wish for that much of a dream.

Knox won't do it—and I don't deserve him to. I know that, too. He doesn't owe me a bloody thing.

"No." I let out a soft sigh. "I'm the one who created this mess with my lies. I can't—"

"You didn't lie!" Bree's defense warms me.

"Maybe not directly. But I kept secrets I shouldn't have. I owe it to Knox to go to him. To explain."

"Are you sure you want to?"

Bree will give me an out, but I can't take it. "Yes. Absolutely."

And I mean that. It might change nothing, but I owe it to Knox. Maybe even want it for myself, though I can't say I deserve it.

For everything that could have been—should have been—I'll take the chance.

The bed in the tour bus's only real bedroom is queen sized. It fills almost the whole space. Knox and I spent some beautiful moments here.

Well, at least some lust-filled moments. I'd like to smile with the memories, but I don't have it in me.

He's stretched out on his stomach, still dressed in his jeans and a T-shirt, stocking-footed. I wonder if Bree's the one who pulled off his boots. His head's turned to one side; his hair falls over his cheek. He's snoring a little.

My love.

Seeing him this way, even knowing he might hate me, I still embrace the truth. On the inside, at least.

I love Knox Gallagher, and I have for a while now. Probably since I first saw how much he's willing to do in order to protect his family. Blood and the others he adopts into his life, automatically making them *family*. It takes a special man to care that much.

And me? I'm under no illusions, have no expectations. I'm not sure he ever cared that way about me, and now he never will. I'll probably never get the chance to tell him how I feel about him, and maybe it's just as well. I squandered whatever rights I might have had with my secret and lies, even if they were *only* lies of omission, and the time may never be right again.

What words might he accept from me? I shake my head slowly, sadly, watching as he shifts and lets out a soft breath. Not telling him about the baby changed everything. He's made that perfectly clear, and it's my job to accept it. Gracefully. Generously. Apologetically.

Can I do it, even with these holes in my heart and soul? Holes left from losing the peanut. And now Knox.

What choice do I have? I have to try to accept them.

I deserve them.

I didn't do right by him, and I can't pretend otherwise. It was selfish and cruel, and even though it made sense to me at the time, it was the absolute *wrong* thing to do.

Worse, I pretty much knew I was wrong about what I was doing to Knox at the time. Even so, I let fear make my decisions for me. Now, I might never get the chance to make it up to him—and if I don't...well, it's my own damned bloody fault!

I stiffen my shoulders, my spine, but only in the recesses of my mind. Physically, I move carefully, peeling off my loose tank top and wiggling out of my yoga pants. Bree brought them to the hospital today, the loosest clothes I own, and I'm glad for them now. The bruised ribs still make certain actions difficult, but I suppose I deserve the pain.

In my plain white bra and panties, I crawl into the bed next to Knox. He sprawls over two-thirds of it, but there's enough room for me to curl up on the far side. I slip under the covers and try to remain still.

What do you think you're doing? a voice of horrified uncertainty demands in my mind.

Truthfully, I don't know. I just know I'm feeling a little brittle suddenly, maybe after seeing Knox in this new and vulnerable way, or facing the unflinching truth of my thoughts. Whatever explains it, I need to be close to him. I won't push myself on him; that wouldn't be right. But if I'm here, close enough to be in bed with him, to draw on his energy, his strength. Even if we aren't touching, maybe it'll help.

I just want to lay here and look at him. Love him. Steal a few peaceful moments. Pretend for a little while.

My eyes water with unshed tears, and I blink them away. Close my eyes. Breathe. And, eventually, I fall asleep. I must have, because the next thing I know, I'm still laying on my side, facing Knox, but his eyes are open. He's looking at me.

Has he been staring for a while? Is that what woke me?

I swallow. "Are you okay?"

He blinks and keeps staring. "No."

On the surface, the word sounds stiff and maybe unfeeling. I know better. Oh, maybe his feelings aren't for me, but I hear the underlying pain and a thousand other emotions that he doesn't want to acknowledge. That doesn't mean they aren't there.

I watch him for a few silent moments before I crawl slowly, carefully, from the bed. "Let me get you some water and aspirin."

I pull on my tank top but forego the yoga pants; I'm just going to the bathroom and the kitchenette. Besides, modesty is something that lives on a sliding scale on a rock band's tour bus. There just isn't enough privacy to get too hung up on it.

I slip into the bathroom first, take care of my own business, check for spotting. I'm clear, and oddly enough, I have to sniff away a few tears. I know intelligently the D and C was the right thing to do medically after the miscarriage, but I hate that all evidence of the peanut is gone from my body now. The spotting felt like I still had some small connection left, but that's gone now, too.

I blink away the last of the tears, wash up, and collect a couple of aspirin. Next I grab a bottle of water from the refrigerator. Rye's watching a movie—I can't tell what—and Bree and Ajia are nowhere to be seen. In their bunks, I guess. The bus is moving, which tells me we're on the way to Salt Lake City.

I glance at the clock on the built-in microwave. Almost eight o'clock.

My eyes pop. Whoa...three hours since I got back from the hospital! Guess I *did* nap.

Knox was out longer than that. Was it long enough that he's somewhat recovered? Enough to talk?

I swallow, knowing what's coming and, just as clearly, that I can't put it off. I did that already, and look how that turned out!

Back in the bedroom, I close the door quietly behind me. Knox is on his back now, still stretched out across the bed, but his smoky gray eyes watch my every move.

"We're on the road," I say as I offer Knox the aspirin and water. "To Salt Lake, I guess."

He pushes up on one elbow, tosses back the painkillers, drinks some water, and otherwise just keeps staring at me. I back away towards the foot of the bed, not sure what else to say or do.

I'm in mid-step when the bus swerves a little. I twist to catch myself against the wall, and pain sears through my midsection. Gasping, I grab my middle, lean forward at what turns out to be an awkward angle, and breathe as deeply as I dare. I count to ten, pant a little, count again.

A handful of seconds, maybe even a minute, pass until the pain retreats to no more than a dull throbbing. I swallow and look up. Knox is watching with that damned unreadable gaze.

"You okay?" he asks, sounding all too distant.

"Yes," I breathe and try to smile. I fail. "It's the ribs. Doctor Brown told me bruised ribs can be almost as painful as if they were broken. I just need to be careful for a while."

He nods once but doesn't say anything.

I finish my walk around the bed, breathing carefully with each movement, and perch lightly on the other side of the mattress. I assume Knox won't mind, but the instant it's too late, I reconsider. I glance around anxiously, but there's nowhere else to sit in the small room.

He's sitting up now, propped against the faux headboard, his ankles crossed. His jeans are stylishly ripped, and his T-shirt is vintage Rolling Stones. His hair flops over his forehead, his shoulders, leaving him looking a little ragged, hungover, and miserable.

How much of that is my fault?

"Can we talk?" I ask softly.

His eyes go dark, and his expression hardens. "I don't know—"

"You've been avoiding me," I interrupt before he can put me off completely. "I know this probably isn't the best time, but I need to say some things." I pause, swallow. "They haunt me…" My voice cracks. "You may think I don't deserve it, but please, let me explain."

I know better than to take a deep breath, so I try to out-stare Knox. Finally, slowly, he nods.

"All right. I'll give you that."

"I…" I close my eyes, sort through my thoughts, gather my strength. With a swallow, I force myself to reveal myself as clearly and openly as I've ever looked at anyone.

I try again. "I didn't lie when I said I was protected, that I was getting the shot for birth control. I was, but I hadn't been on it long. About six months, and I was due for my third dose. Everything I told you was the truth when I said it. I just…got my dates mixed up."

Knox doesn't try to hide his disbelief. "And how did you manage that?"

"I told you about Colin." I wait until Knox nods. "My trips to England got me confused about the dates, I guess. Or maybe it was everything else. Breaking up with him. Graduating from college. Interviewing with the label—and you."

I drop my gaze for a moment, but force myself to look at him again. I might feel weak, but I don't have to show it.

"I don't know," I add with a soft sigh. "All I can say is I *thought* I'd gotten my last shot *after* spring break. Turns out it was before. I didn't know until I went to get the STD test. By then, it was too late."

"And so you decided to get a pregnancy test?" Knox demands, his voice filled with disbelief.

"No." I set my jaw, pretending like I don't recognize his attitude, and shake my head. Maybe his tone *does* irritate the crap out of me, but he's entitled to be pissed. "My doctor insisted I have a pregnancy test when I told her I'd—*we'd*—had unprotected sex. There's some special blood test they can do early. I waited for the results, and they came back positive."

"And then you decided to keep it your own little secret."

His anger slices through me. Enough so that I take a breath, as deep as I dare.

"No." I shake my head sadly, and force myself to meet his fierce gaze. "It wasn't like that at all, lu—Knox."

I link fingers, squeezing them tightly. *Oh, God.* I almost let the endearment slip. As much as I'd like to recapture those soft, gentle words and the feelings that accompanied them, I know better.

Now isn't the time.

"Yes, I *did* want to keep it to myself the first couple of days." I lean forward to recapture his flickering gaze, mine earnest and his...remote. Worse, he seems willing—or able—to look at me for only so long before he turns away.

Does he hate me that much?

"I needed to come to terms with it," I admit. "I was shocked. Overwhelmed. Scared. I'd lied to you, even though I didn't know it at the time. I knew you'd be upset. I...knew about what your ex had done."

He scowls. "They shouldn't have told you about that."

"Maybe." I lift a shoulder. "I was glad then, because I thought it helped me be more sensitive to your feelings. Now...I'm not so sure."

"And after those couple of days? You keep your secret for a lot longer."

I drop my eyelids but open them again almost immediately. My mistakes glare back at me too sharply from the veil of darkness.

"You'd had the call from your—the sperm donor," I correct, "and then the rumor about Noah and the STDs came up right after that. I wanted to wait until that died down, but he—the sperm donor—kept making threats and things stayed...difficult."

Knox stares at me, his lips parted and his eyes narrowed. He leans toward me, just enough for it to seem almost like a threat. I force myself to hold steady.

"And what the fuck does *that* have to do with you telling me you were *pregnant?* With *my kid.*"

I swallow, but my voice cracks, anyway. "I...didn't want to add to everything else. Be another burden. When I told you, I wanted it to be...well, happy news, I guess."

"Happy news?" He shakes his head. "You telling me you were happy about it?"

"I *was!*" I scramble to my knees, pausing to wrap a trembling arm around my middle and pant a few fast, shallow breaths. "You can't fault me over that, Knox. I messed up in a lot of ways. I was scared, yes, and had no bloody clue what I was going to do or how I'd manage, but, yes. I was happy about the peanut."

"The peanut?" A soft emotion flickers through the storm clouds in his eyes, and then it's gone.

I nod. "That's what I called her. Him. The baby was my peanut."

"Your peanut," he repeats. "And what about me? Did it ever fucking occur to you that *I* might have wanted—*needed*—something to be happy about? Something *good* with all the *shit* I was dealing with?"

"I..." But the word fades on a gasp. *"Good?* Is that really how you would have seen it, Knox? Because I remember a lot of that shit you were dealing with. Your father and the rumors about the band weren't enough? What about Zayne's first OD? Can you *really* say that you'd have seen me being pregnant as a *good thing?"*

I read the shaky emotion on his face this time: Uncertainty. Even as it satisfies the part of me that prayed to make him understand, it hurts, too. Yes, I made my mistakes and I'm willing to own them, but Knox's doubt brings all those old feelings back again.

"I thought so." I nod, once.

"What?"

"Now, when it's too late, you wish you'd known about the baby. But you didn't experience it from my perspective, Knox. You weren't scared. You weren't almost paralyzed, not knowing the right thing to do. I watched people take and take and take from you, and I didn't want to do that. I didn't want to be like the rest of them. I wanted to be the *one person* who didn't take advantage."

"No, you didn't fucking take advantage." His mouth is flat. "But you didn't give me the truth, either."

"No, I didn't. I...protecting you somehow became more important than the truth."

"Protecting me?" He jerks back like I hit him or something.

"I guess that's what I thought I was doing. But I was wrong, and I owe you an apology. It wasn't my place to control the information you should have had. You trusted me, and I took advantage of *that.*"

He doesn't say anything, and so I gather up any shred of dignity left to me and push carefully to my feet. I move slowly, one hand on the wall for balance, stopping only when I reach the door.

I turn back to him. "I am *so sorry,* Knox. Words will never be enough to make it up to you. But please know how deeply I regret everything. You were right. If I'd been honest about the baby, things might have been different all the way around. And I'll have to live with that for the rest of my life."

CHAPTER 26

KNOX

TWO DAYS.

Takes me two fucking days to get over that goddamn hangover. Not that I let anybody else know I'm hurting. Last thing I'm gonna do. Doesn't matter, anyway. Shit's still way too screwed up to worry about ridiculous shit like *how I feel.*

The minute we pull into Salt Lake, we hit the ground running. Got a full day of auditions scheduled. Seems like Baz or the label sent every goddamn bass player on the West Coast to Utah. It's just a temporary gig; Zayne might be on the shit list right now for putting us in this position, but he's still Wycked Obsession's bass player. Always will be, unless he wants out.

He says he doesn't.

Noah's still in Austin with Zayne, so only Ajia, Rye, and I are there for the auditions. Well, Bree's there, too, mostly 'cause she's been with us so long. She has a feel for what works and what doesn't. Yeah, and maybe to see if she learned anything in her two years at Butler College.

London stays back at the tour bus. She's working with Baz and the label to put out the fires left from the shitstorm in Boise. Explaining the sperm donor without giving any details, and putting some kind of decent spin on Zayne's bullshit. Whatever that means.

At least she doesn't have to say anything about the baby.

God. My head's finally catching up with my heart, and my gut clenches, my heart skips a beat. Shit. How does she *feel,* trying to write press releases about this shit? Must hurt like a son of a bitch.

I am such an asshole. Been fighting the image of pain, sorrow, the regret in English's eyes. I saw it all. Yeah, she *should* have told me about the baby—it *was* my right to know—but she didn't deserve what the sperm donor did, anymore than Bree or my mom or I did.

And she sure as hell didn't deserve the way I acted.

Haven't been ready to talk about it again, and she made it easy for me. She pretty much stayed in her bunk, no matter how hard Bree begged her to take the bedroom. Selfish asshole that I am, I stayed there instead.

Couldn't quite bring myself to climb into the bunk above her.

Now we're all kind of milling around in the lobby of this stop's hotel. We got to Salt Lake ahead of schedule, so spent last night in the bus until reservations could be changed. Baz and Bree are checking us in, the others are huddled together, and I'm standing off to one side by myself. Wycked Obsession has circled the wagons, like the old-time Western movies. They're protecting London, and I'm on the outside.

Like I deserve.

I lean my shoulder against the wall, cross one ankle over the other, and turn my thoughts off. Well, not off, exactly, but to something productive. Music swirls through my mind, a progression of notes that sound sad and...melancholy. It hurts to hear, but I can't stop listening, hope it will continue.

"Here." Bree interrupts the internal concert and hands me a key card. "From Baz." Her tone's still snippy. Won't deny I deserve it.

"Thanks."

"I'll give London hers."

"Hey, wait." A thought occurs to me. "We're in separate rooms, right?"

Bree steps closer, her green eyes sparkling with anger. "No, Knox, you're in the same room. Don't be an ass about it."

"Jesus, Bree," I snap back, scrambling to make sense of it. "That isn't a...good idea."

"Too fucking bad." I hate when my sister swears. She does it whenever she gets good and pissed, and I seem to do that to her.

"It's the best damn idea there is, so don't fuck this up, Knox. She needs you—and you need her."

"Bree—" But she doesn't let me finish.

"So she made a little mistake. Get over it."

"A little mistake."

I only mean to consider the idea. Sort the observation along with the other explanations English provided. Bree doesn't hear it that way.

"A little mistake," she repeats through gritted teeth. "Can't you give up your damn idea of control long enough to see what all this cost her? Yeah, so you didn't know about the baby. So what?"

She takes a breath and repeats, "So what? In the overall scheme of things, it means nothing."

She steps back, turns, and then returns, her eyes narrow and cold. "If you don't make this right with her, Knox, I will never forgive you. Just get over your fucking self!"

I watch my little sister as she stalks around the lobby, giving everyone else their key cards. She approaches London last. I turn away as they talk.

I've pissed Bree off a lot over the years, but never like that.

She made a little mistake. Get over it.

Give up your damn idea of control long enough to see what all this cost her.

Is my pride, maybe my need for control, keeping me on edge? Holding London at arm's length? Unwilling to forgive her? Staying pissed off when I know damned well it's so much more complicated than that?

I am so sorry, Knox. Words will never be enough to make it up to you. But please know how deeply I regret everything. You were right. If I'd been honest about the baby, things might have been different all the way around. And I'll have to live with that for the rest of my life.

Her apology was real. Very fucking real. I know her well enough to be sure. I saw the tears in her eyes, heard the break in her voice. Heard and saw, and when the pain from her injuries made her wince, I wanted to go to her. Hold her.

But I didn't. The instant I started to soften toward her, I deliberately hardened my heart against it.

And why? Because of Farren and that years-old bullshit?

No. I shake my head with a tiny movement. Can't say that bitch has anything to do with it. London is so different from Farren, and I rarely think about my old girlfriend. Not seriously. Not until Ajia brought her up.

So what's wrong with me? Why can't I just accept her explanation, her reasons? No doubt she meant them, and they make sense.

But...*fuck!* I don't need her to *protect* me. *I* do the protecting, and she—

My thoughts stumble to a sudden, choppy death. Is that *it?* Am I pissed because she wanted to *help* me? What the fuck? I've always *liked* that sense of helpfulness about her.

Oh, yeah. As long as she helps you on your *terms,* a snotty voice inside me insists. *She did* this *all on her own, didn't she? Took the hit for you—literally. What does it matter that she didn't get your fucking permission for what she was doing?*

Fuck.

My heart beats hard all of a sudden, pounding a rhythm that feels a lot like it's saying, *asshole, asshole, asshole.*

No matter what London did or how she handled things, she lost a baby. *My* baby, yeah, but it was a child she was carrying *inside her.* Changing her body. Fucking with her hormones and changing her emotions.

The peanut.

Okay, so maybe I *was* pissed. It fucked with my head to find out I might've had a kid—a real kid and not a figment of some crazy bitch's imagination—but I only knew when it was too late. Yeah, I'll even admit it hurt. But London didn't keep it secret specifically to hurt me...and she didn't come through this shit whole.

Physically or emotionally. And I made it worse.

I'm standing here in the hotel lobby like a damned idiot, but I can't seem to move. My brain's too goddamn busy stumbling over my thoughts like a freaking lab puppy. Legs too long, feet too big, can't find its footing.

I am so sorry, *Knox.*

Words will never be enough to make it up to you.

Please know how deeply I regret everything.

I'll have to live with that for the rest of my life.

And she will, too. She'll take every damn bit of it to heart. God*dammit!*

"Meeting in Noah's room." Rye strolls up to me, his face revealing nothing. Jesus, have we all become goddamn mimes?

"He's here?"

"Checked in early this morning. Room 503. Concierge's taking care of the luggage."

I nod, join everyone else. London stands on the other side of Bree, away from me. Baz is still at the front desk, but the rest of us enter the elevator together. Everybody stays quiet, and even though I don't mind, it pisses me off, too. There's so much to say, at least between London and me...but not now. Not *here.*

Can't get to her, anyway. The others surround her like a team of goddamn Navy seals, protecting her like I'm some sort of terrorist or something.

Fuck my life. I'd never hurt her.

But you have.

It's true, and I know it. I'll never forget the sight of her face, her eyes, when she explained herself to me. The memory makes my gut churn.

I'm almost relieved when we reach the fifth floor, and Rye leads the way to Noah's room. The door's propped open, and Noah looks like...well, shit. Rough. Really bad. His eyes are bloodshot, like he hasn't slept in a couple of days.

Was it that hard to get Zayne settled in rehab?

"Jesus, you look like hell."

Four pairs of eyes look at me with the same expression. *Eat shit and die.* Noah just shrugs.

"Been a rough couple of days."

I snort without quite meaning to. "Rough couple of months."

Everybody looks serious but not disagreeable. Fuck, I don't have to remind them of everything. They lived it, too.

Noah wanders to lean against the dresser while the rest of us settle in. London takes the upholstered chair at Bree's insistence, while she and Ajia take one of the beds. Rye straddles the desk chair, leaving the other bed for me.

"You see the audition tapes?" Ajia asks, straight to business.

"Yeah." Noah nods once. "Played 'em half a dozen times. They all still here?"

Ajia snorts. "Yep. Like good little minions. Told 'em we'd either make our choice or play with 'em today."

Noah nods again.

"Any reactions?" Rye doesn't usually say much, but he's taking an interest in this. Either it's that important to him—them—or they don't want my brand of *control* in this.

"Couple of good ones." Noah shoves a hand in his hair, pushes it away from his face. "Sarge Harman's the best. Hands down. Can we play with him, see if there's any…chemistry?"

"Sure." Ajia pulls out his phone. "I'll text Baz. Have him set it up for this afternoon."

Noah nods, and everybody seems satisfied. I lean back against the headboard, look around the room, pretending to observe while I straddle that fucked-up place between belonging and being on the outside. Not really used to this feeling, and I hate not knowing where I fit anymore.

But, *Jesus!* I wanna smack myself. I'm not an indecisive guy, letting anybody make decisions for me. So maybe it's been kinda screwed up for a few days—partly my fault, I'll admit—but it doesn't have to stay that way.

"Get Zayne settled okay?" I ask briskly and lean forward.

"Yeah." Noah takes a breath. "Nice place, but he doesn't want to be there. Says he can do it on his own."

"Yeah, uh…no." Ajia's not buying it. "He got worse. This business, this tour? Nope."

Noah shrugs. "It'll be a couple of weeks before he can have any outside contact. Baz has the details."

"He in for ninety?" I ask.

"Yeah. He ought to be able to have visitors by the time we get back to Austin."

I hear the words, but I'm more interested in Noah himself. Besides looking like death warmed over, something else is wrong. Paparazzi describes him as larger than life, and it's true. Yeah, he's a big guy, but he's a joker. Never met a stranger. Life of the party. Now it's like he's all turned in on himself.

Fuck.

"What's wrong with you man?" The question's out before I can think better of it.

"Knox," Bree snaps. "Jesus."

"What?" That's it! I'm sick of being their whipping boy. "Noah's acting like his dog just died or some shit. I wanna know why. Was it that bad getting Zayne settled? Or is there something else we should know?"

Noah blows out a harsh breath. "It went okay with Zayne. Well enough, anyway. No, he didn't like it, but he knew he didn't have a choice."

"Okay." I'll accept that. "Then what is it?"

Noah's eyes close, and he looks fucking miserable. Like...well, like I've never seen him.

"Noah?" Bree sees it, too. "Sweetie?"

"Dude?" Ajia asks.

A knot fists in my gut. What else? Jesus Christ, what else do we have to go through this tour?

"C'mon, man," I insist. "What?"

Noah straightens, looks at Bree for a couple of heartbeats. They've always been close. Shit, she's always been close with all the guys, and they worry about her just like I do. Put her ahead of just about anything.

Is it that bad?

He glances towards London, me. *"Fuck!"* he shouts and smacks one fist on the dresser behind him.

"Noah?" London's voice is soft but no denying she means to have him answer. "Tell us what's wrong."

"I...shit! Got another problem we're gonna have to deal with. Fuck my life!"

"What is it?" London asks before I can.

"I..."

Noah's voice dies away, and I stare at him. Never seen him at a loss for words like this.

"What, man? Just fucking tell us!" I demand.

"Fuck, I'm sorry." He shoots a quick look in my direction but pretty much stares at London. "I'm so goddamn sorry, London."

"It's okay, sweetie." She's taken to using Bree's band-wide endearment. "Just tell us so we can deal with it."

"Fuck." He shakes his head. "Fuck, fuck, fuck. Don't wanna do this now. Everything's already a fucking mess and now…"

"Now what?" London prompts.

He closes his eyes for a second. "Now some chick's come out of the woodwork. She got to Baz when I was in Austin. Says she's going to the tabloids next."

Fuck. Can't even guess what this means. I let out a long, weary breath. "What does she want?"

"Whatever she can get." Noah pins a heavy gaze on me. "She's six months pregnant, and she says it's mine."

CHAPTER 27

LONDON

THE ROOM GETS SUDDENLY AND UNNATURALLY QUIET. I look around at the others, none of whom look back. Except Knox. While most of the faces are a mix of shock, confusion, resignation, he looks...I don't know. Overwhelmed. Angry.

And so bloody damned wounded.

How could I *not* have guessed how much a baby would mean to him? He spent most of his life taking care of his family, blood and band. To lose the peanut before he even knew about him or her...

But, no, I can't go there now. It isn't the time or place. My feelings are too close to the way Knox looks, and I have to hold it together. This isn't about me and the baby I—*we*—lost. This is about Noah and his new problem.

But why the bloody hell does it have to mirror my situation so closely?

A hole settles low in my stomach, and I try to breathe around it. I haven't really cried about the baby yet. Not the deep, soul-cleansing tears that I probably need. That doesn't mean I'm doing it now, though, no matter how much it feels like the sperm donor just kicked me in the stomach again.

Noah doesn't need that kind of display, Knox doesn't need it, the band doesn't—and I sure as hell don't.

Not yet.

I take a deep breath, as much as my ribs allow, and drop my eyelids closed. My hands are shaking, I realize, and I clench my fingers into fists.

She's six months pregnant, Noah said with such misery, *and she says it's mine.*

Six months pregnant.

The reality of the words strike me in a new way. A woman I don't know, along with thousands of other women I will never meet, all get to maintain their pregnancies. They didn't get kicked in the stomach by some lunatic who also happens to be their baby daddy's father. They'll have their babies and—

Nope. Not going there. I can't afford it right now.

I blink, swallow, and force myself to look at Noah. He's a nice guy, always sweet, fun, and funny. He holds Knox—all of them, really—accountable when they screw up, and he's not a slacker himself. He contributes to the band as much as any of them.

His biggest quirk is liking to bang more than one girl at a time. Threesomes. It's never meant a lot to me either way, because I'm usually too busy to think about it. The guys mostly hook up with groupies after the concerts, and that's when I'm taking pictures, posting to Twitter, making notes for blog posts. All the PR stuff that makes online fans feel like they're there in real time.

Not sure how I feel about Noah's sexual preferences now.

She's six months pregnant, and she says it's mine.

"*Is* it yours?" I ask, forcing the words out a dry throat. It's not the easiest question I've ever asked, but it's better than giving in to all the things crowding into my heart, swirling through my brain.

I'm really not ready for that.

"No." Noah's answer is low. Rough, maybe. Emphatic for sure.

"Any possibility?" asks Rye.

Noah shakes his head. "None. I always wear a condom. *Always.*"

"Condoms break," says Knox, his tone brittle. He's holding it together like me. Barely, but at least he's doing it.

Noah nods. "Never had that happen. I'm *careful.*"

I swallow, sorting through my jumbled thoughts for something useful. "What do you remember about this girl? Anything that will help us deal with her?"

He blows out a shot of breath. "Fuck, London." He looks almost embarrassed, probably more because of the timing than because of the situation itself. "I don't remember a goddamn thing about her. Don't even know if I fucked her for sure."

"You don't know…?" I can't really think how to finish the sentence.

He shrugs. "Don't always get their names, and their faces…fade."

"Fuck."

That comes from Knox, but I catch a thread of understanding that runs through his voice. He gets it; they all do. It's that way with him, too. They've all fucked a never-ending line of one-night stands. How *could* they remember them all?

"Well, we're keeping *that* a secret," I announce primly, swallowing back a knot in my throat, and I pin a reproving gaze on each of the guys. Bree nods in agreement, and Ajia looks damned uncomfortable. I'd smile if I could. He's running a consoling hand down her arm, like he's trying to make up for his past bad behavior.

Bloody rock stars.

"You said she got to Baz first?" Knox says, phrasing it as a question.

Noah nods. "Yesterday."

Dammit, why didn't he tell me? Warn me? Prepare me?

But I know. It's too soon after the miscarriage. The peanut—

Not now! Not here.

"What's her name?" I ask the first question that pops into my head.

Noah shrugs. "Alice. Elise. Elaine. Something like that."

I take another breath, this one too deep, and I gasp with the pain that shoots through my middle.

"London?" Urgency colors Bree's voice. Knox scoots to the edge of the bed.

I shake my head. "Just the ribs," I say a little breathlessly as a sudden wave of sadness washes over me. The reason for my sore ribs looms large in my mind, and while I pant some shallow breaths, my heart clenches in pain. The thoughts just won't stop, no matter how hard I try.

Poor little peanut. You never got a chance—and neither did I.

Not with Knox, and not as a mother.

I'm afraid to look at him. I'm not strong enough to conceal my feelings, and I'm just not up to sharing my heartbreak, my regret…or my love for him. Especially not in front of everyone else.

I know then, in an instant, that I can't do this anymore.

"You know what?" I push myself carefully to my feet. "Let me think about how we're going to handle this." I paste a smile on my face that I know is fake, but it's all I've got. "I'm going to go to my room, get settled, maybe take a shower." Why the bloody hell am I telling them all this? Who cares? "I'll get ahold of Baz. We'll…make a plan."

I have to pass by Noah on my way to the door. He stops me, bends down, pins me with his always-shocking blue and now very pained gaze, takes my hand between his much larger ones. "I'm so fucking sorry, London. I know the timing is fucked, and it's such bullshit. I'm—"

I cut him off by pressing two fingers of my free hand against his lips. "I know, sweetie." I swallow. "Don't worry. I'm just…tired."

I pull away, make it to the door, relieved that I'm actually going to escape unscathed. A hand settles on my hip, and Knox whispers, "I'll go with you, English."

The shower relaxes me. I need it, even though I'm not quite sure whether it's Noah's news that has me so worked up or the fact that Knox escorted me back to the room.

Our room. I told Bree it was a bad idea to put us together, but she disagreed fiercely.

"You and Knox have something special. Give him a chance to get his shit together. It's best this way."

I expected him to stalk off and get his own room once he discovered we were staying together. Instead, he kept his arm around my waist as he walked me to the door, and then he followed me inside. Nerves churned in my stomach, and I tried to breathe them away.

We didn't say much. Our luggage had been delivered, so I dug around for my shower stuff and fled into the bathroom. It was a decent, if temporary, escape.

Toweling off now, I think about what's next. I wasn't kidding. It might not be noon yet, but I need a nap. Or at least to lie down. Noah's news took an emotional toll, and I just need to rest.

I slip into a tank top and sleep shorts and dry my hair quickly. I don't style it or anything; all it needs is enough to get the dampness out of it. Physically I'm ready, but I still stand at the door, my hand on the knob.

What waits on the other side? Is Knox still in the room? I couldn't hear anything over the shower and then the blow dryer, and now I'm torn. Do I want him there?

The truth is…yes and no. A part of me craves some romantic, even loving attention. Longs for him to put his arms around me, to hold me and say soft, sweet things in my ear. To soothe my rawness with tenderness. Most of me, though, is practical enough to know it will never happen. He's hurt and angry, and he has every right to be.

Remember! A sensible voice inside me speaks up suddenly. *Just because you finally admitted to yourself that you're in love with him doesn't mean anything has changed.*

It's the truth, and I know it. Why would things be different? I can't undo what I've done or the way I've done it, and I definitely can't change the loss I'm responsible for. If I could, I would, but—

No! Stop! I shout inside the privacy of my mind. *Just stop!*

Tears threaten my already fragile control, tears that are never far enough away these days. The news that Noah could be a father, that some other woman is pregnant with a baby that will be born healthy and happy, seems to have released the tight grip I've had on my feelings, and I don't know what to do about it.

I'm *this close* to falling apart; I feel it in every part of my being. Worse, I don't dare take the chance that I'll lose it in front of Knox. I've already disappointed him in huge, unforgivable ways. I can't ask him to share my sorrow.

He has enough to deal with.

Bollocks! Pull yourself together!

I scramble to find the British stiff-upper-lip way of looking at things, stiffening my spine and straightening my shoulders as much as I'm able. My bruised ribs make so many movements difficult, but I refuse to step out of this bathroom acting like a weak, broken mess.

Alone in the hotel room or not, I can't fall apart. Won't.

My mom's advice comes back to me one more time. *Fake it till you make it.*

The bedroom is dark, or mostly so. The drapes are closed, and a bedside lamp is the only light. The room has one king-sized bed, the normal request for the rooms Knox and I've shared.

He's there, sprawled in the middle of the bed. He's covered from the waist down, but his chest is bare. His Wycked Obsession tattoo and the Celtic heart and dragon beckon, and I ache to snuggle up against his broad, muscular body. Rest my hand over his heart. Absorb his warmth and strength.

God. What does that mean, him being in bed? I swallow and stare.

He gives me a serious look. "C'mon, baby." He pulls the covers back. "Let's take a little nap."

"A...nap?"

"You said you were tired."

"Well, yeah." I blink and glance around the room. Everything else looks normal, but...is it? It's like Alice in Wonderland or something. Or maybe...I can't remember the name, but the guy who fell asleep for like twenty years.

"I am," I add after a minute. "But...don't you have to audition those bass players."

"In a couple hours. We've got time. Now come on." He jerks his head to indicate the bed.

I blink. What the bloody hell? Why is Knox acting so normal? Almost...nice?

"Knox...?"

"What?"

"What's wrong?"

His mouth goes flat. "What do you mean?"

"You're so..." What can I say without making him sound like a dick? Yeah, maybe he *is* a dick at times, but he has every right to be pissed off at me. I can't defend myself against it.

"C'mon, baby." He pats the bed.

My body starts moving, whether or not I want it to. *It* wants to be close to him, and so I end up crawling in bed beside him. I lie on my back, stiff and awkward, until he scoots up next to me. He pulls me close, taking care with my ribs, and tucks me tight against his side.

What the fuck, to quote just about every member of Wycked Obsession.

"Knox?"

"Yeah?"

"What's going on?"

"What do you mean?"

"Why are you being so nice to me?"

"Fuck."

He rolls away, leaving me to turn on my side until I can face him. He's lying on his back, one arm thrown over his eyes.

"Knox?"

He moves his arm enough to peek at me through one eye. "I was a dick, okay?"

I stare at him until he finally drops his arm from his face. His gray-green gaze flickers with a couple of emotions that confuse me. Regret? Sorrow?

"I'm sorry," he says after a minute or two of silence. "You didn't deserve it. The way I acted. You didn't deserve any of it."

I rest my hand on his arm, fingers tightening on his bicep. I can't help myself; I need to touch him. "I know you were upset," I start carefully, but he continues before I can.

"Doesn't matter." He moves his arm, and I swallow a small sting of rejection, but then he links our fingers and squeezes. "I knew what the sperm donor was capable of. I should have fucking protected you whether you were pregnant or not."

Pain threads through his voice, and answering tears prickle behind my eyelids. I breathe in through my nose. *God, no!* No crying. Not now.

"You couldn't have protected me from him, luv," I offer softly, the endearment slipping out in spite of me knowing better. "Nobody knew what would happen. What he could do."

"I should have guessed." He's not looking at me anymore but staring at the ceiling instead.

"You couldn't have. No one could." I swallow so I can force the rest of the words out. "And that's really not the problem. It's me. What I did." Or didn't do, but I don't need to go into the details again. Knox already knows them, as well as I do.

He pulls his hand free, pushes up on one elbow and leans over me until I have to roll over on my back. He smooths the hair back from my face, runs the backs of his fingers over my cheek. He watches his moving hand with a strange intensity, as though memorizing each touch. They are light, tender caresses, and real tears gather in the corner of my eyes.

"I'm processing things, English." If he sees my tears, he doesn't mention them. *Thank God!* "Trying to understand. It's been like a perfect fucking storm of shit happening around us, and it's been...tough. I get that."

"But I didn't tell you the truth." My voice is thicker than I want, but I push through. "And I messed up on the birth control."

His fingers trail down over my jaw, my throat, and he draws light, lazy circles over my upper chest. "Don't think you did that deliberately. Like I said. Perfect fucking storm. I got a lot of shit to work out in my head, but I want you to know I don't blame you. And I'm sorry I acted like I did."

"You don't—" I have to pause to breath, swallow, sniff "—hate me?"

"Hate you?" He jerks his head back, that beautiful dark hair falling around his shoulders while his expressive eyes warm to almost green. "I don't hate you, baby. I never did. I might have been pissed off about shit—" his hand returns to my face "—but I never hated you."

"I..." God, I want to say something. Not just anything but the *right* thing. Only...what the bloody hell is it?

I blink, discover Knox watching me with an amazingly tender gaze, and then I do the one thing I promised myself I wouldn't. I collapse with a gut-wrenching sob, and I cry my regret and heartbreak against his warm chest, his arms tight and comforting around me.

CHAPTER 28

KNOX

THE CROWD IS ELECTRIC. It's our last show in Denver. We've practiced and played with Sarge for days now, and he gets better with each gig. He's handling it all like a pro, even the interest from the press, and relief erased my nerves from the early days. It's been ten days since we first played with him, and shit's settling in to a new normal.

Noah still looks a little grim, like some disapproving gargoyle looming over us or something, but Rye and Ajia have stayed calm and easy. Ajia works extra hard to keep the audience focus on him, his fuck-me voice and sexy prowling around the stage overshadowing the rest of us for the most part. Rye's a little more animated than usual, filling in when Noah's not there, and I put everything I have into my guitar solos. I stalk to the front of the stage and play with a passion I haven't had as much of earlier in the tour. Too much fucking else has gone on, but it feels good to be back in the groove again.

Especially tonight.

Tonight.

It's our most current hit, the last song in our set. It's next, and then we're done for the night. Sarge's done great, yeah, but it still isn't the same. Never will be. We got a bond, the five of us, and Wycked Obsession will never be right without the original lineup.

I glance offstage as Ajia flirts with the crowd. My sister watches him proudly, but I don't give a shit anymore. Guess I'm finally used to them as a couple. I see how he cares for her, keeps her safe, and that's enough for me.

I'm more interested in London, anyway. Been watching her like a hawk since the day she broke down in my arms. She's a strong goddamn woman, amazing at times, and she's stayed busy doing her thing these last ten days. I kinda assume she likes the escape of it, and I know her routine by heart. Posting clips to Instagram. Taking pictures for the website and Facebook. Showing us back stage, on stage, panning the crowd. She's transformed our social media accounts.

Tonight she's wearing a dress I haven't seen before. Bree took her shopping on one of our heavy practice days, and she must have gotten it then. It's white, with red roses and green stems and leaves weaving over her perfect-looking body. The skirt's long, almost to her ankles, with a slit that stops just below her pussy.

God *damn,* but I want her.

We haven't fucked in days.

It hasn't felt…right. For once, I don't know what to do. It's been a couple of weeks since the miscarriage. Is it okay to have sex? Then there are her sore ribs. She ices them occasionally, but her movements and breathing seem better. And emotionally…she's less fragile and more herself since she broke down in my arms.

She slept for *hours* after that, and since then has spent every night curled against me. Trusting me in a way I don't deserve. I don't sleep so well. Mostly I lay there with a rock-hard dick that doesn't give me any peace until I rub one out in the shower. Even that doesn't last long.

Doesn't matter, though. I'll take it over not having English in my arms. I want it.

I *need* it—just like I need her.

Spent ten nights like that, but tonight…

Tonight she's mine.

She might not be up for fucking. I get that. She'll have to tell me how much we can do. But however it happens, I'm going to pleasure her and remind her of the beautiful, sensual woman she is. She deserves it…and so much more.

I focus as Ajia raises his arm, Noah counts off the beat, and Rye keys the opening notes of *Tonight.* It's his song, one he wrote about…well, not quite sure what. Or who it's about. Rye's got secrets that go back from before we started the band, and he's never shared a damned hint about them. Not with me, anyway. Had no choice but to leave him alone about it, and if *Tonight* is his way of dealing with it?

Good for him, and good for the band.

I step in with a guitar riff that seems at first shocking as the song picks up momentum, but then it all makes sense when Ajia begins to sing.

It's late and I'm here all alone,
Like I've been since she's been gone.
I pretend but truth is truth,
And that means we're really done.
How did it go, why did she leave?
She kept her truths deep in her soul.
I would have done so much more
If only I could make her whole.

It's a song about loss, but I hear the lyrics in a different way tonight. I pick through the words, find ones that make me think of London. And me. Maybe she *did* keep her truths deep in her soul, but I swear, I'm going to make her whole again.

Me, too.

Tonight.

I can't think anymore, have to concentrate on the complicated guitar outro Rye let me arrange for the song. It's kind of a *Hotel California* ending, something I wanted to try since I first picked up a guitar. Mom is a huge Eagles fan, and I grew up on their stuff, especially since they were getting back together about the time I was born.

Everybody, including the critics, agree it's a haunting ending to the song, and I send an approving smile in Rye's direction as I finger the last riff. He smiles back, and satisfaction practically chokes me up.

Wycked Obsession will be okay. I know it now.

And tonight I make things right with London, once and for all.

Not interested in seeing the groupies or drinking with the band in the green room after the show. Baz has a Town Car waiting behind the venue, just like I asked, and I tell Bree we're leaving.

"You told me to make it right with her." I step up behind my sister and whisper in her ear. "Well, tonight, I'm taking English back to the hotel, and I'm gonna do it. So don't call. Anything happens, call Baz."

She grins like it's Christmas and then hugs me like I'm Santa. "I won't cockblock you, Knox, I promise!"

"Jesus." I shake my head. "Did Ajia teach you to say that?"

She laughs and shakes her head. "No. I'm twenty, Knox, remember? Starting my third year in college this fall. You think I don't hear the same kind of stuff y'all say at school every day?"

She's saved—or maybe I am—when London comes around the corner. She smiles warmly seeing us. She and Bree are close. That's one thing I love about my girl. Family, whether blood or band, is important to her. And she's part of the Wycked Obsession family now.

One thing I love about my girl.

Yeah, I've had to admit my feelings in the last couple of weeks. I love London. It fucking damn near choked me when I first realized it, it crept up on me so slowly, I don't really know when my feelings went from sexual attraction to liking to love. All I'm sure of is that my feelings for her are so foreign to me, they can only be love.

Oh, and I'm *not* sticking to that stupid rule about the relationship ending at the end of the tour. We've got maybe three weeks left on the road, and I'm keeping London after that.

"You two kids have fun." Bree gives London a quick hug, waves her fingers at me, and hurries into the green room.

London looks at me curiously. "What's that about?"

I shrug. "Not in the mood to hang out with the groupies or drink with the guys. I need—*we* need—a break."

"Okay." She says it slowly, carefully, and looks at me uneasily. "Are you okay, Knox?"

"Just fine, baby." I smile easily and sling an arm around her shoulders. "Let's go."

The ride to our hotel is mostly quiet. English sits next to me, and when I pull her close, she snuggles against my side. It's kind of an awkward angle she couldn't have managed a week ago, and relief lightens my mood. I'm glad she's healing, but my selfish side prays to fucking God that her ribs are good enough for some careful lovemaking.

And, yeah, for the first time in my life, I'm gonna make love to a woman, not fuck her.

There's no crowd to notice us when we reach the hotel. The last real paparazzi we had was shortly after Zayne went into rehab. English has been releasing carefully-worded updates, and that seems to keep things quiet. Now we're just hoping that Noah's baby mama—if that's what she is—keeps her fucking mouth shut. Especially me. Every time my girl has to deal with this pregnancy shit, I know it hurts her.

I shake off my shitty thoughts and get London to the elevator with my palm on the small of her back. I keep it there through the ride upstairs, 'cause pushing her up against the wall and fucking her standing up is *not* part of the plan.

English seems a little nervous when I open the door to our room, but she kinda gets that way with me now. We're close and, I don't know…cuddly, I guess, when she allows it, but sometimes she gets nervous. I understand, even though it hurts. Can't say I don't deserve it, though.

"You look beautiful tonight, baby."

She stops just inside the door, stares at me.

"The flowers on your dress bring out the red in your hair."

She blinks, still staring. "Knox…"

I step closer, wrap one hand around her hip while I trace the fingers of my other hand up her leg, to the top of that fucking slit. "I wanted to do this all fucking night."

"Why?"

I stroke my thumb over the soft skin of her thigh. "What do you mean, why?"

Her skin gives a little twitch, and she presses her leg lightly against my hand. "After everything. What happened, and what I did—"

"We talked about that, baby. I don't blame you."

"I know you said that, but..." She takes a breath and steps away, wanders farther into the room.

"But what?"

"You were so cold. So distant." She seems to search for a word but then brings her gaze directly to mine. "Angry."

I blow out a harsh breath and shove my fingers into my hair, squeeze the back of my neck. "Fuck," I mutter to myself but force myself to answer. "It wasn't you I was mad at."

"Who was it, then?"

"Me." I don't hesitate. "The sperm donor. All the shit going on. You were just...convenient."

She blinks, erasing any hint of how she's feeling from those beautiful whiskey-colored eyes. "Convenient?"

"You..." I pause. Fuck. How do I say this without making her feel bad? "The baby...not knowing." I take a breath. "Made you an easy target. I could get pissed about that and not deal with any of the rest of the shit."

Strange, but she shakes her head. "You deserve to be pissed about that."

"No."

"Yes," she disagrees. "I told you, I—"

"Goddamn it, English!" The words sound rougher than I meant them, but it's too late now. "Don't do that!"

Kinda surprised my anger torched so quick. Especially now, when this night was supposed to be about seduction. But...*fuck!*

She swallows. "Do what?"

"Keep blaming yourself. Take it all on yourself. You didn't do anything wrong. *I'm* the one who fucked up."

"No." She holds her hands up, palms toward me. "Knox...luv, of anyone in this godawful drama, you're the one who's innocent. You—"

"Fuck!" It's a shout, but at least it stops her words. Concern darkens her eyes.

"Knox?"

I stalk past her to the other side of the room, pace back by her, and finally end up between the wall and the bed. "We can't keep doing this, baby. Blaming ourselves for shit. We'll never make it if we don't let it go."

"Let it go?" She comes toward me, that fucking slit in her skirt showing her long, slender leg and then hiding it again. She stops in front of me and slowly brings her hands up to rest on my chest. How is it that she's not nervous now, when I just yelled?

"You want to just let it...go?" she asks.

"We have to, baby." My heart's pounding like Noah's goddamn bass drum, and I wonder if she can feel it. "We can't go on if we don't. You were trying to find your footing before you told me about the baby. I get it. And I—" I snort. "I never thought the sperm donor would touch you, let alone..." Fuck, I don't wanna say the words again.

"It wasn't that I didn't trust you." She comes a half a step closer. "That isn't why I didn't tell you. You have to believe that. I was just...scared. Confused."

"I know." I take her hips in my hands, pull her crotch against mine. "You had every right to feel like that. When I had time to think about it, I knew it. Understood it. I just..."

"What, luv?"

"Wish I'd protected you better. From the sperm donor—and me."

"Oh, baby." Her arms slip around me, and she lays her head against my chest. "I don't need protecting from you. You're the last one. You're...I—"

The word ends with a strange gasp, and the body tucked against me stiffens. I glance down but can only see the top of her head.

"What, baby?" I stroke a hand up her spine. "What's wrong?"

She shakes her head against me, but I can't let it go. I tilt her head back, my fingers under her chin. "What?" I ask again.

She swallows, closes her eyes on a long, slow blink, and shakes her head. "You don't wanna hear it. It isn't part of the deal."

"Deal?" I stare. "What deal?"

She lets out a short breath. "The rules, then."

The rules? Fuck my life.

"The rules?" This time I say it. "What the fuck are you talking about, English?"

Something about the words, my tone pisses her off. I don't know what it is, but suddenly she's out of my arms and storming over to the bed. She plops down on the mattress and glares at me.

"The fucking rules, Knox. You know, the ones where we're exclusive through the end of the tour. And then, you know, when it's over, *we're* over."

My blood runs cold. "We are *not* fucking over." I stalk over to her, stop so close she has to lean back to see my face. "Not at the end of the tour, and not...ever."

"No?" She doesn't sound as angry or defiant, but it doesn't matter. *I'm* still hot.

"No." I reach out for the back of her neck, hold her tighter than I should as I bend down until our lips are almost touching. "Hell. Fucking. No. I love you, and I'm not letting you go."

.

CHAPTER 29

LONDON

I LOVE YOU, and I'm not letting you go.

The words echo through my head, and I stare into Knox's heavy gray eyes. I shake my head. Did I hear him right?

"You love me?" It's only a whisper.

He straightens suddenly, steps back, turns like he's ready to run. I grab his hand. "Knox?"

He doesn't look at me. "Yeah."

"Oh, baby." Part of me wants to sit there, hug the memory of the words to me and just let the amazement warm me. The rest of me can't wait for that.

I push up off the bed, slide my arms around his waist, press myself against his back. "Oh, baby, I love you so much." I kiss him between his shoulder blades. "So much. I've never felt this way about anybody before."

He's stiff, his spine straight and his muscles tense. I understand suddenly how hard it was for him to say the words. And *first?*

Wow.

"Me either," he says finally. "Never thought I could."

I kiss his back again and tighten my arms around his stomach. "I was so afraid, baby. So afraid you didn't feel the same way. I didn't want—"

"Dammit, English!" He turns in my arms. "Were you trying to protect me again?"

The question sounds odd. Half like he's irritated, but the rest like he's touched. Both are probably true, and I want to reassure him with a hug. But I have to be honest.

Always.

I drop my head back so I can look him straight in the eye when I say it. "No. I was protecting myself."

I can't miss the flicker of pain that darkens his gaze. "Yourself," he mutters carefully.

Everything's out between us, so it's time to be brave. "It's been there for a while now, but I couldn't admit it to myself until I'd miscarried. You were so upset then, and I didn't want to make it worse. For either of us. I didn't think you could—would—forgive me, so it was better if I kept it to myself."

He lets out a long, low breath, pain clear in its raggedness, and pulls me close. "I'm such an asshole."

"No, baby, you're not." I kiss the place on his chest where his heart's covered by a Wycked Obsession T-shirt. "I know better. You're a man who takes care of those he loves, who protects them, and...sometimes makes mistakes. Just like the woman who loves you."

"Jesus, English."

He hauls me up his chest until I'm on my tiptoes. He takes my mouth in the first real, sexual kiss we've shared since our lives imploded, and I delight in its claiming nature. Knox licks my lips, again, and I open my mouth against his. His tongue pushes forward, and I suck him into my mouth.

Oh, God, the taste of him. I miss it whenever we're apart. He strokes through the recesses of my mouth, around again, and I swirl my tongue up and over his. It remains a blatantly sexual kiss, and I want more.

I follow his lead, my tongue in his mouth, and I imitate the things he just did to me. He sucks on my tongue, pulls me deeper, and a soft moan of need escapes me. Oh, Lord. But I can't help it. He's making me feel things I've never felt.

Knowing he loves me and admitting I love him changes everything.

Awareness settles heavy in my core, and butterflies race through my stomach. *Love.* It doesn't even come close to describing what I feel for this man.

"I need you," he growls against my lips. "Whatever that means for tonight."

I push my hands in his hair, kiss my way from his mouth, his jaw, his neck. "Whatever that means?" I whisper against his rough, unshaven skin.

He palms my ass, and the thick ridge of his cock presses against my mound. Bloody goddamn clothes, always in the way. He pulls back enough to cast a serious gaze over me. "After…everything. I wasn't sure if it's…okay. You know. The physical stuff."

"Oh." I smile tenderly. He's sweet, sounding so uncertain. I know it isn't about having sex; the man who greeted me with his cock on display isn't shy about fucking. It's about the baby, the loss.

"It's okay, luv." I arch up on my tiptoes for another earth-shattering kiss. "The doctor gave me instructions. I just have to be careful of infection, so we have to use a condom."

"Like we should have from the beginning."

"Knox…" He looks as sad as I feel, and I stroke my fingers gently over his cheek. "Not now. Okay? Tonight let's just be us. Together and—" I'm almost afraid to say it "—in love."

"In love." He repeats the words, sounding both growly and almost curious at the same time. *"In love,"* he says it again, and laughs this time. "How the fuck did that happen? What'd you do to me, English?"

"I was going to ask you the same thing."

He kisses me again, and I feel his fingers fumble over my back. "As much as I love this dress on you," he pants when he pulls away, "it *has* to come off."

He tugs the zipper down, pushes the boatneck bodice over my arms, and the whole thing catches at my hips. Knox doesn't seem to notice, because he's staring at my bra. Well, my breasts, I suppose, but they're covered by the sexiest lingerie I own. A see-through scrap of tulle that's decorated with a little bit of lace. My still-hidden thong matches.

Instinct urged me to put them on tonight.

"Jesus Christ." He reaches for me, his fingers light as they run along the upper curve of my breasts, down over my nipples. They were puckered with excitement to begin with; now they're so stiff, they ache. "You are so damn beautiful," he says, and takes my mouth in another mind-blowing kiss.

Panting, I push the dress down my hips, step out of it, and kick it aside. I'm in flat gladiator sandals, easier to maneuver in when I'm racing around backstage, and I've never gotten them off so fast. I toss them across the room.

"Fuuuuck," says Knox when I straighten and stand with unexpected nerves before him. He swallows and rubs his palm over the bulge in his pants. "You're so beautiful, English, you're gonna kill me."

I smile and feel myself grow wet, knowing how much he wants me. How much I want him. It's...different, and a little scary, this first time together again.

I've never wanted anything—any*one*—more.

I push his T-shirt up over his head, kiss a lingering path down his chest until I sink to my knees. I kiss his stomach as I work my fingers at the fastening of his leather pants. Between my trembling hands, his hard-on, and the leather, nothing cooperates.

"Bollocks," I snap as I keep working. "Why do rock stars have to wear *leather* pants?"

He laughs hoarsely and takes over, freeing his cock. He shoves his pants down in mere seconds, but I grab at his feet. "Boots, Knox," I mutter.

He steps back, gets rid of pants, boots, socks, and then he's as gloriously naked as I am.

Finally.

"Up, baby." He pulls me to my feet, his hands supporting me under my arms.

I can see his hard dick, and I try to reach for him, but I can't manage it. "No, I—"

"Uh, uh." He smiles and backs me slowly toward the bed. "Tonight it's about you."

"Me?"

His hands wrapped around my waist, he lowers me to the mattress. He strokes his thumbs up over my ribs. "I know you aren't healed yet, baby. And as much as I would love to tie you up and pound the fuck into you—" he grins "—it's not happening tonight."

"God, Knox." Warmth settles in my core, and my panties are soaked.

He kneels before me. "As sexy as this fucking bra looks on you, I need to see your tits, baby." He pushes the straps down over my arms and flicks the back clasp open. The scrap of fabric falls from my chest, and he tosses it across the room.

His eyes are dark, flooded with desire. Maybe that's what makes me brave. I don't plan it but find my hands on my breasts. I push them together and arch my back, offering myself for Knox's hands, his mouth.

"Jesus, baby."

He takes one nipple in his mouth, swirls his tongue around the areola, moving closer to the center until it drags over the crest. I gasp as he closes his teeth over me, his fingers imitating the same actions on my other breast, until he pinches my nipple and sensation soars straight to my clit.

"You like that, don't you?" he mutters as he switches sides. "You've got amazing, sensitive tits." He does the same sucking, biting, pinching, and I moan my approval as I push my breasts at him.

Knox laughs, does it again, again, and I'm a bundle of nerve endings centered on my nipples, with a heightened connection straight to my pussy. *God.*

"Someday I'm gonna make you come just by sucking on your tits."

I wheeze a ragged breath. "Can...you do that?"

He leans back enough to catch my dreamy gaze. "Maybe most men can't." He strokes a thumb over each nipple, and—God, I can't help it!—I flex my hips. "But you and me, baby? I can."

He drags his hands down my sides, my hips, my thighs, and pushes my legs apart. "Let me in, baby. I need a taste."

"What?" I don't know what I'm saying.

"You." He slips his fingers under the elastic of my thong, tugging, and not even the sound of ripping fabric can bring me out of my stupor. "Let me taste you."

His shoulders widen my legs farther, and then his tongue is there, stroking over my lower lips, my clit. Did that guttural-sounding moan come from me?

"God, baby, you're soaked." He licks me from bottom to top. "And you taste so. Fucking. Good."

His mouth works me, his tongue working up and down and his teeth scraping lightly over my clit. Sensation roars through me, making my legs twitch, and I have to lean back on my elbows. I take most of my weight on my uninjured side, but even if my ribs ached like holy hell, I wouldn't stop him.

His mouth is making love to my pussy.

"Knox," I breathe and rest one hand at the back of his head.

He pulls away long enough to ask, "You like that, baby?"

I nod, but then I lose my breath again when he slips one finger into me. He uses his tongue to toy with my clit, moving his finger in and out, and then, suddenly, there are two. Three.

I groan.

"You like that, too, baby." This time it isn't a question.

I try to say yes, but I can only flex my hips with the movement of his hand. And, yeah, my ribs twinge, but I don't care.

I find a breath. "I need you, Knox. Inside me."

He strokes his tongue over my clit. "Oh, I will be, baby." He gives his own little groan. "Believe me. But first..." His fingers plunge in and out, and his teeth drag over my clit. "First I want you to come on my tongue. My fingers."

He does it again and again, and I can't help myself. I fall back onto the bed, my hands on my breasts as I pluck at my nipples. God, I need this. I need...something. Knox inside of me, but the edge of my orgasm is creeping closer.

How does he do that? Make me come so hard and so fast? No other man has ever done that for me.

But no other man has been Knox Gallagher. And I've never loved anyone the way I love him.

"Knox!" I can't help it. It's almost a scream, and my hand shoots to the back of his head. I hold him there and thrust my hips against his mouth.

"You ready, baby?" he murmurs against me, and then his teeth clamp down hard on my clit.

"Yes, baby. Oh, God, yes!"

His fingers push in and out, and my orgasm rolls over me like a tidal wave. Words tumble from my lips, but I don't know if they make any sense.

Knox.

I love you.

Don't stop.

It could be any—or all—of them, but I can't make sense of anything besides the overwhelming sensation of satisfaction that holds me in its grip. My pussy pulses, my nipples tingle, and my whole body soars.

He kisses me through my orgasm. That is, his mouth stays pressed against my lower lips, stroking and kissing and bringing me back to awareness.

I huff out a quick sigh, brush my fingers over his hair. "Knox. Baby, that was…"

He moves, dragging his open mouth up my body until he reaches my throat. He licks where he must be able to feel my pulse, bites softly at my neck, my jaw. "Speechless, baby?"

"Yeah." I'd laugh if I could, but these amazing little twitches keep my body on edge.

He kisses me, deep and hard, his tongue dragging over mine to fill me with my own taste mingled with his breath, his unique flavor. My body clenches with remembered passion.

"I need you, Knox." I say the words against his mouth. "Inside me."

"Like this?" He teases me with his tongue between my lips.

"Yes. *No,*" I groan. "God, no. I need you to fuck me, baby. You know…"

I've become braver about dirty talk since I've been with Knox. It floods my pussy, tightens my nipples when he does it, so I think he must like it, too. It seems pretty certain when he scoops me up into his arms and slides me to the middle of the bed.

He leaves me with a kiss, fingers stroking over my pussy, his thumb on my clit. My body responds instantly…only to have him disappear.

"Knox?" I whine, and then he's back, standing next to the bed.

Condom. I notice he's sheathed, and I nod once. Jesus, I forgot—but he remembered. Keeping me safe. I can read the importance of it in his dark and stormy eyes.

"See what you do to me, baby?" he asks as he just stands there. "You haven't touched me, and my dick is hard as granite. Fuck, harder. I could cut diamonds with it."

I smile and move with what I hope is a sensual twist. "Forget granite, forget diamonds. Just come inside me and make me feel every inch of you."

He doesn't move, just stares at me like he's never seen me before.

"I could never do it with you," he says sounding oddly awestruck.

"What?"

"All the others? The chicks whose names and faces I'll never remember? I didn't give a shit. I was never *there*. Wasn't even an exchange of pleasure. There was an expectation. I'd make them come, and I could get off. Release some tension or...whatever."

He blinks. Swallows. Continues. "So I figured out how to make it work. Tie 'em up. Blindfold 'em. Spank 'em. Whatever. It added some interest, some excitement, and then there were more expectations. It became my kink."

He shakes his head. "But with you...I could never do it. It was never right. I needed more from you. Wanted to give you more." He sighs. "Just couldn't understand it until I knew I loved you. That shit was okay for a one-and-done girl, but not for you. Not for my English."

"Knox." I swallow back the oddest tears that prickle behind my eyelids and threaten to choke me. I try to smile. "That's probably the most romantic thing you've ever said to me."

He gives a disbelieving snort and smiles, just a little. "Gonna have to work on my game, then, English."

He moves then, kneeling on the bed until he's crouched between my legs. Knees bent, I open them as wide as I can and arch my hips. "C'mon, baby. I *need* you."

He strokes two fingers over my pussy, up and down like he did with his tongue. "You're still wet."

"For you, baby. Only for you."

He strokes some of my wetness over the condom, and the sight of his hand moving up and down his cock gets me wetter. I gasp. Who knew Knox Gallagher could be such a tease.

"You ready?" he demands as he slides the tip of his dick into me.

"Yes!" I arch toward him, and then he fills me, inch by slow inch. Finally, *finally,* he's in all the way.

"Okay?"

"Yes." I breathe suddenly, no clue that I'd stopped. He's so big, I'm so full, and I've never felt more complete.

He pulls back slowly, pushes forward just as slowly, and then does it again. Again. Again. Long, slow strokes that drag over my highly sensitized clit and send a flurry of nerve endings into overdrive.

"Knox. Baby." It's more gasp than actual speech, and I reach for him, wherever I can touch him.

He grabs my hands in his and leans forward, taking my arms with him so they're stretched out above my head. Our fingers are linked, and his tighten around mine as he maintains that slow, maddening pace.

"English." He bends down to kiss me, the same leisurely pace as the rest of his body. "Look at me, baby."

I do, and I see the whole world in his eyes. Love, sorrow, guilt, redemption. It's all there, and it completes me like the last piece of the puzzle that's been my life. We share those things. They make us who we are. They give us the ability to heal ourselves…and each other.

I squeeze his fingers and flex my hips as much as I can. "I love you, Knox."

He smiles, but it's short lived as he surges back into me. "I love you, too, baby."

"Now." I shift against him. "Will you please *fuck* me properly?"

He pulls his hands from mine, leans back, grabs my hips, and thrusts deeper. Deep enough to make me gasp. Deep enough to hit my cervix.

"Always, baby." He drops forward for a kiss that goes deeper. "Always.

EPILOGUE

LONDON

I LIKE AUSTIN A LOT MORE THAN I THOUGHT I WOULD.

I shake my head as the thought rumbles through my brain. It's not the first time I've realized it, but I still feel a little embarrassed. I always considered myself a true international soul, but I guess I was thinking about it from my pretty narrow experience. L.A. and London. And I had the same stupid stereotypes about Texas as half the people in the country.

I don't know about the rest of Texas—it's a big state—but Austin is a great mix of urban and country, the west and the south, Texas and U.S. mongrel, and it's now home.

With Knox.

The tour ended a week ago, and, true to his word, Knox refused to let me go. Well, I wasn't letting him go, either. I had Lucia pack up my room and ship it all to Texas. Knox held my hand when I called my parents with the news. They only said, "Whatever you want, dear," and that was it.

I think Knox was disappointed for me. It made me love him more.

"Fuck them," he'd whispered after I hung up. "You don't need them. You've got me, Bree, my mom, and Wycked Obsession for your family now."

And I guess he's right.

Family. I know I've never had it. Not a real one. And I suppose a part of me knew I was looking for...something. I just never guessed what glory I could find with Knox Gallagher.

We're staying with his mother while we search for an apartment. Bree and Ajia are doing the same. It took every bit of the time I was with the tour, but Knox finally seems to have accepted the relationship between his sister and his best friend.

Noah's kind of fallen off the grid since we got back. Well, not entirely. One of us talks to him every day; he just doesn't want to see us yet. "Let me figure some shit out," he always says, and who are we to argue with him? He's entitled. Knox and I both took our time figuring shit out.

Bree and Ajia did, too, according to them.

Rye says he slept for 24 hours straight. Now he's looking for property to buy. He's got a plan, he says, but he's not going to tell us anything until he finds the right place. He seems more excited than I've ever seen him, and Knox thinks it's a good thing. I'm dying to know what it means.

Zayne...well, we've been able to talk to him, but nobody's seen him yet. I can't figure out if it's because it's treatment facility rules, or if that's the way Zayne wants it. Whatever, we've all taken turns calling him, and he sounds...well, not good, exactly, but not terrible, either. He's been very sweet, even apologetic, over adding to the pain of the whole Mr. Gallagher/miscarriage incident, but I've forgiven him. Knox has, too. Zayne's got a problem, an illness, and we're there to help him.

Whatever that means.

"What are you doing in here?"

Knox steps into the room with a smile. We're sleeping in his childhood bedroom, and I kind of like it here. The walls are covered with his adolescent posters: Jimmy Page, Jimi Hendrix, Stevie Ray Vaughn. A couple of groups made the cut, too: Seether and Green Day. I have to admit I wouldn't have been sure about the identity of all of them if Knox hadn't told me.

"Just admiring your teenage idols," I say with a smile.

"You aren't gonna quit giving me shit about that, are you?"

I grin. "Not for a while. I like getting a peek at the teenager you were."

He prowls up to me, slips his arms around my waist, and tugs me closer. I melt against him.

"And who would I have found on your teenage walls?" he whispers just before he catches my mouth with his.

"Uh…" His kisses always steal my good sense. I pull in a breath so I can think again. "Justin Timberlake," I admit without much interest. "One Direction."

He kisses me again, nips my bottom lip. "Were you a Niall girl?"

I shake my head and return the favor. "Nope." I bite a little harder. "Harry. All the way."

"Oh, well…" He grins and adjusts my hips against his. His erection presses back against me. "I'm good, then. I can take Harry."

"Oh, yes, baby." I arch against him. "You can. In fact…" I pause, tease him with a wicked smile. "I'm thinking about putting that poster of you—the one you took the day we met—on our bedroom wall."

He snorts. "No. Way."

I give him a naughty smile, and we stand in each other's arms for a few minutes, both thinking about the bed just a few steps away. I know he is, because *I* am. It's a full size mattress, a little snug for two people, but neither of us minds too much. Not in the short term, anyway.

"We're getting a king size in our apartment," Knox says suddenly, like he's reading my mind. It creeps me out, the way he does it. But then, he accuses me of the same thing.

We're kind of on each other's wavelength.

"You know what else we're getting?" He pulls back and stares at me, his expression as flirty as it is serious.

"What?"

"Hmmm…maybe some furry handcuffs. Or under-the-bed restraints. Or—"

"Really?" Even I hear the thread of excitement in my voice.

"You *want* that?" He sounds surprised, steps back—or tries to, but I'm right there with him.

I lift one shoulder but keep my gaze trained on his. "I don't know. I've never done it. But I read about your reputation, and—"

"Fuck my reputation." His brows arch down.

I smooth my fingers over his forehead, and his expression eases.

"Shh, baby. I know how you feel. We've talked about it."

And we have. He admitted how he'd earned said reputation, and while I was a little relieved not to have to face that with everything else, at least in the beginning, I was also a little disappointed. The idea of being naughty with Knox sends a thrill of excitement through me.

I sink to my knees and start working at the fastening of his jeans. Thank God he only wears leather pants on stage. I'm well-practiced at freeing his cock by now, and it springs out into my waiting hands. I lean forward, drag a slow, seeking tongue over the tip, down the front to that special place I know will drive him crazy. I lick him there, again and again.

"God*damn* it, English!" His fingers shove into my hair and he holds me steady. "We're supposed to barbecue in the back yard in like *five minutes.*" He groans.

"So we make it in ten. Or fifteen." I peer up at him through the fan of my lashes. "However long it takes."

He pushes deep, and I widen my mouth, relax my throat to take him. He groans again.

"However long it takes," he grunts.

I move my head forward and back, taking him, and reach one hand up to cup his balls, caress them. I balance myself with the other hand on his thigh. I know just how to make him crazy, and I use my mouth and tongue to love him.

I *like* going down on him, love the taste of him, and I moan my approval…only to lose control of things when he jerks me to my feet and tosses me onto the bed. My ribs give a slight twinge as he follows me down, but they're the last thing I care about right now.

Knox…me…our future together.

I reach up, push his hair back from his face, and catch his stormy eyes with mine. "I love you, Knox." More than he'll ever guess.

His eyes darken. "And I love you, too, English. You're mine. Forever. And I'll always take care of you."

"I know you will, baby," I sigh as his mouth captures mine. Then I can't speak anymore as he proves it to me.

THE END

Wynne Roman

___PLAYLIST___

These aren't only the songs I listened to while writing Wycked Rumors, but also songs that describe the Wycked Obsession experience and mean something to the band.

Baby It's You – Smith
Birthday – The Beatles
Bleeding Love – Leona Lewis
Can't Fight This Feeling – REO Speedwagon
Careless Whisper – Seether
Caught Up In You – 38 Special
Dirty Deeds Done Dirt Cheap – AC/DC
Hold On Loosely – 38 Special
Holiday – Green Day
Hotel California – Eagles
Is This Love? – Whitesnake
The Load Out – Jackson Browne
Lodi – Creedence Clearwater Revival
Remedy – Seether
Rock & Roll Band – Boston
Turn The Page – Bob Seger
While My Guitar Gently Weeps – The Beatles
With Arms Wide Open – Creed

<u>ACKNOWLEDGEMENTS</u>

Writing this book was very different from writing Wycked Crush. I still don't know why. I blame Knox.

We argued a lot during the months I wrote this book. I had ideas about how things should go. London was sweet and almost always cooperated. Knox...not so much. And when he didn't get his way, he refused to play.

Midway through the book, I'd learned the signs and knew when to give in. I literally can't take credit (or blame, for that matter) for this book. It's all Knox.

I want to thank my beta readers, brainstormers, and very patient friends who listened to me complain about Knox. Here's to you, Kathy Hafer, Nickie Harman, Sherry Goodman Hughes, David Hunt, Jennifer Kress, Rachael Siegel, Karen Wilson, and Stacy Young. Every time I whined, "Knox is such an ass," you encouraged me with, "Yes, but he's so *hot!*" I hope the rest of you think so, too.

Thanks to the readers who gave Bree and Ajia a shot in Wycked Crush, who followed me on Facebook and joined my little author group, Backstage with Wynne Roman, and who keep anxiously asking, "When can we get our hands on Knox?" I hope *Wycked Rumors* was worth the wait.

Please watch for *Wycked Escape,* Noah's book, coming in late Spring of 2018.

ABOUT THE AUTHOR

Reading and writing have always been a part of my life. I was that odd child who went to the library during summer vacation, reading romances before I realized what they were. My habits are still the same.

I published two historical romance novels as Wendy Douglas. **Shades of Gray** and **The Unlikely Groom** were released by Harlequin Historicals. After a long hiatus from publishing, I returned with a new enthusiasm and a different focus. The **Wycked Obsession** series is the result.

Born and raised in northwest Iowa, I spent most of my adult life in Anchorage, Alaska. I moved to the Texas Gulf Coast to thaw out my bones, where I live with my two very spoiled dachshunds and an assortment of fictional characters who remind me that I'm never really alone.

BOOKS BY WYNNE ROMAN

WYCKED OBSESSION SERIES

Wycked Crush – Ajia's Story *(Available Now!)*
Wycked Rumors – Knox's Story *(Available Now!)*
Wycked Escape – Noah's Story (Spring 2018)
Wycked Redemption – Zayne's Story (Summer 2018)
Wycked Love – Rye's Story (Winter 2018)
Wycked Trio – Baz's Story (Spring 2019)

WRITTEN AS WENDY DOUGLAS

Shades of Gray
The Unlikely Groom

WYCKED CRUSH

Wynne Roman

Wycked Crush

Wycked Obsession Series – Book 1

(Ajia's Story)

Available Now!

WYCKED CRUSH

PROLOGUE

BREE

I've waited so long.

Now, finally, Ajia is touching me. His eyes are soft and…is it love I see in their unique caramel color? I've crushed on him for so long—five whole years—and he's finally seeing me as a woman. Not just a kid who's trailed along behind her big brother and his band.

Me and Ajia. Just like I've always known it should be.

His fingers cup my breast and he squeezes. Hard. But—wait a minute. What? Something's wrong. He's crushing me. Pinching me. It's not…right. Ajia's touch wouldn't be like this.

"I knew you'd feel this way."

The low, guttural voice rips me out of my dream—oh, God, it's only a dream—and I wake up on high alert. I open my eyes to *him* in my room, standing over me.

Not Ajia, the man I want like no other, but Gabe. My stepfather.

I shriek and shove my hands against his chest. He stumbles back, leaving my breasts exposed because he pushed my T-shirt up. Thank God, I'm wearing a sports bra.

I jerk my shirt down to cover my chest. It's an old Pearl Jam T-shirt that belongs to my brother Knox. It's way too big for me—exactly the way I want it. Disgusting as it might sound, I've started wearing baggy clothes so my *stepfather* won't notice me.

It doesn't seem to be working.

He blinks and then his lips curve into a small smile. "I didn't mean to scare you, sweetie." He takes a step toward me. "I just—"

"I don't give a damn what you were *just* thinking." I push up on my knees, and if looks could kill, he should be a pile of ashes by now. "Stay away from me, Gabe. Don't ever touch me again."

"Aw, Bree." He gives me a look I've seen him give my mother a hundred times. Maybe he thinks it's seductive. It makes me sick. "Don't talk like that."

"What the fuck is wrong with you?" I demand. "You're my *stepfather*, for Christ's sake. My mother loves you!"

"And I love her." He gives me that same awful smile. "But you...you're like she must have been as a teenager. Imagine. Fucking both versions of the same woman. And within hours of each other."

For a minute, I think I'll throw up. Gabe's been coming on to me for months now, ever since he and my mom got married. It's been a soft press up until now. Things he always claimed were accidental, or I'd misunderstood his intentions.

He's younger than Mom by about five years, good enough looking, I suppose—or at least I thought so when she first started to date him. Dark hair always perfectly styled, dark eyes, clean shaven. He dressed in suits and cotton pants with button-down shirts. Conservative and professional, I thought.

I was so fucking wrong.

At first I thought it was just a new husband figuring out how to fit in with a ready-made family. A forty-something, never-before-married stepfather learning to live with a nineteen-year-old stepdaughter in the same house. Touching my shoulder, my hip, watching me in that pervy way I now hate. I tried to blow it off. Walk away. Eventually I learned to make sure I was never alone with him.

Most especially, I never meant for anybody to find out. I'd thought I could handle it. Handle him. It was Knox who caught Gabe once, rubbing his hand up and down my spine, grabbing my ass before I could step away. The memory pierces me again.

"What the fuck?" Knox had asked the instant I'd gotten him away from Gabe.

I hadn't been able to meet his eyes. "It's...nothing."

"It didn't look like nothing."

I'd lifted one shoulder. "Yeah, he's been a little too…friendly."

"That fucker coming on to you?"

I'd shaken my head. "No. Not really. Just…well, like what you saw. It makes me uncomfortable, but I'm not sure he realizes what he's doing."

"Fuck that," Knox had snapped. "He knows."

"Knox." I'd grabbed his arm so he'd know I was serious. "I can handle it. It's nothing. I'll be fine."

"C'mon, Bree. You know better." He'd frowned in that overprotective way of his. "He—"

"He's Mom's husband and she loves him. She waited a long time to get married again after Dad took off. I'm not getting in the way of that."

"You aren't doing shit. It's him and his wandering dick."

"Well, his dick isn't going to wander in my direction. I promise."

I'd meant it then, and I mean it now. Every single day. Even if he's getting braver. The idea of even being in the same room with Gabe Richmond is enough to make me want to puke.

After I convinced Knox to let it go then, I've kept as much of it from my brother as I can. Was that a mistake?

"Get out of here, Gabe." A rage is growing in me, and I put every bit of fury into my voice. "I'm not sleeping with you. I'm not doing *anything* with you."

"Oh, Bree, honey." He shakes his head. "You don't know how good we'll be. We—"

"Gabe? Honey, I'm home! Bree?"

My mother's voice rings from another part of the house, and relief floods through me. A tension I hadn't even been aware of eases. It's always like that. I just react however I need to in order to get away.

But I'm safe now. Mom's home, and he won't try anything else.

Not today.

Still kneeling on the bed, I sit back on my heels. Gabe shoots me a dark look. "You won't say a word if you know what's good for you."

What does he think he can do that's worse than what he's already tried? But he's right. I *won't* say anything—and not for his sake.

He's still standing in the doorway when Mom walks up. Everybody always says we're mirror images of each other. Her hair's shorter than mine, shoulder length but the same coffee color, and I inherited her brilliant green eyes. She's dressed in what she calls business casual, a plain gray shift dress and teal-colored blazer.

She looks between us. "What's going on?"

"I just came to check on Bree. She was being awfully quiet in here." He gestures to my bedroom.

I point to my phone, headphones still attached. "I was listening to the new album. I guess—" I swallow "—I fell asleep."

Mom smiles easily. "How many times have you listened to Knox's new album already?"

You can do this. I can look my mom in the face and carry on a decent conversation. "It's not just Knox's album, Mom. It's all the guys in Wycked Obsession."

"Yes, yes, I know. And I'm proud of them all. But Knox is the only one who's actually my son."

She turns to Gabe, her smile softening to one of love. The kind of smile I'll give Ajia someday, if I ever get the chance.

The kind of smile that asshole Gabe doesn't deserve.

"Now, aren't you taking me out for Mexican tonight?" she asks him in a throaty voice and slides her arm through his.

He smiles back, and the whole scene just makes me sick. Sicker than when he touched me—and I didn't think that was possible.

"Sure, honey," he says and then looks at me. "You want to come along, Bree?"

"Uh, no." It comes out too flat, and so I add, "I'm going to see Knox."

Something flickers in Gabe's eyes, and it makes me smile. Does he think I'm going to tell my brother? I don't say anything else.

"Sure." Mom nods. "You want to spend time with your brother before the boys leave on tour, don't you?"

"Yeah. That's it."

Knox and his band have a rental house where they've stayed the last six months. I didn't have any plans to go there tonight; we planned to hook up tomorrow. That's changing right now.

Wycked Obsession's become the biggest band to come out of Austin in years, and I've tried not to be too much of a pest since they got back from their first tour. Things are different now—*the guys* are different. They've had new experiences. Fame. Adoration. Fans and groupies and shit we all used to joke about. It's all real for them now.

But, I need them tonight. Whatever part of their life they can share. I need the guys who are as much brothers to me as Knox. And I need Ajia, however I can get him. Even if he doesn't know how I feel. Will probably never know.

Tonight, of all nights, I want to think about loving Ajia and how I'm going to spend the summer avoiding my stepfather's advances.

CHAPTER 1

BREE

I stand in the driveway of my brother's house and frown.

Shit. Shit, shit, shit.

He's having a party. Well, *they're* having a party.

Why didn't I expect it? A pre-tour party and a chance to celebrate the release of their second album, *Wicked Is As Wycked Does*. This is for their friends and their hometown fans. Different, I guess, from tour parties. Especially *this* tour, when they'll be opening for Edge of Return, just about the biggest rock band in the world right now.

They didn't invite me.

It hurts. I get it—sort of—but that doesn't make me feel any better. Knox doesn't want me hanging out with their musician friends. Groupies and sluts, he calls them, but maybe that's just for my benefit. To get his way and keep me from getting to know people he things might be a bad influence.

Hysterical laughter bubbles up in my chest. I'm living with Gabe fucking Richmond, for Christ's sake! So maybe it's more complicated than that, but I don't give a shit right now. I hate my life—and I *really* hate witnessing the one-night stand hook-up thing that's part of the whole rock star lifestyle.

It's become part of the Wycked Obsession lifestyle, and Ajia's living it every goddamn day.

Well, fuck that. Fuck rock stars and my stepfather and my piece of shit life. I'm crashing.

I stalk up the driveway and through the front door before I can even think about it. Noise overpowers me at once. Voices and the pounding rhythm of music. Not Wycked Obsession's music but…*Highway to Hell* by AC/DC.

Great. They're into 80s metal tonight.

The crowd moves like it's alive, and I slip into the kitchen to stash my purse in one of the cupboards. Why not? They never keep any food there, anyway.

It's hotter than hell in the house, and I notice the open sliding glass door. May in Austin—of course it's freaking hot! Did they remember to turn off the AC with the door open?

I'm stalling, and I know it. Maybe I was brave a few minutes ago, but it's all starting to fade, now that I'm faced with the reality of finding Knox. I'm pretty sure he won't make me leave. And if he tries? Well, I don't want to pull the Gabe card in front of everybody, but I'll do it if I have to.

"Hey, you need a beer?" Some guy shoves a Shiner Bock in my hand, and I smile a thanks. Deliberately, I wander away before he can say anything else.

A corner of the living room's a safe place to watch the action while I search for Knox. He's a couple of inches over six feet tall, so I should be able to find him easily enough. As always, a passing jealous thought reminds me that he has the height. Knox takes after Dad and I, as Gabe so disgustingly reminded me, look just like Mom. All 5'4" of me.

My brother is nowhere to be seen, but I'm not looking as hard as I should. Not for him, anyway. Ajia's the one I really want to find.

Ajia Stone. Lead singer of Wycked Obsession. The hotter-than-hell guy with the throaty, husky voice that generates love, lust, and orgasms, according to fan gossip. He's one of my brother's best friends. One of *my* friends.

And the man I can't seem to get over.

I was 14 when I first met Ajia. He and Knox were putting Wycked Obsession together, and I was the tag-along. Ajia was 19, out of my reach purely because of our age difference, but I crushed on him, anyway.

Well, I'm 19 now, almost 20, he's 24—and just as much out of my reach. He's a rising rock star with access to any girl he wants. Worse, my little schoolgirl crush has become so much more. I never wanted any other guy, and so I'm a 19-year-old virgin who's Ajia's *friend.* Like the band mascot.

Worse, he calls me *kitten,* like I'm some kind of pet.

There's a reason for it, not that I like remembering it. I was babysitting a friend's kitten the day I met him. An unexpected birthday present for my friend Heather, I'd drawn kitten-sitting duty when her family had gone on a planned vacation to Disney World. Knox and I had never had a pet, and I was a little obsessive about making sure that Whiskers went home as healthy and happy as when she came to me. Somehow, that earned me the nickname *kitten,* and I've been stuck with it ever since.

Ajia might be missing, but I spot Noah, the band's drummer. He's huge, like 6'4" or 6'5", with an upper body honed by years of playing the drums. Except for his darker hair, he could give Chris Hemsworth's Thor a run for his money. He even has the long hair and firm jaw that hints at superhero status. I teased him about it so much, he eventually had Thor's hammer tattooed on his bicep. He's kind of become known for it, and now he takes off his shirt about halfway through every show and throws it to the crowd.

I grin in spite of my party-crashing status. I love Noah like a brother, but I'm a realist, as well. He's also kind of a wild man, and right now he has a girl under each arm. Nope. Not talking to him at the moment.

Zayne and Rye aren't too far away, I notice as I sip my beer. They're standing pretty close together, talking to a group of girls. They're a really stunning combination—tatted up, long-haired music gods. Rye plays keyboards, and his pitch-black hair and matching eyes attract more attention than he ever seems comfortable with. Zayne's the bassist, with chocolatey brown hair and striking hazel eyes. He seems to like being noticed just fine.

They're like a couple more brothers to me, but no way am I approaching them with a whole *group* of fans around them. Knox's sister or not, girls don't like me being around their idols. It's jealousy, pure and simple, and it's also so goddamn stupid! I'm the band mascot, after all.

"What the fuck are you doing here?"

The voice comes from the right, close to my ear, and I squeak as I turn.

"Knox. You scared me, you fucker." I have to give as good as I get with these guys.

"Who told you about the party?"

"Nobody."

"Was it Rye?" He narrows his eyes, so dark suddenly they're more gray than blue.

"No! I kind of ended up here by mistake."

"Mistake?" Knox shoves a wave of dark hair away from his face and gives me that piercing look that sees way too much.

"Not really mistake," I correct as I drink my beer. Damn, but I always get nervous when my brother starts his protective thing. It's so freaking unnecessary. Most of the time.

"I…meant to come here," I add, "but I didn't know about the party."

"So you decided to stay."

"Yes."

The song changes to Guns N' Roses, *Welcome to the Jungle,* one of Knox's favorites. Maybe it'll put him in a better mood. He lets out a sigh to go along with the frown.

Is he weakening?

"You know I don't like you around this kind of shit." He jerks his head toward the rest of the room.

"What, watching you and the guys hook up with as many girls as you can convince to sleep with you?"

His gaze sharpens. "Can't say there's much sleeping that goes on."

"Okay." I pissed him off. Fine. He's pissing me off, too. "Then watching y'all hook up with as many girls as you can fuck."

He sucks in a tight hiss. "Goddamn it, Bree!"

I stare at him with what's supposed to be wide-eyed innocence. "You think I don't know how this works? I'm not a kid anymore."

"So?"

"Wycked Obsession is hotter than a Texas summer," I snap, like I'm not proud as hell of the guys. *"Wicked Is As Wycked Does* is climbing the charts, they play *Tonight* on the radio every freaking hour, and you're leaving for three months to tour with

Edge of Return. You're honest-to-God rock stars now, and you're taking advantage of the—perks."

"The perks." Finally, Knox grins. "Wonder what the fans would say if they heard you say that."

I shrug. "They wouldn't care. All they want is to fuck one of you."

His grin dies a sudden, ugly death. "Stop saying shit like that."

"You shouldn't have taught me the words, then."

"Hey, baby." A hand with long, pointy fingernails painted red slides around my brother's chest. The rest of the girl follows, her skirt so short it barely covers her ass and top so low it hardly hides her nipples. "You said you were coming right back."

"I need a couple of minutes." Knox doesn't even look at her.

"Who's this?" she demands, her eyes narrow and angry. Her voice is sharp enough to cut steel.

"My sister." Knox drops his gaze to hers. I can't see his expression, but I know what it means when he says, "Maybe I'll catch up with you later."

So does she. "Knox...baby."

"Later."

She glares at me and slinks away. Later means never when my brother says it like that. She fucked up, and she knows it.

"Sorry." I don't sound it.

"You gonna tell me why you're here?"

I sigh. Knox has a one-track mind about some things, and I learned long ago that I'm one of them.

"Later. I'll tell you later when all this—" I wave one hand "—isn't going on."

"So you're just going to hang out here?"

I take a drink of my beer—a long one this time—and give him a look that says, *Listen to me! For once in your life, just* listen. "Look, Knox. You can kick me out. I'll sit outside on the curb. Sleep in the bushes. Whatever. You're stuck with me tonight, and we'll talk about it tomorrow."

"Bree—"

"Baby girl!"

That's my other nickname. All the guys call me that, even though I'm not that much younger than they are. Ajia's the oldest in years, but they all have worlds of experience over me, so I guess the name fits. It doesn't matter. I've never been able to convince them to stop using it.

"Noah."

I grin at the drummer. His girls trail behind him, looking less pissed than Knox's groupie. Maybe they don't care so much since they're already looking like a threesome.

"I wondered if you'd show up." He grins back.

"She wasn't invited," Knox puts in.

"Asshole," I say just as Noah offers his own opinion.

"Don't be a fucker, man. You know Bree-baby is always welcome."

"Thanks, Noah." I give him a big hug and slide a shitty smile in my brother's direction.

"Uh, the…other guys know you're here?" asks Noah.

I shake my head. "No. Don't think so. I saw Zayne and Rye. Where's Ajia?" I ask as casually as I can.

Noah shrugs, but he doesn't make eye contact with me. I tell myself it isn't because he suspects how I feel about Ajia, but a part of me is afraid he guessed. I've been wondering that for a while now.

"Haven't seen him lately," he finally says.

Knox stares at me, and I know what he's thinking. The same thing I'm thinking. If Ajia isn't around, then he's off somewhere with…someone. Some chick. A slut, I insist to myself, whether it's true or even fair. All I can think of is him kissing another girl, touching her, fucking her.

My breath catches and the bottom drops out of my stomach.

"Look, you guys go do…whatever." I force the words out, but they come easier as I speak. "It's your party. Just ignore me. I'll mingle, and if I get bored, I'll go to the music room. You won't even know I'm here."

The music room is actually the garage, but the guys put some soundproofing in there, keep most of their instruments there, added some furniture and a window AC unit. It's gotta be cooler in there, and I won't have to worry about turning around to find Ajia sucking face with some slut.

"You sure about that, baby girl?"

I smile at Noah for trying to makeup for Knox's shitty attitude. He's protective, too, but in a different way. If nobody gets hurt, if it's legal—or close enough—and everybody involved is an adult, Noah's all for it. My being here pretty much fits all his criteria.

"Go on." I step from in between the guys. "I'm going to get another beer. Don't let me cramp your style." And then I just walk away.

For the next couple of hours, I work my way through the crowd. I talk to a few of the guys' friends, some I know from school and others from the club circuit back when Wycked Obsession played every damn gig they could get. Most of the girls ignore me, but I know a few of them. I even get a chance to talk to Zayne and Rye…and then finally I see Ajia.

He stands across the room from me—with someone. An octopus, I think with a look that should disintegrate her on the spot. She has her hands all over him. I'm sure as hell not going up to him now, but I'm torn. I don't want him to see me like this, all brokenhearted and aching for him, but another part of me wants him to notice me. He doesn't.

He's totally preoccupied with *her*.

Asshole. I'm pissed off and sick, even knowing I have no right to be. *Don't forget what you've always known,* I remind myself. Ajia's flat-ass fucking hot, almost pretty in a handsome sort of way. His features are fine and perfect. His hair is wavy, like Knox's, and they both wear it long, past their shoulders. Ajia's is a golden blond color, his eyes a caramel brown. The combination is unexpected and alluring.

He's tall, maybe 6'2", and muscular. He doesn't have Noah's upper body, but Ajia works out and looks pretty damned impressive. He's also tattooed, sleeves on his arms, part of his chest, and some stuff on his back. Knox told me they'd all added the new album title somewhere on their bodies, but I haven't seen any of the finished work yet.

I have to force myself to look away. No way can I talk to him now. Not with Ursula hanging off him. A smile makes me feel only slightly better, but I like comparing the fangirl to the villain from *The Little Mermaid.* Maybe it's childish, but I don't care.

It's a distraction, but I force myself to listen to Mötley Crüe's *Kickstart My Heart,* Poison's *Every Rose Has Its Thorn,* Whitesnake's *Here I Go Again,* and Warrant's *Heaven.* I've heard them all—dozens of times over the years—along with Classic Rock, Blues, 90s Grunge, Alt. Rock, and Indie Rock. In fact, I can't hear any goddamn song at all without associating the music with Knox, Ajia, and Wycked Obsession.

Hell, I've spent the last two years at the Butler School of Music, going for a degree in Composition because of the band. How fucked up is that?

By the time one o'clock rolls around, I'm done. My emotions are raw, and I never wanted to be a part of the whole party scene in the first place. It only got worse after seeing Ajia like that. Knox made me feel like shit, too, and no matter how hard I try to forget, the thing with Gabe still preys on my mind. I need to get away, sack out in the music room and just get some sleep so I can talk to Knox tomorrow.

The music room *is* cooler and quieter. I turn off the lights and stretch out on the ratty old couch the guys dumped there. I wish I'd brought a toothbrush or looked for an extra one here, but no way am I fighting that crowd again. I'll have to make do until morning.

I don't expect to fall asleep easily, but I must have. One minute there's silence, and then suddenly there are noises. Realizing I'm awake, I lie quietly, listening and hoping it isn't a rat or something. Doesn't matter that I grew up in Texas; I hate that kind of thing!

No, it isn't a rat, I decide. Not the four-legged kind, anyway. The noises aren't right for that. It's people, and they're—

"What the ever-loving fuck?"

The words are out before I can stop them. *Holy hell!* The last thing I want is to be an audience for some couple getting it on.

The overhead light snaps on, and I get my first glimpse of the spectacle. A girl's on her knees with some guy's dick in her mouth. She's sucking, moving her head back and forth and making soft, greedy noises low in her throat. She pulls back, blinking and giving me an unobstructed view of a long, thick, hard cock that looks way more impressive than anything I've ever imagined.

"Ajia?" she snaps, stroking the length of his cock once, twice, but it's too late. My gaze jerks upward and I stare into his face. His caramel eyes look odd, sharp and piercing, as always, and yet heavy with desire. His gaze catches mine and he blinks.

I'm up off the couch in an instant, suddenly on fire and not in a good way. *"Oh, Jesus."*

They stand between me and the door, but I can't stay there. I try to keep from looking down again, but I can't help it. Ajia's dick is still hard, and long, well-manicured fingers still stroke him.

"Jesus." I say it again, and somehow I can finally move.

"Bree," he says in a hoarse voice as I brush past him on my way to the door. I cut it too close, and my shoulder rubs against his.

"Jesus." I'm begging by this time, and then finally— somehow—I'm on the other side of the door.

Ajia and...that girl. She was sucking him off. Stroking him off. I want to close my eyes, but I'm afraid to. Afraid that's all I'll be able to see. Where else can I look? It's all there, and it won't go away.

"What the ever-loving fuck?" I whisper to myself again.

"Baby girl?" Noah suddenly stands in front of me.

"Hey." I want to smile, but I can't.

"What's wrong?"

I shake my head. *I just interrupted Ajia getting sucked off by some chick and it's breaking my freaking heart.* I can't say it.

"I just need a couple of minutes." I clear my throat. "It hasn't been the greatest night." *That* is an understatement—but why did my voice have to sound so goddamn *weak?*

"You—"

Noah breaks off when the door behind me opens. *Shit.* I should have kept moving. Why didn't I? I really don't want to do this now.

"Bree?" Ajia's voice is soft.

I don't look back; I don't have to. It's all on Noah's face. The recognition. The understanding. The...sorrow? Yeah. He knows how I feel. How I *really* feel about Ajia.

Noah hauls me against his chest and gives me a hug. It's comforting, and I hug him back.

"Go to my room," he says against my hair. "Sleep in my bed tonight. I'll take the couch."

I want to laugh, but it won't come. Instead, I pull back from him. "That's sweet, but you know you don't fit on the couch."

His eyes crinkle with a smile, and he winks at me. "You inviting me to spend the night with you, baby girl?"

"You wish." Somehow, I manage a smile.

He nods. "Okay. Go on, then." He gives me a little push, like I'm a kid or something.

Oh, that's right. The band mascot. Like their pet. Their baby girl.

A sad place twists inside me, but it isn't Noah's fault. It's nobody's fault but my own, longing for shit that can never be mine. Like some sort of freaking masochist.

I reach out for a quick squeeze of his hand. "Thanks, Noah."

"Don't mention it."

I walk off without ever looking at Ajia, and then I hear a grunt from behind me. "What the fuck, Ajia?" Noah's voice sounds sharp, like a whip. "Just once, couldn't you learn to keep your dick in your pants?"

CHAPTER 2

AJIA

"Shut the fuck up, Noah." I bite the words off, my jaw clenched, and turn to the girl next to me. Hailey? Harley? "I'm gonna have to take a raincheck, honey. Something came up."

"Yeah. I know just what that is." She rubs her hand over my crotch and smiles. It's probably supposed to be sexy. It isn't.

"No." I push her away. "Something else. Band shit."

"Was it that little bitch who interrupted?"

"Bree's not a bitch," I snap. Defending her comes automatically. It's that way for all of us. Bree is...special. Always has been.

"Okay. Well, I'm not really into threesomes, you know. You got the whole package here, baby." What's Her Name throws her arms wide and shoves her chest out like she's trying to remind me of her fake tits. "If you want her, too, I guess I can put up with a lot to fuck Ajia Stone."

God, she even says my name wrong. It's pronounced *Asia,* like the continent. The spelling of my name has pretty much pissed me off for most of my life. *I* didn't choose it. Can't *somebody* get it fucking right?

The rest of it...I don't even go there. Chicks always want to fuck the rock star. Doesn't matter which one. Front men and guitarists like Knox and me are always targets, but everybody in the band gets more than our share of pussy. It's like a goddamn game or something, and I'm so fucking sick of it.

So why do I keep playing?

But I know why. It's because I'm such a piece of shit. I don't deserve anything better. And now Bree saw this chick sucking my cock. Jesus-fucking-Christ.

"Look, sorry." I don't even try to be nice. She called Bree a bitch. "It's not gonna happen tonight. I got shit to take care of." I stalk off without a look back.

"Where you going?" Noah calls after me.

"I told you! To take care of shit."

He ought to fucking know. We rented a four-bedroom place in Austin after the last tour. A place to share, to practice, write music, and figure out what the fuck we're doing. Our first album took off kind of unexpectedly, and then we started touring to promote it. We didn't have a lot of time to think or even *breathe* on tour, and we finally got the last six months to put together the album that became *Wicked Is As Wycked Does*.

We'd written most of the songs. This was time to polish and record. Time to plan. Time to get to know our manager and the people at our record label. We did all that and more, and day after tomorrow, we're leaving on tour again. Or is it tomorrow already? Whenever, we've got three months across the South, West, and Midwest.

Three months before we'll be anywhere near Austin again. I can't leave Bree with her last image of me being sucked off by some random chick.

Noah's words come back to me. *Just once, couldn't you learn to keep your dick in your pants?*

It beats the alternative. If whipping my cock out for every girl who's interested keeps me from thinking about—well…old crap that can't be changed, then I'm all for it. Besides, it's the perfect description of my life.

Ajia Stone, fucker.

I stop in front of Noah's door and give it a quick tap. I don't wait to be invited in.

The room is dim, the only light coming from a lamp on the bedside table. It creates a lot of shadows. Maybe that's good. I won't have to look Bree in the eye.

She's sitting on the end of the bed, staring at the floor. Sad. Lost maybe. Did I do that to her? I've always known she had a little crush on me, but that can't be enough to make her look like that. Can it?

"Bree."

"Uhm." It takes a minute before she looks at me. In my general direction, anyway. "Hey."

"You okay?"

Her gaze slides away. "Embarrassed, but I'll live."

I sit next to her, almost close enough for our hips to touch. Too much, maybe, but I want—*need*—her to be comfortable around me again. "I'm sorry you saw that."

She nods but doesn't look at me.

"I didn't know you were there." Lame fucking excuse.

Her laugh is cut off, a kind of choked sound. "Yeah, I know. You were...busy. It's funny." She doesn't sound amused. "I thought the garage'd be safer than the bedrooms."

"Bree..." Fuck. How can I tell her I don't bring random hook-ups back to the place I *sleep?* "Kitten—"

"Don't worry. I know I wasn't supposed to be here. Knox already bitched me out." She sounds hurt. "I didn't mean to crash, but—"

"Ajia, you fucker!" Knox barges through the door. So Noah tattled.

"Shut up, Knox. I'm talking to Bree right now. I'll deal with you later."

"You'll deal with me right fucking now. Leave my sister out of this. She's—"

"Right here, Knox. I can speak for myself."

I swallow a smile. One thing about Bree, she can hold her own against her brother.

"Look, Bree—"

"No, you look," she interrupts and throws her head back to glare at Knox. I've seen Bree in lots of different moods. This is her pissed off one. The one she brings out when her brother gets on her last nerve.

"Just stop this *protective shit.*" Even Knox can't miss how furious she is—can he? "I'm sick of it. I don't need it. Not where the band is concerned. So I woke up to see Ajia getting a blowjob. At some point, I could have caught you doing the same thing, or

Zayne eating some girl out, or Noah in a threesome. So the fuck what."

I choke off a strangled sound. Damn. I've always admired Bree's honesty, but...Jesus! Where the fuck did this shit come from?

She stares at Knox, but he only shakes his head, his eyes bugged wide. "Goddammit, Bree, you're not supposed to know about that shit."

Exactly.

Her shoulders slump. "Knox, you dumbass. I'm nineteen now. *Nineteen!* Twenty this summer. You know I'm at least as old as most of the girls you guys fuck around with. Older than some."

He blinks, his mouth open but nothing comes out. I can't help laughing. "She's got you there, dude."

Me, too, actually. She's at least as old as Blowjob Girl. I mean, I know I'm an asshole, but have we really been pretending that Bree isn't grown up, same as us?

I slant a glance in her direction. She's dressed in some baggy white shorts, but—damn! She's got legs. Tanned and sleek, they go all the way to heaven.

Holy shit. I am *not* thinking that way!

At least she's wearing an old Pearl Jam T-shirt of Knox's. It's way too big for her, and I can't tell anything about her shape underneath it. Good thing.

He starts to laugh all of a sudden, a weird, stupid sound. I look at him, equal parts relief and confusion, but he's staring at Bree. "Jesus, you're right," he says, shaking his head. "It's fucking insane! I keep thinking you're still the kid you were when we started this thing."

"I'm not. You grew up, and so did I." She points to her chest.

"Yeah, okay." Knox lets out a long breath. "I get it. Fuck." He shakes his head. "Look, I'm not going to change overnight, but I'll try to do better. Okay?"

"Yeah." She smiles, the first I've seen since I flipped on the light in the garage. Maybe she doesn't need to be protected from real-life shit, but—

Wait. What did she say? *Just stop this protective shit. I'm sick of it. I don't need it. Not where the band is concerned.*

"Hey, just a minute."

"What?" Knox and Bree look at me. I stare at her.

"You said you don't need protecting where the band is concerned. So what *do* you need protecting from?"

Maybe she didn't mean the band in general. Did she mean...*me?*

Her eyes pop wide, and I notice them for the first time. Kind of a dark green, or maybe sort of brownish? The shadows make it hard to know for sure. Why didn't I ever pay attention before? And why am I looking now?

"Bree?" Knox asks.

The wheels are turning in her brain; I can almost see it. Something's going on, something she doesn't want to say. Shit.

"Well..." She has kind of a swagger in her voice, a sure sign she's nervous. "I was wondering. I thought maybe I could, you know, housesit for y'all this summer. Stay here in the house and just, like, watch over things."

"You wanna stay here?" Knox repeats.

"Yeah. It'd be...great."

"You want to party or something?" So maybe it isn't about me, but it pisses me off to think about her partying without the rest of us there to look out for her.

"No, it's not like that." She shakes her head. "I just—"

"Doesn't matter," Knox interrupts. "We can't say yes even if we wanted to. The lease is up. We let it go for this tour."

"You're moving out?"

"Movers are coming tomorrow afternoon—well, *this* afternoon. Everything we don't take with us is going in storage."

Bree sort of sinks into herself, almost like she's folding up, trying to find some strength or something. She's *never* acted like that before.

"What's wrong, kitten?" I can't catch her gaze.

"I was just...well, I hoped—" She shakes her head.

"Bree?" Knox sounds concerned, but at least he isn't pushing too hard. It's like a goddamn miracle or something. Maybe he really *is* listening to her for a change.

She doesn't answer, just stares at her lap and her twitching fingers.

"Baby girl?" I try again.

She looks at me then, her eyes damp and almost stricken. When she drops her lashes, the tears spilled down her cheeks.

"Aw, don't cry, kitten." I haul her into my arms and shoot a fierce glance at Knox. *What the fuck?* He shakes his head like he hasn't a fucking clue.

"Bree?" He kneels down in front of her. "What's wrong? What happened?"

She sniffs but doesn't move. Her arms are around my waist, her breasts soft against my chest. She has a little more upstairs than I realized.

Nope. Should *not* have noticed that. I should push her away and get the hell out of there. I don't, of course. No way can I.

"It's…Gabe," she says finally.

Gabe? As in Gabe Richmond? Knox's and her stepfather?

"That motherfucker." Knox shoots to his feet as he swears. "That son of a bitch tried to touch you again, didn't he?"

"What the hell?" I look between siblings. "Are you telling me that Gabe—" I can't even fucking say it.

"He came into my room this time," she whispers against my chest. I think she'd push herself inside me if she could. "I was sleeping. I—" she swallows "—woke up and he was touching me."

"I'll kill him." Knox whirls toward the door.

"I'll help." I try to peel Bree away from me.

"No! Stop! You can't!" It's almost a scream.

Knox glares at her. "Why the fuck not?"

"You…know why." She sits up and pulls away from me. Some part of me doesn't want to let her go. "We've talked about this, Knox."

"You've talked—" I look between them. "This isn't new?"

She shakes her head, and her long brown hair dances around her shoulders. I've never noticed *that* before, either.

"No." She doesn't look at me. "It's been happening for…a while."

"Since he moved into the house," adds Knox grimly.

"I've been trying to avoid him." Fuck. She sounds so desperate about it. "Never be alone with him. You know."

"And it's not working," Knox puts in flatly.

"Wait a minute." I aim for clarity. "He's a grown-ass man and you—" I look at Bree "—grown up or not, you're still technically a teenager. What the fuck's he think he's doing?"

She shudders. "Today was the worst. He told me...he wants Mom *and* me. The younger version."

"That's fucking sick."

"You haven't told your mom?"

She shakes her head and sends a pleading look at Knox. "We *can't* tell her. We've talked about that."

"Tell me, then." I grab her hand. For her or me? I only know this whole thing has my gut churning.

Bree dips her head. "Dad broke Mom's heart when he took off, A." A spark of relief soothes me if she can call me by the nickname only she uses.

"It took her a long time to get over it," she adds after a second. "She worked like hell as a single mom to support us. When she found Gabe...it was like she came back to life. I'm not taking that from her."

"Sis—"

"No!" Bree straightens her spine but doesn't pull her hand from mine. "I told you. There are two outcomes if I say anything. One is that she doesn't believe me and it ruins our relationship. Two is that she believes me and it ruins her marriage. Either way, she loses, and I won't be a part of it."

"You really want your mom to be with a guy like that? If he tries shit with his own...stepdaughter—" goddamn, it's hard to *think,* let alone *say* "—you think he won't try with somebody else?"

Bree swallows hard. "I don't know, but I can't be the one to break her heart. *I can't.*"

Fuck. I get it. That doesn't mean I like it, but I let it go—for now.

"Okay...so..." I can't think of anything else to say.

"I don't know." Bree sighs. "I got rid of him today, but he's pushing. Getting braver. I don't want to spend the summer around him. You know, with you guys gone."

Knox slumps against the door and shoves his hands into his hair. "Son of a bitch. You're right. Okay." He stiffens, straightens. "Then we do the only thing we can."

"What's that?" She sounds so goddamn tired.

"You're going on tour with us."

WYCKED CRUSH

Wycked Escape

Wycked Obsession Series – Book 3

(Noah's Story)

Spring 2018

.

Wynne Roman

PROLOGUE

Paige

"YOU READY, BABY?"

My boyfriend looks at me with a grin on his face. Biggest grin I've seen on his face in a long time. But why not?

It's Noah's eighteenth birthday, and he's getting what he wants.

A threesome.

I swallow and try to force myself to smile. I can't match his expression, so I do the best I can. And, I encourage myself, it's okay if he sees that I'm anxious. A seventeen-year-old girl who had to be talked into this deserves to be nervous.

"Is this really what you want?" I pin my gaze to his. He's got bright blue eyes with the longest lashes I've ever seen, and I've come to depend on the truth I can always find there.

He pushes my hair back over my shoulders and tries to contain his excitement. I can see the effort, and a part of me appreciates that something in him is attuned to my feelings. The rest of me...well, I admit it.

Most of me is just freaking scared.

"You know it is." His tone sounds encouraging, but it doesn't really fool me. Yeah, maybe he *is* trying to reassure me, but it's not because he wants me to feel better. He's doing it because he wants me to go through with it.

"We talked about it," Noah adds a minute later. "I thought you were okay with it."

We *did* talk about it. So often that I wonder if he just wore me down.

But…no. That isn't fair. He made his case, I asked questions, and eventually I agreed. Not the first time, no, but the longer we talked, the clearer the benefits—and the risks—became. I can't pretend now.

I knew what I was getting into, and I said yes, anyway.

From the day Marlie Davis showed up in school, she's been after Noah. And why not? He's tall, taller than most boys in school, and more muscular, too. He has a smile that lights up the world, a great sense of humor, and fills a room with his presence when he enters. He's hot, the best looking guy in town, and everything he is hints that sex with him could change your life.

It's true. He's mine, and has been for two years now. My first boyfriend. The first guy I said *I love you* to. The guy who got my V card.

And now Marlie wants him. Worse, she's offering something no eighteen-year-old boy in his right mind will turn down.

A ménage a trois with her, him, and…whoever. He picked me.

Of course he picked me. I'm his girlfriend. We've been together for almost two years. But the sultry look of excitement on his face when he told me about it guaranteed one thing: if I didn't agree, I risked losing him. To Marlie, and maybe even some other girl who wanted to ménage with them.

So I said yes, and here we are. In a motel room, because Marlie wanted a *special place.* Noah agreed.

"C'mon, baby, you ready yet?"

That's Marlie's voice, and she wraps an arm around Noah's waist as she slips into his embrace. She's wearing only her bra and thong panties, both from Sluts R Us, if I had to guess. And why is she calling him baby? He's not hers. He's *mine,* and he calls *me* stuff like that.

She's just here to fuck.

My uneasiness robs me of breath, and emptiness fills my chest. This isn't good. I know it, especially when Noah grins and then slaps her on her ass. Emotions, awful and desperate, claw through me. Fear? Disappointment?

Anger?

"Just giving Paige a second to get ready," Noah says and glances back at me. His eyes are dark, pupils dilated, and he blinks away a flash of impatience.

"Well, c'mon," says Marlie. "Let's get this party started, then."

She throws her arms around Noah's neck and goes up on her tiptoes to kiss him. She grinds her pelvis against his, his arms are around her, and I hear Noah's low, guttural moan. One I've heard before.

But only when he kisses *me.*

Oh, God. This is a mistake!

But even if that's true, there's nothing I can do about it now. Noah pulls himself free of Marlie and grabs my hand.

"C'mon, baby."

He drags me down onto the bed, reaching behind his head to pull off his T-shirt, as he grabs hold of my tank top. He disposes of both our shirts and then kisses me like I've come to expect.

I kiss him back, remind myself to make it hot and deep and real, but it doesn't feel the same somehow. My imagination tells me I can taste Marlie on his lips; my brain keeps flashing the image of them kissing over and over in my mind's eye. I tell myself to forget about it, to let it go and just get into it, that'll it'll all be okay in the end, but I can't make myself forget.

Noah sweeps his tongue into my mouth, and he kisses me the way he always has. It sets my heart pounding and butterflies race through my stomach, just like they've done since the first time he snuck me into the boy's locker room and pinned me up against the wall. It smelled like sweat and grimy clothes that had been worn too long, but all I could see, hear, smell, touch, and taste was Noah.

It's been the same every day ever since.

It'll be all right, I tell myself now, and try to relax enough to give myself over to his kiss.

"Hey, big boy. Let's get those pants off you." Hands snake between us at the same instant Marlie's voice destroys the moment.

Big boy? I'm repulsed by the stupid name and want to be irritated, but I can't concentrate when this girl is working at

Noah's belt buckle. She gives a throaty laugh as she pulls his pants over his hips, down his legs—and he helps her!

Marlie crawls up behind him, and I can't seem to force myself to look anywhere else as she kisses his back, his shoulders, his jaw. He pulls away from me and turns, taking her mouth in kiss that is nothing if it isn't sexual.

She's naked.

She arches so that her tits are pressed against his back, her hands come around to his chest, and then she slides them down to wrap her fingers around his dick. Her knuckles, hard and bony, brush against my hip as she strokes him.

Noah groans, flexes his hips, and Marlie laughs deep in her throat. She pushes her tits against his back and licks his neck.

What am I supposed to do?

I shift uneasily, for no real reason except I need to move. To find...what? I can't say, but it seems to draw Noah's attention back to me. He grins and dips his head, licking my lips before he kisses me again. His hips flex, but Marlie's fist is between him and me. I feel her, not him, but I swallow my disappointment. Instead, I try to make sense of my confused feelings by kissing him back.

"That's right, baby," he murmurs against my mouth and pulls back with a heavy grin. "Here, let's get these off you."

He twists until he frees me of my panties. They aren't a slutty thong like Marlie's, but I'd liked them when I put them on. A sexy mix of white ribbon and lace, teasing and promising, and then I saw what Marlie wore. Now they feel outdated. Old-fashioned. Conservative.

Ugly.

"I love your pussy," Noah groans as he drags hard fingers over me, and his needy tone warms me. Encourages me. He loves me, and I love him. He knows exactly where and how to touch me, the secrets of my clit, and I will always respond to him. Forget everything except his touch. His scent, his smell, his very presence.

Until I hear the sound of kissing.

I open my eyes to see Noah's head turned away, his tongue twined sensuously around Marlie's. His fingers still touch me, but they only rest there. They aren't moving at all.

My sexual excitement, my physical response, my sense of being desired, all die a sudden, painful death.

I want to look away, but I can't seem to make myself do it. Not when they continue to kiss passionately, when Noah's hands leave my body and move to grip Marlie's breasts, play with her nipples, when they sweep down to toy with her pussy. Heat pours from his body, still crouched to straddle one of my legs.

Does he even remember I'm here?

"What do you want, baby?" Marlie moans against his mouth, and he growls in return.

"Fuck," he grunts. "I need to fuck."

She reaches behind her, grabs a condom I didn't know was there, and rips the packet open with ease. She rolls the condom over Noah's dick, stopping long enough to kiss him when he thrusts himself against her hands.

"Jesus," he mutters against her mouth, and I wonder if I'm going to be sick. Was this really what I signed up for?

He looks at me suddenly, his smile wolfish. "Are you ready, baby?"

Me? Ready? For what?

The words won't come. I can't think well enough to form a response, don't even know what to do or say or feel. Then it's too late, and Noah moves. He's closer, between my thighs, and he brings my ass up to rest against him, just above his knees. He spreads my legs and drags the tip of his dick up and down over my pussy. I'm not wet, not like I usually am, and definitely not like I was a little while ago, but he doesn't seem to notice.

I'm not sure he remembers it's me at all.

He's kissing Marlie again, and in a minute, he shoves into me. Hard and deep and quick. It hurts like it hasn't since I was a virgin, but I'm too dry and Noah either doesn't know or doesn't care. He just keeps thrusting, kissing Marlie, fondling her tits and pulling on her nipples, and then sucking them. Shoving his hand down to play with her lower lips, her clit, and shoving his fingers inside of her.

I groan just a little as I try to make myself more comfortable, and Noah must take that as a sign of something it isn't. Rather than hearing the discomfort, he thrusts harder and picks up his rhythm.

The harshness becomes easier as natural lubrication comes to my rescue. I may not be turned on or excited or anything; I can't imagine I'll actually come. This is more about endurance than a race to the finish, but at least my body knows how to get me through it.

My mind isn't so calm. Inside, I'm screaming. Crying. Hating every fucking second of watching Noah's tongue plunge in and out of Marlie's mouth. Watching him suck her bottom lip, her ear lobe, her nipples. Watching him pull his fingers free of her pussy and suck the juices clean. All the while pumping in and out of me like I'm...a hole.

A glory hole.

Noah told me about them, showed me a porn video once. I admit it turned us both on a little bit, but only because we were snuggled up together, and I knew that, when we fucked, I had his full attention.

Now, I have nothing. He's moving, fucking me, because his dick demands the movement, the pressure, the friction, and he wants to come. What's turning him on, though, making those demands of his body, and moving him closer to orgasm, is the fact that he's making out with Marlie, touching her, being touched by her.

"Hurry, baby," she mutters against his mouth. "Come so I can have my turn. I want you to go down on me."

"Oh, I will." Is that Noah's voice? It's rough and raw and doesn't sound like him at all. His hips snap against me, his dick goes deep, and I feel something inside of me break. The pieces disintegrate when he says, "I'm going to eat you like you've never had before, baby."

Noah finishes with a roar, comes inside me, but I don't feel it. I don't feel anything at all. I just lay there unmoving until he pulls out, tugs himself free of the condom, and ties it off. He kisses Marlie again, flips her onto her back next to me, and she shoots me a triumphant gaze.

I lay there in a stupor, realizing that I'm still wearing my bra. No need to take it off. Noah never touched my breasts, never even tried. Never touched anything at all except to shove his dick inside my glory hole.

I glance at Marlie, despite knowing I shouldn't. And when I catch sight of her face, her head thrown back as Noah kneels between her legs, I understand. I get it all.

She won, I've lost him, and who's the slut here?

The one he *wants* to be with, or the one who just got fucked because she happened to have the right hole in the right place at the right time?

CHAPTER 1

Paige

THE BRIDGE SENIOR CARE FACILITY SITS IN A PARKLIKE SETTING
IN THE SOUTHERN PART OF AUSTIN. I love it here, especially the
view of the cypress, mesquite, and oak trees that fill the
landscape. My favorite sight is that of a Mexican plum tree that
sprawls in front of my office window. My *new* office window.

I've had this office for—I glance at my wall calendar—a total
of 37 days. One month and one week. I'm currently employed as
the *acting* Activities Coordinator, or, as the residents call me, the
cruise director. One of them coined the title from the old 70s TV
show, the *Love Boat,* and it stuck.

It makes me laugh. It makes me feel…wanted. Like I belong.
I'm important. Those are things I've come to value over the years.

I know what it's like to feel worthless, and I never want to
feel that way again.

I smile crookedly to myself. It might seem weird to some that
I found my acceptance with a group of senior citizens, but it
makes perfect sense to me. Seniors know what's important.
They're done with all the bullshit of youth and middle age and go
straight for the truth. The things that matter.

And they make me feel special.

They didn't have a nickname like mine for my predecessor
and former boss. She was far more reserved and serious than I am.
A little older, in her late thirties. Stella always loved her job, she
told me when we first met, but working with the elderly had
slowly become almost foreign to her. Gradually, I'd taken on
more of the personal interaction with the residents.

I understood it. She'd explained it from the very beginning. She'd hired me because her biological clock had begun ticking louder and faster, and we'd met in the middle of her years-long struggle to get pregnant. When her third *in vitro* had taken, she'd given her notice immediately.

And so, after two years as Stella's assistant, I'm five weeks into proving myself as a suitable *permanent* Activities Coordinator. I even have Grace, my own brand-new assistant. She's about my age; a full, lush figure; blonde hair; and with kind of strong features that I think are beautiful.

She doesn't, but I can't argue it with her now. She's smirking at me from my office door.

"It's Mrs. Hurley again."

I smile to myself but try to keep my outer expression relatively bland. "What is it today?"

Grace holds up a finger. "Her TV isn't working." Finger number two. "There are strange people lurking in the hallway." A third finger. "She doesn't have the right equipment to refill the postage meters."

I shake my head with a small sigh. "So she's cycling back to the post office construct."

"Yes. And she won't talk to anyone besides you."

"That's because I'm the Postmistress."

Grace grins. "Yep."

"All right." I stand and smooth my burgundy pencil skirt over my hips and thighs. "I'll figure this out."

"Did she ever really work at the post office?"

"Yes, actually, she did. For years." I smile softly. "She wasn't a letter carrier—she'll tell you that right off. She worked in *the facility* for thirty years, longer than everyone else."

"Do you think it's true?"

"I know she worked at the main post office." I shrug. "I don't know exactly what she did or if she was actually there longer than anyone else."

Grace follows me from my office. "Why does she listen to you but everyone else upsets her? You've never said."

I stop near Grace's desk, partitioned off just outside my office. It used to be my cubicle, and I still find comfort there.

Reassurance. Almost strength. Emotions that come from being appreciated.

I close my eyes for a second. Why does Mrs. Hurley listen to me? Feel safe with me? Treat me differently from the way she is with everyone else?

His face pops into my mind, but I give a quick shake of my head to erase it. I've been having to do it more often lately than seems fair, especially after all this time, but I don't know how to change it. Fix it. I can't exactly ask Mrs. Hurley to stop talking about her grandson. Even if she *could* remember the request, she wouldn't understand it.

"Paige?"

I blink and glance at Grace. My half-smile is rueful. I know it, because that's exactly how I feel.

"I've known her for a long time," I admit with a heavy breath. "I...went to school with her grandson."

"Her grands—" The words die a hard, sudden death. Grace stares at me, her eyes wide and mouth open. "Her *grandson?*" she repeats.

I nod.

"You know...*him?*"

I nod.

"As in...Noah Dexter."

I nod again.

"Wycked Obsession's drummer?"

I nod one more time.

She sinks down onto a nearby lobby chair and stares at me. *"Oh, my God."* It's a whisper. *"You know Noah Dexter?"*

I take the seat next to her. "Yes. And I'm guessing you're a Wycked Obsession fan."

"A fan?" She places her hands splayed over the middle of her chest, one on top of the other. "Like, their *biggest* fan."

She squirms in her seat, and I can't help but smile. Noah and I might have a history—a shitty history that I prefer to forget as much as possible—but Grace is still cute in her adoration.

"They are all so *hot,*" she gushes. "Ajia is so sexy, like he's gonna have an orgasm when he sings. Knox is a guitar god, but he's kind of intimidating, too. Rye's so mysterious but kind of sad. I love Noah and his flirty ways, but Zayne..."

Noah's flirty ways? *Fuck that!*

I don't swear very often; it's rarely appropriate in my daily life. But this time it fits. In fact, it feels so good, I'll think it again.

Fuck Noah Dexter and his flirty ways.

Not saying any of that out loud. The last thing I want to do is have to explain any of it to Grace.

Instead, I try to relate to her as one fan to another. "So, Zayne's your crush?"

"Yes! God, yes. He's so hot and...I don't know—tortured? But now..." Her voice fades, and her expression falls.

I've heard the rumors. Everybody has. Not just about Zayne Prescott, but other, questionable stuff. Orgies with Knox Gallagher's sister, Bree, before she and Ajia Stone hooked up. Then some groupie claimed Noah gave her an STD. Unfortunately, knowing Noah, it isn't that hard to believe. Then Zayne ended up in rehab after almost ODing.

Who'd have thought being in a rock band would be such a...challenge?

I can't guess how Noah feels about it all. Life has changed for him; he's a celebrity. For an ordinary person like me, it wouldn't be all that easy. How *does* a person manage the kind of notoriety that Wycked Obsession's success has brought?

Again, those thoughts are more personal than I want to share with Grace, so I keep my comments focused on the man she's most interested in.

"I hear Zayne's in rehab," I say, trying to sound encouraging. "Supposedly here in town." I gesture with one hand. "They're all from around here, and the band formed in Austin."

"I know." Grace's eyes go all soft and dreamy. "Did you know Noah then? Meet the others?"

I shake my head. "No, that happened after—high school." I catch myself at the last second, reforming my words. "We'd...lost touch by then."

"But he'd remember you?"

Would he? A part of me thinks yes, of course he would! We were together for two years. I wasn't his first girlfriend, and not even his first sexual partner, but he was mine. He'd remember *that,* wouldn't he?

Knowing the things he's done since then, the women he's had, the *threesomes* he's famous—or infamous—for…would he really remember some silly girl from high school who couldn't stand to be a part of a ménage a trois? A three-way relationship that meant she had to share him.

"I think so." I finally say the easiest thing.

"Maybe he'll come to see his grandmother. Maybe—"

"Oh, Lord!" I jump to my feet. "Mrs. Hurley. She's been waiting, and you know how she hates that."

Grace blinks and then wrinkles her nose with a little chuckle. "You better get going."

I wave behind me as I start down the hall.

"Tell her you were in a meeting with the Postmaster General," Grace calls. "Maybe she'll accept that as an excuse."

I laugh to myself. When has *any* excuse been good enough for Mrs. Hurley?

Lorraine Hurley's room is at the end of a long corridor on the east end of the building. She has what we call a studio apartment, a large main room with a sleeping alcove and a bathroom. It's furnished with a small sofa, a comfortable recliner, a bookcase, table and chairs. Her television is mounted on one wall, while opposite is a pseudo-kitchen with built-in cabinets and a small, under-the-counter refrigerator. No other cooking facilities are allowed in the room.

"Good afternoon, Lorraine," I call as I push open her door.

"Miss Hamilton!"

She's standing in the middle of the room, her mostly gray hair a tangled mess. Her blouse is buttoned crookedly, and her pants are stained. I make a mental note to speak with the nurse on duty. We have measures in place to help our residents dress and groom themselves when they need additional assistance. Especially our dementia patients.

No one needs to look like an unmade bed, as my gran used to say.

"You can call me Paige, you know." I move into the room with a smile. "I told you that."

She looks around uneasily. "Are you sure it's all right? As the postmistress—"

"It's fine," I interrupt her, hoping I can sidetrack her post office construct. "We're a lot less formal these days."

She nods slowly, as though considering the idea. "All right."

"Now, why don't you tell me what's wrong."

"Wrong?"

"You complained, said you needed to see me."

She looks confused, so I smile.

"Here, Lorraine." I reach for her buttons and begin to refasten them properly. "It's a lovely day out," I say with probably more cheer than she'll understand. But if it keeps her distracted, it's worth it. "A little warmer than I'd like, but it's just the middle of September."

"September?" Her eyes cloud a little, like she's trying to place herself. Maybe not where, but when.

"Yes. It will be fall soon. Halloween, jack-o-lanterns, and pumpkin spice." I take her arm and lead her toward the sofa. "And pecan pie has always been your favorite."

"Oh, yes." Her face goes dreamy. "My beautiful pecan tree." Her eyes close, and when she opens them again, she pierces me with a surprisingly sharp gaze. "You and Noah used to collect the pecans for me."

I smile with the memory. "We did. But that's because we both loved pecan pie almost as much as you do."

She closes her eyes again, linking her fingers together, as though trying to hold a memory close in her mind. I've seen it often enough in her and others like her. Tears no longer sting my eyes, but my heart clenches all the same. Lorraine Hurley was always a strong, vibrant, and independent woman. Seeing her in this state just breaks my spirit a little bit.

I slip away into the bathroom for a comb and a warm, damp cloth. Lorraine is still seated when I return to the main room, and I resume my seat next to her. She smiles as I gently wipe her face, and then I separate her hair in small sections.

"May I comb your hair for you?" I ask quietly.

She blinks, reaches for her head. "Does it need it?"

"There are a few snarls. Will you let me take care of them?"

Her eyes track from side to side. "Yes. I need to look...professional for the customers."

Customers. So she hasn't completely given up on the post office theme for today.

"Yes, we want you to look your best," I say mildly, and begin carefully pulling the comb through her tangled gray hair.

She closes her eyes, and her head moves with the tug of the comb. I'm gentle, remembering my own mother's ruthless hairdressing skills, and Lorraine sighs with what I hope is pleasure.

"Lolo, my love, how are you today?"

My hand stops in mid-comb, because I suddenly have no air in my lungs. I can't breathe, can't think, can't stop the trembling in my hands.

I'd recognize that voice anywhere, anytime, for the rest of my life.

Lolo, my love, how are you today?

I love you, Paige. You'll always be my girl, sweetness.

I drop my hands to my lap, close my eyes for a heartbeat, and then slowly turn to face the doorway. I know what—who—I'll see, but even expecting it can't prepare me for seeing Noah Dexter again. It's been five years, and while everything has changed, it's also true that nothing has.

He's taller by an inch or two, and he was almost 6'3" in high school. His arms and chest have filled out to an adult masculinity, and his chestnut brown hair is long, almost halfway down his back. His trimmed beard is a shade darker and somehow doesn't disguise the sharp cut of his jaw. In fact, it accents the fullness of his bottom lip.

How many times did those lips find mine? Wrap around my nipples? My clit? His mouth knew my body almost as well as I knew myself, and the memories I've been running from for five years come roaring back.

God, how I've missed this man!

I can't bring myself to look into his eyes, even though I'll never forget the startling blue that always seemed somewhat out of place when paired with his brown hair. Instead I take in his tight, ripped jeans and a white button-down shirt. He still favors the same type of biker boots he used to wear, and he looks...stunning. Exactly like a rock star god should look.

Rock star god.

Drummer for Wycked Obsession, the hottest band to come out of Austin, and making a name for themselves with hot-as-hell guys turning out some amazing rock songs that have topped the charts for months now.

How do I know all this? Everybody in Austin knows about Wycked Obsession. Their ups, their downs, their successes, their failures. Everybody has a story about one of the guys, how they met them, partied with them, fucked them.

Fucked them. I avoid those stories most of all.

And me? I have all those stories about Noah—and more. How I loved him and he loved me. And then how he threw me away, moved on to bigger and better things, and never looked back.

I take a breath, long and deep and more ragged than I'm willing to admit. I force my gaze up to his and say the only words I have.

"Hello, Noah."

CHAPTER 2

Noah

THE GIRL IN FRONT OF ME IS BEAUTIFUL. A bit above average height, maybe 5'6 or 5'7, and with a smokin' hot bod. She's slender, a little on the small side on top and with slim hips. The body style I'm most attracted to, if I have to choose. It makes me feel all protective or caveman or some shit.

She's dressed in a maroon-colored skirt, a fitted white blouse, and low heels in plain black. Very conservative and proper—and totally wrong for the innate sensuality of this woman.

Her hair's long and straight, kind of a coffee color but darker. Maybe like espresso. Her eyes are light brown, possibly hazel. She has the clearest, smoothest skin I've ever seen, a really cute, slender nose, and lips that curve seductively but aren't too full.

All in all, the perfect package for me. If I hadn't recognized her before—and I did...instantly—her husky voice would have given her away.

Paige Hamilton.

"Paige!" I grin, surprised by the flash of appreciation I feel, and move closer. "Hello, sweetness."

I take her in my arms and pull her close, until she's pressed against my chest and pelvis with every bit of her softness. The fit and angles are a lot like I remember, even though it's been— what? Maybe five years. Her head tucks under my chin, her cheek rests against my chest, and I like the way it feels. It's been a long time since I've held a girl close and tender like this.

Fucking doesn't require it.

Well…maybe I've held Bree this way, but that doesn't count. She's like a sister to me, and nothing I feel for Paige is sisterly. Never was.

She isn't the first girl I ever fucked, but she was among the first. She *is* the one I stayed with the longest. The longest in my entire life, actually. We dated for almost two years, and she told me she loved me. I said it, too, and probably even meant it at the time.

That's how shit goes in high school.

She's also the only girl to ever break up with me. Makes me want to grin a little bit now, but it pisses me off at the time. I get it. I've grown up, learned not everybody is cut out for my kind of lifestyle. That's okay; they don't have to be. It's better when everybody wants to play, anyway.

Paige? It was too much for her. But me? I've played a lot.

She feels kind of stiff against me, I realize. Like she's…uncomfortable? Is that possible? Really don't know for sure, but I release her and step back.

Her smile shocks me, fake and almost awkward, and she only pretends to look at me. Her gaze lands somewhere around my shoulder, and she doesn't acknowledge my stare.

Does she really feel like it's been that long since we saw each other? Or is it the fame thing? Why the hell else would she be so standoffish?

"I…" Her voice drops off, and then she starts again. "I'm surprised to see you here."

"Why? I visit Lolo a lot." Maybe not every day, but three or four times a week when I'm in town.

"You…usually come at night."

"You keeping tabs on me, sweetness?" I tease, but she doesn't smile back.

I don't mean to keep using the old high school name I had for her, but it just pops out. It's so damned natural. It started as a joke, a naughty one, back from the first time I went down on her. I told her she tasted sweet, she called me a liar, and she became sweetness after that. I couldn't resist.

Does she remember?

I open my mouth to say…something. Not sure what. Not like I can ask her if she remembers when I used to eat her pussy. Not in front of my grandmother. Then it doesn't matter when Lolo saves the day.

Sort of.

"Who are you?" she demands.

I glance past Paige to where Lolo squats on the sofa. She doesn't sit in a relaxed, comfortable way. She's kind of hunched and anxious-looking. Her appearance is a little messier than it was two days ago. Her clothes look dirty and don't fit right, and her hair is only partly combed. I swallow a sigh.

Fuck. I struggle to keep my expression neutral. So this isn't one of Lolo's better days, apparently.

"It's me, Lolo. Noah." I move around Paige, get a little closer—but not too close. I learned the hard way that crowding Lolo's personal space is a bad idea. Especially on a bad day.

"I'm here a little early," I add, "because I have plans tonight."

She stares at me, her blue eyes faded and cloudy. Is she trying to process what I said? Still figure out who I am? Or just trying to decide if she believes me?

"A maintenance man shouldn't hug the postmistress," she sniffs disapprovingly.

"Maintenance man?" I look at Paige. "Postmistress?"

Paige angles her head slowly toward me, as though giving me some sort of instruction that I don't understand. I lift my shoulders to say, *what the fuck?*

Paige huffs out a short breath. "Why do you think he's a maintenance man, Lorraine?"

"He's not wearing a letter carrier's uniform. It's disgraceful! But..." She blinks, narrows her eyes, and looks me over from head to toe. "Do they let mechanics and maintenance men wear something different?"

"Only letter carriers can wear that uniform," Paige answers without looking at me.

"Yes." Lolo nods. "I suppose that makes sense."

I'm...confused. Lolo worked at the post office for years, yes, but it's also been almost ten years since she retired from there. A lot has happened since then; I graduated from high school, joined the band, started touring.

And *Papi* passed away. Maybe that's why she goes back to a happier time?

"Do you see Lolo often?" I ask Paige, still considering my ideas.

"Young man! Don't be impertinent with Miss Hamilton."

I blink, look between them. "Miss Hamilton?"

"Lorraine, would you mind if I spoke to Noah alone?"

Lolo blinks, looking suspiciously between us. "Is he in trouble?"

"No." Paige smiles. "We just need to talk."

"All right." My grandmother nods like she's the queen of the world. For a long time, she was.

Queen of my world, at least.

Paige starts for the door, and I follow, wondering how often they visit. I didn't even realize Paige knew Lolo was at the Bridge.

"My grandson's name is Noah," Lolo calls just as we reach the door.

I turn back, but she continues to speak before I can say anything. "Maybe he'll grow up to be a big, strapping man like you. He wants to be an airline pilot or a truck driver." She laughs. "We'll see how he feels about that when he's old enough to get his driver's license."

A small, empty place opens up in my throat, and I swallow it down. Lolo rarely knows who I am now, but I treasure the times she recognizes me. Today isn't one of them. I must be ten or twelve in her mind.

Losing our connection while she's still here breaks my heart. Especially now, when things are kind of fucked-up in my life. And it's been—what? A year and a half since *Papi* died?

Why does everything have to change? Why can't it all just stay the same?

"Follow me." Paige leads the way down the hall. She takes a couple of turns, staying far enough ahead of me that conversation doesn't really work, and then she arrives at a small office area. A desk is partitioned off and sits outside the Office of the Activities Coordinator, according to the sign on the door. She escorts me inside.

"You work here?"

She nods. "Since college."

"And you're the Activities Coordinator?"

"Acting."

I angle my head and wait.

"I've got six months to prove myself worthy of the job. Uh—" she glances at the calendar on the wall "—make that four months and three weeks."

"Wow. Impressive, sweetness!" I smile my you-know-you-want-me smile, but she doesn't respond.

I try again. "How are you?"

"Fine, thank you. I don't have to ask about you. Everybody in Austin knows about Wycked Obsession."

I stare as she takes a seat behind her desk. What does she mean by that? *Everybody in Austin knows about Wycked Obsession?* Is it the success? Zayne's stint in rehab? The rumors?

Especially the ones about me?

Her expression reveals...nothing. Her dark eyes are distant, her mouth pressed tight in a thin line.

Seeing me isn't something she likes.

Breath deserts me for a second, but I search for air and pull it deep into my lungs. Paige doesn't want to see me?

The idea never occurred to me until now. I mean, I know we didn't end under the greatest circumstances. We didn't like the same things anymore, and so she cut me loose. Aren't *I* the one who should still have hard feelings?

But I know that's bullshit. It wasn't that we just *didn't like the same things anymore,* as much as I might try to convince myself of it. I was in sexual discovery mode, finding out what I liked, what turned me on, what I wanted more of.

Being with two girls at once was the big one. Once I went there, I didn't want to go back...and Paige said she didn't want to share. I was disappointed. Fuck, yeah, I was, but I tried to respect her decision. We broke up, and that was that.

Wasn't it?

"So, how do you like being known as the sexiest drummer to ever come out of Texas?"

Made in the USA
Middletown, DE
31 October 2021